WHITE HARVEST

ALSO BY LOUIS CHARBONNEAU

Stalk
The Ice
No Place on Earth
Night of Violence
Nor All Your Tears
Corpus Earthling
The Sentinel Stars
Psychedelic-40
Way Out
Down to Earth
The Sensitives
Down from the Mountain
And Hope to Die
Barrier World
Embryo
From a Dark Place
The Lair
Intruder
The Brea File
Trail

AS CARTER TRAVIS YOUNG

The Wild Breed
Shadow of a Gun
The Savage Plain
The Bitter Iron
Long Books, Hard Boots
Why Did They Kill Charley?
Winchester Quarantine
The Pocket Hunters
Winter of the Coup
The Captive
Blaine's Law
Guns of Darkness
Red Grass
Winter Drift
The Smoking Hills

WHITE HARVEST

LOUIS CHARBONNEAU

DONALD I. FINE, INC.

NEW YORK

This one is for
Marilyn and Ray Karabela with love

PROLOGUE

At the edge of the world, where the barren sweep of the Alaskan tundra met the gray waters of the Chukchi Sea, a finger of a peninsula hooked outward to form a buffer against the icy winds and the smashing waves. Over countless years the pounding of the surf had pulverized the base of the bluff, creating a rocky shelf within a sheltered cove, protected from the sea's unending blows and the blasts that roared unimpeded across the Arctic wastes not far to the north.

For three days in mid-September this northern Alaskan coastline was buffeted by high winds and rain. In the early hours at the end of the third night the storm pattern broke. When the winds subsided and the sea grew calm, a deep crashing sound jarred the small cove, as if a giant beneath the waves were hurling himself against a massive door. For several minutes the heavy knocking continued. Then, after a brief silence, a strange song began. It rose and fell, echoing eerily off underwater rocks and the submerged cliffs that formed the sea wall, as if bells were tolling beneath the surface of the ocean.

The belling ceased. Within the cove the sea heaved upward beside the shelf of rock. A huge walrus hauled himself out of the water. Weighing at least two tons, he dragged his great bulk onto the rock by hooking his long tusks over the edge of the shelf. This habit was responsible for the walrus's scientific name, *odobenid,* the Tooth-Walker. His thick skin, normally a deep rose, was white from the near freezing cold of the water. In the pale morning light he looked like an enormous ghost of the sea.

Young walrus bulls in a herd practiced their mating song for hours in the stillness of the night, but they invariably swam in

1

packs of four or five, belling in chorus. The huge old bull swam alone, and sang alone.

Eskimos who had seen him when they were children—or claimed to have seen him—estimated his age at no less than thirty years. He was larger than any other bull in the male herd that gathered around him. When he dragged his body out of the water, or used his flippers to lumber across the rock to his chosen spot, he moved slowly, cumbersomely. In the water, although walruses were not renowned as swimmers, he swam with a ponderous grace that belied his size and weight. On land he was clumsy—and more vulnerable.

What set the great bull apart from the others, in addition to his age and size, were the magnificent tusks extending almost straight downward from his jaws. They were so long that he could lie comfortably only on his back or on his side. Often he rested his head over the edge of his small table, allowing the tusks to fall clear. Each walrus, female as well as male, bore tusks, the canines locked into the upper jaw. Those of the mature males in the herd averaged from two to three feet in length. The tusks of the old bull were spectacularly larger. Remarkably, though yellow with age, nicked and scarred and striated, they were not worn down or broken. They measured four-and-a-half inches in diameter at the jawline, and nearly five feet in length.

The Eskimos who inhabited this northern Alaskan coast had caught glimpses of the huge bull many times. For an entire generation their most skilled hunters had devoted whole seasons of their lives to the hope of claiming this greatest of all prizes. Old men told stories of their attempts to hunt him. His skin, more than an inch thick and armored with lumpy tubercles, carried the scars of a score of bullet wounds. To the awed hunters he seemed impervious to their weapons, as if he were invincible, a god of the sea.

The natives called him Muugli. The Great One.

In the morning, fog shrouded the beach for several hours. Outside the cove the sea rolled in, cold and gray, pounding against the flatter shoreline in a ceaseless tumult, or crashing against the rocks and broken cliffs, where it lifted in thirty-foot fountains of foam and spray. But at midmorning the fog lifted. A pale, late summer sun washed the shore. It turned the sea a deep blue. The very air seemed to glow.

Within the cove where the male walrus herd had paused in its fall migration, the sunlight bathed the rocks in its soft light. The shelf seemed to come alive, for it was covered by the massed bodies of the walruses. There were about two hundred of them. They ranged in color from pink to rusty red, some of them mottled with dark patches of hair where the new winter coat had not yet filled in. The old bull who slept by himself, undisturbed, on a small table, had changed in color from ghostly white to a dark reddish brown, as the blood that had retreated while he was in the icy water moved toward the surface of his skin to dissipate the heat.

For some time the shelf stirred with activity. There was a steady grunting and snorting. Barks and bellows shook the air. Some of the mature males jousted, using their tusks as weapons, but the day was too warm for serious fighting. Others slipped off the rocks into the sea, where they scoured the muddy bottom for the clam beds that had prompted them to pause in their migration. But as the day warmed, almost the entire herd piled onto the narrow shelf, heaping on top of each other, completely covering its surface with their bodies. Some lay on their backs, their flippers languidly waving. Others sprawled on their sides, or leaned against the rocks, or draped their heads over the armored backs of neighbors. They pushed and shoved, and settled down, and slept.

There was nothing to disturb them within the sheltered cove. On the landward side, the steep cliffs, thrusting seventy feet high, made the shelf inaccessible. The sea itself presented no immediate danger, for the walruses' only enemy of the deep was the killer whale, which swam in open waters. The real enemy lived on land: man. And the cove was hidden from human hunters by the jutting finger of land.

At the beginning of this century the walrus herds of the north Pacific had numbered more than two million. Arctic Eskimos, the Inupiat and the Yup'ik, traditionally hunted them, but only for need. A single walrus might serve a native family for a full winter, providing food, skins for their boats and for making ropes, and ivory for carving and trading. Then a different kind of hunter came, light-skinned, hunting not for subsistence but for ivory or, even more perversely, for sport. In the annual slaughters that followed, more than ninety percent of the entire walrus population in the Bering and Chukchi seas was plundered. When the very survival of the species was threatened, laws were finally passed against wholesale killing of the walrus for ivory, or trophy hunting. Only the Eskimos' traditional subsistence hunting was still allowed. So was their sale of the small quantities of ivory they carved to sell to tourists.

Poachers quickly recognized and exploited this breach in the law. Eskimos became their cover for their own illegal harvesting of ivory. Outside the law, the slaughter continued.

During its brief summer sojourn, ranging as far south as Bristol Bay, Muugli's herd had been unthreatened. Now it was traveling north to meet the descending pack ice, and to reunite with the female herds and last spring's calves, who were following the accelerating progress of the pack ice from northern Arctic waters toward the Bering Strait. During the summer the females remained in Arctic waters, near the pack ice in the northern Chukchi and Arctic seas. Male herds scattered, riding drifting islands of ice southward to choice seabottom feeding grounds. Some browsed and fed in the southern Chukchi Sea, while other herds ventured up to two thousand miles south, where they were frequently seen on Round Island and the Pribilof Islands in the southern Bering Sea. It was during these few months that the males built up the thick layer of fat that would enable them to survive during the winter, when the sentinel males might go for weeks or months on the ice without food, living off their own fat.

When the scattered male and female herds were reunited in this fall migration, they would travel together to their breeding grounds near St. Lawrence Island, some two hundred miles west of Nome in the northwest sector of the Bering Sea, within sight of Russia's Siberian mountains on a clear day—a rarity in the vicinity of that island. For Muugli's herd the arduous northern journey had been over fifteen hundred miles. That journey was near its end.

The cove they had found seemed safe. Even if Eskimo hunters had discovered the herd while it rested there, the shelf was normally impossible to reach in small boats because of the turbulent sea outside the cove. At peace, the walruses dozed in the sun.

A mile from the cove, on orders from the white hunters, the outboard motors powering two long Eskimo skin boats were shut down. Although walruses had no external ears, they could hear fairly well in the open, and remarkably well under water. Beneath the surface the sound of the motors could easily travel a mile or more.

There were five natives in one boat, six in the other. One white man crouched in the stern of each boat, hunched against the wind. The Eskimos worked the oars. The open sea was rough, the current strong enough to make the men grunt and strain at the oars.

Billy Mulak, in the second boat, didn't like the look of the sky behind him, but Travis Mayberry, the white hunter in command of his boat, was unconcerned. He had eyes only for the wall of rock as the two boats worked closer to the tip of the peninsula.

The native boats were *oumiaks,* narrow open boats about twenty feet in length and covered with walrus skins. Each was capable of carrying a half-dozen men with their equipment. The boats were remarkably durable and seaworthy, but Billy knew that the weather could change in an instant. Five-foot waves could become towering walls of water, swamping them.

The appearance of the sun that morning had brought the boats out. The white men had been three days at the village, increasingly edgy and bad-tempered, while rains and heavy seas battered the coast. They wouldn't listen to the possibility that this morning's break in the pattern was only a lull. They had to go after the walrus herd that had been spotted from the air just a few days ago, before the storm drew a curtain over the coast-line.

This was no ordinary hunt. They were after Muugli, Billy re-minded himself. The name, with its weight of legend, brought an exhilarating edge of excitement to the hunt.

Billy thought of the reward Mayberry had promised him for the capture of the Great One's tusks.

He brushed off a flicker of guilt, his thoughts shunting away from the questionable nature of the hunt. Billy had been taught to hunt by his father in the traditional way of his people. They killed only for need. They respected, even revered, the animals that provided them with their means of survival. For the Yup'ik and Inupiat Eskimos of Alaska's northern coast, the seals and the walruses were gifts of God to their people, without which they would never have survived. In consequence the natives of the region did not kill wantonly, or for sport, or to prove their mastery of nature. They knew better who was master.

The white men didn't hunt in the native way. They brought many weapons, with great firepower. They did not honor or respect their victims. They did not care how many were killed.

This morning all of the men carried weapons, Eskimos and whites, although at least two men in each boat would have to continue to man the oars unless the inlet was very calm. Travis Mayberry, and one of the natives in the second boat, had Chi-nese-manufactured AK-47s, assault weapons that fired a hail of bullets. Billy Mulak, who was armed with the rifle his father had given him when he was still a boy, envied the man from his village who had been given the AK-47 for this hunt. And yet . . .

Billy felt his heart hammering against his ribs. His stomach churned at the prospect of the carnage that lay ahead.

He thought again of what Mayberry had promised him. Noth-ing else mattered.

The first boat was nearly level with the last rocks. Billy could see an edge of the cove just around the tip of the peninsula. At a signal from Wolf Simpson, the white hunter in the lead boat, the natives working the oars kept the oumiak in position, wait-ing for the second craft to work closer, until it was almost abreast . . .

* * *

On the shelf the old bull lifted his massive head. He blinked at the phosphorescent sunlight. A feeling stirred within him, an old instinct of danger. But the sun was warm and he was sleepy. Normally he could smell humans hundreds of feet away, but the wind was carrying their scent away from him. Although the sky was black against the horizon, the sea remained calm. A group of four walruses swam across the cove toward the shelf, returning from feeding. With their keen underwater hearing they would have sensed any unnatural sound. Nothing threatened them.

The Great One let his long tusks drop over the edge of his bed of rock.

After a moment he raised his head again. The feeling of unease persisted. There had been a growling or buzzing some time earlier, almost muffled by the familiar pounding of the surf, but the sound, so thin and distant, had not alarmed him. Danger was a white bear encountered on polar ice, the massive shape of a killer whale looming out of the blackness of the ocean deep, or men, small creatures hiding behind long, whale-like shapes that floated on the surface of the sea, whose sting was quick and sharp and far-reaching.

The boats appeared without warning at the mouth of the cove. Even as Muugli bellowed his warning, one of the small creatures was clambering up on the rocks at one side of the cove, from which he could look straight down at the herd.

The bulls near the edge of the shelf lunged for the water. A number of them reached it. In the manner of their kind they turned to face the common enemy together, presenting a kind of wall of tusks, a pathetic act of bravery against the awful terror about to be unleashed against them.

The men were standing now in the boats. Up on the rocks, Billy Mulak trained his rifle on the huge old bull at the end of the shelf nearest him. He was awed by the bull's size, the magnificence of his tusks, the defiance of his roar.

Anxiously Billy took aim. He heard the AK-47s begin to chatter. He mustn't shatter the tusks, he'd been told. He must shoot to kill . . .

For the next ten minutes the cove was bedlam. The crack of rifle fire, oddly thin in the cold air, punctuated the harsher rattle of automatic weapons. Densely packed onto the shelf, most of the walruses were trapped. Scores died in the first volleys of fire. Some wounded reached the water to die. Others were cut down before they could cross the shelf. There was a ceaseless din of roaring and bellowing from the wounded walruses, and a churning of the waters inside the cove. Mayberry and Simpson were yelling at the native hunters and each other. Outside the cove the wind had picked up, unnoticed by the hunters, and ten-foot waves slammed against the walls of the peninsula, adding to the chaos.

Up on the rocks Billy Mulak stood frozen, unable to move. Travis Mayberry was screaming at him. Wolf Simpson shook his fist. Billy was certain that his first shot had struck the huge old bull. Simpson had fired at Muugli simultaneously. But in spite of being hit twice—they could not have missed at this distance, Billy kept telling himself—the bull lumbered across the shelf toward the water. His undulating movements were clumsy but surprisingly quick. Again Billy took aim. The wind made his eyes water, and fear of failure made his hands shake. Just as he fired again the big walrus tumbled into the water.

Was he badly wounded? Billy stared down in rising panic. He waited for the wounded old bull to surface. Fragments of old tales of Muugli's capacity for survival jabbed at his memory. The waters that had closed over him were darker now, red with blood, and dark from the reflection of black clouds scudding overhead.

Below Billy, some of the other Eskimo hunters had leaped from the boats onto the shelf. A few of the wounded and beleaguered walruses charged toward them. In centuries past the charge of an angry walrus had been a fearsome thing, but these hunters carried rifles, and they fired quickly, usually stopping one of the mammals with a single shot. One of the AK-47s chattered its own deadly song, raining bullets in a scythelike sweep across the shelf. The charge was broken. The few survivors of the walrus herd tried to escape to the water. More bullets stopped them.

And at last the panicky bellowing was silenced. More than a

hundred walruses lay dead on the shelf or in the roiling waters of the cove.

The older, more experienced Eskimos went quickly to work on the carcasses heaped across the shelf, using their razor-sharp knifes and short-handled hatchets to chop the tusks free of their anchors in the upper jaw, or sometimes to sever the entire head. On a traditional hunt they would have paused to cut off a hunk of the black flesh and thick white fat and drop it into the sea as a tribute to ancient gods. Now there was no time for such superstitious offerings. There would be no taking of walrus meat to save for the winter. A stack of tusks and heads at one end of the shelf grew larger. The shelf itself was awash with blood.

All of a sudden one of the older Eskimos began to yell at the others. His finger jabbed toward the sky. The others became aware of a new danger. Consternation spread among them. The first native ran toward the nearest boat.

In the noise and excitement, no one at first had paid attention to the darkening of the sky overhead, or heard the rising winds keening in the rocks, least of all Travis Mayberry. He had been too choked with elation over his success in actually hunting down the legendary Muugli. The old bull's tusks were even more spectacular than Mayberry had imagined—priceless!

When the first heavy raindrops lashed his face, Mayberry turned toward the sea and gaped. His heart thudded. A black wall of rain marched toward him across the water. The waves in the open sea were already heaving twice as high as his head.

On the shelf the natives had been skillfully at work separating the tusks from the dead carcasses. A large pile of carefully stacked ivory, along with a number of intact walrus heads, had grown at one end of the shelf. But as Mayberry turned back from the open sea, the Eskimos abandoned their work almost as one. They scrambled toward the boats. Mayberry yelled at them, ordering them back. They ignored him. They feared his anger, but they feared being caught by the storm even more.

Wolf Simpson, standing in one boat, shouted at Mayberry across the water. The wind shredded his words. "—God's sake! Trav! . . . gotta . . . ge . . . outa here!"

"The ivory!" Mayberry shouted. "Load the goddamn ivory!"

But his angry command went unheeded or unheard. The natives, normally so indifferent to the hazards of the sea, were clearly alarmed. Wolf Simpson had caught their panic. Mayberry was jolted into the first clear sense that they understood the danger better than he did.

"It'll be . . . safe here!" Simpson yelled back. "Get going! . . . gotta . . . save our asses!"

"Muugli!" Mayberry screamed. "Where's Muugli?"

It was already too late. The hunters were all in the boats. Even Mayberry couldn't stop them. One of the outboard motors caught. The other quickly followed. The fringe of the curtain of rain reached them as they cleared the tip of the peninsula and ran before the storm, racing toward the open beach, racing for their lives.

ONE

From HIS office on the second floor above his Front Street saloon, Travis Mayberry could swivel around in his high-back green leather chair and look out through rain-streaked windows at the Bering Sea. It was a week since the richest harvest of ivory Mayberry had seen in years had been aborted by a series of storms. The view from his office windows for those seven days had suited his mood—a gray, angry sea, lowering clouds, rain lashing the beach and the sorry, soggy row of buildings that made up Nome's principal street.

Mayberry's rages caused those around him to walk very softly and, if possible, stay out of his way. Even Marie Lemieux, his current summer woman—who had confounded locals by lasting not only through one summer but a winter and a second summer as well—had made herself scarce. Usually she could brighten one of Mayberry's black moods with a wiggle of her hips. Not this time. He seemed obsessed by the loss of one particular walrus he'd been hunting. Marie couldn't understand why anyone would be in such a temper over a couple of walrus tusks, but she knew better than to press the issue.

Mayberry was a powerful chunk of a man, with a thick chest and arms like small oak trunks. His forearms and chest and shoulders were covered with curly black hair. His face was square and heavy, with wide-set brown eyes and a full, wide mouth that could settle into a deceptive appearance of geniality. Although many of his activities were illegal, the saloon being an exception, Mayberry ranked near the very top in the hierarchy of the citizenry of Nome, Alaska. He held no official title—he had turned down the chance to run for mayor three differ-

11

ent times—but little was done without his knowledge and approval.

A sting operation mounted by the Fish and Wildlife Service the previous year had snared two men known to be Travis Mayberry's employees. The discovery had done nothing to diminish his stature. Nome's tradition of tolerance for debauchery, drunkenness, gambling and violence had begun with the gold rush in 1899. A century later it was still said that Nome was a good destination if you were running from the law.

The city was home to fewer than four thousand residents, three-fourths of them Eskimos. It stood at the edge of the continent, facing a view of the Bering Sea that was usually shrouded in fog or rain or sleet, and rarely offered beautiful sunsets. The climate was abysmal pretty much year round—dusty and windy and rainy in the brief summer months, cold and windy and foggy in winter, when the rain turned to icy sleet or snow and everything froze. The terrain was bleak in every direction—a flat coastal plain, barren of interest. The nearest tree was about eighty miles inland.

There had never been a good reason to go to Nome, much less settle there, until gold was discovered in 1899. By the following summer, a tiny settlement of some two hundred souls had become a raucous city of thirty thousand people seeking their fortunes. Men were quite willing to go to a frozen hell where you could walk along the beach and stub your toe on a nugget of gold.

Now Nome was notable primarily as the destination point of the annual Anchorage to Nome Iditarod Trail Sled Dog Race, a winter ordeal across one thousand and forty-nine miles of snow- and ice-covered mountains, frozen rivers and some of the world's most hostile terrain. The race commemorated an historic 1925 rescue in which twenty mushers with their dog teams risked their lives to rush serum to Nome in the face of a diphtheria epidemic.

Though comfortable with Nome's casual view of the law, Mayberry didn't think of himself as a criminal, or even a particularly violent man. He had a temper, sure, rock-hard fists, and was rumored to have killed more than one enemy with a knife or a gun. But Mayberry considered his brushes with authority as occurring in the normal way because he stood up for himself and made the best of his lot, doing what a man had to do when he didn't have his life handed to him on a platter.

Mayberry had fought in Vietnam. He'd tried his hand at peddling drugs in the Lower 48, but had run into trouble with more organized and dangerous gangs. Drifting north, he had eventually come to Alaska. There he had fallen into his trade by a chance encounter with Delbert Hicks, a seller of illegal ivory who took a fancy to him. Hicks was long since gone, disappearing under mysterious circumstances that Mayberry was careful not to inquire into too closely when he met Hicks's boss, Harry Madrid. Mayberry guessed that Hicks was a victim of his own greed.

Because of Hicks, Mayberry had found his calling. He was a poacher, supplying a variety of illegal goods to Harry Madrid—chiefly walrus ivory, but also including polar bear pelts, and the gallbladders of brown bears because in some societies they were regarded as a cure for impotence, and the talons of grizzlies, and anything else in Alaska, from eagles to snowy owls, that was exotic enough to bring a good price.

In Mayberry's experience, most goods that were of significant value were illegal, not because there was anything intrinsically wrong with selling them but because governments were bound and determined to interfere with normal trade. Everything Mayberry did that the United States Fish and Wildlife Service regarded as illegal had, at some point not very far back in history, been perfectly legitimate. His only problem, as he saw it, was that he had been born into a time when the bleeding hearts and environmental crazies were in the driver's seat. He was only technically engaged in criminal activity. In another, more enlightened time he would have been viewed simply as an enterprising merchant.

The past year hadn't been a particularly good one for Mayberry. The poachers caught in the Fish and Wildlife Service's sting operation, including the two who had worked for Mayberry, had come to a show trial over in Anchorage. That sting had taken place right here in Nome, the Federal agents setting up a false storefront where they posed as ivory buyers. The trial had been melodramatic enough for Perry Mason or Matlock,

heroes of two of Mayberry's favorite television shows, in the re-
runs that made up most of the TV schedule pulled in on
Nome's satellite dish. Mayberry hated scams by the Feds.
"They're fuckin' dishonest!" was his sour verdict.

Then something happened that looked like it would turn
Mayberry's year right around.

For at least two decades poachers dealing in walrus ivory in
Alaska had heard Eskimo tales about an enormous old walrus
with monstrous tusks that were, depending on the teller, four,
five or even six feet long. He was called Muugli, the Great One.
The stories had been largely discounted, brushed off as native
legend, the stuff of tall tales old men told their grandchildren.
But the stories persisted. In time they filtered along the network
of poachers, from the hunters in Alaska to their buyers and
bosses in America to the overlords of the trade in Asia. If they
were never quite believed, they were not forgotten.

Then, in May of this year, during the spring migration of the
male walrus herds southward through the Bering Sea from their
winter breeding grounds, a wildlife photographer flying over a
tiny strip of beach on a small island in Bristol Bay snapped a
long-range picture of a walrus herd. In one corner of the beach,
lifting his head toward the plane and the excited photographer's telephoto lens, was a huge old bull with enormous tusks.
When the photo was published—ironically, in a small magazine
devoted to ecological concerns—the scene on the beach was
blurred by distance, but the walrus's tusks were distinct. It was
possible to estimate their size with a fair degree of accuracy.
The measurement left no doubt. Muugli was more than legend.
He was alive.

In late July a copy of the magazine reached Hong Kong. Gate-
way to the Asian continent, that great city was the center of the
hugely profitable international trade in ivory and exotic animal
artifacts. At the heart of this traffic was the Chang family, one of
two powerful Chinese families that dominated the illegal trade.
The picture in the magazine was spotted by Deng Chang, the
youngest son of Madam Lu Chang, the matriarchal ruler of
the organization. Intensely ambitious to claim a larger role in
the family business, Deng had begun to read Western maga-

zines and newspapers, gleaning them for any information that might be useful in the ivory trade.

At sixty Madam Chang was as renowned for the cruel efficiency of her methods as for her delicate, parchmentlike beauty. Deng waited for the right moment, approaching her after her morning massage, when she was usually in a good mood. It was a warm, bright morning, and she was on the terrace of her hilltop estate overlooking the crowded heap of skyscrapers below and Hong Kong's glittering, teeming harbor. Her cheeks and lower eyelids had been carefully rouged, making the pale skin appear more white, almost translucent.

She watched Deng's approach with a small smile, recognizing his eagerness. "What is it, my son? You have something that would interest me?"

"I am sure of it, Honorable Mother."

He handed her the magazine, opened to the striking photograph of the walrus on the beach. She studied it for what seemed a long time, holding the magazine in her thin, long-fingered hands. A three-inch, carmine-colored fingernail traced the outline of the tusks in the photo. Watching closely, Deng Chang saw a flicker of emotion in his mother's black, almond-shaped eyes. Where first there had been tolerant skepticism, now there was a much stronger emotion: greed.

The walrus tusks were magnificent, at least five feet long, as large as many elephant tusks. If they could be captured intact, there would be nothing to compare with them in the world. Lu Chang's clients included a rich Taiwanese collector of rare ivory and an equally affluent Japanese with the same passion. The two could be played off against each other. It would be like auctioning a newly discovered Monet or Van Gogh to jealously competitive art collectors.

"You have done well, my son," Madam Chang murmured.

"Are they not beautiful?" Deng could not conceal his elation. "I have never seen such walrus tusks."

"Very beautiful."

"You must have them!"

"That remains to be seen." She spoke without visible passion, but her son's excitement awakened an answering tremor within her. He was right in bringing the photograph to her. He would be suitably rewarded. But in the meantime all she had was a picture.

That afternoon Madam Chang placed a call to a New Jersey warehouse, to the office of one Harry Madrid, a kingpin in the North American traffic in ivory and other exotic items. It was only the second time in five years that Lu Chang had personally spoken to Madrid. The effect was electrifying. Yes, Madrid had men in the field in Alaska, the very best poachers. The search for the walrus with the extraordinary tusks would begin at once. If he was anywhere in or near the Bering Sea, they would find him. Harry Madrid guaranteed it.

Madrid's call to Travis Mayberry in Nome, if not as terrifying as a personal call from Madam Lu Chang, nevertheless built a fire under the poacher. The hunt began at once.

For the next month Mayberry and his agents scouted the male walrus herds that thronged the islands and shores of the Bering Sea. The hunt was as covert as possible, careful to avoid drawing the attention of Fish and Wildlife agents, but it was exhaustive.

There was no sign of the walrus the Eskimos called the Great One. Wolf Simpson, Mayberry's second-in-command, grew weary of endless flights in a small plane, especially since they frequently required going up in miserable and dangerous weather. He complained that it was a wild goose chase. Photographs could be faked, he argued. Simpson was one of those skeptics who were half-convinced that television film of the United States moon landing had been manufactured in a secret government studio somewhere in Georgia. Mayberry tersely ordered him back into the air.

In late August the male herds began their northward migration, at the same time as the female herds with their calves followed the progress of pack ice south from northern Arctic waters. The hunters intensified their search, even at the risk of detection by Federal investigators. Under pressure from Harry Madrid, Travis Mayberry even took his own plane up, while Simpson flew with a hired bush pilot in a chartered plane. With summer's passage, time and patience were running out. Winter, with its violent storms and frozen seas, would soon make observations by sea or air impossible.

In the first week of September the chartered plane, with Wolf Simpson aboard nursing a hangover and cursing Mayberry in a variety of inventive ways, quartered the rocky coastline in the northern reaches of the Bering Sea. After a fruitless morning, it continued northward, following the coastline of the Seward Peninsula for a hundred miles through the straits to the edge of the Chukchi Sea. Here the coastline was more rugged and inaccessible, the seas rougher, the sightings of seals and walrus more rare.

The grizzled pilot, an Alaskan veteran named Les Hargrove, kept a close eye on his fuel gauge. In the early afternoon he told Simpson their run was over for the day. The poacher didn't argue. He was cold and hungry, and his headache had never gone away since morning.

As they turned about, Simpson spotted a single large fur seal on an island beach about a mile from the mainland. Alarmed by the buzzing of the airplane's engine, it flopped toward the water in an undulating motion. Simpson reached for the high-powered Remington Magnum rifle at his side. "Catch him!" he urged. "I can get beaucoup bucks for that fur!"

The bush pilot shared the stubborn independence of his kind. He refused. He didn't like Simpson anyway, and he was being paid to look for walrus, not fur seals. If he diverted, he said, Travis Mayberry would have his balls for breakfast.

The seal reached open water and disappeared into the sea. Les Hargrove ignored the curses from the man at his side.

As he flew closer to the mainland Hargrove's eye was drawn toward an odd crook of land to the north. It extended into the sea like a finger before hooking back. The pilot glanced again at his fuel reading. A close call, he thought, maybe too close, but what the hell. "No risk, no gain," he muttered aloud.

Acting on a hunch, he flew toward the peninsula. Coming in low over the bluff, he passed directly over an inlet rimmed by a narrow rock shelf. The shelf was completely covered with the bodies of walruses.

As the plane buzzed overhead, bulls near the edge of the

table began to spill into the water. Scanning the scene through binoculars, Wolf Simpson felt astonishment, then elation. He refocused the binoculars, as if he couldn't believe his eyes. He gave an involuntary whoop. "It's him!" Simpson yelled. He pounded Hargrove's shoulder. "Look at the size of the bastard! It's him, by Christ! It's Muugli!"

Remembering the scene in the cove, the prize almost literally at his feet, almost near enough to touch, Travis Mayberry flushed with renewed anger. He had been so close. Close enough to see the texture of the rough tubercles on Muugli's hide, to measure those tusks with his eyes. But Simpson and the native kid had bungled the hit. Both claimed to have got in clean shots. The old walrus had been wounded. There was blood on the rocks to prove it. But somehow he had managed to slip off the shelf into the cove, diving out of sight.

And the storm had struck without warning. The hunters had had to flee for their own lives.

That had been a week ago. The storm had battered the coast relentlessly. There had been one window of calm two days ago, but Mayberry had been frustrated because the bush pilot, Hargrove, had taken off for Anchorage at the beginning of the week. Although he was an experienced pilot himself, like many Alaskans, Mayberry didn't trust his skill enough to go up in threatening weather. And the sea remained too rough for the small but seaworthy native boats needed to gain access to the walrus cove and haul the ivory out.

Mayberry swiveled away from the windows at the sound of footsteps on the stairs leading to his office. He glared toward the open doorway, as if he were ready to pounce on anyone with the nerve to face him. Wolf Simpson's lean, long face, the kind of narrow, Anglo-Saxon features familiar in the Appalachian hills where he had been born, peered around the edge of the doorway, followed by his thin whippet's body with its narrow shoulders and bony chest.

Simpson's given name was Clyde, though few people knew it. He had acquired his nickname from his predatory enthusiasm for hunting wolves from the safety of a helicopter, a sport that had in times past been popular in Alaska, and was threatening to make a comeback, with the support of the state's legions of hunters and the politicians who catered to them. Only an unexpectedly loud uproar from the Lower 48, and even from animal activists in other countries, had caused the governor to cancel an open season on hunting wolves by air. Angry hunting enthusiasts, like Simpson, argued that thinning out the wolf packs was essential for the good of other game, particularly caribou, that wolves preyed on. It was good wilderness management, he said. And the next time the proposal was revived, he promised darkly, it would be done more quietly.

Simpson was Mayberry's right-hand man. In many ways he was slyer and meaner than his boss, but nowhere near as dangerous. His was the threat of deception and betrayal rather than direct confrontation—of the knife in the back or the shot in the dark.

Satisfied when his appearance did not spark an immediate tirade, Simpson kind of sidled into Mayberry's office. "Uh . . . we got a problem, Trav."

Mayberry glowered at him. "I don't need any more problems. This storm is enough problem." When Simpson was prudently silent Mayberry said, "Seven days to create the whole fuckin' universe, and we've been sitting here seven days with our thumbs up our asses, doing nothing, while the biggest fortune in ivory we've ever seen is sittin' out there where you let it get away."

"It wasn't my fault," Simpson whined, though he knew the futility of defending himself. "I hit the bastard, but I didn't have a good angle from the boat, you know that. That stupid Eskimo kid had the shot. He was up on the rocks, lookin' right down his sights at Muugli. No way he could miss him."

"He says he didn't, but neither one of you stopped that bull goin' in the water."

"He was hurt. He wasn't goin' anywheres. We get back there, I guarantee you we'll find him tossed up on those rocks."

"The natives say he's been hit before, and he always gets away. They say you can't kill him."

"You don't buy that superstitious bullshit," Simpson protested.

"Maybe I do and maybe I don't. But we're damned sure gonna find out in a hurry. This storm's breaking up. The TV weather guy says there's clear behind it, maybe late tonight, tomorrow for sure. Did you get hold of Hargrove? I want him here early tomorrow morning."

"That's the problem," Simpson mumbled in a very low tone, as if he didn't want Mayberry to hear.

"What'd you say?"

"Hargrove's gone."

"Hargrove's gone? Whata you mean, he's gone? I know god-damn well he went back to Anchorage. Get hold of him and tell him to sober up and haul his ass back here."

"That's what I'm tryin' to tell you. Hargrove's not comin' back. He's bailed out. He's gone back to the Lower 48. The son of a bitch said he'd had enough."

"That's crazy, those guys never have enough." Mayberry scowled in disbelief. "You ever hear of one of those old bush pilots could walk away from it?"

"Hargrove did. Said he was gonna go and lay on some beach in California. He's gone, Trav. Took his fuckin' little plane and flew south."

Mayberry blew. If he had been a volcano, Simpson thought, there would have been ashes falling from Barrow all the way to Juneau. Having survived similar eruptions before, Simpson knew the best and safest course was just to hunker down and wait it out. Downstairs in the saloon, there was a sudden, listening silence. A stranger started to chuckle, until the whole room turned threateningly toward him.

When the worst was over and Mayberry, red-faced and breathing hard, slammed a broad palm on his battered walnut desk and fell back into his leather chair, Simpson said, "He recommended this other guy, lives over in Fortune, flies a Cessna."

Mayberry was silent a moment, staring at him. "You gonna spoon-feed me these little tidbits of information one at a time? Or is this one of those good news, bad news things?"

Simpson flushed. "We don't know the guy."

"Did Hargrove know him? Did he say he was okay?"

"Yeah, but . . ."

"But what?" Even as he grunted the automatic question, however, Travis Mayberry was sifting the news, examining it cautiously, like a demolitions expert peering at a package that might or might not contain a bomb. He didn't like unexpected changes. In his business, changes in personnel were the most suspect. "What's his name, this pilot?"

"Robie, Rorie, something like that. Jeff. Jeff Rorie, I think that's it."

"These Alaskan bush pilots, they're all the same," Mayberry said thoughtfully. "They're all a little crazy. And they're a goddamn fraternity. The guy's been around, Hargrove would know him."

"That don't mean we can trust him."

"Um. You got any better ideas?"

Simpson admitted he hadn't. He argued that he ought to check the new guy out first, that another few days wouldn't make any difference. Mayberry said it couldn't wait. First chance, he wanted a flyover to see if the giant walrus with the special tusks could be spotted. Simpson could run a check on the pilot later.

"Hargrove knew the score," Mayberry said. "He wouldn't vouch for the guy if he wasn't right."

"Hargrove wanted out. Maybe he'd say anything to keep you from comin' down hard on him."

"How'm I gonna do that if he's in California?"

Simpson stopped arguing. The important thing was that Mayberry had forgotten his rage. He was being almost reasonable.

"Get hold of him," Mayberry said. "Tell him he wants a job, he'll be here at six in the morning. If he's not, don't bother coming." He swung his swivel chair toward the rain-smeared window. He stared at the gray lid of clouds that clamped down over the angry sea, leaving only a narrow strip of dirty white to define the horizon line. "Dead or alive, I'm gonna find that long-toothed son of a bitch . . . and then maybe I'm gonna go and lie on some sunny beach."

"Is one pair of tusks worth that much?"

"Not just any pair of tusks," Mayberry said, swiveling around. "Just the biggest walrus tusks in the whole goddamn world!"

*   *   *

When Wolf Simpson left, Mayberry stared after him for a long time, unseeing. The angry optimism he had summoned while talking to Simpson faded away.

Harry Madrid had called twice when Mayberry was out, both times leaving urgent messages.

Mayberry hadn't told him about having to leave the ivory haul out on the edge of the Chukchi Sea for a week. Madrid, who shuttled between his million-dollar condo overlooking Central Park and a seaside pink villa on Key Biscayne, didn't understand about weather in Alaska. He didn't understand that flying a Cessna into an Arctic storm, or trying to maneuver an Eskimo boat in those raging waters, wasn't a walk in the park or a trip to Disneyland. He didn't even want to hear about such things. All Harry wanted was his ivory, or his polar bear pelts or grizzly talons, or whatever it was he had an order for. Anything else was excuses, and Harry Madrid didn't want to hear excuses.

Mayberry didn't want to return Harry's calls and tell him he couldn't get the ivory yet because it had been raining here.

In a way Madrid was like a spoiled child, Mayberry thought sourly. What he saw he wanted, and if he didn't get it he threw a tantrum. The only time Mayberry had ever been physically present when Madrid had a tantrum was that time when Madrid paid an unexpected visit to Nome and caught Delbert Hicks keeping two sets of books, one for the stuff he sold Harry and another for a small portion of ivory and other items Hicks had been setting aside for himself, dealing on the side. It didn't amount to much, maybe no more than five percent of the illegal plunder Hicks had been providing to Madrid and the international poaching organization he represented. But Madrid had reacted the way the owners of Las Vegas casinos responded to finding a blackjack dealer skimming off the top for himself. The heirs and descendants of Bugsy Siegel and his friends had a great big empty desert all around for any such necessary employer-employee conferences. Harry Madrid had gone off with Delbert Hicks for a heart-to-heart talk out on the lonely tundra. No one had ever seen Hicks again.

That was, in fact, how Travis Mayberry came to be promoted to being Madrid's Number One Man in Alaska.

Mayberry stared glumly at the phone on his desk.

He knew he couldn't be out if Harry called a third time.

TWO

A HUNDRED fifty air miles north of Nome, beyond the Bering Strait, the week of persistent storms in mid-September brought hard winds and rain lashing inland from the Chukchi Sea. The nights dipped below freezing and the rains turned to sleet that froze on the ground. A frozen crust hardened the single muddy street of the Yup'ik village on the river.

When the sky cleared and the temperature climbed, the crust thawed and the street turned to an ooze that sucked at John Mulak's boots as he plodded through the muck toward the river. Head down in gloomy thought, he did not glance at the modern government houses on either side of the street. Mulak had spent his early childhood in a sod house with dried seal gut over the one window, a mud floor in the single room where the whole family slept, a kerosene cooking tank, smoky seal oil lamps for light. The government houses, products of the brief period of prosperity brought by the Trans-Alaska pipeline, had changed village life forever. Each house had three separate bedrooms, a furnace, a stove, refrigerator, washer and dryer. Storage tanks fueled the electric generator that provided power for the entire village. A disk antenna brought television to every living room, dominating family life.

A blare of sound from a log house at the center of the village, a relic from earlier times, caused Mulak to lift his head. Even at this early hour the village's recreation center, with its wall of arcade games, would be crowded. Mulak supposed that was where Billy had gone when he stormed out of the house.

Mulak welcomed the clear day. It gave him a chance to get away from the village to hunt or fish. His daughter Ruth, along

24

with his brother's family, were off berry picking, one of the favorite activities of the village people. The salmonberry bushes, their branches heavy with berries in August, were now bare, but patches of the tundra not far from the village were laden with blueberries. In another week the crowberries and cranberries would be ripe, the last of the treats the tundra offered before the barren emptiness of winter.

The quarrel with Billy had started over the berry picking. Mulak had said that Billy should go along with Ruth. His son refused.

"Ruth should not be the only one of our family to go," Mulak had said. "The berries will be shared by all."

"No!" Billy cried. "You want some fuckin' berries, you go pick 'em yourself!"

Billy was nineteen. The Yup'ik people did not believe in striking children, who were generally sunny-tempered, as Billy had once been. In that moment Mulak felt very close to striking his son, and he had to turn away, his face dark with anger as Billy slammed the door on his way out.

In the last year Billy had changed. His moods swung wildly from exaggerated laughter to sullen irritability. He had lost interest in fishing or berry picking. He spent most of his time watching TV, or down at the arcade, or out on the airstrip that served the village, searching for a sign of the plane that would bring the white men seeking ivory. They paid Billy and a dozen other young men of the village to hunt with them—paid them more than most of them had earned in their lives. These whites ignored the Eskimos' subsistence hunting rule, which was not spelled out in the law but left to the natives themselves. In Mulak's village the agreed limit was four walruses per boat in hunting season, a total that might cover two or three families.

Reaching the bank of the river, John Mulak pulled the tarpaulin cover from his kayak, checked the skin boat for any damage from the storm, and dragged it down the dry gravel incline toward the river. Although the kayak was nearly four times his size, he handled it easily.

Mulak's father had built the kayak with the help of his grandfather. The latter, whose name was Eli, had been an Inupiat, a native tribe living on the fringe of the Arctic Sea north of the mountains. He had been a hunter of whales, and in the course of his pursuit he had ventured south to the Yup'ik village on the river that fed into the Chukchi Sea where Mulak's grandmother had lived. They had soon married and, in an unusual choice among the people of both Eskimo tribes, Eli Mulak and his new wife had stayed in the village of her people, not his.

Eli Mulak was a hunter and fisherman, trained by his own father in ancient survival skills and crafts passed on from one generation to another. He made fishnets and small animal traps by hand, tools and spears of bone and ivory, snares to catch birds, sleds and boats to travel in. Among these crafts was the making of the light, fast, highly maneuverable and seaworthy skin boats used by his people long before the coming of the white men. The kayak he had helped John Mulak's father make was twenty feet long and about three feet wide at the center. Its original whalebone frame, which was covered with sealskins, had been reinforced over the years by wooden supports. The deck was completely covered except for the cockpit, and even here John Mulak had a skin shirt inherited from his father with fringes that could be laced into the edges of the opening, sealing out the water. Although Mulak seldom wore his father's old shirt, which was precious to him, his boat was still watertight and safe even in heavy seas. An expert kayaker, like Mulak, could even roll completely over in his boat without sinking or taking on much water.

He pushed off the bank into the swift current. It felt good to be out on the water, good to feel the pull on his back and shoulders. His paddle flashed silver in the sunlight with each stroke. But he did not find his usual joy in his boat and the river and the feel of the wind in his face. An uneasiness followed him all the way down the river to the sea. Billy had been moody and sullen-tempered since the last time he had been out hunting with the white men, just before the latest series of storms. Some of the hunters bragged that Muugli, the Great One, had been slain in the hunt, but no one knew if this was true. Whatever had happened, John Mulak thought, something was very wrong with his son.

*   *   *

Late that afternoon, far north along the coastline, working his kayak skillfully through the rough waters at the edge of the sea, John Mulak rounded a pile of rocks fingering out from the shoreline and, entering an unexpected cove, came upon the carnage without warning. First the bloated body of one dead walrus, headless, lying against a pile of rocks. Then others, piled like driftwood along a rock shelf or lumped in shallow water. The long shelf and the tumbled rocks at the edge of the peninsula were dark with blood, and the familiar sea seemed darker, colder, more menacing, as if a shadowy evil lurked beneath the surface. The sharp cold air seemed to hold the smell of gunsmoke as well as blood, and he thought he heard the bellowing and roaring of the dying mammals, their clamor so real that he sat motionless in his skin boat, appalled, listening.

Only the waves beating against the shore. Only the screams of scavenger birds frightened by his passage, wheeling in agitated circles overhead.

He paddled toward the shelf. Here the walrus colony had dozed in the sun, heedless of danger, their inlet protected by the finger of rocks. Riding up onto a flat rock, Mulak jumped out with an agility that belied his sixty years. He pulled the kayak halfway out of the water. The blood was pounding in his head, a drumbeat of shock and anger.

And fear.

For a half-hour Mulak walked slowly along the shelf, picking his way among the dead bodies like a stray soldier blundering upon the scene of a recent battle. He was a short, blocky figure. He wore L.L. Bean rubber boots and a plaid hunter's cap with flaps turned up so they did not cover his ears. His quilted nylon parka had a sealskin fur cape sewn onto it, matching his hand-sewn sealskin pants, which were worn over thermal underwear ordered from a Sears catalog. His was an incongruous mix of traditional native garments and others that were manufactured in what he thought of as the Outside, a world he had never seen in person but watched now regularly on television, a world whose goods came to the village in the twice weekly flights bringing supplies, mail, news, officials and sometimes tourists from Anchorage.

Or white poachers from Nome.

Mulak had left the village that morning dressed for what he considered a mild, sunny day. Although the wind blowing in off the sea was sharp, the temperature close to freezing, he did not feel cold. The cherished summer days of the midnight sun were over, but this was still early autumn, after all. The cold, dark winter would be here soon enough without hurrying it along.

He counted the bodies of the dead until, after the first fifty and more, the numbers became so great his mind rejected their grim reality and he stopped counting. He thought of the hunters, picturing them in boats at the mouth of the cove or standing on the rocks that looked down on the shelf, holding their automatic weapons, their cheap Chinese-made AK-47s, firing until the sea itself was churned up into foam by the rain of bullets.

Walruses, unlike the wilier seals, had few enemies. They were wary of humans, but slow to panic. That had always made hunting easier for the Eskimos. But Mulak's people, for untold generations leading back into the mists of time, had always hunted only for what they needed, as they did even now. They did not slaughter greedily. Like the Indian tribes to the south, they killed for food, for clothing, for the oil used to light their lamps and cook their food. If an animal had horns or tusks, as well as meat, fat and skin, these too were saved, shaped into utensils or tools or the points of spears, or carved into artifacts. Seal or whale or walrus at sea, salmon in the rivers, caribou on the vast tundra, each was an essential part of the Eskimos' life from birth to death. Without them he could not have endured for long in his harsh environment. Each was respected, as the earth itself was respected, the land and the sea and the sky.

This kind of killing was the gussak's way, Mulak thought, but the knowledge that white men were responsible did not ease his mind. White men might have organized this hunt, but when Mulak pictured the hunters he saw them in skin boats like his own, probably the larger boats called oumiaks. The men standing up in the boats holding their fearsome weapons had brown faces like his. The white men had learned to employ the Eskimos' knowledge and expertise, not only because Eskimos were superb hunters but also because it was legal for Alaska's natives to hunt walrus, as they had for countless generations, and to carve and sell the ivory they obtained, where it was forbidden to non-natives. Seeking to exploit these skills and their cover of legality, the white man had come first with goods, with utensils and canned fruits and medicines. Then he had brought rifles to trade for the walrus ivory tusks. Then whisky, which was cheaper for him and soon more desirable to the Eskimos . . .

Eskimos did his hunting now. The young, restless ones, those who had watched the flickering life shown on the television screen and were no longer content with the ways of their elders. Those who had briefly held and then lost their jobs on the pipeline, in the meantime becoming accustomed to thick rolls of money in their pockets.

Even, Mulak thought with anguish, his son Billy.

The poachers had abandoned the shelf in haste, Mulak decided. But they had completed much of their work before they were interrupted. The tusks taken from the dead walruses had been stacked against the wall of the bluff like wood. Each tusk weighed five pounds or more. Most of them measured from two to three feet in length. Some were pale white, some the creamy color of polished ivory, others yellowed or stained. At least a hundred pairs of tusks, Mulak guessed. Alongside them were a dozen severed walrus heads still carrying their tusks, the wet ivory pale against the blood that had congealed on the rocks. These heads had been saved because they carried the longest, most valuable tusks. After a week on the shelf the roots would have begun to lose their grip, and these tusks could be pulled out more easily without the risk of damage.

Mulak had attended the village school, taught by a white woman brought in by the government, and his arithmetic was good. He quickly calculated that he was looking at a thousand pounds of the ivory so coveted by the white hunters who came to the village. He had no idea of the value of so much ivory on the Outside.

In the shadow of a small pile of rocks outside the cove, beyond the tip of the peninsula, some movement caught Mulak's eye. He walked toward the end of the shelf to see better, scowling. Fog was rolling in from the sea, turning the long afternoon into a gray murk like early twilight. The cold shroud made it hard to see clearly. He climbed onto the rocks until he was close to the end of the finger of bluffs, close enough to hear the waves smashing against them from the open sea just below him. Now he saw the small pile of rocks more clearly. It was a tiny island little more than a hundred feet from the peninsula. The surf spilled over the top of the rock pile and cascaded in foaming rivulets along the seams and cracks. And over a pair of huge tusks that gleamed like a monstrous smile, mocking him from the shadows.

The old Eskimo stared in wonder. The huge old walrus on the island appeared to be the only survivor of the slaughter Mulak had stumbled upon. He did not plunge immediately into the sea, which suggested that he might be wounded. He did not bark or bellow, but seemed to glare at Mulak accusingly across the narrow bridge of water that separated them. What held Mulak transfixed was the size of the tusks, larger than any he had ever seen, so large as to confound belief.

"Muugli," he whispered.

Although Mulak had never before seen the huge walrus, Muugli had been part of his life since he was a young man, the hero of countless stories, the object of dreams. When the word came to the village that the walrus herds were migrating, always a time of great excitement, tales of the Great One resurfaced. Mulak had always known he was there, sharing the harsh life of the north, a part of the Eskimos' world.

Mulak waited, motionless as the wind tugged at him and the waves pounded the bluff until it shook beneath his feet. He was captive of the awe he felt for this wondrous creature. After what seemed a long time Muugli moved, drawing deeper into the shadows of his little island, until he could no longer be seen. Either he had retreated behind the rocks, or he had slipped into the sea.

Turning away at last, Mulak stared at the greedy slaughter on the shelf behind him. He began to shake with anger.

Mulak was not an impetuous man. His children, three of whom survived, called him stolid and unimaginative. The way of survival for his people had always included death and danger as

intimates, but that familiarity had made Mulak, like his ancestors, prudent and wary, not given to impetuous actions or need-
less risks. But Mulak's decision had been forming earlier as he
counted the tusks on the shelf. With each number his anger
deepened. Now the sight of the Great One, wounded and
mourning, brought an overwhelming sadness, confirming his
resolve.

It was a decision that would make him an outlaw—for which
no word existed in the Yup'ik dialect of his village.

He had to work quickly. The poachers would have planned to
take their harvest of ivory out by air or by sea—there was no
overland road within a hundred miles. He decided they must
have been driven from the scene of the harvest by the storm
that had blanketed the area for the past week with heavy rain,
winds and fog.

The passing of the storm had brought Mulak out in his boat
to fish. The ivory hunters would not be far behind. Was that
why Billy could not go berry picking? he wondered. Was he
waiting for the white men to return?

Most of the traditional kayaks used for centuries by Mulak's
people had room only for the paddler in a round cockpit near
the center of the boat. Mulak's boat was slightly different in
providing a cockpit designed to accommodate two people. The
design caused little loss of maneuverability or increase in
weight, and the extra space offered useful storage for hunter or
fisherman if there was only one paddler aboard.

The larger cockpit made an excellent cargo hold. Into it Mulak carefully placed several of the severed heads bearing the
largest tusks, handling them with something like reverence.
Then he crammed as many of the other tusks as he could into
the opening.

When he left the cove the kayak, overloaded, rode very low in
the water. It wallowed in uncharacteristic fashion with the
swells, and icy water spilled into the cockpit. Digging hard with
his broad-bladed paddle, Mulak worked his boat through the
heavy surf for a mile north of the inlet until he reached the
mouth of a river. From there, turning inland, the going was

easier even though he was paddling upstream. He left the river where the current was strong and threaded his way through tidal flats laced with innumerable marshes, ponds, narrow creeks and streams. Mulak knew them as he knew the veins on the back of his hand, as he knew each line and scar. The fog closed in behind and then enveloped him, swallowing the treeless landscape, smothering sounds. The little finger of Mulak's right hand, which bent like a diverted creek away from the enlarged knuckle, experienced the fog as a spray of tiny needles. He ignored the familiar pain.

Mulak's paddle dipped into the shallow water, making its small, rhythmic ripple in the silence, each thrust propelling the slender craft without apparent effort. For Mulak the muffled scene was never completely silent. He heard the fish breaking the surface of the water as he slid smoothly by, the muted thunder of a flight of geese passing high overhead, the whine of a small cloud of no-see-ums through which he quickly passed. It was late in the year for those pesky, biting, nearly invisible gnats that lived along Alaska's inland waterways, as much a part of the brief summer as the movement of the caribou herds over the tundra, the glut of salmon in the rivers or the migration of thousands of walruses in the neighboring seas.

Though he continued to paddle inland for most of an hour, Mulak was never lost for a moment even before he outdistanced the fog, always knowing exactly how far he had come, which tributary stream would lead him back to the river, how far he was from his village.

Once he spotted two brightly colored tents pitched near the river. Obscured by the brush along the riverbank, he drifted by the small camp, his paddle still. There was no one in sight. A gussak camp, he thought, wondering what white men were doing here this late in the year.

Not long after seeing the tents he came to the spot he had chosen. He left the kayak wedged into the bank of the stream and, in a series of trips, carried the ivory across the tundra into some low foothills. Beyond them, their tops lost this afternoon in a mantle of low clouds, loomed the formidable crags of the Brooks Range. The tundra, though it appeared to be covered only with low grasses and brush, was in fact very difficult terrain for walking. The hummocks of grass twisted underfoot, and the boggy ground between the tufts sucked at his boots. In spite of his age and his burden of tusks, Mulak moved back and forth from the hills to his boat without pausing to rest. Only when the last of this load of ivory had been safely stored inside a cave in the hills did he stop to look out over the tundra toward the ocean.

Though the escarpment on which Mulak stood at the mouth of the cave was less than a hundred feet above sea level, it offered a panoramic view in every direction. Nothing within his sight moved but the grasses stirring in the wind. For more than fifty miles south of the river the tundra extended in a flat, featureless plain, empty, without a tree or a visible rise. On a clear day the great mountains that thrust high above the plain seemed near enough to reach out and touch them. Today they were obscured by mist and clouds. There was no boat on the river or within sight of the seashore, which was obscured by the fog. No plane dotted the sky. No sound broke the silence but the ceaseless wind and the scream of a lone eagle soaring above the foothills, following the line of the river. No one had seen Mulak at his surreptitious work. No one had followed him.

He thought of the gussak camp. Its presence was unexpected, and he would be careful rowing past it. But even if he were seen he believed he would simply be another native in a kayak.

It was late afternoon when Mulak returned to the cove where he had first stumbled upon the horde of walrus ivory. Even though he had seen no sign of anyone, he approached the inlet cautiously. The white men who were responsible for the walrus slaughter were cruel beyond imagining. He knew they would not value the life of an old Eskimo who attempted to interfere in their plans.

The cove was empty of men but not of life. The scavenger birds were still busy. They rose in a cloud, squealing and crying, when Mulak came around the breaker of rocks. He ignored them. He searched for Muugli on the little island but there was no sign of him. Mulak prayed that he was not mortally wounded, and that he would leave before the white poachers returned to search for him.

Was the failure to kill the Great One behind Billy's anxious, ill-tempered mood? He had been present at the hunt. What a prize Muugli's magnificent tusks would have been! How frustrated they must have been over his escape. Perhaps the white men, thus far denied the fruits of their hunt, had in turn denied Billy and the others their share of the spoils.

Mulak turned grimly to the cache of ivory. Once again he loaded his cockpit until the kayak rode dangerously low in the water. Always he watched and listened for the drone of an aircraft approaching, the plume of smoke out to sea that would warn of a large boat's passage. He was a man who had never stolen a thing in his life, or even thought of it. Goods were shared in his village. No one went hungry if others ate. No one needed to steal. Now, in spite of his anger, he felt like a thief. It was an uncomfortable feeling.

He made four trips before full darkness came. Each time he looked in vain for another sign of the Great One. Each trip took well over an hour of punishing labor, paddling the overladen kayak first through the surf and then among the twisting warren of creeks and streams where he could not be seen except from the air. Each time he drifted silently past the gussak camp, and once he glimpsed a slight figure in a red parka trudging across the tundra toward the camp, accompanied by a large dog. The dog surprised him.

Though he had begun in the late afternoon he gave no thought to how long he was laboring into the night. For an Eskimo, to use every minute of summer's light was common. When Mulak was a boy, and the long summer evenings stretched into eternity, he and his companions used to play all night. Such times were too precious to be wasted. A little over a month ago, in early August, the sun had stood above the horizon for twenty-four hours of the day. This night there would be four or five hours of relative darkness. By late December there would be no sun at all, only the endless darkness and the cold.

He slept just inside the mouth of the cave. By then he had moved most of the ivory. Perhaps two more trips, he thought. If the poachers did not return in the morning.

He prayed again that Muugli would escape, because there was nothing he could do to save him. He was a Christian, but at moments like this, ancient beliefs of his people resurfaced, and he hoped the god of the sea would intervene.

He also hoped the bear in whose cave he slept did not decide to return before morning.

THREE

Around two in the morning a smothering fog lifted over the tundra, revealing a small camp with two bright yellow tents pitched a short distance from the river. Here, north of the Arctic Circle, the September darkness was not yet total at this hour, relieved by a kind of halo visible above the horizon, where the sun rolled just out of sight. With the lifting of the fog, and the absence of the foul weather that had battered the tiny camp for most of the past week, a deep stillness settled over the scene.

In that stillness a wolf howled.

Kathy McNeely woke suddenly. For a moment she was disoriented. She was instantly aware of the silence, and as she shook off the clinging webs of sleep she thought it was the unusual silence that had awakened her, the absence of tearing winds and rain pelting the roof of her tent. Then she heard Survivor whimper, a kind of low moan back in his throat. The husky preferred sleeping just outside the entrance of her tent to the relative warmth inside. Kathy rolled halfway out of her sleeping bag and reached out to open the flap. Survivor was on his feet. She saw a tremor pass along his flank.

The wolf howled again, startlingly close. The sound rose, and peaked, and died away. This time smaller yips and cries formed a muted chorus to accompany the soloist's soaring call. Kathy felt the hairs rise on the back of her neck, and a chill trickled along her spine.

Carefully, as if afraid of shattering the moment, she eased out of her warm cocoon of polyester and down, and crawled over to the opening of her tent.

Just as she peered out, the wolf's long, haunting howl poured over her, and she froze in place.

36

The first thing she saw in the pale light was a man standing naked at the edge of the river, knee deep in the icy water, a bar of soap in one hand. Like her, Jason Cobb was transfixed, his head tilted slightly as he listened to the cry of the wilderness. Kathy stared, no more capable of averting her eyes than of closing her ears to the wolf's call.

Cobb was a tall man, over six feet, lean and handsome and fit. His body seemed to catch all of the soft, pre-dawn light, silhouetting him against the silver ripple of the river and the black bulk of distant mountains. Kathy thought of a nineteenth century painting of a lone, naked savage pictured in the vast beauty of the Western wilderness, an idealized canvas so extravagant and romantic as to seem unreal.

The silence returned. Jason Cobb lifted his head. Across the thirty yards between the tents and the river, his eyes met hers.

Kathy ducked back inside her tent. Her cheeks burned in spite of the cold. She slipped back into her sleeping bag, shivering with sudden anger. He had deliberately chosen to make her uncomfortable! She was annoyed with herself for the strength of her reaction. Annoyed with Cobb for choosing to bathe so openly without forewarning her. Annoyed with herself again for the logic that told her he'd bathed in the middle of the night precisely to avoid any discomfort for either of them. Such moments were inevitable in their isolated situation. You coped, that's all. She managed an occasional, awkward sponge bath in the confines of her tent, pre-heating a pan of water until it was bearably tepid. She was compelled to admire Cobb's fortitude. My God, the river was freezing!

At length she began to smile in spite of herself, struck by the ridiculousness of the situation and her reaction.

Far from sleep, Kathy listened for the spine-tingling cry of the wolf. Once, outside the tent, Survivor whimpered, as if he too remained awake, listening intently. But the long, mournful howl did not come again that night.

For a long time Kathy lay wide awake. The sky was fairly light, and she had to check her watch to make certain that it was still the middle of the night. During the heart of the summer, in their first weeks near the Arctic Circle, the sun had never set, and the absence of any darkness was disorienting, her body's

clock unable to match its normal rhythms to the presence of
the midnight sun. With autumn the night was beginning to define itself, and she had adjusted somewhat. Still there were
times, like tonight, when after being awakened she had no
sense whatever of the time of day or night.

She saw Jason Cobb's lean body, white in the Arctic night,
and shook off the image, scowling. Then she had to smile again,
ruefully acknowledging her confusion. Jason Cobb was the last
man on earth she would have expected to step boldly into her
fantasies.

She had first met Cobb on the flight from Seattle to
Anchorage in the first week of June. They had flown over what
was known as the inland route to Alaska, popular for tourist
cruises because of the spectacular proximity of the passing
cruise ships to dramatic, sea-flowing glaciers. The Alaskan Airlines 747 flew low enough to offer breathtaking aerial views of
the unfolding panorama below—dense green forests yielding to
snow-capped granite peaks, and the stunning vista of great rivers of ice flowing between the flanks of mountains toward the
ocean. The day was clear, the sky almost cloudless, and one
glacier after another appeared in the distance, glittering white
in the sunlight. Most of Alaska's great glaciers were in the
southern part of the state, Kathy recalled, where there was annual rainfall of up to two hundred inches. Where she and her
group of scientists were destined, up around the Arctic Circle,
there was barely a tenth of that, little more precipitation than
you would find in the Sahara, far too little to feed the glaciers . . .

Captivated by the spectacle, Kathy had been peripherally
aware of someone taking the empty seat beside her and peering
past her shoulder. "There's your twentieth century view for
you," a deep, confident voice said. "Antiseptic, remote and
safe."

"It's still beautiful," Kathy replied, controlling a slight irritation.

"But not very personal." When Kathy glanced toward him,
she recognized Jason Cobb instantly. She had met him briefly at
the airport, but knew him well by reputation. He was one of the
driving forces behind ASSET's Alaskan expedition.

Cobb smiled. "I'm thinking of John Muir approaching one of those ice massifs in an Indian canoe a hundred years ago. Listening to the crack and roar of ice slides, chunks of the glacier sheering off, feeling the ocean move, not knowing if he was going to get away alive. And still forcing his Indian guides to take him closer." Cobb paused. "Not quite the same, is it?"

He was a strikingly handsome man in his early forties, tall and broad-shouldered. His dark hair was gray at the temples, and he wore a short, neatly trimmed beard that was mostly black with clearly marked crescents of gray framing his chin and the corners of his mouth. The effect was so striking as to appear contrived, as if he had his beard streaked. Very effective on television, Kathy thought. Cobb was an environmental scientist at Berkeley, one of those who was frequently trotted out as an expert in brief segments on the nightly television news whenever an environmental crisis made headlines. His arrogant self-assurance was backed by a legitimate academic reputation, but he had become a media favorite largely because of his telegenic looks, she thought. She was instantly uncomfortable with the glib assessment. That was one trap she, of all people, should avoid. Her own brief media fame, stemming from a widely publicized Antarctic adventure, had earned her some gratuitous sniping by jealous colleagues.

"Like Muir, you've been there, Dr. McNeely," Cobb said. "Not many of us have survived an Antarctic blizzard, alone and unaided."

"Not unaided," Kathy murmured.

Cobb brushed the protest aside. "A wilderness adventure, all the same." Staring through the small window at the slowly unfolding panorama of another frozen river splitting granite peaks, he added thoughtfully, "They say if you can get there by car or tour bus, or even on foot, it will never be a genuine wilderness experience. It's an outdoor experience—like playing golf. For the real thing, you have to fly or boat in, and have the plane or boat leave, so you're alone in the wild. If you meet a wolf or a bear, it's on his terms—and his turf."

"That's what we're here for, isn't it? To try to help preserve one small corner of the earth where man in the twenty-first century will still be able to have that kind of experience?"

"Of course, Doctor." The environmental scientist seemed amused. "We're fortunate to have the Bird Woman with us . . . someone who's been out there on the edge."

Kathy sensed the hostility concealed within the polite sheath of his words—including the reference to the Bird Woman. It was a nickname she had accepted amiably enough at first, until, in the aftermath of Antarctica, it became a relentlessly repeated media catch phrase. She had degrees in marine biology and ornithology, but the former didn't lend itself quite as well to catchy Capital Letters. And birds were the reason for her Antarctic journey, prompted by the plight of a colony of penguins caught in an oil disaster on that continent of ice.

"Antarctica isn't Alaska," she said quietly. "And we're all fortunate to be able to take part in what we hope to accomplish this summer."

He's one of them, she thought with sudden prescience. *One of those who opposed having me join the expedition. My God, is he afraid I'm going to steal some of the attention? Or is he one of those who thinks a woman's place is in the kitchen, or at best the laboratory?* Like most women in scientific disciplines—it was hardly different in law or medicine or engineering, she was sure—Kathy had routinely encountered resentment and opposition from some of her male colleagues.

"Of course," Jason Cobb said again, with the same sardonic smile. "I hope we have a chance to work together."

To her relief he returned to his own seat. She turned her attention back to the window and the view it framed. But her cheeks felt warm, and her thoughts strayed back to the spring visit from a delegation representing ASSET. There had been an undercurrent even then, in that first meeting, a sense that the decision to invite her had not been unanimous—and not entirely motivated by her credentials. The all-too-familiar backbiting and political intrigue was the one aspect of academic life she despised. But the chance to come to the Alaskan wilderness, on a mission she wholeheartedly supported, had been immediately tempting. If it hadn't been for Brian Hurley, she wouldn't have hesitated for an instant. And then he had made her decision easy . . .

She had been approached by ASSET in April, first by mail

and then by phone. ASSET was an acronym for the Association of Scientists to Save the Environment. The activist group was organizing an expedition of concerned scientists to dramatize the damaging environmental impact of a proposed new Alaskan oil pipeline, approved by the President, that would bring oil from a new field on the Northern Slope over the Brooks Range and across the unspoiled tundra to the Chukchi Sea. Congressional hearings on the proposed development were to convene in Anchorage in November. ASSET's goal, through field research that summer along the actual pipeline route, was to identify, catalog and dramatize the reasons for its opposition to the pipeline. Kathy, she was told, would be an asset to ASSET's mission. She was a professor in the Department of Marine Biology of the University of California at Santa Barbara. Her area of special interest was sea birds—like the penguin. And something like ninety-five percent of all the world's sea birds were in Alaska, many of them congregated along or near the Bering and Chukchi seacoasts where their habitat would be threatened by the new demands of an oil-hungry civilization.

She had agreed to talk to a delegation from ASSET because an old friend and mentor from UCLA, Carl Jeffers, was on the committee. The group had arrived in Santa Barbara on a Thursday late in April. They all had dinner together that night, Brian Hurley one of the party but withdrawn, listening thoughtfully and saying nothing. On Friday Kathy spent most of the afternoon with the committee in her office on the UC campus, discussing their proposal. And resisting it. It would mean putting her own research on hold. And it would mean separation from Brian . . .

She had first met Brian Hurley at McMurdo, the United States station in Antarctica, during a Christmas break from her work. Kathy had gone to the continent at the bottom of the earth with a group of other scientists to investigate unexplained oil damage to a colony of penguins. Brian was an adventurer training a team of huskies for a one-man dog sled expedition up the Hartsook Glacier and across the ice cap to the South Pole. His attempt at a record-breaking run was being filmed for showing on U.S. television.

They met again when Brian brought an injured dog to

Kathy's camp. The husky had broken a leg when he tumbled into a hidden crevasse. In Antarctica's severe conditions survival seemed improbable. Kathy had fought to save the dog, setting his leg under primitive conditions while a blizzard roared outside her tent. Surprisingly, the husky had pulled through, earning the name Kathy gave him: Survivor. And Kathy had won Brian Hurley's admiring attention.

When Brian left her camp that time, Kathy knew that what had started between them was more than a holiday fling. At the age of thirty-one she had reconciled herself to a life that met her personal priorities, allowing her to make her own choices. Brian threatened to change all that.

Kathy was back at work at the university when Hurley came to Santa Barbara for another Christmas holiday—and stayed on. Setting tongues wagging in Marine Biology. Turning her focused, career-oriented life upside down . . .

Carl Jeffers did much of the talking for the ASSET committee during that spring meeting. Jeffers had been her mentor during her graduate studies at UCLA. Mentor, model, cherished friend. Their friendship compelled her to hear him out. "They're planning another rape of the Alaskan wilderness," Jeffers had argued with typical vehemence. "The President has given his approval—Alaska's governor and his development cronies suckered him! They're going to drill in what was supposed to be permanent wildlife refuge, bring a new pipeline over the mountains, then run it west all the way to the sea—and hope to God the ice doesn't close their goddamned port for most of the year!"

"It sounds like a disaster in the making," Kathy admitted.

"Damned right it is!"

Although Kathy needed little convincing, Jeffers had laid out all the arguments for the expedition. Its purpose was to stop further exploitation of the last accessible American wilderness by focusing a harsh light of publicity on the project and exposing its potentially devastating effects on wildlife refuges, Eskimo hunting and fishing grounds, and coastal wetlands favored by millions of birds. "You can help us there, Kathy," Jeffers pointed out. "You can help document the impact on one of the largest and most varied concentrations of birds not just in North America but on earth."

"I understand what you're trying to do," Kathy said. "I'll support you any way I can, but . . . why me? I can think of at least a dozen others with better credentials—I know you can, Carl."

"No," he said bluntly. "There's no one else."

"What are you talking about?"

"Well . . ." His hesitation was uncharacteristically awkward. "Hell, Kathy, what's wrong with Alaska? You'll not only be helping us, you might have a chance to look into the poaching business up there."

Jeffers had touched a nerve. Kathy had recently published an article on worldwide poaching activities. She had concentrated on depredations against wild birds in South America and Africa, and eagles and owls in North America, but her review had also touched upon the recent increase in illegal poaching of walrus ivory in Alaska. Even though the focus of her study had been statistical, Kathy recognized that the lack of firsthand field observations was a weakness. So did Jeffers, she thought.

"What Dr. Jeffers is trying to say," another man commented, "is that you can make a unique contribution to the public side of our expedition."

The speaker, a marine biologist from Ohio State named Berwanger, was one of those in her field who had been critical of all the publicity given to Kathy's Antarctic experience. Berwanger himself had done extensive research in Antarctica with little or no fanfare. Straightforward science didn't stand much chance against an exotic tale of oil spills, coverup and murder, the ingredients of her summer on The Ice that nearly cost her her life. She understood Berwanger's resentment without forgiving it.

"I'm not sure what that could be."

"Because you can get us some attention. Let's face it, Dr. McNeely, after that Antarctic affair, you're a sort of celebrity. More to the point, an anti-development icon."

Kathy tried to control her temper. Her investigation of the oil injury to penguins in Antarctica had led to the discovery of an accidental oil spill at a remote research site, where an energy

conglomerate was carrying out secret uranium mining in violation of the Antarctic Treaty. The development company's over-
zealous field agents, desperate to cover up their operation, had
tried to stop Kathy's dogged probing. When Brian Hurley abandoned his polar run to help her expose the truth, the story
acquired a romantic twist that made headlines. For a brief period—proving Andy Warhol right, Kathy said—she was a celebrity.

Berwanger flushed at her direct stare. "I don't mean that you
sought notoriety, Doctor. What I'm trying to say is . . . we
need media attention. The President can summon a hundred
reporters at the snap of his finger to extol the virtues of a rich
new source of energy. But we're not news. We're a bunch of
eggheads who don't live in the real world. You can help us crack
that barrier."

Carl Jeffers, she saw, was furious with his colleague, but Kathy
tried to brush her feelings aside. Berwanger wasn't the issue.
Although she wasn't comfortable with the notion of being used
for publicity purposes, she was realist enough to admit that was
how the world worked. In science as in any other field. Environmental concerns could not be divorced from economics or politics.

"Think about it, Kathy," Carl Jeffers urged. "Take the weekend. Give it a chance."

Her agreement had been reluctant, as if she were afraid of
the answer and its consequences . . .

Six weeks later she was in a 747 bound for Alaska, with Jason
Cobb and the rest of the ASSET team, a collection of fifteen
men and one other woman, with various scientific credentials.

During the busy days in Anchorage, in addition to the com-
plicated logistics of obtaining and organizing food, supplies and
transportation for the expedition, there had been the endless
meetings and conferences that academics thrived on. Meetings
with officials from the Alaskan Department of Fish and Game
and the United States Fish and Wildlife Service. A conference at
the University of Alaska. Press briefings and Sunday morning
news shows. During that period Kathy had little personal contact with Jason Cobb. And when the expedition went into the

bush and set up its base camp in the foothills of the Brooks Range, near the pass where the proposed pipeline would cross the mountains, the size of the group had limited direct interaction.

Then, in the first week of July, the members of the expedition had been briefed on their individual assignments. Kathy was to travel downriver toward the coast. Her particular mission was to document the varieties and numbers of birds that might be adversely impacted by the proposed invasion. The scientist who would supplement her observations with his own assessment of the environmental impact upon the land and its wildlife was Jason Cobb.

After ten weeks on the river with him, Kathy's feelings about Cobb remained ambivalent, but so far their relationship had been professional. They had worked out unspoken accommodations that allowed for privacy and personal space—no easy task in the circumstances. And they had functioned well in the field together. They were building impressive documentation, Kathy felt, for the devastation that the pipeline and service road would visit upon this entire waterway. There would be worse than the sorry spectacle of bears hovering near service roadways, as they did along the Trans-Alaska pipeline route, like beggars waiting for handouts. Much of the terrain would be irreversibly altered. Habitats would be bulldozed out of existence. Near the coastline, breeding and nesting grounds for millions of birds, there would be pipelines, huge storage facilities, refineries, service roads. Two thousand people now lived at Prudhoe Bay. As many or more would converge on the new port site at the edge of the Chukchi Sea. From the pass over the mountains to the sea, a raw scar, several miles wide and nearly four hundred miles long, would forever alter a part of the rapidly disappearing wilderness.

Once Jason Cobb had pointed out some parallel depressions in the tundra that ran for miles. They resembled the "canals" visible on Mars that suggested the presence of intelligent life. In this instance, Cobb observed dryly, very little intelligence had been involved. The depressions were vehicle tracks, probably made half a century ago during World War II, going no one knew where. The heavy vehicles left deep ruts in the boggy earth. Over time the tracks sank down and water filled them. In the permafrost above the Arctic Circle, where the thin top layer of soil melted and froze, over and over again, the scars would never heal. "What they call a green wound," Cobb said.

In time Kathy accepted the fact that Jason Cobb was more than a television showboat. His passion for the environment was genuine and knowledgeable. Only occasionally did his sharp tongue or the arrogant dogmatism of his opinions irritate her.

She had never caught him bathing in the buff before, tall and white against the dark bulk of the far mountains, as if he were an actor on location, spotlighted by artfully deployed, low-key lighting . . .

She must have dozed, because she sat up with a start. It was light inside her tent. How late had she slept? Why hadn't Cobb awakened her? Damn it, if he was going to make an issue of that incident last night—!

She dressed quickly, and emerged into the first blaze of dawn. Like that unearthly howling in the night, the sight stopped her in her tracks.

Since they had arrived in this low river plain two weeks ago, she had rarely glimpsed the sun. Now she watched the sunrise over the tundra with awe. It began with a backdrop of light, reflected from the clouds above the eastern mountain peaks. The light slowly brightened, like the controlled illumination behind a stage set. It turned from pale pink to fuchsia to red. In the luminous air the colors were not vivid but softened. Almost in an instant, the red glow leaped from the clouds to the snowy peaks below them, limning their jagged outline as if they were on fire. The flames crept down the flanks of the highest peaks, descending range upon range toward the shadowed hollows and canyons, slowly filling them like lava. In all that splendid vista nothing moved. A great stillness poured around the rapt observer.

She looked around the camp, eager to share the wonder of the moment.

Jason Cobb was nowhere to be seen.

Frowning, she rejected the quick thought that Cobb's independent junketing was another evidence of his arrogance. He really hadn't been that bad. And she saw that he had built up their fire and put coffee on.

She surveyed the sweep of the tundra. No doubt he would be back soon. They would have to take advantage of the day, which was clear and bright. Though the morning air was cold, and the offshore wind that never really stopped blowing carried a bite, the warmth of the Arctic sun made a tremendous difference. This would be a day to wear layers that could be shed one by one—first the parka, then the wool sweater beneath it, down to comfortable flannel shirt and underwear. With the outer layers kept handy to put on again the moment the sun disappeared.

She walked down to the river. Survivor trotted along at her heels. She squatted beside the stream to bathe her face in the icy water. The shallow water was so clear she could see the varied colors of the gravel bed, a feathery trail Cobb had identified as the mark of a salmon's tail along the bottom as it swam upstream. A few feet away, the big husky broke a crust of new shore ice with his paw in order to drink.

While Kathy crouched there on the riverbank, half hidden by brush and bunch grass, Survivor lifted his dripping muzzle, suddenly alert. Kathy stiffened, remembering the wolf cry. The husky growled.

Something large slid by them on the river. Startled, Kathy jumped backward and fell off balance. By the time she scrambled to her feet, she was able to catch only a glimpse of the pointed stern of a native kayak before it fishtailed around a gravel bar and disappeared downstream.

Her first impulse was to scramble for higher ground to see if she could get a clearer view of the skin boat and its occupant. Although the treeless tundra was not nearly as flat as it appeared at a distance, having many small dips and humps, it was nonetheless flat enough, and the autumn grasses were tall enough, to hide the outline of the river. The nearest rise that would offer a better vantage was a good quarter of a mile away. By the time Kathy reached it, the kayak would be far downstream.

It had bobbed lightly on the water as it slipped silently past her.

Not the way it had been the previous day. Assuming it was the same boat, of course. Then it had seemed overladen, riding so low that its deck was only a few inches above the water. She had marveled at the lone paddler's expertise, progressing upriver against the current more rapidly than she had been able to walk on land. She had wondered where he had been and where he was going. She and Cobb had passed no Eskimo camp or village on their way downriver. The nearest village that she knew of, having flown over it on her way to ASSET's base camp, was far to the south on another river. Glimpsing this Eskimo for the second time in two days, her curiosity was piqued.

She was munching a raspberry-flavored granola bar, and enjoying her second cup of coffee, when Survivor's sweeping tail announced Jason Cobb's return. He seemed more animated than usual, and his dark eyes warmed when he spotted her beside the fire.

"Good morning, Doctor Cobb. You were up early."

"Couldn't sleep." He grinned. "All that damned howling. I found the tracks of a mother wolf and several cubs." He pointed toward the foothills behind them. "I think she's been watching us for a while."

"I wish I could see her."

"Not much chance of that unless she wants us to. But I don't think we have to worry about her." Cobb helped himself to coffee and stood beside the fire, sipping from his mug and looking down at her.

"I did see that Eskimo again this morning."

"Your mystery man in the kayak?"

Kathy nodded. "I'm sure it must be the same one we saw yesterday. What do you suppose he's up to?"

"Fishing, I suppose. Or hunting—last chance before winter sets in." Cobb brushed the question aside. She saw a gleam of excitement in his eyes. "I have a surprise for you. Spotted it while I was searching for our wolf." He waited, savoring her curiosity and the gift he was about to reveal. "How would you like to see a snowy owl in her nest, Kathy? Up close and personal?"

Only later, as she eagerly followed him across the tundra, did the thought strike Kathy that it was the first time, in the four months she had known him, Jason Cobb had ever called her by her first name.

FOUR

A SMALL cluster of bars, a hardware store, beauty salon and barber shop, a drugstore, market, bank, and a combination city hall and jailhouse, comprised the town center of Fortune, Alaska. East and west of the town center, the single road was flanked on either side by a collection of houses that looked as if they had been built on impulse with whatever materials were handy. They had wood or tin siding, or a mixture of both. A few had tin roofs. Here and there a solid log cabin stood, in that company looking as if it ought to be featured in Architectural Digest. The dirt road became a mud road in spring and fall, and an unevenly crusted frozen road in winter. South of town it connected to a paved highway that led to Anchorage, forty miles away.

West of the single row of houses the forest crowded close. On the east side, however, was an open meadow. Here, behind the ramshackle houses and shacks with their doors that stuck and windows that wouldn't open, was a collection of small planes— several Aeronca Champs, a Bellanca Citabria, assorted Cessnas and vintage Piper Cubs—and at least two helicopters. They were parked behind the homes like campers in the working class neighborhoods most of Fortune's residents remembered from their days on the Outside. The meadow, unpaved but reasonably flat, served as the landing strip. It was probably busier than many small airports in the Lower 48.

Alaska was a mecca for pilots of small aircraft. The fact that four-fifths of the state was wilderness, and the road system rudimentary for the sparsely settled parts, meant that many areas were accessible only by air. Alaska had more pilots per capita than any other state, or any country.

50

Jeff Rorie was one of them.

He was a compact man, not big but well made, with the slightly bowed legs of a man who'd spent his boyhood on a Nebraska ranch and a lot of time in the saddle. He had clear blue eyes and light brown hair, worn longer than was currently fashionable and tied at the back in a short ponytail. He wore a short beard, not neatly trimmed but kind of hacked short all over. He whistled softly to himself as he stood behind his small shack and squinted at Mt. McKinley, one hundred twenty miles distant. He always looked at the mountain first thing when he stepped outside. It was almost a religious thing. This summer he had spent much of his time ferrying tourists up to the climbers' landing area on Kahiltna Glacier, over seven thousand feet up the mountain. The glacier flowed down from a saddle at around eleven thousand feet between Mt. Foraker and Mt. Mc-Kinley—only about halfway to the top. To say that McKinley was the tallest peak in North America was like saying King Kong was a large gorilla. It did little to suggest the mountain's immensity, or the emotional impact it made on anyone seeing it.

The morning was crisp and clear. Rorie was relieved. He couldn't stall Travis Mayberry another day if he wanted the job. Mayberry didn't sound like someone you could push around.

Mayberry had wanted him in Nome yesterday. It was clear in Nome, he said. But it hadn't been clear in Fortune, and Rorie had a bush pilot's respect for Alaskan weather as well as Alaska's mountains. Small plane crashes were a commonplace in Alaska, but in Rorie's experience such accidents, whether here in the far north or down in the Lower 48, were almost always a result of pilot miscalculation. Usually going up in bad weather, or encountering some condition you hadn't counted on. Rorie shared the *mañana* philosophy of his peers. There was always tomorrow. Unless you were careless or reckless today.

He walked toward his Cessna 185, feeling the small lift of pleasure it always gave him. Called a Skywagon by Cessna, the 185 was a workhorse utility plane familiar throughout Alaska's bush. It wasn't as pretty as some, or as fast, but its 260-horse-power, fuel-injected Continental engine enabled it to climb over a thousand feet per minute—often crucial in mountainous territory. It had an add-on STOL package—Short Takeoff and

Landing—that enabled it to take off and land in places that smaller and lighter aircraft had to pass by. It was a cargo hauler unexcelled in the bush, and its 84-gallon fuel tanks enabled it to cruise 800 miles at 150 mph even with a load.

Except for the STOL modification and the amphibious floats he had had fitted, Rorie's plane, built in 1979, was a standard 185. The special floats enabled him to land on grass or glacier shelf or mountain lake alike with reasonable confidence. The aircraft was nicked and scarred, it shook and rattled like a ten-year-old pickup truck, and it was badly in need of a paint job. But it always started, and up to now it had always got Rorie where he was going.

This time he was going into unknown territory, and he needed every small reassurance he could find.

The small plane climbed slowly toward the pass. As usual Rorie felt dwarfed by the magnificence of the peaks surrounding him —Mt. Hunter at fifteen thousand feet, nearly four thousand feet taller than Washington's Mt. Hood, and Foraker, off to the west, seventeen thousand feet high. Soaring towers of snow and ice and rock, all of them satellites to the mighty McKinley, whose mass seemed to push against the tiny aircraft struggling past it.

Behind him the Susitna River Valley dropped away, a green and pleasant farming valley. Ahead, as he found the pass through the first tier of the Alaska Range, was a different world entirely, with no familiar landmark, forever frozen, windswept and cold. The endless march of snowy crags, and the bulk of McKinley dominating everything, captured the feeling of immensity that was so much a part of the Alaskan landscape.

Rorie had had his early flight training with the Air Force over the flat plains of Nebraska and West Texas. He had discovered the joy of being alone in the sky. You could lose yourself in that magical feeling, as if it might go on forever. Alaska was different. This wasn't recreational flying. The weather was completely unpredictable. You could take off in brilliant sunshine, fly through rain, sleet and snow, and back into sunny skies, all in a two- or three-hour flight. And the hostile wilderness below

meant that you couldn't figure on making an emergency landing if you got into trouble, and walking to the nearest telephone box. Here, if you went down, in most places you couldn't
walk out. And there were no telephones.

Three hours out of Fortune, Rorie began to feel the first
twinges of anxiety. Earlier he had passed over what he identified as the Kuskokwim River, west of McGrath, the last community he had seen. Bearing west across the Kuskokwim Mountains, he had come eventually upon another river that,
according to his reckonings, should have been the Yukon. After
following its course northward for an hour, he was no longer
sure. The Yukon was one of the main arteries of the state. It ran
for hundreds of miles inland. The stream below him was thinning out to a trickle.

Travis Mayberry wasn't going to have much confidence in a
pilot who got himself lost on the way to Nome, Rorie muttered.

Nome had to be west of him; at least he knew that much. It
shouldn't be too hard to find the Bering Sea, and if nothing
else he could follow the coastline north to the Seward Peninsula. The only trouble was, west of him the clear, sunny sky
disappeared. Clouds piled, tier on tier, as high as McKinley. He
couldn't climb over them. Alaska had done it to him again. He
was flying into rain . . .

"I'd about given you up," Travis Mayberry said.

"When that first squall hit, I was thinking I wasn't much bet-
ter than a lottery pick," the pilot said. "Lucky it didn't last, and
I flew out of it, and there was Nulato down below, and the
Yukon. Never thought a river would look so good to me."

"I was expecting you yesterday."

Rorie shrugged. He didn't seem ruffled, Mayberry thought,
or anxious. He was like any veteran bush pilot, in fact. He acted
like he didn't give a damn one way or the other. "Today was a
little wet," Rorie said. "Yesterday, over the Alaska Range, was
what I'd call a storm. Know what I mean?"

"Yeah."

Mayberry toyed with the foot-long piece of polished bone on
his desk. Rorie recognized it as a walrus penis bone. A popular

Alaskan desktop artifact, as common as mounted longhorns in a Texas bar. Mayberry studied Rorie appraisingly. "You knew Les Hargrove?"

"We flew some together last summer up around Prudhoe Bay."

"You flew those oil people around?"

"The pay's good, and you can't beat the food." He grinned across the desk at Mayberry. "I sampled one of your steaks downstairs while I was waiting. I have to tell you, you can't hire me with the food. What was that, anyway? Moose?"

Mayberry chuckled appreciatively. Most men didn't have the nerve to needle him, even gently. "Maybe it was bear steak. What you can get locally, you're not always sure what it is. Most of my meat I have flown in frozen from Anchorage," he added. "If it's not walkin', my customers generally don't complain. Hargrove tell you much about my business? What you'd be doin'?"

"Not much," Rorie admitted. "He said you paid on time, and you didn't try to cheat him. That's all I asked about."

"Good," Mayberry said. "Lemme show you around. I got a trophy room downstairs, private room, you'll get some idea."

Wolf Simpson had been leaning against the wall by the window with his back to the light, watching the newcomer with narrow-eyed skepticism. He was aghast. "You're not showing him—!" Mayberry's clamped-mouth expression stopped him.

"Keep your pants on, Wolf," Mayberry said. "Mr. Rorie here, he doesn't seem like he'd get skittish seein' a polar bear skin on the floor, am I right?"

"You got a fireplace to put it in front of?" Rorie grinned.

"I got just about anythin'," Mayberry said. "But no fireplace in the trophy room."

They went down a narrow back stairway off Mayberry's office, which was not visible from outside the building. It led to a damp-smelling, windowless passageway that ended in a steel door with a heavy padlock on a chain. Mayberry unlocked the padlock and the chain fell against the door with a loud clang. Rorie was aware of Wolf Simpson behind him, scowling in disapproval. *You better watch your back with that one. The man doesn't like you much.*

Mayberry had the opposite reaction to the bush pilot's insouciance. Where it heightened Simpson's habitual suspicions, it reassured Mayberry. He liked bush pilots in general, they were mavericks as he was, and Rorie was true to type.

The steel door swung outward on oiled hinges. Mayberry led the way, flipping a light switch as Rorie stepped through the doorway. Rorie jumped.

Mayberry whooped and laughed. Even Simpson snickered. Recovering, Rorie stared up at the bald eagle that seemed to swoop toward him. Stuffed and hanging from a pair of thin chains attached to the high ceiling, wings spread as if in full flight, the bird of prey had a span of six feet. Its beak had been painted a bright yellow—almost the only immediate sign that it was not alive.

"Gotcha!" Mayberry chortled. "Just be glad you're not a nice fat salmon."

"That thing's real enough to make you duck," Rorie said.

He was looking around, taking inventory of the remarkable trophy display. The room was about twenty feet long and nearly as wide. Every inch of it was crammed. Wooden crates were piled up to the twelve-foot ceiling on a platform facing what appeared to be double shipping doors. Stacks of boxes took up another wall. The rest of the floor and wall space was littered with boxes, wall mounts, bear and wolf rugs piled in a stack six feet high, a stuffed Arctic fox, piles of horns, deer and moose antlers, an eagle feather headdress, a box full of whale's teeth. And, as if allotted one corner of the room to themselves, a jumbled heap of walrus tusks, most of them bound in pairs and tagged. Maybe two dozen pairs of tusks, Rorie guessed. The room had strong, pungent animal smells mingled with the smells of blood and rot. Death smells, Rorie thought.

He didn't have to guess what Mayberry's business was.

Mayberry was watching him. The smile still lingered on his wide mouth, like a shadow, but his eyes were all business.

Rorie whistled softly between his teeth. "You hunt a lot?"

Mayberry chuckled. "You might say that."

Rorie glanced up at the eagle. Its glass eyes glittered back at him, catching the light from one of four pairs of six-foot fluorescent tubes in frames hanging from the ceiling. "You won't believe this," he said. "I carry a rifle in the plane, case I ever go down in the bush a long way from a grocery store, but I'd probably starve to death." Rorie grinned suddenly. "But I guess you're not hiring me to be a hunter."

"Just to fly," Mayberry said.

"And mind your own business," Simpson said.

Mayberry scowled at him. He began to point out some of the trophies. He had to edge along a narrow aisle between stacks of open boxes. "Natives sell most of this stuff to us. I got no need to do any huntin' myself. Isn't that a beauty?" He pointed at another dead eagle, this one lying on the plastic bag in which it had evidently been carried after being shot.

"Isn't some of this stuff illegal?" Rorie asked.

"Depends who's asking. That bother you?"

"I'm not looking to go to jail."

"There's ways around the law. I hire some Eskimos to do a little carving, and some to do some legal hunting for me. Then you take that ivory over there in the corner, I got tags to cover it. Old tags the government gave out to the Eskimos . . . hell, ten years or more ago. I keep them around just in case. Who's to say when I bought some tusks from a native showed up at my door? Who can tell one pair of tusks from another set? There's dozens of people buyin' and sellin' ivory in this town." He paused. "It's not something you need to worry about."

"You must sell this stuff on the Outside. I mean, there are tourists, but . . . you got a lot of goods here."

"There's always buyers."

"How do you ship it? You must have—"

"You don't need to know."

"Hell no, just curious, is all. But if I'm going to be carrying anything illegal, I have to know it. I need to know what I'm getting into. I mean . . . it makes a difference, what I'm getting paid for."

He saw the glint of satisfaction in Mayberry's eyes. He'd said the right thing.

"If I was to charter your plane to fly a load of contraband out of Alaska, that'd be a separate deal, okay? Right now, I need you to fly me and Wolf here down to the coast, to this village. Nothin' illegal about it, okay?"

"Sounds good to me. When do we leave?"

"That little squall chased you in here, looks like it's blown over. We got an empty sky and three, four hours of good daylight left. That's enough to get us there."

Travis Mayberry didn't waste any time, Rorie thought. Either he was an impatient man, or he had reason to be in a hurry.

FIVE

In 1971 the Alaska Native Claims Settlement Act brought to a conclusion the claims of Alaska's natives against the United States government for its ancestral lands. In the settlement the Eskimos received a total of $1 billion, and forty million acres of land to be theirs in perpetuity. The Eskimo territories were divided into twelve regions. The natives of each region set up a corporation to manage its communal funds, and to help bring its people into the twentieth century. Some of the corporations were very successful. Their native managers traveled regularly to Washington, D.C. and to New York. Their faces were familiar in prominent brokerage houses. Others squandered their resources, or invested foolishly. But for a time all Eskimos benefited, and their lives were altered dramatically.

Ruth Mulak, who was twenty-six, could remember the excitement of those early years after the settlement. Though she had comprehended little of what was happening or why, she had watched the new homes being built in the village to replace the shacks and log houses and sod ivruliks in which the people had always lived. The village acquired a generator to produce electricity. Ruth remembered her mother's joy when a washing machine was brought into their new house, even though she did not know how to use it. It was a symbol. The way of life of the people was changing. Everything would be better for them now.

Ruth's mother had been dead for seven years. Now the house had an oil furnace, a bathroom with a tub and shower, and even a freezer as well as a refrigerator. Sometimes, when she would take caribou or seal meat from the freezer, Ruth would think of the white man's joke about the salesman who was so good that he could sell a freezer to an Eskimo. This might have been funny in the old days, but no more. Even modern-day Eskimos were hunters, and the freezer really was a wonderful way to keep meat from the hunt from spoiling for a long time.

Her mother would have liked the freezer, Ruth thought. But if she could visit the village now, Ruth wondered if she would still think everything was better than in the old days.

"Ruth! Come and watch!" her father called from the living room. "It is time for 'Magnum.' "

"I can't, Papa, I'm fixing dinner. It'll be ready soon. Where's Billy?"

"I don't think he will be home for dinner," John Mulak said after a moment. "He and his friends are having a meeting. The white men will be coming back soon."

Ruth walked slowly over to the kitchen doorway. Her father was in his favorite recliner chair in front of the television set. His eyes were no longer keen, and he always sat too close. Ruth had read somewhere that it wasn't good to sit too close to the screen. Her father had been one of the great hunters of the village, and was still honored for his skill, but he pretended to see much better than he did. It was cunning and experience that enabled him to hunt successfully now.

"What is it, Papa? What's wrong?"

"Why do you ask such questions?"

"You know why. Billy's been acting . . . I don't know, like he's crazy. He's not like himself."

Her father was silent for a moment, watching Magnum on the small screen. It was in color, and Hawaii was always beautiful, so beautiful it seemed unreal, and the stories were like fairy tales of good and evil. Her father loved them. Someday he would like to go to Hawaii, he said, and to meet Magnum.

"Something went wrong on the hunt," John Mulak said.

"But that was more than a week ago. Billy and his friends took their boats out yesterday, right after you returned from fishing. It was only when he came back that he acted so crazy. What happened? What are they saying in the village?"

"I don't know. You will have to ask Billy."

She stared at him, puzzled. It was not like her father to be indifferent to anything relating to his family—to his brothers and sisters, his uncles and aunts, and especially his own children.

Especially Billy, she thought. Her brother Paul, two years older than she, had died when he was only six. Billy was her father's only son. Like all Eskimo fathers, John Mulak had always taken great pride in the son who bore his name. Billy, in turn, had always revered his father, the hunter.

Not lately. Billy has changed.

"What is it, Papa?" she repeated. "What's wrong? You and Billy both, you are acting so strange."

"It's nothing for you to know."

"Because I'm a woman?"

He glanced away from the pictures of Magnum in a bright red car chasing someone along an avenue of palm trees. There was pain in his eyes. "It's true. Sometimes there are things a woman shouldn't be involved in. Your mother wouldn't have asked such questions."

"I'm not my mother."

Her father nodded, as if this were something undeniable. Unlike most of the villagers, Ruth had not studied only in the village school, learning the rudiments of reading, writing and simple arithmetic. She was bright, and her teacher, who was a government-assigned white woman from the Outside, took an interest in her. Ruth was sent to a larger high school in Bettles, and then on to Anchorage for two years of college. When she came home, she was restless. She loved her family, her friends, the closeness of everyone in the village to each other. But an unimagined world had opened up to her. She dreamed of traveling, of seeing the places and people she had read about. There was so much out there in the world that she had never experienced—would never experience if she remained where she was.

That spiritual division continued to torment her. She was the village's teacher now. She touched the lives of every family. She felt important, needed. And stifled.

Her father had caught some fine whitefish on his solitary trip, which she grilled in a little seal fat and seasoned with fresh herbs. But they ate in unnatural silence, which diluted the pleasure of the meal. Eskimos were generally cheerful people, who enjoyed talking and joking. But Billy did not appear for dinner, and his cousin Joey and Joey's wife, Linda, and their two children, who often came for dinner and were always cheerfully noisy, were visiting elsewhere. There was only John Mulak and Ruth, and the old man was lost in his own thoughts. Brooding, Ruth sensed.

For dessert she had fresh blueberries the size of large hailstones, an inch in diameter, which she had picked the week before—the last such berries of the season. They were just finishing eating when John Mulak tilted his head alertly, listening. He left the table and turned off the television set, which he had left on all through the meal. Ruth heard it then—the buzz of a small aircraft. For some reason the familiar sound brought a tug of apprehension.

Her father was at the front window, peering out. Ruth approached him tentatively. She saw some of the youngsters and young men of the village running toward the flat strip of tundra that served as a landing area for the mail and supply planes that came regularly to the village. But this was neither the mail nor the supply plane. It was an old Cessna, painted yellow. She couldn't see who got out of the aircraft, but she felt her father's tension.

"There's trouble, isn't there, Papa?" she asked softly.

"Yes."

"Does it have to do with the white men?"

"It's always the white men," John Mulak said.

"What do you mean, the ivory's gone?" Travis Mayberry said in a terrible voice.

"We went out in the boats yesterday," Kirfak said. He was one of those who had participated in the slaughter of the walrus herd. "The ivory is gone—all of it."

"That's impossible! You went to the wrong place. How the hell could you miss it?"

"It was the right place," Kirfak insisted, his pride wounded. "There were the carcasses of many walruses there. The blood of the walruses who died has not washed away. It was the right place."

Mayberry stared at him, then at the others, all of whom shared Kirfak's discomfiture and unease. None of them had been paid after the hunt. Mayberry had been angry because they had fled in the boats, leaving the ivory behind. Now their worst fears were realized. They saw the seriousness of the loss mirrored in the white man's disbelieving eyes.

There was a roaring in Mayberry's head. He tried to calm himself. The pilot was watching him, puzzled. There were villagers all around, including women and a flock of children, who were always drawn by the arrival of an airplane.

"We can't talk here," Mayberry said hoarsely. "You," he said to Kirfak. "We gotta talk. Is that storeroom open?" Mayberry's glance picked Billy Mulak out of the crowd. He recognized him as the one who had been assigned to shoot Muugli. "You, too. Goddamnit, this can't be happening! We gotta talk!"

The storeroom was actually one of the oldest buildings in the village, constructed of logs, once home to a large Eskimo family. Several of such older, durable buildings were now used as storage or utility sheds. One housed the generator, another had been converted into a recreation center jammed with video games. Mayberry waved the two natives into the building in front of him, along with Wolf Simpson and, after a momentary hesitation, the bush pilot, Jeff Rorie.

After shutting the door Mayberry stood for a moment in silence. The storeroom was cold. There was a strong smell of fish. In the light from a naked bulb overhead, Mayberry's breath puffed in visible clouds. He was breathing hard, his rage threatening to explode. "All right, let's have it. What's happened to that ivory?"

"We don't know," Kirfak said nervously. He glanced toward Billy Mulak for support. He wished he hadn't spoken up outside, causing the white men to single him out.

"There was maybe a couple hundred tusks stacked on that shelf. Shit, that's over half a goddamn ton of ivory! It didn't just walk away."

"The storm was very bad." Kirfak shrugged helplessly. "We went to find it as soon as it was safe for the boats. It's gone, that's all I can tell you. The sea must have claimed it. We weren't meant to kill so many . . . to have so much ivory. The sea took it back."

"Don't give us that superstitious bullshit," Wolf Simpson said. "You trying to hold us up?"

"No! It's gone! Tell them, Billy—you saw. None of us believed it could happen, but it did."

Mayberry glared at young Mulak. "You're the hotshot hunter, the one we were told was the best shot with a rifle. What about Muugli?"

"He was not there," Billy said anxiously. "But I know I hit him! Twice, I'm sure of it. He is wounded. He could not go far."

"He could be at the bottom of the fuckin' ocean," Simpson snarled.

"No, if he's dead, he would wash up on the rocks. We can find him." Billy felt desperate. Now the white men would withhold what they had promised. Billy was trembling, not so much in fear of the white men's wrath as with his own craving. "I'll go back with you. I'll find the Great One if he's there. And the ivory. Maybe it's in the sea inside the cove. It must be there!"

There was a long, prickly silence. In the cold shed the men's breath made little white puffs of moisture in the air. Travis Mayberry was trying to think more rationally. The enormity of the loss of the ivory was sinking in. Harry Madrid was pressing him hard. He'd made promises. Talking big to Harry, he had built up the size and value of the white harvest, at the same time minimizing any problem there might be in bringing it in. And he had hedged over Muugli's disappearance. Harry had been insistent. Muugli's giant tusks were the prize of prizes. Harry had given assurances that he could deliver them to some very important people. *Very* important, Harry said. He wanted Mayberry's assurance that the prize of prizes hadn't been lost. Mayberry had given that assurance.

He felt the cold inside the storage shed touch the back of his neck.

"I don't buy any of this shit," Simpson said. "That ivory didn't just walk away. Somebody took it . . . and nobody else knew it was there . . . just us and the hunters from this village."

"What about the Feds?" Jeff Rorie asked.

Mayberry stared at him. He'd almost forgotten about the pilot being there. "What about 'em?"

"Well, maybe they found this haul. Isn't that what they're always trying to do?"

Mayberry turned to the two nervous Eskimos. "Have there been any other white men here? Any buyers? Government people?"

"No, no! Nobody!" Kirfak and Billy Mulak spoke in unison.

"They're lying!" Simpson said.

"Why would we lie?" Billy said desperately. "We couldn't get so much for the ivory from anyone else even if we wanted to. And we made a bargain. None of us would take it . . . and the others would have seen if anyone tried to steal for himself."

Mayberry saw the young native's desperation, and his need. Billy wasn't talking just about money. Mayberry had made other promises, and young Mulak was one of his most eager protégés.

"He's not lying," Mayberry said, his tone dangerously soft. "He wouldn't take the chance."

"Damnit, that much ivory didn't just float away!" Wolf Simpson protested.

"No," Mayberry agreed. "That means somebody else took it. Maybe we got some entrepreneurs trying to muscle in on the ivory business. Maybe some Eskimo has some big ideas of going it on his own. Whichever, we got to find who it is. And find that ivory." He fixed his gaze on Billy Mulak for a long moment. "I want Muugli," he said softly. "Whoever finds him for me, I'll take good care of him, you understand?"

"Yes," Billy whispered. "I promise . . . I will find him!"

SIX

Kathy McNeely and Jason Cobb took advantage of the crisp, clear morning—a rarity so far this month—to make detailed observations of the animal presence as they walked across the supposedly empty tundra. They noted the sign of ptarmigan, lemming, fox and, of special interest after the night's concert, a wolf pack. Cobb pointed out the tracks of the female, each track the size of Kathy's hand, and those of five pups. Two sets of these footprints were almost as large as the mother's. "Males," Cobb observed. "Probably three or four months old."

"Only one adult."

"Yes," Cobb agreed thoughtfully. "For whatever reason, she's alone with her litter."

"Why was she howling last night?"

Cobb shrugged. "Perhaps for our benefit. Or to let other wolves know that this was her territory. Or even . . . to attract a male, if she's really alone. I wondered if Survivor might be a puzzle to her."

"Survivor?" She stared at the big husky, who had spent ten minutes eagerly sniffing at the wolf tracks. "My God . . ."

As they moved on, Survivor ran ahead, conducting his own inventory of the terrain, never losing sight of them as he explored fascinating new scents and tracks. The absence of bear tracks, Cobb observed at one point, didn't mean there were no bears in the vicinity. The entire Brooks Range was grizzly territory. A single bear required a territory of about a hundred square miles. The fact that they had not yet come across any bear sign offered no certainty they wouldn't encounter an angry grizzly behind the next clump of brush.

They were moving west, toward the sea, and Kathy's excitement grew. In the wetlands near the coast, and in the nearby foothills and bluffs, millions of birds nested during the summer. In the past few days alone, even this late in the year, Kathy had observed solitary eagles, great flocks of geese, puffins, clouds of arctic terns and other seabirds, and an astonishing variety of smaller birds. But until now she hadn't seen one of the most spectacular residents of the tundra, the snowy owl.

It was almost noon before Cobb gestured to her to stop. He pointed at Survivor and raised an eyebrow. Nodding, Kathy called the husky over and ordered him to lie down. He was well trained, and he obediently stretched out beside a soft hummock of grass, his pale blue eyes curious. "Stay!" Kathy said quietly.

Jason Cobb led the way up a gentle rise. They crawled the last few feet to the edge of a slightly elevated knoll. Cobb pointed. Silently Kathy took her binoculars from their case and began a methodical sweep of the tundra in the area Cobb indicated. Their elevation was no more than ten feet above the flat coastal plain, but it offered a strategic observation post. "I don't see—"

She broke off, her heart leaping in her chest. She had glimpsed movement in the grass. The autumn colors of the tundra were gold and red. What she saw was small, clumped, brown, almost perfectly camouflaged, and nearly hidden by the grasses and low brush surrounding it. "I can just barely see . . . it must be the nest, and the chicks . . . but I don't see the mother."

"She's probably off foraging for food. Her chicks must have voracious appetites at this stage."

"They'll be demanding food all day long," Kathy said, just as one of the chicks began a shrill, plaintive whistling, quickly joined by the others.

Kathy glanced back down the shallow slope toward Survivor. The dog lifted his head, ears pricked as he listened to the cries of the young owls, but he stayed put.

"Here she comes!" Jason Cobb exclaimed.

Kathy glanced up quickly, shielding her eyes with one hand. Even though the midday light over the tundra was remarkably soft, she was forced to squint. Suddenly she saw the snowy owl, hawklike in flight except for the distinctively larger head and heavier body. The bird was a brief dazzle of mottled white as she swept in low above the grass. With a swift, astonishing spread of her wings—their span was a full five feet—she skidded in the air and slipped lightly to the turf, where she was greeted with a flurry of movement and piping cries.

Anyone would have found the sight breathtaking. For someone like Kathy, with her training in ornithology, it was the kind of vision that crystalized years of aspiration and study into a single unforgettable moment. Behind her, even Survivor sat up, a low whine in his throat.

The snowy owl was one of the few birds known to nest in the open tundra, perhaps because she was one of the few large and aggressive enough to defend herself and her young against those predators that might threaten them. Even after she landed, the nest was almost invisible. The three chicks, whose feathering was dark brown at this early stage of life, were now out of sight. The female's white plumage, unlike the male owl's immaculately white feathering, was accented by blackish-brown bars. Her coloring enabled her to blend almost perfectly into the background.

Kathy's heart still beat rapidly from the elation of that brief vision of the owl as she braked in midair. Like a reflex she felt another quickening, this of anger that such a wonderful creature could be not only an object of awe and delight but a mercenary hunter's target.

"How could anyone kill a creature so beautiful?" she murmured rhetorically, keeping her voice low to avoid alarming the bird.

"Because she's so beautiful," Cobb replied in the same hushed tone. "That's the irony. Her beauty is what makes her so marvelous to see in the wild—and so valuable to poachers."

Kathy was well aware of this bitter truth. The wing and tail feathers of the snowy owl were prized on the black market, like those of the bald and golden eagle. Whole specimens of a snowy owl, in good condition, would fetch as much as five thousand dollars in the Hong Kong and Taiwan underground. There were a great many hunters, Kathy knew, who would kill *anything* for a lot less.

After a moment's silence she said, "I saw one at the Fish and Wildlife Service's Forensics Laboratory in Oregon on my way north."

"A snowy owl?"

"They have all kinds of specimens of birds and exotic animals they've recovered from poachers."

"Ah yes, the poaching thing. One of your interests here in Alaska, isn't it?"

Kathy nodded. She picked up her binoculars again, trying for a more intimate view of the owl at her nest. She could see the mother's white head bobbing as she offered up lunch for her chicks. "At the lab they showed me a huge freezer chest filled with dead eagles stacked to the ceiling—both golden eagles and bald eagles—almost all of them killed illegally."

A sharp whistle from the owl's nest interrupted her. Clucking sounds followed, then another whistle.

"She knows we're here," Cobb suggested.

"She's known from the moment she got back to the nest. I think she accepts the fact that we're not a threat."

"Amazing the nest hasn't been found. I mean, take those fox tracks we saw this morning . . . he or she must have been out scavenging."

"I'm sure predators find the nests sometimes, but I imagine she'd be a force to contend with, even for a fox or a wolf."

They fell silent. While Kathy, completely absorbed, watched the snowy owl's nest, Cobb's gaze strayed off to the south, across the sweep of the tundra toward the first range of hills to the southeast. More than fifty miles away, granite hills heaved up abruptly from the coastal plain. Beyond them, blue in the far distance, rose much mightier crags, mantled in snow, their peaks disappearing in mist, so the mountainous mass seemed to fill up the sky.

"Magnificent, isn't it?" Cobb murmured, half to himself.

"I think it's the scale of it all you can't be prepared for. I know I wasn't, in spite of all the books."

"Wasn't that true in Antarctica?" he asked, genuinely curious.

"Yes, but . . . it's not the same. So much of Antarctica is one great sheet of ice. Often there's nothing for the eye to compare to, you know? Here . . . there's too much to take in all at once. Valleys so long you can't see the end of them, and huge mountain ranges dwarfed by others, one after another."

Kathy's eyes lit as she spoke, recalling the stunning images. Cobb was moved—but not only by the spectacular scenery around them. More and more frequently these days, he found himself covertly staring at this young woman who shared his days and nights. At night, in his solitary tent, he had no trouble calling up the picture. She wore no makeup in the wild, except for something to protect her lips from wind and cold. Her dark, curly hair, cut short, framed an appealing face with a straight, no-nonsense nose, lively, intelligent hazel-green eyes, and a generous mouth that seemed always on the verge of a smile. Next to someone as tall as Cobb, her slender figure, of average height, made her appear slight. Over the last few months, however, Cobb had seen enough to know that she was neither frail nor weak.

He felt wry chagrin over the fact that he was one of those in ASSET who had opposed including Dr. McNeely in the expedition. He had known of her only through newspaper and television stories about her Antarctic experience, with their references to her as the Bird Woman. Most of Cobb's ASSET colleagues had argued convincingly that such prominent media exposure, identifying her opposition to exploitation of the environment in Antarctica by a rapacious energy conglomerate, would bring to ASSET's Alaskan expedition something it badly needed—publicity. Their arguments had prevailed.

Well, Cobb mused, he didn't mind admitting he'd been dead wrong.

Watching her rapt expression as she focused on the snowy owl, Cobb found his thoughts stumbling over a hard fact, like someone stubbing his bare toe on a rock. McNeely hadn't been alone in Antarctica—or in Santa Barbara, for that matter. That adventurer, Brian Hurley, was part of the picture. Out of focus right now, but in the background.

But Hurley was at the other end of the world, Cobb and Kathy were here. And ASSET's expedition was far from over . . .

A shadow passed swiftly over the tundra, arriving with startling suddenness at the little knoll where Cobb and McNeely were stretched out. They became aware of it at the same time, and their startled gasps were almost simultaneous. Black clouds tumbled toward them, driven by high winds, where moments earlier there had been clear skies. The first winds tugged at their clothes and brought moisture to their eyes. To the west they could see the grasses and brush bending and whipping before the gusts.

"Time to call it a day," Cobb said quickly. "Looks like we're going to have a wet hike back to camp."

Kathy swallowed her instinctive protest. Watching the snowy owl and her brood was a once-in-a-lifetime experience, one she was reluctant to give up. But Cobb was right, of course. The tundra was difficult enough for hiking without being caught in a storm.

The mists obscuring the coastline began to change their shape and substance. A gray wall of rain whirled in from the sea. Alaska's weather was changeable everywhere, but nowhere more than along the northern coast.

"I hate to admit it, but you're right," she said.

They moved carefully so as not to alarm the nearby owl. As they crept down the knoll out of her sight and rose to their feet, Survivor joined them.

They were about five miles from their camp. They had covered less than a mile, climbing away from the river into low foothills to avoid a marshy area beside the river, when the full force of the storm reached them, and the long gray twilight darkened into premature night. The temperature dropped twenty degrees—between strides, Kathy joked. While the sun was up at midday the temperature had been in the low forties, and she had shed her parka. Now, with the air closer to twenty degrees and getting colder, she shivered with all of her layered clothes in place. The wind was adding a chill factor to the cold.

The rain enveloped them as they were working their way back down a long slope toward the level tundra. The descent was not difficult except for the footing. In addition to the thick tufts of grass that yielded and twisted underfoot, and the earth made soft and slick by recent rains, there were patches of loose shale. Survivor found these hikes a lark, regardless of the conditions.

The cold didn't bother him, and his dense undercoat kept out the rain. He bounded over tussocks and threaded his way easily across boggy or uneven terrain. Rocky hillsides were simply another diversion. But for Kathy and Jason Cobb the going became increasingly laborious as the ground quickly melted into muck.

Kathy felt a stinging in the rain—bits of ice. It was turning to sleet. She could see no more than thirty feet in front of her. Stay close to the river, she thought, or they could easily become lost in the storm.

Near the bottom of the slope Cobb's foot slipped on loose wet gravel. He caught himself, bracing one arm against the ground to avoid falling. His ankle twisted, and pain shot up his leg.

In the tumult of wind and rain, Kathy did not hear Cobb's scuffling struggle to keep his balance, or his gasp of pain. She was marching on ahead, the hood of her parka protecting her face but also limiting her vision. She had already begun thinking of hot cocoa back at the camp, and the snug dryness of her tent. Cobb felt the cold even more than she did, she thought idly. No padding of flesh, as that night vision had reminded her.

Twenty yards behind her now, Jason Cobb limped across the treacherous tundra. His ankle hurt, but he could still walk. He was breathing hard, his heart thumping. The air was very cold now, the wind hard enough to drive the icy rain in horizontal strings that cut where they lashed across his face.

Cobb's startled cry cut through the wind. Kathy whirled about. Cobb was floundering in an almost comical way. His long arms flailed the air in a pinwheel motion. Favoring his ankle, he had tripped awkwardly over a thick tussock. As he struggled to keep his balance, his right foot skated over bare earth that had been hard ground an hour earlier and was now a spongy ooze. His feet skidded out from under him. Momentum flipped him into the air in an ungainly somersault.

He fell hard, sprawled on his back, spread-eagled over a clump of grass, his face turned up into the rain.

Kathy was at his side in an instant. She was alarmed by the whiteness of his face. "Dr. Cobb! Are you all right?"

For a moment he couldn't speak. The fall had knocked the breath out of him. He lay motionless, his arms flung out. When she tried to help him sit up he made a hissing sound, and pushed her hands away.

"Sorry!" he gasped. "I . . . I can't move."

"Don't try. Just lie there."

She thrust her pack under his head, which was tilted back awkwardly by his position. It was then she discovered that he had not landed on a soft clump of grass but on the hard protrusion of a large, concealed rock.

"It's . . . my back," Cobb said calmly, having regained his composure. "So damned clumsy."

"Don't talk rubbish. We'll get you back to camp and call the base for help."

"That may not be so easy, Doctor . . . Kathy." The rain ran in rivulets off his upturned face. There was a glitter of pain in his eyes. "I'm afraid . . . something's broken."

SEVEN

HARRY MADRID was not his real name, but his creation. Like an obscure English actor named Archibald Leach, who created Cary Grant to such a degree of perfection that he *became* Cary Grant, Madrid had erased all evidence of a Peapack, New Jersey street kid's speech, appearance and style. He had replaced him with an urbane, sophisticated New Yorker who moved easily in the most cultured settings. Harry Madrid now lived on Central Park South with a nice view of the park. He could walk to the Metropolitan if he chose. Harry wore very expensive English wool suits custom tailored on Savile Row. His shoes were English wingtips by Church, which seemed much more elegant to him than Italian tasseled loafers. Harry was a dealer in fine arts and collectibles. His shop was just off Park Avenue. His name and face were recognized at the Four Seasons and other posh Manhattan eateries. He was a bachelor, and Manhattan hostesses were delighted to tap him to fill out a party or dinner guest list. "He'll fit right in," was a frequent judgment.

The kid Harry had once been had started out stealing hubcaps when he was ten. He had graduated to stealing and stripping automobiles, then to peddling crack for small-time street dealers. He learned quickly. One of the lessons he learned was that there were some very nasty people in his line of work, some of whom had a capacity for cruelty that Harry could not even imagine equaling. You could try to compete with them, relying on quick wit and a great deal of luck, or you could do the safe, sure thing and work for them. Harry's choice was easy. He was a survivor.

Eventually he began smuggling tax-free cigarettes across state lines for people with very heavy muscle. Most of the time he didn't even have to worry about the police hassling him. By then he was earning enough, and he had grown shrewd enough, to begin observing how successful men looked and dressed and acted. He decided learning their style wouldn't be any more difficult than some of the other survival skills he'd had to learn.

Harry rarely thought of his petty criminal past now, or the skinny punk who had committed those crimes. He didn't exist anymore. Two years ago, when Harry's cousin Leo was killed in a knife fight in a bar, Harry reluctantly attended the funeral. Leo had stolen hubcaps with him when they were kids, all those years ago. But at the funeral, looking around, Harry asked himself what he had to do with any of these people. He was offended by the uncouth language, the tasteless clothes, the bad breath, the vulgar funeral jokes at Leo's expense. Harry Madrid didn't belong there. He told himself he would never come back again.

Nevertheless, Harry's early lessons on the street had served him well over time. It had helped to shape the man he had become. Perhaps the key lesson Harry retained was that, as a successful businessman, you had to deal very firmly with those who worked for you or depended on your business. Conversely, you didn't try to cross the heavy players. You worked for them. Their muscle became your muscle.

Harry's art dealership was a legitimate business, one that provided him with a suitable entree to Manhattan society, but it was essentially a front. It offered a useful way to launder money otherwise obtained—much more money than his fine arts and collectibles could possibly generate. It created a plausible reason for shipping and receiving goods to and from the far corners of the earth. Harry's real business, which would have astonished any number of Manhattan hostesses but not agents of the FBI or the United States Fish and Wildlife Service, was trafficking in exotic animals and the pelts, skins, feet, tusks, horns, teeth, talons, bladders, glands or other valuable parts taken from them.

On this September morning, across the river from his next-to-Park Avenue store, and a world away, Harry was expansively introducing a group of potential buyers to the abundance of illegal goods he had in stock. The old brick warehouse near the docks, nondescript on the outside, was a city block long. Its shabby exterior didn't suggest the presence of anything valuable enough to make the building a target. It did not reveal the elaborate security alarm and surveillance systems that protected the warehouse, or the unobtrusive presence of well-armed guards.

The devastated area approaching the warehouse had caused an exchange of uneasy stares and murmurings among the three tiny Japanese men in the plush leather back seat of Harry Madrid's Mercedes limo. Harry smiled. A few moments later, when the heavy steel door clanged shut behind them and Harry flipped on the banks of fluorescent lights that illuminated the main warehouse, the uncertainty gripping his guests turned to exclamations of awe and excitement.

Harry Madrid had gotten his start in the poaching business by default. A man named Louis Durand, from the steaming bayous of Louisiana, had come nosing around the New York waterfront, hinting that he had some valuable goods to sell in a discreet way. He was bearded, rustic, hadn't washed in a month, and had a funny French accent, but word of him filtered up to one of the Mob figures controlling the docks. A check on the Louisianan was made through family connections in New Orleans. It turned out that Louis Durand was a well-known poacher of alligator hides. If he said he had the goods, he could be trusted, up to a point. Which meant that he wasn't an undercover Fed, but you should get a good look at each hide before paying.

The Mob wasn't really interested in handling illegal alligator skins. The payoff didn't seem to be worth the risk of attracting yet another government agency. But someone thought of the elegant, smooth-dressing Harry Madrid. Didn't he used to wear alligator shoes? Harry wasn't what was called a "made" man in any Mafia family, but he was known as an okay guy, a sometimes useful player. Tipping Harry off to the man from Louisiana was considered a favor returned for favors received.

Initially dubious, Harry began to become very interested after talking to Louis Durand for three hours one night in a waterfront bar. Harry didn't even know that alligators had been declared an endangered species, and therefore killing the gators and selling the hides were both illegal. Ninety percent of Louisiana's population of a million and a half alligators vanished in the killing frenzy of the forties and fifties, Durand told him. "But they bounce back quick," Durand said. "He is hard to kill, that one."

Durand, however, was an expert at killing them. He could supply barrels of skins, salted down and ready to ship. "Thing is, you can't keep 'em long, or freeze 'em. They get freezer burns, the Japanese won't buy 'em. They want quality hides."

The Japanese, Durand said, were the largest buyers, and they were not overly concerned about the fact that the hides were illegal, as long as the transaction could be carried out without publicity. Harry didn't have to be told the details. Most of his customers were shy about drawing attention to themselves. He could use a freight company as an intermediary to forward the boxed hides, loading them on a ship at the last moment to avoid close customs scrutiny.

Harry remained skeptical. "It's not my line," he said. He had handled stolen clothes, he admitted, whole truckloads that had been hijacked, but that was different. Clothes didn't smell or spoil, and were not instantly recognizable as illegal goods.

Then Louis Durand mentioned money. An average alligator, he said, measured about five feet long. His hide could be sold for about fifty dollars a foot, maybe more to foreign buyers. Durand could deliver five hundred hides within two weeks to any place in the New York area that Harry named. He would sell 'em wholesale.

"Why me?" Harry Madrid asked, while doing some rapid arithmetic in his head. "Sounds to me like you've been in this business awhile. How is it you come sniffing around the docks here looking for a source?"

Louis Durand shrugged, showing his chagrin. His best sources were in jail, he admitted. Fish and Wildlife Service agents had caught up with them. But that was in Louisiana. Here in New York, Madrid was out of the danger zone. Durand would be handling the risky part of the arrangement—killing the alligators, skinning and salting the hides, and trucking them to New York. All Harry had to do was act as the middleman. For that he would get sixty percent of the handle, which Harry had already calculated to be one hundred fifty thousand dollars for a single shipment of hides.

Louis Durand lit another cigarette from the burning ash of the last one and blew smoke at Harry while he waited. Harry couldn't believe that anyone was still chain-smoking. If he was going to do much business with Durand, Harry thought, the second-hand smoke could kill him.

"Let me look into it," he said.

That was how it started. Before long Harry was handling not only alligator skins but bear, otter and wolf pelts, eagle feathers, deer and moose antlers, whale teeth, elephant foot ashtrays, rhinoceros horns and—especially—ivory.

Ivory, in the international market, was number one. The demand was insatiable, especially in Japan, Taiwan and China, and the profits were enormous. Native poachers in Kenya or Zimbabwe would sell a pair of tusks for a few dollars—tusks that Asian buyers would pay four or five thousand dollars for. The more Harry learned about it, the more he saw this area of illegal marketing as a vacuum that had been waiting for him all along. The whole network seemed to him such a hodgepodge of amateur ineptness, a loose arrangement among poachers, carriers who would get the ivory to the African coast, buyers and middlemen who would ship the cargo to Asia or the United States, each one in the chain taking his cut.

After buying a load of ivory and selling it off to one of his Japanese alligator-hide clients at a handsome profit, Harry decided that he had been thinking too small. The ivory trade needed him. The way he saw it, there was no problem of moving in on someone else's territory, the way you had to be so careful in the States, where significant crime was well organized. Africa was a bunch of small, newly independent states, most of them in tribal turmoil. At the time the Convention of International Trade in Endangered Species had just listed the African elephant, but Harry didn't see that as a major concern. There would always be poaching. Poachers could only operate openly in Malawi and Zambia, which refused to ban the trade in ivory, and in at least two states, Kenya and Zimbabwe, poachers were being shot on sight. It didn't matter, Harry knew. Free-lance hunters would still be going onto the savannah or into the remote forests looking for elephants. Where the population was already thinned out, like in Somalia, poachers simply crossed over the borders into neighboring states.

The laws would actually work to Harry Madrid's advantage, throwing the whole ivory business up for grabs. Harry heard there were some major dealers linked to Asian buyers, but Africa was a big continent. There was room for everyone. Harry would set up his own pipeline. However, since the major buyers were in the Orient, Harry decided to emulate Willie Sutton. He would go where the money was. In this case, that meant Asia.

Obtaining the names of potential sources proved to be surprisingly easy. Harry Madrid was becoming known in the business. He was making his mark.

Thus it was, four years after inhaling Louis Durand's second-hand cigarette smoke for three hours in a dingy Brooklyn bar, that Harry Madrid found himself flying in to Taiwan. As the Singapore Airlines jet circled for a landing at Taipei's international airport, Harry stared across the Taiwan Strait toward the great mass of the mainland of China. For the first time in his life, Harry felt, he was no longer a bit player in the game. He was going big time.

Harry checked in at the Hilton, where he ate dinner that first night. He might be going international, but he wasn't going to eat fishheads or anything he didn't recognize. He waited impatiently for a phone call.

Harry had made his contact through one of the middlemen on the West African coast who shipped ivory and other items to buyers around the world. The man had seemed almost eager to help. Probably hoping to get a cut of Harry's action.

The call came early in the morning after Harry's arrival in Taipei. A name was mentioned, the only name Harry had yet heard: Chang. A meeting was arranged for that night. A taxi would pick him up at his hotel. "Where are we to meet?" Harry demanded.

"It is not necessary for you to know," the polite voice answered. "The taxi will be there at eight o'clock."

The caller hung up before Harry could protest.

He was angry. He thought about canceling the meeting—but the contact was all coming from the other side. He had no way to cancel. He considered just not showing up at eight o'clock. That would establish his importance in the eyes of the Chinese players he was about to meet. Asians set great store on face, he remembered. Would they lose face if he didn't show up, and would he gain stature?

By late afternoon Harry had simmered down. His eagerness colored his thinking. He had flown halfway around the world to set up this connection. And maybe his Chinese hosts knew what they were doing, after all. This was their territory. The arrangement they would be discussing involved smuggling illegal goods not only into Taiwan but also to mainland China. Rich Taiwanese, Harry had been told, were gobbling up art and art objects, Rolls Royces, diamonds and other signs of wealth. They coveted the exquisitely wrought ivory statues, fans and jewelry made by the world-class carvers centered in Hong Kong for hundreds of years. Like many other Asians they also believed that powdered rhinoceros horn could cure male impotence and increase sexual prowess. And with China becoming more open to the Western world, vast new market opportunities were opening up there not only for ivory but for other exotic items that Harry Madrid could supply.

A clandestine meeting made good sense. Taiwanese government officials no doubt frowned on the kind of arrangement Harry was hoping to set up. Harry decided he should bottle his anger. There would be time enough to establish his role. Harry was now seeing himself very much as an international mover and shaker. His Chinese connection was only the beginning.

The taxi arrived in front of the hotel at exactly eight o'clock. Harry Madrid was waiting.

Taipei surprised Madrid. It was more glitzy than he had expected. With its bright lights and its glut of modern high-rises, it was also much more like New York. The driver also drove like a New York cabbie. He shot from zero to fifty miles an hour as if he were doing a road test for Car and Driver, tires squealing as he rocked back and forth, changing lanes to shoot around slower-moving traffic. Harry felt the same mixture of thrill and anxiety he experienced during a typical ride from Kennedy Airport to Manhattan.

Soon, however, the character of the city changed. The neon lights fell behind him, and tall modern buildings gave way to narrow, crowded streets jammed with small shops, open stalls and street vendors. The noisy traffic yielded to mobile armies of bicycles. The crowds thinned out, and in the darkness Harry glimpsed low bungalows with odd-shaped roofs along with blocks of apartment buildings.

Then the taxi was in the countryside, speeding past empty rice paddies, cheek by jowl with sleek new factories whose parking lots were filled with small cars and bicycles. Working around the clock, Harry guessed, churning out memory cards for computers and VCRs and TV sets. He hadn't seen a building yet, however small or shabby, without a television antenna.

The driver was a young Chinese. He hadn't spoken since they set off, ignoring Harry's brief attempts at conversation. Maybe he didn't speak English, Harry thought with resentment.

An hour later the vehicle nosed through the narrow, twisting streets of a harbor city. When it drew near the dock area the fish smells were overwhelming. Harry didn't know it yet, but this was Quanzhou, an ancient seaport on the island that was formerly known as Formosa.

Harry was beginning to feel a little uneasy as he followed the young Chinese along a rickety wooden pier. There were dim lights strung along posts, but the night was overcast and the darkness was thick beyond the feeble glow of the lights. The air was muggy and warm. The harbor was clogged with junks and sampans and other fishing boats, so close together it seemed you could step from one to the other without getting your feet wet. Whole families seemed to be living on many of these boats, as nearly as Harry could judge from his glimpses of women and children as well as men on the shadowy decks. The waters of the harbor were muddy and foul-smelling. Harry wondered if the boat dwellers used the harbor as a cesspool.

Near the end of the pier Harry stumbled on one of the uneven boards. He swore automatically, and from the darkness came soft laughter. Harry glared at the sound. His earlier anger resurfaced. He was losing his enthusiasm for his Chinese connection.

His guide stood beside a boat, some kind of junk, Harry guessed, having picked up the word from a travel brochure. The young man beckoned Harry to follow him. They stepped onto the boat. He saw several figures in the shadows of the deck, but he was led toward steps leading down into the cabin.

The boat was larger, the cabin below decks more spacious and better furnished, than Harry had expected. The orange glow from two lanterns revealed three men in the cabin. All stared at Harry in silence. Two of the men were smoking, and the air in the confined space was choked with smoke. Harry could feel his eyes burning.

"Which one of you is Chang?" Harry asked truculently. He didn't think he was being treated like a major player.

None of the men answered him. They didn't look like major players, Harry decided uneasily. They looked like Chinese thugs. And they didn't appear friendly.

Harry turned. The Chinese driver had positioned himself so he was blocking the stairs—the only way out except for two small portholes whose windows looked as if they hadn't been opened in decades.

"What's going on here?" Harry blustered. "If you think you can muscle me without it raising a stink—"

"You have no reason to be concerned," the young man said, in clear, polite English. He didn't look like the others, Harry realized. They wore long baggy black overshirts and rubber boots—fishermen's outfits, Harry thought. The taxi driver wore a pair of Dockers pants and a white shirt, open at the collar. His hands weren't calloused, and his fingernails were clean.

"Where are we?" Harry asked. "What is this place?"

"You are in Quanzhou. It is on the Taiwan Strait. The boats you see around you are fishing boats. Quanzhou is a very busy port."

"Where's Mr. Chang?" Harry demanded. "I don't know how you people do business over here, but—"

"My name is Deng Chang," Harry's guide said.

"You're Chang?" Harry tried to hide his disappointment. He hadn't come all this way to do business with a kid.

"Madam Chang will be here very soon."

Harry stared at him. *Madam Chang?* Nobody had said anything about a woman.

He heard footsteps on the deck above. The three thugs in the cabin all reacted instantly, as if coming to attention. A moment later Harry heard light footsteps coming down the stairs. He watched the small feet appear, clad in black slippers, followed by a long silken red dress, elaborately embroidered with gold thread.

She was a diminutive woman, less than five feet tall and very slim. She appeared very fragile, like a porcelain figure. Her hair was as black as night, caught up in a tight bun at her neck. Her features were delicate and flawless. She wore what seemed to Harry to be elaborate makeup, especially around her almond-shaped eyes, and there was high color in her cheeks and vivid red on her lips. Harry's first thought was that she was the most beautiful woman he had ever seen. His second thought was that she had the coldest eyes he ever wanted to see.

"I am Madam Lu Chang," she said in a thin, singsong voice. "You are Mr. Madrid?"

"That's right," Harry said, beginning to recover from his astonishment. He could handle any woman. "Harry Madrid."

"We must talk," the woman said.

"That's right," Harry answered smoothly. "I understand you need ivory. That's the first order of business. I can supply as much as you want. That's what I'm here for."

She glanced sideways. A chair was instantly brought for her. She sat erect on the chair. The slit on the side of the red dress revealed a perfectly shaped ankle and slender calf. The men in the cabin all stared at her as if she were the Queen of England, Harry thought. He wondered how old she was. Forty-five? Fifty? He couldn't tell. It was hard to imagine how beautiful she must have been when she was younger.

"Let me speak plainly, Mr. Madrid. I considered having you killed without discussion. You are interfering in my family's business affairs, and that is unacceptable. However, my son suggested that you might not be aware of the nature of your transgression. That is why I agreed to this meeting."

Harry's mouth fell open. He couldn't believe what he was

hearing. *Killed without discussion!* A trickle of fear raised the hairs at the back of his neck. She meant it. She spoke as if his life were of no more importance than the time of day. He might have been a piece of lint on her spotless dress.

"I don't understand what you're saying. I'm not trying to interfere with your business, I'm here to negotiate a deal. I have a pipeline set up in Africa—"

"Allow me to finish, Mr. Madrid!" Madam Chang cut him off in an icy tone. "The ivory business in Africa is my family's business. There are others in Japan and Hong Kong who buy and sell ivory in Asia—but not in Africa. We have permitted you and a few petty thieves to make minor arrangements, particularly for sale of small quantities of ivory in Europe and the United States. The indulgence is perhaps the reason for your misunderstanding. But now you wish to intrude directly into my family's affairs. That is unacceptable."

Her cold black eyes fixed on Harry's, holding him captive. He thought of a snake's eyes. He was sweating. Suddenly he knew that he was in over his head. In a matter of seconds he reverted to the street-smart punk who had learned the lessons of survival.

"I thought you wanted . . . I was told . . ." Harry floundered. He had been told what Madam Chang wanted him to hear. He had been led by the nose.

"There will be no negotiations," Madam Chang said. "My son has suggested that you might prove useful to us . . . not in Africa, but in the United States. You have established shipping and storage arrangements. You also have, I understand, sources for items other than ivory for which there might be a market in Asia. If you wish to work for us, it is possible that an association may be mutually beneficial. Otherwise . . ."

Her words brought a flicker of hope. The thugs in the cabin —his judgment had been accurate, Harry realized—were watching him eagerly, as if they hoped he might make a threatening move.

"Yeah, well . . . I can see where I might have made a mistake," Harry said to Madam Chang. He was just short of fawning. "I don't see why we can't have an . . . association."

Madam Chang offered him a very thin, carmine-colored

smile. "You are wise, Mr. Madrid. But I'm afraid your agreement was too hasty. I fear that so ready a concession cannot be
trusted."

"Hey, Harry Madrid's word is good."

"We will see." She gave the briefest of nods. Two of the heavily muscled thugs in long black shirts moved instantly. Before
Harry knew what was happening each of the men had hold of
one of his arms. They wrestled him over to a narrow bench seat
and shoved him down. One arm was twisted and locked behind
his back. The other was jerked straight forward, and his hand
was slammed down onto the polished table in front of the
bench. It was a pedestal table, bolted to the floor.

The two thugs had Terminator's arms. Harry couldn't move.
He was terrified. Part of his dinner had erupted into his mouth,
and his throat burned.

"What is this?" Harry gasped. "I came here in good faith—"

"You came as a conqueror," Madam Chang said coolly. "It is
necessary to dispel that illusion. Permit me to make your choice
clear, Mr. Madrid. You may work for the Chang family, if I so
choose, while carrying on your own affairs as long as they do
not interfere. Or you will die. It will not be quick, and I can
assure you it will not be painless. Perhaps you are aware that the
Chinese have developed techniques of killing by inches, pro-
longing the exquisite agony until death becomes the most desirable of ends."

"There's no need for this," Harry said. "I made a mistake, I
didn't know, you have to believe me!" He was babbling.

Madam Chang stared at him for a long minute in silence.
Then she nodded slowly. "I believe you speak truthfully."

"Yes, yes—I swear it! On my mother's grave!"

"Very good." She turned toward the third of the thugs, who
had been watching quietly, and gave another brief nod. He
stepped over to the table, drawing from a scabbard at his waist a
long, very sharp knife.

Harry Madrid began to jerk convulsively, trying to free himself. The robot grips on both arms were unyielding, steel fingers
digging into his flesh. He felt as if the top of his skull threatened to come off.

"You must understand, Mr. Madrid, that, if you were permitted to challenge the Chang family in its enterprises, others would perceive this as a weakness to be exploited. It is necessary to send such people a message. I have decided to permit you to join our organization. However, there must be a small penalty, a visible sign. I think, perhaps, a finger . . ."

Harry began to whimper. The man holding his left arm slammed his hand down flat on the table, spreading the fingers. The thug with the knife seized Harry's ring finger. He twisted the garnet ring in its heavy gold setting to free it.

Harry screamed. "Not that one! Oh my God!"

"The small finger will be sufficient," Madam Chang said.

Harry Madrid didn't have time to feel relief or gratitude, or even renewed terror. Before he knew it was actually happening, the man with the knife pinned his little finger to the table and struck with the knife, as simply as severing the head of a carrot. Harry stared in horror at the little finger that jumped away from his hand and landed a few inches away on the table.

Harry went limp. He sagged against the arms holding him. His head swam. He was dimly aware of someone packing the wound on his left hand to stop the flow of blood. Deng Chang placed some kind of ointment on the short stub and bound it tightly. The man with the knife efficiently wiped the polished top of the table until there was no sign of blood.

Madam Chang was talking to him, Harry realized. It became desperately important for him to listen to her. "Our association can make you a very rich man, Mr. Madrid. But I must caution you. You must never think, because you are in the United States and not on a small boat in the Taiwan Strait, that you are beyond my reach, and that you might safely have second thoughts. Do you understand?"

Harry Madrid understood very well.

He had been given a chance to stay alive.

"Huh? What?"

The Japanese buyers had exclaimed over some of Harry's showpieces—a magnificent polar bear rug and an eagle feather headdress spectacular enough for a Sioux chief, and a stack of tiger hides. But they had been most excited examining the ivory samples he displayed for them. So impressed that they talked animatedly among themselves in Japanese, momentarily forgetting Harry. Such moments were a poignant reminder of the bargain Harry had made with Madam Chang. He could have sold these Japanese buyers *anything*. They wanted raw ivory—a lot of it. Ivory to be carved into figurines, jewelry, Japanese signature seals, netsuke, canes, fans delicately carved in filigreed panels, and more. Much of the ivory Harry sold now, or shipped to Chang warehouses in Hong Kong, was ivory that *he* and his accomplices had bought or otherwise obtained, without any help from the Chang organization. No matter. He remained only the middleman, not the major player he had hoped to be. His share of the spoils had made him comfortable, but not really rich—and never in control. He could have had it all. For just a moment, lost in bitter reminiscence, Harry had also lost his aplomb.

"What is wrong?" the Japanese buyer repeated, this time in English. "Are you perhaps ill?"

"No . . . no, I'm fine. It was just . . . business. Just business, that's all."

The Japanese spokesman bowed. All three Japanese then bowed in unison, as if to confirm that they all understood how a business matter could be a concern.

"We would like perhaps to see more ivory," the spokesman said. "Our order is a large one—ten thousand pounds. But it must be of the highest quality, suitable for carving."

Harry had to swallow his reaction. By one calculation, that many tusks accounted for more than three hundred slaughtered elephants, or seven hundred walruses, or a suitable combination. By Harry's reckoning, even at fifty dollars a pound, the Japanese order came to a half million dollars. And Harry might be able to jack the price up to sixty dollars.

"I don't have that much in this warehouse," Harry said. Smiling, he added, "It's not wise to keep all your tusks in one basket. But that much ivory is available—at the right price."

He showed them a room filled with African ivory, most of it new. The tusks were not as large as those typically taken from elephants killed on the veldt. "Most of these were forest elephants," Harry explained knowledgeably. "The elephants there have adapted to a different environment. They're smaller, and the tusks are smaller. They average about four feet. But as you can see, the ivory is of the best quality—very hard, smooth, without striations, perfect for carving."

The room held most of the elephant tusks Harry had in stock, about three hundred pairs of tusks. A little over half the order, he quickly estimated, maybe six thousand pounds. But African ivory was becoming harder and harder to obtain. Mayberry would have to come up with the rest in Alaska.

"I also have a large supply of walrus ivory, excellent for carving. It's being shipped to me now," Harry said, stretching the truth.

The Japanese buyers exchanged glances and a rapid volley of words in Japanese. It struck Harry that Japanese speaking their own language always sounded angry. But these buyers ended up smiling.

The spokesman bowed at Harry. By this time Harry had concluded that the other two clients spoke no English at all.

"We are satisfied," the buyer said.

"Let's go back to my office," Harry said. "I like my customers to do business in comfort. Would you believe, I just happen to have some Suntory in the fridge?"

"Thank you," the buyer said politely. "We would prefer Scotch."

There was a message from Travis Mayberry when Harry and his clients returned to his Manhattan office. Harry had to ignore it while he took care of business. An hour later the Japanese had agreed to pay him fifty dollars a pound for ten thousand pounds of raw ivory for delivery within thirty days, including both elephant and walrus tusks. Harry bowed them out of his office—his version of a bow was an awkward jerk of his head. Then he put the call through to Nome, Alaska.

"It's about time you got back to me," Harry said without preamble as soon as Mayberry answered. "I've just got a big order. You'll have to go to the secondary storage." The latter was Harry's coded designation for the remote cabin where Mayberry stored the bulk of his poached walrus ivory awaiting shipment. Harry did not wholly trust the Feds not to tap into his long-distance telephone conversations. "We're probably going to need all that new stuff, too. This is a ballbreaker of an order, Trav. And Madam C. is champing at the bit to get those big ones, you know what I mean. The special order. She's making it personal." Harry had received a hint of just how personal. The bidding for the legendary Muugli's mammoth tusks was rumored to have started at a quarter million U.S. dollars. If on actual inspection they were what they were reputed to be, there was no telling how high the price would go.

"That's what I called about," Mayberry said. He didn't sound happy, and Harry went very still. He had a survivor's instinct for something going bad, and he felt the foreboding now. "It's missing."

"What do you mean, it's missing?"

"Gone, that's what I'm saying. All of it."

Harry's mind refused to believe what he was hearing. "You can't be serious!"

"I'm telling you," Travis Mayberry said, starting to whine a little and hating himself for it. "Someone's stolen it."

Harry Madrid lost it then. He forgot all about the Federal agents who might be listening, the secretary in the adjoining office, the customers in the gallery and showroom downstairs who might be able to hear him screaming.

When Harry finally calmed down enough to be intelligible, Mayberry remained frozen in silence, awed by Madrid's fury. "Who is it?" Harry demanded finally, his voice squeaking. His screaming had irritated his throat. "Who'd do it?"

"I don't know," Mayberry admitted.

"The Feds? They could have someone planted in your organization."

"Why would they take it? They'd rather catch us with it. They don't care about the damned ivory, they want to put *me* away for five years."

Harry Madrid's mind raced, sifting possibilities, rejecting them. "Someone's trying to cut into our action."

"Could be. But if there'd been strangers around, white men, the villagers would have seen 'em, unless they came and went by boat."

"The Russians? Some of those people are desperate."

"I don't think so. We'd know if they came nosing around. Besides, any outsiders, they'd of had to know about the harvest, where it was and all."

"Who knew?" Harry said coldly. He was in control now, which made his anger more deadly.

"Nobody else. Just me and Simpson . . . and the natives."

There was a prickly silence. Mayberry waited it out uneasily. He hoped Harry Madrid didn't decide to make a personal visit to Nome, the way he had once come to check on Delbert Hicks.

"Find out who," Harry said. "Find those fucking thieves and make an example of them. You hear me, Mayberry? I don't care how you do it. You take care of them. And find that goddamn ivory!"

EIGHT

MAYBERRY HAD flown back to Nome to report to Harry Madrid, leaving Simpson at the Eskimo village to begin interrogating the natives. "Looks like more rain coming," Mayberry had said, "but Jeff thinks we can outrun it. If I get hold of Madrid right away, and the storm blows on through, we'll be back tonight. Tomorrow we start hunting for that ivory, and I want some answers."

Simpson started easy. He had unloaded a case of vodka from Jeff Rorie's plane. A thirsty Eskimo would sell a pair of good quality walrus tusks for a bottle of vodka. All Simpson wanted was information. He made it a social occasion, all of the men from the hunt gathering together at the village school. It was late afternoon and classes were over for the day, but the schoolteacher was there. She was fairly pretty for an Eskimo, Simpson thought, with dark eyes and a nice smile, and she wasn't too fat, the way she would probably get when she was older. Wolf told her he and the hunters needed to borrow the school for a meeting. She looked as if she was ready to give him a hard time, but Billy Mulak jumped in and talked to her. He halfway pushed her out of the building.

Eskimos, like most North American Indians, easily acquired a craving for alcohol once it was introduced to them, but had little tolerance for it. They got drunk quickly. Simpson poured generous splashes of vodka into small paper cups he found in the school's supply room. He got the Eskimos talking about the hunt, and what a great day it had been, and how much money and whisky they were all going to have when the ivory was found.

After a while Simpson singled out the hunter called Kirfak.

He was a little older than the others, but he had one of those round, packed Eskimo faces that made it hard to tell if he was thirty or forty. After only two drinks Kirfak had trouble focusing on Simpson. His speech stumbled.

"You think that much ivory could've just washed off that shelf?" Simpson asked him, earnest and friendly. "I'd hate to think we lost it all."

"No way," Kirfak blurted. "Too much ivory . . . we find it!"

"Well, that's the thing, ain't it? If it didn't wash away, I mean, what happened to it?"

Kirfak tried to cope with the question, while his eyes tried to focus. He grinned. "The sea . . . take it all back."

"We went over that," Simpson said. "There aren't any sea gods out there protecting the walruses. If there were, we wouldn't have been able to kill so many of the bastards, would we? What I figure is, maybe some of you hunters went back for the ivory. Am I right?"

Kirfak stared at him. He looked very wobbly. His normally brown native face was a dark red from the alcohol.

"Did the great hunter Kirfak go back there? I mean, before yesterday?"

Kirfak shook his head. "I think . . . Kirfak gonna be sick."

The Eskimo stumbled to his feet and weaved toward the rest-room, which was at the back of the schoolhouse next to the supply room. Watching him in disgust, Simpson thought that he might have to take some of these natives into the little back room for some one-on-one.

The social occasion grew boisterous after a while. Some of the Eskimos became entangled in long, boastful, drunken arguments, each trying to outdo the other in elaborately descriptive insults. This was a kind of game with them, igniting much jeering and laughter. One older Eskimo tried to show Simpson a traditional native dance, but when he fell down he couldn't get up. Several of the men fell asleep, sprawled over children's desks or, in one instance, curled up under a table.

Wolf Simpson kept prodding and digging. Three hours into the party, with only three or four of the great Eskimo hunters still able to string a few intelligible words together, Simpson's patience was running out. He glared at one Eskimo who had wandered into the schoolhouse late. He wasn't one of those who had been on the walrus hunt, he was only there to cadge a free drink. Simpson was about to throw him out when he thought of a key question. This native was still sober enough to make sense.

"Did any of the men in the village go out fishing or hunting during the storm?"

The Eskimo shook his head. "Bad time, not safe for fishing or anything. You got good vodka?"

"Maybe, if you tell me something interesting. Did anyone leave the village right after the rains stopped? You see anyone go off? Maybe two or three men to fish or hunt?"

The native eyed the bottle on the table in front of Simpson and licked his lips. "Some go out, sure. When storm is over, even the women and children go. They go pick berries."

Simpson poured vodka into the last of the paper cups he had. He held it for a moment, out of reach. "Who went? You remember anyone in particular?"

"Sure. Mulak go fishing. He likes to go alone."

Simpson turned quickly, trying to find Billy Mulak. The young Eskimo had stumbled out of the school about an hour earlier, he remembered, looking green around the gills. Another one who couldn't hold his liquor. "Billy Mulak? He went fishing alone?"

"No, no, not Billy. He's not the one. John Mulak. He has a good boat. I saw him that morning when the rain stopped. I saw him go down to his boat."

Simpson pushed the cup of vodka toward the eager Eskimo and hurried from the building.

He found Billy Mulak huddled on the steps outside the schoolhouse. He looked woefully sober, and there were stains on his parka where he had vomited.

"I've gotta talk to you," Simpson said.

He hauled Billy back into the building and escorted him roughly to the storage room in the rear. Simpson turned on an overhead light and closed the door. In the silence he stared at Billy. "You sober enough to know what's goin' on?" he asked.

"Sure. I got a little sick, that's all."

"You could get sicker fast. I thought you told me no one left the village before you and your friends went back for the ivory."

"What do you mean? Sure, I said that."

"Wasn't true, though, was it? You was lyin' to me, Billy."

"I wasn't lying! Why you say that?"

"Tell me about your father, Billy. He went fishing alone . . . the day before the rest of you."

Billy looked disconcerted. Not scared, Simpson thought, watching him narrowly. Not worried yet.

"Well, yeah . . . Pop isn't scared of anything. He'll go out in his boat when nobody else will. But that doesn't mean anything. He always does that."

"You should of told me, Billy."

"But he knows nothing! He wasn't even with us on the hunt."

"How come he's not even interested?" Simpson wondered aloud. "He's the great walrus hunter of the village, ain't he? That's all I been hearing, ever since we started comin' to this village, what a great hunter John Mulak was."

"But he knows nothing of the hunt, or the ivory."

"And you never mentioned it to him? Seems kind of funny. I mean, it was such a successful hunt. How many times did your old man ever kill that many walruses in one day? And you never even told him? You shot Muugli, the Great One, and it wasn't important enough even to mention it to your old man?"

Billy averted his gaze, uncomfortable with the question. "I could not tell him. My father would not approve."

Wolf Simpson had one of his intuitions then. A little nudge of inspiration. It was like when he was hunting a wolf from a chopper, harrying him back and forth. Sometimes he would get inside the wolf's head, until he would actually *know* which way the wolf would veer. And when the wolf actually did what Simpson knew he would do, he would have his sights already lined up, waiting for the kill . . .

"I tell you what, Billy. I think we should have a talk with your old man."

* * *

The rain squall that Jeff Rorie and Travis Mayberry outran that afternoon on the way to Nome was the same icy rain that caught Kathy McNeely and Jason Cobb in the open tundra on the way back to their camp.

After his accident, Kathy made Cobb as comfortable as possible under the circumstances. His injury was in the lower back or hip. With some misgivings, knowing the risk of moving anyone with a back injury, she managed to ease him onto more level terrain. Unfortunately, it was also muddy from the rain. She used a thin plastic tarpaulin from his backpack both as a ground cover and to partially shield both of them from the rain. Their condition remained cold and miserable.

After an hour the rain swept on. She could see the main body of the storm marching eastward across the tundra, a solid gray curtain. It left behind only a fine, intermittent drizzle.

She made her decision. "I have to get you back to camp."

"I don't see how that's possible. You'd better get back yourself . . . call for help."

"It's going to freeze tonight. I think it's already freezing. You can't stay here."

Neither of them mentioned the possibility of predators coming upon him. During the course of that day they had seen the tracks of a fox and a wolf pack. She thought of Cobb's arrogant refusal to carry a weapon of any kind when they left the base camp together. "I'm not a hunter," he'd snapped. "Isn't that partly what this trip is about?" At the time she had rather admired him for his stand. Now it seemed quixotic.

"There's no point in two of us being in jeopardy," Cobb said. "That's simply stupid."

"That may be, but you're in no position to argue."

She had both a knife and a small hatchet in her pack. Peering through the gray murk of early evening, she saw no brush higher than her waist along the riverbank, or to the south across the tundra, which was laced with a network of creeks and waterways that made it almost impassable on foot. Her choice was to climb into the foothills, small steps leading to the hard crags of a westernmost finger of the Brooks Range. The mountains were brown and gray masses of rock topped by snow and ice. There were no real trees as far as she could see. The camp, which was perhaps four miles away, might as well have been forty.

She had to be cautious about distances. There appeared to be larger shrub growth in the foothills not far away, even a few substantial willow thickets. But how far? The massive thrust of the mountains, like the vast emptiness of the tundra, altered perspective. Distances were dwarfed. Were those willows, or the tangled brush, two miles away? Or more like five? Would they move further away from her, as so many landmarks did in this country, when she tried to walk toward them? She couldn't be sure.

"I'll be back," she said. "Survivor will stay with you."

"I don't like you going off alone—"

"Tough," she said.

She ordered Survivor to stay, then set off without another word. She didn't look back. Let Cobb get angry, she thought. It would take his mind off being cold and wet and in pain.

The tangled shrubs that had caught her eye were actually no more than a mile away, but they proved disappointing when she reached them. None of the branches nor even the thickest stems were large enough or strong enough for what she had in mind.

She glanced north, up a barren slope toward a few thin willows, tough survivors in the autumn brown of the foothills. How far? Another mile? Had she guessed wrong? There were poles in their gear at camp that would have served her purpose.

Staring back along her trail, it took her a full minute to find Jason Cobb, a tiny speck of red in that endless sweep of sodden turf and earth and water. She couldn't see Survivor, but he hadn't followed her.

The soft, rain-drenched ground and wet grasses dragged at her feet as she plodded on. Fifteen minutes later she reached the first of the willows she had targeted. The largest trunk was neither long nor thick enough. But a thicket of willows fifty yards farther up the slope answered her prayers.

She selected four willows about the size of tall Christmas trees. From these, after trimming off all the branches, she fashioned four slender poles, each a little over eight feet long, tapering from about an inch and a half at the base to a thin, flexible tip. She needed only two, but spares were necessary. She wasn't sure how the slender trunks would hold up, and she wouldn't be able to go back.

It took her forty minutes to return to the river, both time and distance surprising her. Over the last half mile the four poles became a torturous burden, and she ended up holding two under each arm and letting the ends drag along the ground. Exactly as she planned to have Survivor do it.

She overshot the point where she had left Cobb, and felt a momentary panic. Then she spotted the big husky near the riverbank a hundred yards to her right.

Jason Cobb looked pale and drawn when she reached him. He stared at the rough, mud-clogged poles. "I suppose you think you know what you're doing, Doctor."

"Yes, I do," Kathy answered, more cheerfully than she felt.

She worked quickly. She wasn't sure how much twilight was left—two hours at most, she thought—and she didn't relish the prospect of finishing the trip ahead of them in the dark. She used two straps from her backpack, along with Survivor's collar, to rig a harness with loops large enough to hold the heavier ends of two poles. Then she folded the plastic tarpaulin into a long panel draped over the poles and tied at the ends.

"What do you suppose you're making?" Cobb asked finally.

"The Indians used to call it a travois. Survivor is used to pulling. You should be no problem for him at all."

"I'm not riding on that thing. Didn't you hear what I said? I think something's broken in my back."

"You're not walking," Kathy said, deliberately feigning indifference. "You can't stay here, and I can't carry you. That means you ride."

What she had fashioned was a crude stretcher. She laid it flat on the ground and gingerly wrestled Cobb onto it so that he was lying flat on his back with his head at the forward end. It was a struggle fitting the poles into the harness while lifting Cobb's dead weight. When it was done, however, she saw that Survivor carried the burden without apparent effort. In fact, he acted excited, prancing and whining eagerly.

"I don't think he can do this," Jason Cobb said, paler than before. He hadn't said anything of his pain, she thought, while she pushed him around.

"Piece of cake for him," she answered. "But I have to tell you, Cobb . . . you're going to hurt some."

"No kidding."

Kathy led the way. Most of the time she sought out the most level terrain, and the firmest, even though it meant constant detouring. Sometimes, unavoidably, she slogged across stretches of muddy bog. Survivor, pulling the travois on which Cobb lay, easily kept up with her. He seemed to her to be pushing her from behind, as if they were in competition. He was excited to be back in harness, doing something he had been trained to do from birth. Lolling around camp was all right, she thought, but this was what he was made for. It wasn't a chore, it was a joyous fulfillment.

For Jason Cobb the husky's enthusiasm had a price. The quicker pace meant a more jarring ride. Every bump or lurch to the side sent pain rocketing through his hip and lower back. And no matter how carefully Kathy McNeely tried to pick their route across the tundra, there were no smooth, level stretches. The thick, yielding hummocks seemed to reach out to grab the trailing tips of the side poles.

Cobb could not see ahead the way he was traveling, but he readily pictured Kathy bundled inside her sweater and parka and ski pants, her layers soaked through by now, as his were, grimly plodding on ahead. At least she had listened to his suggestion to lash the spare poles to the sides of the travois, rather than carrying them herself. Today's woman, he thought truculently. You couldn't tell her what to do. You could only offer advice.

He thought of how she had refused to leave him on the tundra and go for help, insisting on hiking off to chop down trees and make this infernal stretcher.

Cobb stared up at the sky. Patches of midnight blue showed through the clouds, a night sky not totally black but awash in stars. To take his mind off the painful jostling, he made a stab at picking out some of the constellations he remembered. Everything looked different so close to the top of the world. It was like looking out upon a familiar city from a different vantage point, a tall building far uptown. No need to grope around for the north star, though. There—

A tearing sound. Something gave way beneath him. One of the poles of the travois twisted to the side, and the improvised stretcher collapsed. Cobb cried out as he slammed to the ground.

It was a moment before he could talk. Kathy McNeely tried to ease him onto his back again before inspecting the damage to the travois. He pushed her hands away angrily. "Goddamnit!" he gasped. "I told you this thing wouldn't work! What I don't need is some amateur playing games with a broken back. My leg is numb! I can't feel anything!"

"You took a hard fall." Kathy's face was as pale as his. "And I don't think your back is broken. I'm not playing games, Dr. Cobb. I'm trying to help."

"You could help a lot more if you went ahead and radioed for someone competent."

She stopped trying to repair the stretcher and glared down at him. "You listen to me, Doctor. I know this isn't any fun. And there *is* some risk in moving you. But if I'd left you back there while I went back to camp and waited for help, it wouldn't have been any walk in the park for you. The base is going to have to call for an emergency plane, and God knows when that will get here. Certainly not tonight. Maybe not even tomorrow. Have you really thought what it was going to be like alone out here? Not just for a few hours, but all night, in the freezing cold? I know you like to prance around naked in icy rivers, but—" She broke off, her face flushed now, warm in spite of the sharp cold in the air. "I'll compromise with you, Doctor. We're only about two miles from camp. If I can't get you there, get you under cover and warm, I'll bring the camp here."

"No," Cobb said tersely. "Do what you have to. Fix this damned thing and let's get going."

They studied each other. Cobb thought she looked especially beautiful in that moment.

"I guess I don't have any more secrets from you," he said.

"Not a one."

"Okay. What can I do to help?"

"Just be quiet. And pray a little."

In a matter of minutes she had the stretcher more securely fastened to the twin poles and secured to Survivor's harness. The husky waited impatiently. He shifted his feet and gave a sudden bark.

"Take it easy!" Kathy snapped, her anxiety showing.

"He isn't barking at you," Jason Cobb said, his voice oddly strained. "My God, look at that!"

She turned to follow his gaze. Gave an involuntary exclamation. Stood there, staring at the night sky. The cloud cover to the north had lifted completely, and a vast portion of the sky was dancing with light. Swirls of color ebbed and flowed, twisting ribbons of pink and lavender and green and yellow. Kathy thought of a painter's brush in the hand of a Disney artist, leaving sparkling trails of colored light as the brush darted swiftly across the dark canvas of the sky.

Neither had to be told they were witnessing the aurora borealis, a phenomenon of the Arctic night, particularly in autumn and winter. The weather had been so bad through September, thick cloud cover so common, that they had not previously been treated to the anticipated spectacle.

"Is this a sign?" Jason Cobb said. "Are you some kind of witch doctor, after all?"

Kathy grinned. "You'd better believe it. Now you just relax and enjoy the show. We're getting you back where we can make a fire. I do that, too."

With the passing of the squall the sea became calm, and within the sheltered cove that had witnessed the carnage of the walrus hunt, there was a stillness. Just outside the cove, on the tiny island a short distance from the tip of the peninsula, something stirred, a shadow so bulky it appeared as if a portion of the island were breaking away.

Muugli slipped quietly into the water.

A day earlier he had heard and smelled the hunters when they returned. He had heard the mutter of their outboard motors and smelled the men even before they reached the cove, and he had not moved. The instinct of one who had been both hunter and hunted saved him. He was hidden within a cup of rock shaped by the relentless pounding of the waves. The hunters in the boats did not see him.

He was weak from loss of blood, but still alive. The wounds themselves had closed, healed by the freezing water. Now he was hungry. He also felt alone. Most of the herd had been killed. A few other survivors, unhurt, had fled.

Walruses were convivial animals, and primitive urges were becoming stronger in the old walrus. There were slabs and wafers of ice in the water: for Muugli, these were familiar signs of the encroachment of pack ice from northern waters into the Bering Strait, harbingers of winter's frozen seas, and of the time of reunion and mating.

He was hungry, and the floor of the cove was a banquet of mollusks—mostly clams and a few crabs. He would forage along the ocean floor, using not his long tusks but his tough whiskers and snout to sense and root out the clams. He could eat a half-dozen clams a minute. He would eat for the next two hours, diving repeatedly, storing the prodigious quantities of fuel he needed to regain strength.

Afterward, when he was rested, he would turn north. The ice was coming. With it came the main herds that traveled with the ice—the females, the young, the male herds that had summered in the Chukchi Sea.

He would find his own kind, and he would survive.

If the hunters did not find him first.

NINE

"HE JUST wants to talk to you, Pop," Billy Mulak said. He appeared nervous, and he would not look into his father's eyes.

"He is a friend of yours? I would not refuse to talk to your friend."

"Not here," Wolf Simpson said. He was standing in the doorway of John Mulak's house. There were a half-dozen Eskimos in the small living room, including two young children. They all stared impassively at Simpson. The scene looked too domestic, too comfortable, too safe. Simpson wanted to unsettle the old man, to have him nervous and rattled. Right now he was much too calm. "We're having a meeting. I figure the great hunter Mulak might help us. Come along, Pop."

At that moment Ruth Mulak appeared from the kitchen, hearing voices. She was startled. "Billy! Papa—what is this?"

"I am going to a meeting," John Mulak said.

Simpson stared at her, then at Billy. "The schoolteacher! You never said she was your wife."

"She's my sister!"

"Ah!" Simpson eyed her, grinning. The young woman looked appealingly domestic, too, her round cheeks warm from the kitchen, a dew of moisture on her upper lip. "Maybe we can have a talk later."

"You don't have to go with them, Papa. They have lost their ivory—the talk is all over the village. It has nothing to do with us." Only with Billy, she thought, seeing the guilt and confusion in her brother's eyes.

"Yeah, he needs to come," Simpson said. "You see, this is kind of a village problem. Everybody's involved. If one of you is

101

a thief, or a bunch of you, it's important to the whole village that we find out who."

"This is *our* village! Not yours!"

"Yeah, well . . . it was *our* ivory. We hired your village hunters to find it, not steal it."

"No one in this village would steal what wasn't his! We're not like that. This isn't a white man's city!"

"Then there's nothin' to worry about, is there?" Simpson became impatient with the argument. Who the hell did she think she was, trying to insult him? "Come along, Pop."

"No!" Ruth cried out, stepping toward them.

For the first time John Mulak spoke firmly. He sensed the violence in the white man, the evil hiding behind the smile. "This is not for you to say," he told his daughter. "I will speak with Billy's friend—"

"He's not a friend! Not to any Eskimo!"

"I will talk with him about the hunt, and the ivory that is missing, and the killing of the great Muugli. It is right that he should ask me. It is right that I should know about such things, of which my son has not spoken to me." John glanced at Billy, his expression revealing nothing of his grief. *What is the hold they have on you?* he wondered.

John Mulak followed Simpson and Billy out the door and along the street toward the schoolhouse. The night had turned cold, and the muddy surface was hardening in thick crusts and furrows. There was a feeling of snow in the air. Soon there would be snow, Mulak decided. The rasping motors of snowmobiles would fill the air with their roar. The walrus herds would migrate far to the west over the frozen Bering Sea, and the white men would stay away, until the herds began to move again in the early spring. And maybe he would have his son back again.

To Billy's surprise, Wolf Simpson didn't take his father to the schoolhouse where many of the other men of the village still sprawled in a drunken stupor, but to the old log building that now served as a village cold storage shed. Built nearly a century ago, long before the modern government houses that now defined the village, the building had been laid on log supports at the corners that lifted it three feet above ground. Otherwise the building would have settled unevenly, twisted out of shape as the ground constantly froze and unfroze over the underlying permafrost. Over the decades corner supports had sunk slowly into the ground, until the main structure of the hut touched the surface. Recently it had been shored up, but its two windows would no longer open and had been boarded over. The single heavy wooden door had had to be refitted several times over the years. But the building was so solid and sturdy that it was virtually impregnable.

At the doorway Simpson grinned at Billy Mulak. "Go get yourself a drink, Billy boy. You might find one or two of those bottles back at the school ain't empty."

"No, I should stay. Pop knows nothing of the hunt—"

"That's what you told me. Now I got to talk to Pop. Just him and me. It's important we have this little talk, just so's we don't have any misunderstanding here."

Simpson flipped on the single overhead light in the storage shed and shut the door in Billy's face. The building was unheated, and the room was very cold. Simpson grinned at the old Eskimo, who regarded him impassively. "Not scared, are you, Pop? Not nervous, either. I'm impressed."

John Mulak did not fear the white man, and he was not a coward. He wasn't as tall as Simpson, but he was compact and sturdy, and his hard life had built hard muscles. In a fair fight he could probably have overpowered Simpson. However, he had seen the weapon Simpson carried in a holster underneath his parka, an automatic pistol. He also knew that other white men would return soon, carrying more weapons, and Mulak's village would be hostage to any act of violence.

"Billy tells me you weren't interested in the hunt for the Great One. That puzzles me, Pop. I thought you were the great village hunter."

"I don't hunt in your way."

"Yeah. I guess you don't approve of our ways, like that pretty daughter of yours. You should teach her not to smart-mouth people like that."

Mulak smiled. "Nowadays, young people don't listen."

"Ain't that the truth. You know anything about that missing

ivory, Pop? I'd think you would hear things, an important man like you."

"I'm an old man. Not so important."

"Billy says he didn't tell you about the hunt because you wouldn't approve. Made me wonder . . . what would you do about something you didn't like? Like steal the ivory for yourself, maybe, so we wouldn't have it?"

"That would be foolish."

"Yeah, it would be foolish, all right. But maybe you didn't think it through at the time, you know?"

"How do you know your ivory didn't wash away in the storms?"

"Why would it do that?" His suspicions fastened on Mulak's question. "How come you know it was where it could wash away?"

"Billy wouldn't tell me, but the other men of the village talked. I know how you killed many walruses, and stacked the ivory on a shelf in a cove. And you shot Muugli, but he escaped. I know these things because I was told about them. But that's all I know."

He didn't act guilty, Simpson observed, scowling. Not ready to admit that his hunch was wrong, Simpson decided to push a little harder. "I think you're lying to me, Pop. And that makes me ask, why would you lie?"

Simpson drew a different weapon from one of the deep side pockets of his parka. It was a narrow leather pouch, about eight inches long, filled with coins. A thong at one end slipped over Simpson's wrist, leaving the loaded pouch dangling. John Mulak stiffened, but he did not retreat.

"I tell you what, Pop, we're gonna be here awhile. I think you have something to tell me, but you're a stubborn old coot, am I right? It's cold in here," he added musingly. "The colder you get, the more it hurts if you get hit with something hard. Like on the hand."

He surprised Mulak by reaching out and jerking one of his mittens off.

The old man reacted. He tried to shoulder Simpson aside as he rushed for the door. Simpson brought the loaded pouch around in a swinging arc. It slammed into John Mulak's shoulder blade with such force that it knocked him against the side wall of the cabin. While he staggered, Simpson swung the leather bludgeon again. It struck the back of the Eskimo's bare hand. A bone broke. Pain rocketed from his hand to the back of his brain, and Mulak sank to his knees.

Panting, Simpson stood over the old man. Rage consumed him, as if the Eskimo were somehow to blame for forcing this issue, making it tough on everyone.

"You're gonna talk to me, you old bastard. Make up your mind. Sooner or later, you'll talk!"

Travis Mayberry returned to the village late that evening in Jeff Rorie's Cessna. He found Wolf Simpson in a sour mood. His interrogation of the villagers had gotten nowhere. Most of the younger natives who had been on the walrus hunt were still in the schoolhouse, sleeping off the effects of their drinking. A few were on their feet again, watching Mayberry with vacant eyes, as if they hoped he had brought more whisky.

The rest of the village seemed deserted. Even though the night had turned cold, with a cutting wind, the emptiness along the single street was unusual, especially with the arrival of the plane, always an event.

"Where is everybody?" Mayberry didn't like the brooding atmosphere.

"The old ones, and the women and kids, they're all playing hidey-hole. Like I was bringing them the plague or something."

"You get a little rough?"

"Hey, I just asked questions. Nobody knows anything. Nobody's saying anything. I tell you what, though. I think one old man knows more than he says. Billy Mulak's old man. I got a hunch about him. I found out he went out in his boat alone a day before the others did. Far as I can tell, he's the only one was off by himself, missing for a whole day."

"Billy's father?"

"Yeah. He's supposed to have been a great hunter in his day. Stubborn bastard."

Mayberry looked at him, sensing something. "Where is he?"

"I got him locked up in that log storage shed. I wanted to give him time to think things over."

Mayberry sighed. "You worked him over? Is he hurt?"

"Hey, he'll survive. And I think he knows where that ivory is."

Mayberry didn't like being heavy-handed with the Eskimos, that could backfire on him. At the same time he had to have the missing ivory, no two ways about it. "It's cold in that shed," he muttered.

"He's an Eskimo," Simpson said. "He's used to being cold. Besides, he gets cold enough, his answers might get warmer."

Mayberry slapped his gloved hands together, and hunched his shoulders, frowning. The bush pilot wandered over from tying down his aircraft. Mayberry didn't think Rorie had been close enough to monitor the conversation, although sounds carried remarkably in this brittle air.

"Man, it's cold!" Jeff Rorie said. "Where are we supposed to bed down tonight? I don't suppose there's a village Hilton."

Mayberry grinned. "No, but there's an empty house we can use. Got two bedrooms. The family moved out, and it's kind of a bed-and-breakfast for visitors. The locals use it to put up visiting relatives." He pointed the house out to Rorie, a frame building about thirty yards up the street. "The door's open. They don't lock things up around here. I'll be with you in a bit. Gotta talk to some people."

The pilot glanced curiously toward the schoolhouse. "You find any of that vodka left, bring a bottle with you."

"You got it."

Simpson frowned as he watched the pilot trudge through the freezing mud toward the one-story house, one of those prefabricated units that might have been found in small-town suburbs in the Lower 48, or in military housing anywhere. "I don't know about him," Simpson said. "I still want to check him out."

"He's okay," Mayberry replied. "And I need him. Where's Billy Mulak?"

"In the school."

Billy Mulak was obviously agitated, Mayberry saw. He had been drinking earlier, but when Mayberry offered him another drink he shook his head. "My father knows nothing," he mumbled. "How can he tell you what he doesn't know?"

"Sometimes Wolf has hunches about these things. Hey, if he's wrong, that's all there is to it, okay? Do you know anything you're not telling us, Billy?"

"No!"

"You're sure? You know where your father went in his boat?"

"He brought home fish. He was fishing, that's all."

"I know what you need," Mayberry said quietly. "You need to calm down, kinda look at this thing the right way."

He fished a ziplock plastic bag from his pocket, opened the seal at the top and extracted a cigarette. It looked like a hand-rolled cigarette, which it was.

"Here you go, Billy."

The young Eskimo stared at the cigarette. When he reached for it, his hand trembled. Mayberry snapped open a battered old Zippo lighter and held the flame to the tip of the cigarette.

After a moment Billy leaned back against the wall of the schoolhouse, inhaling deeply. Mayberry watched the pinched, strained look around Billy's eyes begin to ease.

"Nepali gold," Mayberry chuckled. "Best grass in Alaska. You just sit back and relax, and think about things, Billy. Nobody wants to see anybody hurt. I don't want to see you hurt, or your old man."

He waited a moment, watching the youth. Billy's eyes held the misery of the universe, but they were not moving around so frantically. An average Eskimo would sell a good pair of walrus tusks for an ounce of marijuana. But Billy Mulak had discovered an even stronger craving.

"I tell you what, Billy. I've got a little of the white powder with me, a little coke. And it's yours. I know you didn't earn it, not until we find that ivory, but that's okay. You do a little something for me, I do a little something for you. You know what might work? After your old man has a chance to think things over, you could have a talk with him, you know? You can make him understand. If he knows anything about that ivory, anything at all, he has to tell you, or you're in big trouble. A father wouldn't let his son down, would he? You have to make him understand, Billy . . . either he talks to you, or he talks to

Wolf. It might take a while, but either way, eventually he has to talk.''

Billy stared at him. He took another deep drag on the marijuana cigarette, holding it between thumb and forefinger. His actions were in slow motion, and his hand no longer shook.

TEN

THE STRANGE, luminous darkness of the Arctic night closed in during the last weary quarter-mile, but by then Kathy had spotted the two yellow tents on a little rise above a gravel beach that identified their camp. Survivor also knew they were almost at their goal, and she had to hold him back. Jason Cobb had taken enough punishment on the travois.

She got Cobb inside his tent and lit the Coleman stove that also served as a heater. Earlier, they had gathered as much firewood as they could find near the campsite, most of it logs and driftwood rescued from the river, forest debris ferried, some of it for hundreds of miles, from the tree-covered mountains where the river began. Kathy built a roaring fire near Cobb's tent. She chopped up the four travois poles, which had served their purpose, and added them to the fire.

Jason Cobb was a little feverish by then. She gave him a painkiller from their first-aid kit and, after some hesitation, antibiotics for the fever.

She had him lie on his back on top of his sleeping bag. "We have to get you out of those wet clothes," she said.

"Hell of a time to make an offer like that."

"Uh-huh. I guess you're not in such bad shape."

She was able to pull off his parka and a wool sweater, and unbutton his shirt, which was wet. His pants, protected by an outer cover of nylon, were another story. If his back was seriously injured, he had already been moved around as much as they could risk. Kathy had bullied him into riding on the travois only because it was the only way to get him back to the camp. She found scissors in her gear and cut the wet shirt and slacks

109

away. To her considerable relief, his thermal underwear seemed reasonably dry.

"Am I supposed to just relax and enjoy this?" Cobb said.

"Something like that."

When she had the wet clothes off, she wrapped him in a blanket topped by her own down-filled sleeping bag.

"Where are *you* going to sleep?"

"I guess I'll just have to stay in here with you and keep warm. I don't plan to sleep much."

"Why do I get the feeling that your intentions aren't entirely amorous?"

"Because you're a wise man, Dr. Cobb."

She left him alone while she used the short-wave radio to raise someone at the ASSET base camp, two hundred miles upriver. There was a long delay before someone answered, long enough for her anxiety to build. Then a voice broke in. "ASSET base. Come in."

"Riverboat One," Kathy said, identifying the call name she and Cobb had been given. "This is Dr. McNeely."

"Dr. McNeely! We've been wondering about you two. Tried to call you earlier but there was no answer. Everyone's up late here. Have you seen our light show?"

"Yes, it's spectacular."

"Really incredible, Doctor. Some of the photographs should be—"

"I'm sorry," Kathy cut him off. "There's been an accident. Dr. Cobb is hurt. We need to get him out of here and to a hospital as quickly as possible."

"Oh my gosh! The plane isn't here, Doctor, but I think it's supposed to be back tomorrow. If not, I believe the nearest emergency flights are out of Fairbanks. I'll get right on it. We'll get you both out of there as fast as we can."

"Just Dr. Cobb," she said without thinking. "I won't be leaving just yet. I still have work to do."

At that moment, from the shadows of the tundra nearby, a wolf began to howl. Kathy looked up in the direction of the spine-tingling sound.

She saw the wolf then for the first time. She stood on one of the mounds that distinguished parts of the tundra, about a hundred yards away, her head lifted. She was large, at least as tall as Survivor, although she appeared to be thinner and longer-legged. Her coat was almost pure white. It seemed to Kathy that she looked directly toward the camp for a moment, then threw her head back and howled again.

Survivor, on his feet with his hackles rising, moaned deep in his throat.

"I don't think the committee would approve of leaving you there alone," the voice on the radio was saying.

"That's as may be," Kathy replied. "Dr. Cobb is the issue right now. He has a severe hip or back injury. Call me as soon as you know about the plane."

"You've got it, Dr. McNeely."

Cobb was watching her when she reentered his tent. "You're something else, McNeely. A bird woman of a different feather."

She felt her fatigue descend upon her like a roof collapsing. "Wet and wild," she said with an effort at humor. "Wet, anyway."

"You should get out of those clothes. I won't mind."

Kathy grinned. "I've heard about troublesome patients. My sister's a nurse."

"Occupational hazard. You go around saving people's lives, you have to take the consequences."

"I didn't save your life, Dr. Cobb. I'm not even sure I did the right thing."

"I am, and you did."

Cobb was silent for a moment. Kathy was aware of a difference in their relationship, a subtle, unspoken alteration from working colleague to friend.

"What's with this guy Hurley?" Cobb asked finally. "Are you in love with him?"

"That's . . . personal."

"I know. But if everything were perfect, I think you'd say so."

"We have a ways to go," she admitted. "But we're working things out. I've never been very good at relationships. It's something I have to learn."

"I don't believe there's anything you're not good at, not anything important. And if you were my girl, I wouldn't be off in Antarctica chasing rainbows. I'd be wherever you were."

Kathy smiled. "Well, you're here now, and a lot of good you are to me. Anyway, Brian isn't chasing rainbows. A dream, I guess, or a challenge he couldn't pass up. You see, he has this marvelous dog team, he's trained them for three years, and it's something they do together, racing against others who've tried to meet the same challenges. Survivor was part of the team until he broke his shoulder. Brian's going to climb the Hartsook Glacier, and race to the South Pole, trying to set a record. It's something he would have done over a year ago, that's what he first went to Antarctica for, but he gave it up because I needed his help. I think it's something he has to finish, or he'll always regret it."

"And after that?"

"After that . . . we'll see."

It felt odd, hearing herself defend Hurley to Jason Cobb. Defending what she had once attacked so vehemently. She remembered the last angry exchange with Brian. It would have been different, she'd argued, if he were going wherever his work took him—Hurley's training was in archeology—even if it meant having him go off to Borneo or Tibet. But he was going to the bottom of the world just for kicks, she'd said. On a whim.

It was the word *whim* that got to him. It wasn't a goddamn whim, Hurley raged. It was something he'd given several years of his life to. It mattered. He didn't care about the television coverage, he cared only about doing what he had set out to do, doing something better than anyone had ever done it before him. If that was frivolous, he'd wear a big letter *F* on his shirt. His dogs could wear smaller *F* tags on their collars.

It was the worst argument they had had, and the timing couldn't have been worse, coming the night after the ASSET committee arrived in Santa Barbara to talk to her about the Alaskan expedition. They had got over the anger, but they hadn't resolved the conflict. There hadn't been time.

She stood, restless, surprised at how much she had opened up to Jason Cobb. She felt tired and clammy in her wet clothes.

"I'm going to change into something dry. But I'll be back."

"Good. I don't fancy being alone tonight."

Outside, the air sharp and cold after the warmth of the tent, Kathy stared at the northern lights, remembering similar if less

fantastic displays of light and color in southern skies over Antarctica. Was Brian watching them now, thinking of her? That
question, she decided firmly, wasn't going to help *her* get
through the night.

In her tent she recalled Cobb's last words with a grin. She
had something to hold over him. Something she would be able
to tell all his friends and colleagues, and his adoring public.
The formidable Jason Cobb was human and vulnerable, after
all.

John Mulak rested inside the storage shed. He had moved a
crate against the wall and sat on top of the crate with his legs
drawn up close to his body, making himself a compact ball, as
warm as he was going to get. He kept his left hand under his
parka. After the white man Simpson left, Mulak had retrieved
his mitten to cover the broken hand. The hand was warmer
now, and didn't hurt as much. It throbbed, though. Only hurts
when my heart beats, he thought with dry humor.

The life of an Eskimo, especially when Mulak was younger,
had never been easy. Pain and hardship were familiars, cold
even more so. Life was never as far removed from death as it
appeared to be on the Outside, at least from what Mulak had
observed on television. And the violence in nature was an everyday experience, accepted without anguish. Still, Mulak's interrogation by Simpson had been unique. He had encountered
anger among his own people, but he had never known, or even
witnessed, the calculating, vicious cruelty Simpson seemed to
enjoy. It was a phenomenon to puzzle over. What was it in the
white man's nature that made such indifference to the human-
ity of other men possible? It was a question to occupy his
thoughts while he sat there. Better than thinking about the cold
inside the shed that seeped under your parka and your shirt.
Because there was no movement of the air in the room, the
cold seemed to envelope him more than it did in the open.

He thought about what he had done to create his present
predicament. The white man was right, he had stolen what was
not his. And he had lied about his actions. Neither fact gave
him comfort. Both actions were alien to his nature, but he had

seen no alternative. He saw none now, nor any escape from his situation. The white men would return, asking more questions he would not answer.

"If you know where the ivory is, Pop, why won't you tell them?"

They had sent Billy to gain the answers Simpson could not get from him. His son, but a stranger. There was a brightness in Billy's eyes that was not normal, a nervous energy about his movements. When he entered the storage shed, he couldn't stop pacing back and forth, bouncing on the balls of his feet. He spoke excitedly, not looking at his father directly, pacing back and forth. Mulak wanted to tell him to be calm, to sit down and they would talk. But Billy never stopped moving.

Mulak would reveal nothing to this stranger.

Billy talked about the hunt, about how exciting it was to see Muugli. How he, Billy Mulak, had been chosen by the white men to kill the Great One because he was the best man in the village with a rifle. How the men in the boats, and others who had leaped onto the shelf in the cove, had killed great numbers of walruses, at least a hundred! It was a hunt, Billy boasted, that Eskimos would talk about for years to come.

"You did not kill Muugli," Mulak said.

"Yes! Yes, I did!" Billy insisted. "I shot him twice. I couldn't be mistaken."

"But you didn't kill him."

Billy stared at him. "How can you know that?"

The old man was silent, thinking that he had said too much. It was easy to betray himself when he was talking to his son, rather than to the stranger.

"What do the white men give you for all this killing?"

"They'll pay us, but only for the ivory. Do you know what happened to it, Pop?" Billy didn't really believe his father could have taken the ivory. There was too much of it. But it seemed possible that he knew something he wasn't telling.

"That's our ivory," Billy pleaded. "Without it we get nothing. And we have nothing to prove the story of the hunt. No one will ever believe us without the ivory to show for what we did. No one will believe that Muugli is dead."

"This hunt," John Mulak said after a moment. "Is this a story you would tell your children and your grandchildren? The white men are not hunters, they are butchers. They care nothing for those they kill. They don't respect the walrus. This isn't the Eskimo way. Eskimos do not kill what they don't need."

"It's for the ivory! We've always killed the walrus for ivory. What's wrong with that?"

"Only what we needed," his father said simply.

The stubbornness in John Mulak's face increased Billy's desperation. His pacing became frantic. His arms flailed the air in agitation. "You've got to tell them what you know, Pop. They won't stop until you tell them. They're very angry. You don't know them, Pop. You don't know what they might do."

"Yes, I know them."

Billy didn't know about the bone in his father's hand broken by Simpson's blackjack. He didn't know about the painful bruise on Mulak's shoulder, and another that had left his arm numb. But he saw the bruises on the old man's face, the cut and swollen lip where blood had dried. Billy began to tremble.

"Tell them, Pop. Whatever it is they want to know, tell them. Do it for me."

"I am doing this for you," Mulak said. "And for all our people."

He saw the shock of his words register in Billy's eyes. "Oh my God!" his son whispered. "You did take it. You stole the ivory."

"You know nothing," John Mulak said. "Go away. I will not talk to you anymore. Tell your bosses you learned nothing."

Hours later, the white men had not returned to the shed. Mulak wondered what Billy had told him about their talk, and what they had given him in return. He thought he understood now what had changed his son. For the past year or more he had heard talk in the village about some of the hunters selling ivory for marijuana, preferring it to dollars. And lately there had been whispers about another drug, the white powder called cocaine. Mulak knew about cocaine from watching TV. Everyone in Los Angeles and other great cities on the Outside used it, rich and poor people alike. They would destroy their lives to possess it. They would willingly destroy others, even their families. This was something Mulak couldn't comprehend. He knew about whisky, because he had tried it. Even one drink made his face hot and his tongue thick. But he didn't understand the hold the white powder exerted over men's minds and hearts.

Alone in the shed, Mulak thought about his son, remembering him as a boy, eager to learn everything his father taught him. He had been a cheerful child. His mother was alive then. Her laughter filled the house, the older house with no heating and no washing machine. Her laughter made everyone around her happy. The house was made warm by people, not a furnace. It was always full of people eating and laughing and telling stories.

Mulak thought about what the white men were doing to his son, and he knew that he would never tell them where the ivory was.

He dozed after a while, his bones and muscles stiff and aching from the cold and the blows he had taken. He woke suddenly, so stiff that he felt he couldn't move, and he wondered what had awakened him.

A rattling at the door.

The door was secured by a sliding bolt and a simple padlock on the outside. Mulak had tested it earlier. The door and the lock were too sturdy to break down.

He heard the scratching outside the door. Simpson was returning.

In spite of himself, Mulak felt a twisting in his belly, a sign of weakness. He steeled himself against the fear. And waited.

The crack was so loud it caused Mulak to jump. He slid off the crate he was sitting on, jolting his wounded hand. His heart pounded.

Nothing happened. The door didn't fly open. Neither Simpson nor the other white man was standing there to confront him. Nothing. The night silence returned.

After a moment Mulak approached the door. It was no longer firmly shut. He tested it with his good hand. The door swung open slightly.

Someone had broken the lock. Not the lock itself, Mulak saw as he examined it, but the wood frame to which the lock and the sliding bolt were secured. It had been pried open. A crowbar lay on the ground, as if to provide evidence of what had been done.

Mulak picked up the crowbar and slid it quietly into the shed, leaving it on the floor. The white men might think he had found the bar in the shed and pried the door open himself.

He stood beside the entrance to the log building, under the shadow of the roof overhang. The sky shimmered with light. It made Mulak think of pictures he had seen of cities on the Outside, like the gambling city, Las Vegas. But the northern sky was more beautiful. It wasn't the same garish neon of the cities. More like there was a city of lights somewhere below the horizon, and what Mulak saw was a reflection of all that color and glitter, winking and dancing across the sky.

The village street was empty. So was the boardwalk that defined the cluster of civic buildings—town hall, post office, the arcade where the young people of the village now spent so much of their time instead of playing games outdoors. Lights glowed here and there in scattered houses. A dog foraged. Otherwise the village slept.

Mulak circled the log shed, keeping it between him and the houses up the street, including the house where the white men customarily slept when they stayed at the village overnight. At first Mulak was surprised that no one was watching the shed. Then he realized there had been no apparent need. With the door padlocked, how could an old man escape?

There remained a mystery: Who had broken the lock? Who other than his son? Would anyone other than Billy have taken such a risk? Mulak felt a surge of renewed pride in his son.

It was best that Billy had not remained near the shed. The white men would suspect him of aiding the escape.

Mulak didn't like leaving Billy to face that suspicion alone, but remaining at the village would mean even more trouble— for himself, for Billy, for the entire village.

Mulak angled to his left, toward the river. The ground was frozen, which meant that he left no tracks. The last few mornings the puddles left over from recent rains had had thin skins of ice. This morning they were frozen solid. Without tracks, the white men would not be certain he had left the village. Mulak knew the delay would be brief, however, lasting only until they discovered that his boat was missing.

On the narrow beach where he had pulled his kayak out of

the water, Mulak paused. But there was no other way for him to have any hope of escape. How far could he travel on foot across the open tundra before searchers in an airplane found him?

He broke a thin crust of ice at the edge of the stream when he slid his kayak into the water. The crackling of the ice seemed very loud, almost as loud as the lock breaking away from the door frame. He glanced back toward the sleeping village. No one stirred. Mulak lifted his paddle awkwardly, favoring his left hand. He had identified the fractured knuckle at the base of his left forefinger, and he had wrapped the hand tightly with a strip of cloth. He couldn't grip the paddle firmly with that hand, but he could use light pressure to guide the paddle, relying on his good hand for strength. He would have trouble if he encountered rough seas.

He glanced for the last time toward the village. He watched and listened. He saw no one, but the sensation he felt was inescapable.

From the moment he left the storage shed, someone had been watching him.

ELEVEN

RUTH MULAK was up early as usual. She often used the early morning hours to prepare for the day's classes. Other times there were household chores, or she could work on one of her crafts. She was a basket maker, a craft she had learned from her mother, and she had been laying in a supply of the wild rye grasses she preferred to use for the long winter nights when she could work on a basket while she watched television. Most of her baskets she gave to friends or relatives, but there was a store owner in Anchorage who paid fifty dollars for the smallest baskets, and twice as much for the larger baskets with lids.

Ruth had also learned and practiced other traditional everyday skills of her people. She had cleaned, salted and filleted most of the fish her father had caught on his last fishing trip, for example, and hung it up on the fish rack behind the house to dry. Although there was frozen fish most of the year, either in the freezer or in the old fish house out back that was shared with several neighbors, the dried fish, oily and chewy, was a delicacy favored by all Eskimos, almost as tasty as smoked salmon.

She also had three sealskins stretched and hanging on racks. Two of these her father would use this winter to re-cover his kayak. The third skin was ready to use in her skin sewing class. It had been dried, scraped, soaked and worked until it was soft and pliable. She planned to take it to school today, along with a supply of dental floss for sewing—a modern substitute for thread made of animal sinew.

The house was quiet. She missed the busy feet and cheerful voices of her cousin's children, who had visited the day before.

And she missed hearing her father begin to stir around in his room. Like her, John Mulak was usually up early.

There were mornings when Ruth felt the loneliness of her life. She didn't mind looking after her father's house, but she would have liked a home of her own, and children. She knew she was attractive, but so far the young men of the village had been intimidated by her. She was different. She had left the village to be educated, not only through high school but two years at the University of Alaska as well. She was not as compliant as most of the young women in the village. She raised troublesome questions about the Eskimo wife's role as simply a helper for her husband and mother of their children. She didn't accept some of the arrogant ways the young men acted toward women, as if they were inferior, and she had strong opinions of her own she was unwilling to smother. She was only twenty-six, but already she was beginning to be regarded in the village as too old for marriage.

Ruth removed the tanned sealskin from its rack, shivering in the cold air. The sky was gray after partial clearing during the night, but there was a difference from recent stormy days. This was like a winter sky, and the ground was frozen hard.

Billy entered the kitchen silently as Ruth was wrapping the sealskin in a cloth. The skin was very soft and workable now, but also tough and waterproof. Sealskins had been favored by the Eskimos for generations for some articles of clothing, including pants and shirts, and especially for the boots called mukluks. Ruth was going to use this skin to show her students how to make a pair of plain, knee-high boots. When finished, the boots would be for her father.

"Why do you bother with such things?" Billy said suddenly. "No one needs them anymore."

"You're wrong, Billy. I don't see you throwing away your old boots. Anyway, this is to show the children how to sew with skins, and how Eskimos have always made a pair of boots."

Billy helped himself to coffee. He looked like death, she thought. There were dark shadows under his eyes, as if he had not slept well. She wondered how much he knew about what was happening with their father.

"Do you want something to eat?"

"I'm not hungry." He continued to watch her fold and wrap the sealskin. "Why do you live in the past? Maybe if you paid more attention to the present, you could find a man."

"Maybe I don't want to find a man who lives only in the present."

"You will be an old maid."

The prediction stung. "I'm teaching the children useful skills. They are things our people have always been able to do. It would be wrong to let them disappear. Anyway, I've never seen you turn down salmon in December or January when the fishing is bad."

"You're like our father. He lives in the past. He doesn't understand that way is dead. We live in the white man's world now."

"No, we don't!" Ruth retorted. "We still live in our own village, with our own people."

"Don't tell me you're happy here. I've seen you reading your books, and watching the TV. You wish you could go away, to be like the gussak women you see, with their fine clothes and their cars and all the rest. You envy them, just like I do!"

"No, I don't!" Ruth retorted. Billy was wrong, but he had penetrated her fantasies shrewdly enough to surprise and disturb her. "I would like to see more of the Outside—there are so many wonderful things I've never seen. There is so much history that isn't part of our history, so much to know. But I wouldn't live there. I belong here. So do you, Billy."

"You think I want to stay here all my life? I want more than this."

"What has this to do with Papa? He didn't come home last night. What do these white friends of yours have to do with Papa?"

Billy became evasive. "You don't need to know. It's not your business."

"It's not my business? He's my father! Where is he? What have they done to him?"

"Nothing. He's in the storage shed. They locked him in there to teach him a lesson. They think he stole the ivory from the hunt, or at least knows where it is."

Ruth was momentarily shocked speechless. Her father locked

up like a criminal! It would have been bitter cold in the storage shed last night. Even worse for him, she thought, would be his feeling of shame.

"Papa would never do such a thing. He's not a thief."

"He stole it! Or if he didn't take it himself, he knows what happened to it." Billy's tone became sullen. "He's a stubborn old man, a foolish, stubborn old man! If he doesn't tell these white men where the ivory is, we will all suffer. None of us will be paid for the hunt. There will be no—"

"No what?" Ruth demanded when he broke off. "No more whisky? No drugs? Is that why you work for these men? Is that all you want? Oh, Billy, don't you see what they're doing to you? They're using you and the other men, and they don't even pay you properly. They give you whisky and grass cigarettes, and you get drunk or high, and when it's over what do you have? Nothing! They have all the ivory, and you have nothing but a hang-over."

"What am I, anyway?" Billy burst out in anger. "I am nothing! You're a teacher, at least you are something. But what am I? Our people don't need hunters anymore, the way they did when Pop was younger. We can have all the food we want. We don't need your dried salmon or your sealskin boots. We can buy just as good. And if we have no money, the government, or the village council, will still give us what we need."

The passion in Billy's words came from anger and frustration, but there was something else, and his sister read it clearly: guilt.

"Tell me the truth. What have they done to Papa?"

"Nothing! I told you, he's in the shed. They think when they let him out, he'll tell them what they want to know."

"If he did what you say, he had a good reason," Ruth said quietly. "He won't talk. Not if he doesn't want to."

"He's a fool!" Billy cried.

"Did you help them? Did you turn against your own father? Is that why you're so angry?"

"You don't know anything about these things. I'm not one of the children in your classes."

"Are you not even a son? Is what the gussak gives you so important as that?"

She saw that the accusation was truer than she had guessed.

Billy became agitated, his eyes darting about as if he were look-ing for a way to escape from his own thoughts. "You don't know anything about it. You don't understand—"

A heavy pounding on the front door silenced him. They both jumped. Ruth's first thought was of her father. But he wouldn't have knocked. This was his house.

A fist pounded on the door again, hard enough to make it vibrate. "Mulak? Are you there?"

Ruth recovered first. A little apprehensive, she went to the front door. Three white men stood outside, two of them on the small porch, the third one hanging back. The latter was the airplane pilot, a man Ruth had never seen before. But the two men on the porch, both of whom appeared angry, were familiar figures in the village. Sometimes they bought furs, but mostly they came for ivory. Ruth despised them for what they were doing to the people. She had been raised as a Christian, and she knew it was wrong to hate. But she was as close to hatred as she could ever be.

Travis Mayberry's eyes narrowed, as if her deep hostility was immediately transparent to him. "Where's John Mulak?" he de-manded.

"I don't know," Ruth said. "Why do you come here looking? You took him away last night."

Billy appeared at her side. There was consternation in his face. "Pop's not here." He looked past the men in the direc-tion of the log storage building. Disbelief replaced the worry in his eyes.

"He's gone," Mayberry said harshly. He glared at Billy with suspicion. "Somebody broke the lock and let him out. You wouldn't have started feeling sorry for your old man, would you? And let him out?"

"No, I swear it!"

"Well, somebody in this village did. Tried to make it look like Mulak did it himself from the inside, but that door was pried open from outside. Then the old bastard took his boat. He's gone!"

Ruth's elation was banished by the white man's next words.

"You're coming with us, Billy. You know where he'd go. You're gonna help us find him. Him running away like this clinches it. That old man took the ivory for himself. He stole it, and he's gonna give it back. . . . or this whole village is going to pay!''

That morning, Jason Cobb felt much worse. All movement was painful, but he was not—as he had feared the day before—paralyzed. He was able to move the leg that had felt numb. What he wasn't able to do was relieve himself while lying on his back. And like many arrogant, self-sufficient men, he hated being incapacitated. When Kathy tried to offer suggestions, he snapped, "For God's sake, leave me alone. Just give me a pan and get out of here. I'm not helpless!''

Kathy choked back a retort, swallowing her irritation. She tried, without much success, to put herself in his place. What was obvious was that she couldn't give him the medical attention he needed. Wilderness wasn't only communing with nature, and being a long way from a 7-Eleven. It also meant being hundreds of miles from the nearest doctor or hospital, and with no way to get there in an emergency.

A little later, when she brought Cobb some crackers and cheese, and a mug of hot coffee, he was ill at ease. He couldn't quite bring himself to apologize, but he grunted his thanks. "You having coffee?''

"Yes, I was just going to . . .''

"Out there by yourself?''

"I'll be back in a minute.''

Over coffee she felt the closeness they had enjoyed the night before return. "When's the plane going to get here?''

"Soon, I hope. I talked to base an hour ago. The regular supply plane can't get back here for another day or two, for whatever reason. It's in Anchorage. But they were able to talk to a pilot who's picking up some sport fishermen this morning who've been in Alaska on a package tour. They've been at a lodge in the Brooks Range about fifty miles from a place called Bettles. He's going to divert this way and pick you up.''

"Great, I can listen to fish stories all the way to the hospital.''

"Stop complaining, it'll take your mind off things, like missing all this camp food.''

"I've been doing more than my share of that, haven't I? Complaining . . ."

"Oh, I don't know. For a man with a broken back you haven't been too bad."

He studied her quietly. Her face was flushed from the cold outside. It was, he could see, a gray, cold morning, but at least it wasn't raining. He thought that what he was going to miss most was not the camp food, the incredible scenery and wildlife, or even the work he had come to do, but the growing intimacy between himself and this sensible, caring, desirable woman, whether it was sharing that intense moment when the snowy owl swooped down to her nest, or a quiet cup of coffee in the morning.

"Kathy—"

"Don't, Jason. You're in a weakened condition," she added lightly. "Don't say anything you'll regret later."

"I'll regret not saying anything."

"But I'll feel better if you don't. Anyway, it's not as if we're not going to see each other again. You'll probably be on your feet in no time."

"Maybe." His disappointment was plain. He covered it by saying, "I heard you talking on the radio last night. You aren't serious about staying here alone!"

"I'm not joining the tour with you and your fishing friends, that's for sure. Survivor and I will be fine. We haven't finished what we came here for, Jason, and we're running out of time before winter chases us out. Those hearings in Anchorage are only about six weeks away."

"I'm going to talk to the ASSET people. They can't leave you here—it's too dangerous. That she-wolf, for instance . . . she was back last night. I don't like that."

"You weren't worried about her before. I think you were right then . . . she likes our company. She's not threatening us. Anyway, I'm sure our colleagues will feel the same as you. They'll be sending someone to join me, or insisting that I pack it up. I'll be fine for a day or two."

"Stay close to camp—stay out of trouble."

"You sound like a parent," Kathy said, amused.

"I care about you, Dr. McNeely."
"Yes," Kathy said. "I know."

At Jason Cobb's insistence, Kathy managed to slide his improvised bed out of the tent before the plane arrived. The pilot had
relayed a message through the ASSET base camp of his impending arrival, and Cobb didn't want to be found lying in his tent
like an invalid. It was a floatplane, and Cobb and Kathy watched
the pilot pass over their camp and continue downstream a short
distance, examining the river and the lacework of canals and
marshes to the south. In this part of the wilderness, a plane
equipped with pontoons could land safely on water or, if the
lakes and waterways froze and snowpack covered the ground, it
could set down on skis. There was no place for a safe landing on
wheels.

The plane made a second pass before coming in for a rough
landing in the middle of the river, flying upstream against the
current. The craft taxied toward the camp, working gradually
closer to the shoreline, and stopped a few feet from the riverbank. Two grizzled men in thigh-high boots, red plaid parkas
and caps with fishing flies attached to them joined the pilot as
they waded ashore, calling out cheerful greetings. Jason Cobb
groaned aloud.

"Cheer up," Kathy whispered. "Just think, you'll be the first
one to hear their stories . . . it'll be like a premiere perfor-
mance."

"Need a lift?" the bush pilot called out.

TWELVE

"FELLA BACK at the Nome airport was telling me Mayberry has some wings of his own in a private hangar there."

Wolf Simpson's habitual suspicion flared. "Yeah?"

"Truth is, I took a peek at it. A Piper Super Cub, about a 1980 I'd guess, fitted up as a floatplane."

"A man could get into trouble, peekin' where he hasn't been invited."

Jeff Rorie shrugged. He glanced toward the river, where Mayberry was talking to some Eskimos. A group of the native hunters were to return to the walrus cove by sea to search for the missing ivory, while Mayberry and his sidekick flew along the coastline in Rorie's plane. Mayberry seemed to have several items on his agenda: looking for his ivory, trying to spot a walrus with huge tusks that had supposedly been wounded or killed during the recent hunt, and searching for the Eskimo who had escaped from the log shed in the night. The main item on Rorie's agenda was the weather, which was cold and gray and had a feel to it that he didn't like. The weather report said nothing about a storm, but that could change along the north coast of Alaska about as fast as you could think it.

"Just interested, that's all," Rorie said easily. "That's a nice little plane. He fly it much?"

"What's it to you?"

"Wonderin' why he needs me to ferry him around if he's got wings of his own. I wasn't lookin' for just weekend work."

Slightly mollified, Simpson glanced toward Mayberry and grinned. "He cracked up about eighteen months ago. Got hit by a crosswind touching down, and it blew him off the strip into a ditch. He walked away from it, but ever since then he hates to

127

fly on his own. There's times he has to fly places on his own, and he'll take her up when he has to, but not when he can get somebody else to chauffeur him."

Rorie wondered what those trips might be that Mayberry had to take on his own, even though he hated flying solo.

Mayberry joined them, with the young Eskimo Billy Mulak in tow. "Let's get her up. That old man's got a good start on us."

Taking off, the Cessna felt the tug of southerly side winds, but the landing strip ran east to west and Jeff Rorie had no choice but to ignore the winds and point the aircraft's nose to the east in the direction of distant purple mountains. He could feel the drag of the floats in the wind.

Once airborne, he swung about in a wide circle and flew back over the collection of houses and huts that made up the Eskimo village. Scattered along the twisting course of the river, the settlement resembled a question mark from the air. The largest thing in sight was the village dump, which collected everything from garbage to tin cans to empty oil barrels to snow machines abandoned because they would no longer run. The dump was too near the river for Rorie's liking, the river being where the Eskimos got much of their water.

A number of villagers were outside, watching the plane take off. Some of the children waved. The adults just watched, faces tilted toward the sky. Rorie put faces on those little blurs, impassive brown faces, betraying nothing. Eskimos were friendly people, but they were taught from birth to contain their feelings. No way to tell what they were thinking unless they wanted you to know. Rorie wondered how much hostility had been generated over the treatment of John Mulak.

The winds gusted. They became stronger as the airplane headed out over the coastline and, at Mayberry's direction, turned north along the rim of the Chukchi Sea. Rorie scanned the horizon to the west, looking for telltale blackness, but the gray cloud cover extended to the end of the world. He trusted his small plane, but he didn't trust that sky. No matter what Mayberry said, Rorie meant to keep an eye peeled on the horizon.

To the left, under that surly sky, the sea stretched out gray and bleak, but its northern rim, and a crust along some of the shoreline, was white—a frosting of ice. The ice pack was moving down, Rorie thought. Here and there below him he saw slabs and pancakes of floating ice. Within a month, maybe sooner, the pack ice would be jamming up at the entrance to the Bering Strait. In two months you could walk to Russia.

The Cessna 185 was a six-seater. Rorie had removed the two rear seats, which were cramped for adults anyway, to create more storage room. Wolf Simpson sat in the front next to Rorie. Behind them were Travis Mayberry and the Eskimo. The kid was troubled, Rorie thought. And scared. The four men were packed so close together in the little cabin that Rorie could hear most anything that was said, especially since speakers had to raise their voices close to a shout to be heard over the droning of the engine, the wind scream from the vents, and the assorted vibrations and rattles and squeaks of an airplane that had fifteen years of pounding behind it.

"Where would the old man go?" Mayberry asked Billy.

"I can't be sure . . ."

"You can take a guess. What are the other villages he might go to? Old man like that must have a lot of friends or relatives. Anyone he'd likely run to?"

"Nobody. He knows many people, he has many friends, but their villages are all inland. They aren't close, but he might have gone that way."

"I tol' you I think his hand's hurt," Simpson said. He swung about in his seat and shouted above the airplane's racket. "No way he's gonna paddle a hundred miles upstream with one hand just to hide out."

"You're sure about the hand?"

Simpson grinned slyly. "Yeah, I'm sure. What I say is, he's gone where that ivory is. I say he took it, and stashed it someplace, and that's where he'd run to."

There was a silence for a while. Rorie hadn't wanted to inquire too closely into the ivory they were talking about, which was almost certainly illegal and none of his business. Simpson was already skeptical about him. But he'd heard some of the talk at the village. What it added up to was, a major harvest of walrus tusks from a recent hunt had disappeared before the ivory could be brought to the village and then shipped to Nome or wherever Mayberry wanted it to go. The suspected thief was the man who had escaped from the locked shed during the night. Had one old Eskimo really stolen all the ivory? If so, why? And where would he have taken it? It was an interesting puzzle.

"Where does he like to go fishing?" Mayberry asked after a time.

"There are many places . . ."

"You're his son. Where did he take you fishing? Old man like that, he has to have his favorite spots."

"The rivers . . . there are several places he likes to fish. I can't be sure which one he likes most."

"Goddamnit, don't hold out on me, Billy! Now where the fuck would he go?"

Billy Mulak cringed away from the burly white man, but in the narrow cockpit there was no room to escape the physical pressure or the hard, suspicious eyes that watched him closely, waiting for his answer. Billy wished desperately that his father hadn't done this stupid thing. Stealing from men like Mayberry and Simpson was crazy! It would be better for everyone if the ivory was found. They wouldn't care about an old Eskimo once they had the ivory. And they would pay what they had promised . . .

Billy felt jittery this morning. His stomach was queasy. He didn't like the way the small airplane dipped and tossed about in the wind. When he was able to get the white powder, like the sample Mayberry had given him last night, there was no feeling like it. He was on top of the world, up there all by himself where nobody could reach him or sneer at him or make him feel like he was nothing. But the mornings were always worse after being up so high. He was tired and jumpy, and he didn't want to think.

"There's some creeks just ahead there, you can see them." Billy pointed toward a broad sweep of marshland laced with innumerable creeks and streams. Inland, a shallow lake was visible. In that limitless coastal plain it seemed a small lake. In reality, it was five miles across. "And there's another river to the north, past the walrus cove, where he catches big whitefish."

"He bring any whitefish back from that fishing trip?"

"Yes."

Mayberry grunted. A marsh might be a good place to hide for a time, but not to stay. The old man would want to find solid ground sooner or later. Mayberry wondered if Mulak had taken time to stock up with food for a hideout, or if whoever had let him out had also provided something for him to eat and take with him. He should have checked on that before leaving the village. Simpson should have thought of it.

"We'll give this area a look-see." Mayberry tapped Rorie on the shoulder and pointed. "Take us down, and cruise along slow as you can fly without stalling out."

"You've got it."

"I know that river he's talkin' about," Wolf Simpson shouted at Mayberry. "Maybe the old man's got a place up that way he could've stashed the ivory. Maybe there's an old shack, or maybe an abandoned old village. You'll see some of those along the rivers. He had to have some place to hide all those tusks. No way he'd dump 'em in this marsh."

"If he's got them." Mayberry was feeling less certain than he'd been before setting out.

"He's got 'em!" Simpson yelled. "I could tell the way he looked at me last night he was lyin'. We find him, we get what we came for."

Listening to these exchanges, hearing most of the words above the engine's roar and easily able to fill in the missing pieces, Jeff Rorie wondered what Mayberry was giving Billy Mulak that was desirable enough for him to betray his own father. The pilot had an idea what it was . . .

He banked and flew down over the marsh, and a small cloud of white-winged terns rose up as if to greet him.

Kathy McNeely watched the small rescue plane dwindle into the far distance, as if it were carrying away part of herself. She watched until it was only an imaginary speck. She wished Jason Cobb well. A smile lingered at the thought of the two hearty trophy hunters who had enthusiastically taken Cobb in tow, the first audience for their adventures in the wild.

At last she turned away. She was alone. "No offense, Survivor," she said to the husky, speaking aloud as if she felt the

need to announce her continued existence. What was that co-
nundrum about a tree falling in the forest, and was there any
sound if no one was there to hear it?

Until someone from the ASSET base joined her, she was on
her own. She could set her own priorities. Jason Cobb had been
more than cooperative, especially toward the last. But even with
a colleague who proved surprisingly easy to get along with,
there were always adjustments, compromises on both sides. Today she could do what she wanted.

The sense of freedom was overwhelming, like the space
around her. Everything suddenly took on a different perspective—the long march of the tundra, the towering mass of the
mountains, near and far, that framed three sides of this long
river valley, the clear rush of the river itself—she viewed them
all as if for the first time. Perhaps it was true, she thought, that
you couldn't have a real wilderness experience unless you were
alone. Whatever you encountered, you had to draw upon your
own resources, coping with elements that had been unchanged
for a thousand years.

She thought about that Eskimo in his kayak. Having him slide
by on the river was not quite the same intrusion of civilization
upon the wilderness as following a mountain pass to a pristine
valley and coming abruptly upon an architecturally perfect
A-frame log lodge with an airstrip, comfortable rooms and a
dining room that served up the creations of a chef trained at
the Cordon Bleu—which had happened in the Brooks Range
not far from the ASSET base. By contrast, that Eskimo belonged
here, like the fox, the wolverine, the lemming, the snowy owl
and ptarmigan. Like that female wolf and her pack, or that
peregrine circling over the tundra on the south side of the
river. She watched it ride the air currents, admiring its power
and grace.

Where had the Eskimo been going?

She had come down the river with Jason Cobb. There was no
settlement anywhere near the river. In fact, there had been few
signs of human intrusion. Some abandoned tin cans and old
ashes that showed where some careless campers had stopped
some time ago. The remains of a pair of Eskimo fish racks at a
fork in the river, alongside a roofless shack so weathered the

wood was rotting. But the man in the kayak hadn't gone far, judging from the intervals between trips. And he had been intent on some specific mission. She wasn't sure how many trips he had taken, because it was unlikely that she had seen him each time, but there had been several. Always with his boat laden down with cargo on the way upriver, empty when he returned. As long as she was documenting this habitat anyway, it made sense to discover what he was up to.

She recognized that she was rationalizing a decision she had already made unconsciously, perhaps from the moment she had known Jason Cobb had to be flown out to a hospital. Cobb had dismissed the Eskimo. Kathy couldn't dispel her curiosity.

"Something new and different, Survivor," she murmured. "We're going for a walk."

She took along a light pack, including some raisins, nuts, chocolate and granola bars, a can of Spam and a packet of crackers, biscuits for the dog, a knife, a flashlight and a ground blanket. She didn't intend to stay out late, but over the past two months in the Alaskan wilderness she had learned not to count on anything going exactly as planned.

Walking, she gave herself to the land and the sky, savoring everything she saw and heard. The fascinating bird life of the northern tundra was beginning to thin out as the weather turned cold. There were still great flights of snow geese heading south, though not as many. Two weeks ago she had focused her binoculars on some murres nesting on a rocky promontory, thousands of them, as thick as bees in a hive. She hadn't seen one since. But in the first hours of her walk on this gray morning she caught glimpses of ptarmigan, turning white for winter; loons from China or Europe, soon to be heading home; wheatears all the way from Africa; and, standing in marshy water beyond the river, a speckled, long-legged godwit. There had been so many other species all this summer, more than she would have seen in a lifetime in any other place. Seeing them alone made the trip worthwhile. Being able to document the potential damage to their habitat from the proposed pipeline was a bonus.

Walking on the tundra was, as usual, frustrating and tiring, although the ground was firmer than it had been recently. It would be frozen solid soon—there was floating ice in the river today. That would make the terrain difficult in a different way, spiny and uneven as the mud froze. She remembered something from the journals of Lewis and Clark during their epic journey across an uncharted American wilderness nearly two hundred years ago. At the time of reading it she had marveled. Meriwether Lewis, in particular, couldn't get enough of exploring every aspect of the great land he was discovering. After a morning fighting his way upriver in one of the boats, or an even longer, more arduous afternoon, his first thought on stopping for the midday meal or camping for the night was to take a walk. Fifteen miles during the dinner break was routine, across unspoiled terrain where no boot had ever trod.

"We've lost something, Survivor," she commented, yielding to the new habit of addressing the husky out loud. "We've turned into softies."

Enjoying himself, the dog gave a bark in answer, as if to say, "Speak for yourself."

She stopped to rest in the early afternoon. She had some of her nuts and raisins, and one of the granola bars. She let the sense of space pour around her, felt and listened to the wind, sensing that the grasses were more alive than usual. The sky remained overcast, gray to the horizon. Did that mean another storm on the way? The possibility did not alarm her, but it was something to consider. She told herself the Eskimo couldn't have gone much farther. Had she missed the signs along the riverbank where he might have come ashore? She didn't think so.

She walked on, captivated by the sense of being little more than another stem in a universe of brown and beige and red grasses bending before the wind. This is a match for what you saw, Meriwether, she thought, as unspoiled and beautiful as that American West that became your obsession. Unless we trample it under the wheels of trucks, and smear it with oil . . .

Several times during the afternoon she thought of turning back, realizing that she had perhaps come too far to make it back to camp before dark, but her stubbornness drew her on. Another mile, she told herself. She was making notes as she went, some of them in a small notepad, others in her head. Nothing she saw would be wasted.

She almost missed the tracks leading from the river. They had filled with water from the rain, and hardly looked like human footprints until she inspected them closely. Then she followed them to the river, and saw where the Eskimo had drawn his kayak onto a narrow beach.

The tracks led inland, away from the river. The land rose, gradually at first, then on a steeper rise toward a broken crest. The mountains moved closer to the river here, and the foothills straggled almost down to the river. *This is where he was coming,* she thought. Obviously it was a place he knew.

She followed the tracks more cautiously. Here and there she lost them, where he had stepped on grass mounds that had bounced back or on patches of rocky ground. But each time she found them again, climbing higher. What was he carrying? she wondered. She was acquiring a deeper appreciation of his repeated journeys up the river.

Near the crest the tracks vanished.

Kathy examined the ground carefully, frowning. He wasn't a magician, she admonished herself. He didn't just vanish into the earth. But where could he have gone?

The surface was hard near the crest, mostly rock. Between the hard surface and the intervening rains, he might simply have left no tracks to indicate where he had gone.

Her disappointment was so keen she refused to give up. She ascended a few feet to the crest and walked along it, looking down, examining every change in the terrain just below her. Turning back, she did the same for thirty yards in the other direction. Survivor had been trotting ahead of her, and suddenly he disappeared.

She found him sniffing at an opening into the hillside. At first it didn't seem like much, being half covered over with stunted brush. Then she realized that there was a flat spot just inside the opening, a kind of level ledge. And that the hole was much larger than it appeared from above. Large enough for a man, crouching, to step inside.

She felt a tension in her stomach as she bent to peer into the hole. It was dark inside. She fumbled her flashlight out of her pack and clicked it on.

The yellow beam startled her. It leaped into a cavern at least a dozen feet across. It was a natural cave, helped along by someone or something, she thought, that had pushed or scraped or shoveled dirt out of the way to enlarge the opening. The floor of the cave was several feet below the mouth. With her heart hammering and her stomach quivering, Kathy slid down this short ramp into the hollow in the hillside.

It was even larger than the first sketches made by her flashlight beam had suggested. Old, dried animal droppings covered much of the floor. One corner of it, to the left of the opening, was elevated where a large burrow had been dug out several feet higher than the floor. An animal's bed. My God, she thought, a bear's!

Fear seized her. She had to fight it back. Trotted out her common-sense reassurances: there was no bear here now; she hadn't followed the tracks of an animal, but those of a man; there was nothing to be afraid of. They helped a little, but didn't slow the racing heartbeat.

She turned her attention toward the back of the cave, which had remained in gloom. Shone her flashlight toward it, and jumped a foot off the ground.

Heart pounding, Kathy McNeely stared at rows of walrus tusks, scores of ivory teeth arrayed along the wall in a monstrous grin.

THIRTEEN

IT WAS afternoon when the Cessna flew over the walrus cove, after spending hours exploring every stream that wound into the tundra from the coast, examining every stretch of beach where a small boat might come ashore, sometimes doubling back when Mayberry or Simpson had a hunch, or when the young Eskimo aboard remembered a creek where his father sometimes fished.

Mayberry had Rorie circle over the cove, as low as he could safely fly—close enough, Rorie thought, exaggerating only a little, to catch some spray on the windshield from the waves battering against the little peninsula. He saw the lumpy carcasses of dead walruses on a rock shelf along one edge of the cove, as if large sacks of grain had been dumped there. A congregation of scavenger birds sat on the rocks or wheeled about the area. They scattered before the noisy airplane.

Mayberry had him come about for another pass, then a third. He had his binoculars fixed on the scene below, scanning the rocks and the shoreline and the surrounding sea.

"What are we looking for?" Rorie asked, raising his voice to be heard.

"Biggest damned walrus you ever saw!" Mayberry shouted back. "With the biggest damned teeth."

While they were still circling, Rorie spotted a small boat to the south. Mayberry waved him toward it. Flying over, Rorie recognized the Eskimo oumiak that had been seen at the village that morning. They had left it far behind, but with all their circling and wandering inland and backtracking, looking for one Eskimo in a smaller kayak, the hunters from the village had caught up.

"Any place you can sit down around here?" Mayberry asked.

Rorie considered the question seriously. He wasn't going to try to land in heavy seas, and there was no clear beach level enough and sufficiently long for a safe landing.

"I could put us down on one of those little lakes in the tundra marsh. I see one there, off maybe a mile or so. But I wouldn't want to wade all the way to those rocks through those wetlands. That peninsula is probably the first place you could stand for more than thirty seconds without sinking."

Mayberry scowled. Rorie hoped he wasn't going to push it.

"Let the Eskimos look down there," Simpson shouted. "We gotta find that fuckin' thief."

They flew north after that, Mayberry always sweeping the sea and the shore, forcing Rorie to fly over every slab of floating ice he spotted. "Walruses aren't great swimmers," he argued, half to himself. "They like to hitch a ride on the ice. If Muugli is hurt, and there's ice to be found, he'll show up there."

"I say he's dead," Simpson answered. "He'll pop up on a beach somewhere, sooner or later."

"Harry Madrid wants those damned tusks. I never should've told him about them."

"We find the rest of the ivory, he'll simmer down."

Harry Madrid? The curious bush pilot knew better than to inquire about Harry Madrid or his connection with the ivory.

Late in the afternoon, calculating that they were close to reaching the point of no return, Rorie suggested they should think about turning back. Mayberry, whose mood became more savage as the fruitless search continued, turned on the Eskimo. "Where the hell is this river your old man goes to? The one where he catches the whitefish?"

"We're almost there. Look, you can see it." Billy pointed ahead.

The river was a gray ribbon at the edge of an infinity of marshy tundra. Beyond the river bottom to the north, the land rose, climbing through smoothly rounded foothills toward craggy mountains whose white shoulders thrust up through the cloud layer. The peaks were invisible.

"Flying this slow, we've used up more than half a tank of

gasoline," Rorie pointed out reasonably. "That river might have to wait."

"I'm not waiting. That old man's got to be down there somewhere."

"One man in a kayak, we could've missed him way back. He could be anywhere. I doubt he'd have got this far."

"I'm payin' you to fly, not argue. We'll look at this river."

Beside Rorie, Wolf Simpson grinned. "I thought you bush pilots didn't worry about anything. Don't you have a saying, somethin' about flying the smallest piece back?"

"This pilot worries about keeping all the pieces together."

At Mayberry's demand Rorie flew over the network of smaller creeks that webbed the tundra near the coast, as intricate as Irish lace. He had come to the mouth of a river, a quarter-mile wide where it met the sea, when the first snowflakes smacked the windshield of the Cessna.

"What the hell!" Wolf Simpson exclaimed.

Rorie knew instantly that he had been paying too much attention to Mayberry, and not enough to his own instincts. An Alaskan pilot was always trying to outguess the weather, and as often as not he was wrong. But the worst sin of all was not to pay attention.

He tried to climb out of the front. There was no buildup of snow on the wings, but the air was heavy. As he gained altitude Rorie realized that he was not readily going to fly out of this storm going up. It was incredibly deep.

He turned inland. Visibility was down to a dozen feet. The snowflakes were not large and wet, which was good in a way because the snow didn't cling. The powdery stuff blew on by. Rorie hoped he could outrun the storm, but it was moving very fast. That was how it had caught him by surprise.

He could feel the tension inside the small cabin. Billy Mulak looked as if he were going to be sick; he was terrified. Wolf Simpson's knuckles were white where he gripped his seat. Rorie glanced back at Mayberry. His wide mouth was set in a rigid line, jaws clamped. Rorie remembered a line from a Thomas Hardy novel: lips that met like the two halves of a muffin. Thomas's English muffin, he thought. The byplay was a means of taking his mind off the fact that he was now flying blind in a full-fledged whiteout. The condition was a pilot's worst nightmare. It took away his directional sense, which was what small aircraft flying was all about even with instruments. There was nothing but white all around. He had lost not only the sense of left and right, which meant he could fly in a circle without knowing it. He had also lost the up-and-down sense that kept a pilot from flying straight up (gravity would soon help him there, as pieces of the cabin began to fall toward the earth), or plummeting down into the ground, all the time thinking he was straight and level. Rorie kept flicking glances at the artificial horizon and directional gyro, praying that they didn't freeze up or otherwise betray him. He could land in total darkness on instruments, but he always felt better about it if there was some visual landmark, some spot of darkness or light to confirm the readings.

A downdraft pushed the plane toward the ground like a giant fist. It dropped five hundred feet in seconds. Simpson swore, and pieces of gear slammed around inside the cabin, bouncing off walls. Rorie confirmed his altitude. Over the coastal waters he had been wave-hopping so Mayberry and Simpson had clear views of anything below them. He had climbed to a thousand feet when he tried to get above the front, and he had leveled off close to six hundred. The draft had shoved him down within a hundred feet of the ground.

An updraft picked the Cessna up and threw it skyward like a toy balloon. Rorie was ready for it, even anticipating it, but his passengers weren't. Someone screamed in panic. Rorie guessed it was Billy Mulak, who had probably never flown in this kind of weather. On the seat next to Rorie, Simpson was swearing steadily, savagely.

"Get us out of this!" Travis Mayberry raged at the pilot.

"My sentiments exactly," Rorie muttered, not caring if Mayberry heard him. It was a big front. He knew he could probably get out of it if he kept going inland long enough. But there were mountains that way, and closer to the north. He didn't like flying toward mountains he couldn't see. And he didn't like the idea of having a teaspoon of gasoline left when he did get out of it. Heading south offered no better alternative. For fifty miles or more he would be over nothing at all if he had to sit down.

He raised his voice. "I'm going down to find that river, and we're going to get our feet wet."

He was talking more to himself than to his passengers, but Mayberry heard him. "You're gonna get us all killed!"

"Shutup!" Rorie's control momentarily snapped. To himself he added, *I'm not the one who kept us out here past the time it made good sense.* He knew he was going to have to concentrate, using every trick he knew about flying, and he couldn't do that with someone yammering in his ear.

Simpson stared at him with his mouth open. Mayberry, who actually seemed to have some common sense, fell silent. Rorie shut out the sound of the young Eskimo whimpering. Then there was nothing but the airplane, of which he was a living part, and the whirling snow through which he flew on blindly. He thought about the company he was in, which was not the company he would have chosen to accompany him into the hereafter, and about the reason he had taken this job and was here in a wilderness that was less hospitable for an emergency landing in a storm than any place on earth. He had no regrets, but he felt a stubborn resistance to folding his hand at this time and place and in this game. Damned if he would!

He dropped back down below a hundred feet, flying slowly but not slow enough to stall out, noting the red warning of the stall indicator every time it blinked on, and compensating for it. The roar of the engine seemed muffled in the storm. Inside the cabin the silence was thick in his ears. He dropped to fifty feet. Not much room to maneuver. Along most of these tundra rivers there was nothing taller than willow brush along the banks. But was he above the river? Was his compass reading accurate? Was he still flying east, or had he swung toward the hills to the north? He kept looking for a shine of water, a glimpse of brush through the white curtain, anything to tell him where the river was—if he was still near it.

A gap tore in the curtain. It closed almost instantly, but not before Rorie saw two small bright patches of yellow on the tundra—tents! And a gray worm of river beside them. He dipped toward the river reflexively. He was going down. He could land on water or mud or even a gravel bar and probably walk away.

At the last moment the real world reappeared suddenly, a

world of solid objects, of light and dark and color. He was over
the water. The tents he had caught a saving glimpse of were
ahead and above the left bank. The river was about fifty feet
wide at this point, shallow over a gravel bed, but he didn't need
much water for his floats. He throttled back, and was aware of
the stall indicator blinking, of the snow streaming past his windshield like white water. He remembered to keep the nose up.

In an airplane landing on wheels or skis, there was always
some give involved from their springs. But float landings were
harder, and water was as hard a landing surface as any airport
tarmac. Rorie felt the first jolt as the floats struck water. Then
the plane was skimming along on the leading edges of the
floats. The stall warning sounded as the floats took hold. Rorie
fed a little more gas and rode through some hard, choppy
pounding. But the aircraft was still all in one piece and it was
slowing fast, under control.

He picked out a splash of yellow above the riverbank and
taxied toward it. Cutting power at the last moment, he ran out
of water and onto mud, anchoring the floats in the riverbank.

In the sudden, muffled silence, Rorie heard the metallic tick-
ing from the hot engine, and the hoarse rattle of someone
breathing hard. He couldn't control the grin that spread across
his face.

Kathy McNeely was not aware of the storm when it began. The
snow fell noiselessly over the river, and upon the slope leading
up from the river to the cave. It filtered silently down upon the
small ledge at the opening. She was so absorbed in her assessment of the awful harvest she had stumbled on that she didn't
look out or sense any change in the atmosphere. When she
finally did, what she noticed was silence.

Moving quickly to the mouth of the cave, she was stunned by
the sight of snow falling thick over the tundra, blotting out her
view of the river below, isolating her.

Her first thought was of returning to camp. She might still
make it before full dark. Then she realized that light or dark
meant little in this blizzard of snow. Visibility was no more than
a few feet. She might easily become lost.

She turned reluctantly back into the cave.

She was sheltered here from the storm. She had food and water for herself and Survivor.

Like it or not, this was where she would spend the night.

The old walrus heard the droning of the aircraft engine long before it passed overhead. He was riding on a cake of ice in open water. The ice drifted away from the shoreline, moving out toward the opening of the Bering Strait. Muugli had been traveling north, but the movement of the ice was now carrying him back where he had come from, back toward the inlet where the rest of the herd had died.

He was not yet at full strength, although his wounds were continuing to heal. He was slow to react to the droning sound, which was different from anything that had previously threatened him directly. It was, moreover, an airborne sound, and he didn't hear as well in the open as he did underwater.

He had shuffled over to the center of the ice cake earlier, where the ice buckled and rose higher out of the water. Now he lumbered toward the edge. The noise was louder now, resembling the rasp that sometimes came from the boats in the water. Two tons of ungainly flesh, the walrus would never have made it to the edge of the ice before the plane passed directly overhead. But a gust of wind brought a whirl of snow between them. Within seconds the snow became a white curtain blowing in the wind.

The old walrus lifted its round, whiskered head and small, hooded eyes, peering upward into the snow as the droning engine passed overhead.

FOURTEEN

KATHY MCNEELY woke to a total stillness, and felt a moment's claustrophobic panic. Blood pounded in her ears. She was in some kind of an earthen hole, walls closing in on three sides of her. The cold was a physical force, like a fourth wall.

Awareness came in a rush. She remembered stumbling upon a cave late in the day. She remembered this little nook around a corner at the side of the cave, so neatly shaped it might have been dug with a shovel. She remembered the blanketing snow that had reduced visibility to an arm's length, forcing her decision to stay the night in a bear's den.

Most of all, she remembered the astonishing horde of ivory. She could see a portion of it now in the dimness at the back of the cave, assorted tusks stacked and piled against the earthen wall, forming a dense bulwark several feet high and nearly twenty feet long.

She rose, stiff with cold, and suddenly realized Survivor was nowhere in sight. To her right, around a jutting elbow of rock, the floor of the cave caught a spill of light flooding in from the opening. Kathy had been afraid the heavy snowfall might completely cover the cave's mouth.

She heard a muffled sound. "Survivor?"

White powder filtered down into the cave, whirling in the shaft of light. Stepping forward, Kathy came in sight of the entrance to the den, which was almost at eye level.

A man crouched on the flat ledge at the opening, his bulk filling the hole. His brown face hinted at distant Mongolian ancestors. It was unsmiling, the black eyes that studied her unreadable. He had a swollen lip, and what looked like dark bruises on one cheek. She was jolted by the realization that he blocked the only way out of the cave. She was trapped.

Survivor's big head appeared beside the Eskimo, who stared down at her. The husky looked happily into the man's face, gave a tentative lick, and accepted a pat on the head.

Kathy felt immense relief. She trusted Survivor's instinctive judgment of a stranger. He wasn't frightened by a difference in color or speech or clothing.

"Who are you?" Kathy asked.

"I'm a human being." An Eskimo did not readily identify himself by name to a stranger.

"I can see that," Kathy answered dryly. "Is this your cave?"

"This is a bear's cave," the man said seriously. Then, after a pause, "You're not a bear."

"No, I'm a human being, too."

The native nodded. "You are a hunter of ivory?"

"No, I . . . I watch birds. And study sea animals."

He was silent a moment. She wasn't sure if he found her answer perfectly reasonable or preposterous. He was a short, sturdily built man, round-faced, wearing a mixture of native fur garments and store clothing from the Outside. His hat was typical. It was a Seattle Mariners baseball cap with wolverine fur earflaps attached. His age was indeterminable—she would have guessed anywhere from forty to sixty. He did not appear threatening, but he had not moved away from the cave mouth.

"There are many porcupine droppings in the cave," he said. "Bears like to lie on them. But there aren't any birds. And no sea animals, either."

"No, there aren't." Kathy became bolder, encouraged by what seemed to be ironic humor in the Eskimo's words. "But there's a great deal of walrus ivory. It's yours, isn't it? I've seen you before. I saw you in your boat coming and going on the river." She glanced over her shoulder into the gloom of the cave. The stacked rows of walrus tusks smiled back at her. "Your boat was very low in the water when you came upstream. You were bringing all these tusks here. Walrus tusks . . ."

"I didn't expect anyone to see me." The Eskimo nodded appreciatively, as if she were a slow student who had unexpectedly given a good answer. "I remember passing by a small camp, and once you were there beside the river with your dog. You are a good watcher."

"Your boat was very full each time you came this way. And you made many trips."

He nodded again. "There are many dead to make so much ivory."

Kathy was appalled. "You killed them all?"

"My people don't kill that way." For the first time the native's voice roughened with anger. "That is the gussak's way."

"The gussak?" *White man,* she thought. "I don't understand. If you didn't kill for the ivory, how did you get it?"

Instead of answering, the Eskimo slid down the shallow ramp into the cave, bringing with him a small avalanche of snow. She could smell the snow, and vague smells of fur and leather and sweat from the man who now confronted her. He was an inch shorter than her five feet six inches, but much bulkier in his fur-lined parka. Survivor scurried down the ramp after him, gave Kathy a perfunctory greeting, and eagerly turned his attention back to the stranger, who took off one mitten to scrub the husky's head.

"So much ivory has to be illegal. Where did it come from?" Kathy asked quietly. "Do you know?"

"Yes, I know." The Eskimo's expression became brooding as he peered toward the small fortune in walrus tusks in the back of the cave. More comfortable now with this stranger, he said, "I am John Mulak. I come from a village on another river, a half-day's boat ride to the south."

Kathy speculated over what lay behind the Eskimo's somber mood. If white men were responsible for the terrible slaughter that had produced this bloody harvest of ivory—poachers, she thought with a spurt of anger—how had this old man come into possession of it? My God, he must have stolen it!

"Are you in trouble? With the gussaks?"

Mulak smiled. "Not anymore."

"What do you mean?" She studied the bruises on his face, the puffy mouth. He had also winced when he took off his mitten, favoring his left hand. Those marks weren't from a fall, or an accident in the river. He had been beaten. Her anger deepened.

She was a scientist familiar with the cycles of birth and preda-
tion and death throughout the natural world. She understood
the need for culling and thinning out many species, even the
African elephant in some parts of the veldt. Nature did not
always take care of such adjustments in the best possible way,
however much sentimentalists might wish to believe it. Nature
was often indifferent, prodigal, cruel. Species regularly disappeared from the face of the earth, in remarkable numbers. But
once all that was recognized, human poachers remained the
most brutal, violent and savage enemy of far too many species.

You could understand the needs of African tribesmen who
poached for ivory, as their ancestors had done for centuries,
often as their only available source of income. Even now such
poachers sold elephant tusks for as little as a dollar and a half a
pair. Just as you could understand how a poor man with a family
in Thailand might hunt a rare, beautiful snow leopard and sell
the skin for thirty dollars—more than he could earn in a year
any other way. What Kathy could not forgive were the plunder-
ers in America, Japan, Taiwan and Hong Kong, far from the
sight or smell of blood and death, who reaped not a few dollars
but millions from the wanton killing of endangered animals for
their hides, their teeth, their glands, their horns, providing
imaginary elixirs or wall trophies or material for art objects
meaningful only to rich collectors.

The walrus was not yet endangered, though its numbers were
drastically smaller than they had been even a quarter century
ago. Eskimos, she knew, were permitted to continue subsistence
hunting, and to sell the small quantities of ivory they obtained.
But what she saw in the cave was something far more drastic, far
more threatening to this unique animal of the sea. It could only
mean that the ivory markets, concentrated largely in Asia, were
now turning to walrus ivory to fill the demand as the supply of
elephant tusks diminished because of the international ban on
the raw ivory trade.

"They must find me," Mulak said. "Then I will be in trouble
again."

Kathy frowned. "I found your cave," she said slowly. "Are
these poachers searching for you?"

"They have been hunting me, and they are close. But they

didn't see me on this river. You're the only one who can tell them.''

"They might still find your tracks."

"There are no tracks now," the Eskimo said. "Today there is only snow."

She moved past him and scrambled up the short ramp that led into the cave. On the narrow ledge just inside the mouth, she crouched. A dazzlingly different world opened out before her, an immensity of whiteness assaulted the eye. The river, gray under a gloomy sky, was almost the only interruption in the soft white cover that lay over the tundra, erasing its contours and autumn vegetation. The mountains fifty miles to the south were ghosts in a white mist. But less than twenty feet away, on a little mound scoured free of most of its snow by the wind, a stubby little lousewort incongruously poked into the open, its pink flowers vivid against all that purity of snow.

Even though the sky was overcast, this new white world, extending as far as she could see, made her eyes ache. She had felt small and vulnerable yesterday, alone in the wilderness. Snowbound in an infinitely vast, empty, white landscape without beginning or end, without definition, she felt even more fragile and insignificant.

No tracks marred that empty landscape, except for a few Mulak had made at the entrance to the cave, and some footprints that Survivor had left nearby. No animal tracks of any kind. Any trace of her passage over the tundra the previous day had been completely covered over.

She turned back into the cave, startled. "How long have you been here?" No tracks, she thought.

"I came before the snow stopped. You were sleeping, and I didn't want to disturb you." He spoke with simple dignity, as if the answer were self-evident.

"Are you hungry, Mr. Mulak? I have a little food."

He smiled. The suggestion was one an Eskimo might have made. Instant hospitality to strangers, the sharing of whatever one had, was a tradition among the people. "I have not eaten. I left my village in a hurry."

"I'm beginning to guess why."

She had eaten most of her raisins and nuts the previous day, but she had, still unopened, a small can of Spam along with some water crackers. She dumped the contents of the can of Spam onto the metal plate she carried in her pack, cut it into wedges and opened a packet of crackers. "We'll have to share," she said.

"Of course." Mulak beamed at the Spam. "I have this at my house. I like it. It's very salty, very good. Mostly I like Eskimo food, but this is good. It won't make me turn white, I don't think."

Kathy squatted on the floor as the Eskimo did. The wedge of Spam on a dry cracker tasted marvelous. "Is that what Eskimos think about our food?"

"Some of us think that. I'm not sure that it's true."

"What is Eskimo food?"

"Salmon and herring and whitefish. Caribou and moose. Sometimes walrus meat. Berries that the earth gives us. But we eat a lot of your food, and it's good, as long as we have enough salmon and caribou to take away the whiteness."

She thought he might have been joking with her, but wasn't sure.

After a while, when the Spam was gone and most of the crackers and the last of her chocolate bars, which she divided with the Eskimo, she said, "Tell me what happened to you. Tell me about the ivory."

Mulak was silent. His apparent reluctance made her wonder if he completely trusted her. But the answer, she soon learned, was more personal and painful. "There was a great hunt. It was organized by the white men who come from Nome to collect ivory from my people. A large number of walruses had been seen. It's not usual in this season to see so many of them near our village. The white men were excited over finding so many. My people were excited, too. My son was one of the hunters."

"Your son?" she prompted, when he lapsed into brooding silence again.

"My son Billy. He is a very fine shot with a rifle. I taught him to shoot when he was a boy. Eskimos have always been hunters and fishermen."

"But you weren't in on this hunt."

"No. I don't hunt with these gussaks." He chose to express

his thoughts carefully, and she was becoming accustomed to his pauses. She could hear the wind whistling at the mouth of the cave. It blew a fine powder of snow inside that hovered in the air like particles of dust. "The walruses were sleeping in a protected rock formation near the edge of the sea. The hunters came in their boats, and found them sleeping. They sleep like children in a small house, many of them in one bed, all piled on top of each other for warmth and companionship. There was one very old walrus among them who is famous among my people. He's called Muugli, the Great One, because he is so old and large and has such fine tusks. They are the largest tusks any of us has ever seen. The hunters were all excited about seeing Muugli."

"I remember . . . there was a photograph of such a walrus in a magazine this past summer. It came out after I was in Alaska, and one of the men in my group obtained a copy. There was a lot of talk about the size of the tusks."

"Yes, they are very fine." This time Mulak remained silent for so long that Kathy thought he wasn't going to finish the story. Then he said, "The white men brought guns that shoot many bullets very fast. They used these guns, and rifles the Eskimos have, and they sought to kill the entire herd of walruses. There was much ivory taken . . . all that you see here. But they had offended the sea from which the walruses come, and a storm came. Everyone had to get into the boats and run from the storm. They couldn't take the ivory with them. They left it behind.

"The storm went on for many days. At the village I heard talk about the great hunt, and about Muugli being killed. My son was one of the hunters who was given the honor of shooting the Great One."

"Oh, no!" Kathy whispered. "Was he killed?"

"They shot at him, but it's not certain he is dead. He is hard to kill, that one. Many hunters have tried to kill him for almost as long as I can remember, since I was as young as you are."

Kathy smiled. The momentary pleasure faded as Mulak went on, speaking softly. "When the rains stopped, I was the first to leave the village. I wasn't looking for the walruses, or the ivory, but I found them. The killing was done without giving honor to the walruses. It was without respect. I saw all these tusks on a ledge in a cove, waiting for the hunters to come back, and I became very angry. I thought these hunters shouldn't have the tusks. There should be no reward for such killing. So I became a thief."

"You took it . . . alone . . . and brought it all here in your boat." The prodigious physical effort involved in what the Eskimo had done strained credulity. He was not a young man—on closer inspection she now put his age at closer to sixty than forty in the brackets she had originally guessed at. Moreover, she had observed him while he ate the Spam and crackers, using only his right hand. How was it possible for anyone to do what he had done alone? But she had seen him on the river. And she had no doubt whatever of his honesty.

"It's not the way of my people to take what isn't ours."

"I know that. But what you did isn't stealing. You did what was right. Slaughtering all those walruses was illegal. These white men are poachers. They can be arrested."

Mulak looked at her skeptically. "They have been doing this for a long time."

"Some poachers were caught selling illegal ivory in Nome over a year ago. They were brought to trial. That can happen to these men, too. Do they know you took it?"

"I think so. They didn't know at first, but they think so now. That's why they locked me up."

"They locked you up?" Kathy's voice rose.

"They wanted me to tell them where I had taken the ivory."

The bruises were explained. Kathy McNeely's outrage toward the poachers was growing by the minute, as intense as her sympathy for the unique animals that had been so cruelly destroyed, and for this Eskimo who had defied the killers. It was true that natives had been involved in the hunt, but the white men were the instigators. Like the natives of Zimbabwe and Kenya and Somali, the Eskimos had simply been exploited by greedy outsiders.

"How did you escape?"

For the first time Mulak seemed puzzled. "Someone broke the lock. I think it could only have been my son." The pride in the old man's voice was restrained by anguish. "The gussaks have given him whisky and drugs to hunt for them. They have changed him . . . but perhaps he could not accept that his father would be put in a cage. I believe that's what happened."

He *wanted* to believe it, Kathy saw. "Drugs," she said. "It gets worse."

"Yes. At first it was the marijuana, but now it is what you call cocaine."

"Oh, my God!"

"They are searching for me. It might be that, if there had been no snow, they would have found me."

"Listen to me, Mr. Mulak. I can help you. These men have broken the law. They can be brought to justice. You're safe here —they'll never find this cave. As soon as I get back to my camp, I can radio my people—the other scientists who came to Alaska with me. They all feel the same way I do about preserving this environment and the animals who belong here, in the sea as well as on land. They'll feel the same anger I feel over what's being done to your people. We can reach the authorities—the Fish and Wildlife Service, and Alaska Fish and Game—the FBI may even have jurisdiction."

Mulak smiled. "I have seen the FBI on television."

"The point is, we can have these men arrested. They won't be able to touch you."

Mulak was silent a moment, studying her with approval. "This may not be easy," he said.

"Why not? There's no question they're violating the law—"

"When the snow came yesterday, I passed your camp by the river. I saw the tents, but you weren't there. I was coming to the cave. I heard the airplane behind me, and I hid to watch. The airplane landed on the river near your camp, in the storm. The pilot is very good."

"What!"

"I believe they are staying there until it is safe to fly again. I don't think they were following me, I believe they landed because of the snow. The airplanes don't come to our village when it snows. It's dangerous for them." He paused, observing her consternation. Then he added simply, "So you see, it may not be easy to arrest these gussaks. And my son is with them."

FIFTEEN

"THIS IS a very old cave," John Mulak said. "I have known of it myself for a long time, since I was a young man and I first found it. But the bears have known it for much longer."

"Grizzlies?"

"Yes, that's your gussak name for them. I think it was a male who slept here last winter. There was no sign of cubs when I visited the cave in the spring after the bear left."

"Don't grizzlies usually den at higher altitudes?" Kathy Mc-Neely asked.

The Eskimo shrugged. "I'm not an expert on bears. What you say is true, I think. But sometimes they must come down where there is plenty of food when they must fatten up before winter, and if winter comes quickly they will stay where they are. This cave is high enough it will never flood. And that place where you slept is a good one, above the floor and warm." As he glanced around the cavern, Mulak's expression altered slightly. Kathy thought of someone in a church gazing at an altar. "This has been a bear's cave since long before I was born, and before my father and my grandfather were born. It must be a good place."

"It's about to become a famous place, once I get through to my people and tell them what's here."

"You must be careful," Mulak said. "These are bad men."

"They won't harm me. They have no reason to. There's no way they could guess I know anything about the ivory, unless they can track me back to this cave after I leave."

"There will be no tracks," the Eskimo promised. "It is snowing again. It is light, but it will fill your footsteps quickly, and mine, long before you reach your camp."

153

"By the time I get there, they may be gone," Kathy said hopefully.

"I don't think so. This pilot is a good one. He won't want to fly until it's safe." Mulak had watched bush pilots come and go for more than half a century, and he respected their courage and skill at something he could not even comprehend doing himself.

"What about you?" she worried. "They'll never find you if you stay here. I'll contact my people by radio as soon as the men leave my camp. They'll get in touch with the authorities. But we'll need you to tell them everything that's happened. You'll probably have to testify in court, eventually. Does that bother you?"

"I'm only an Eskimo," Mulak said slowly. "I'm not sure about this justice you talk of. I think there is justice for the white men, and there is justice for Eskimos. I don't think they go together much."

"You're wrong—I promise you, they'll listen. I'll make them listen! Anyway, this isn't just about white men or Eskimos, it's about the wholesale slaughter of walruses for their ivory. There's no question it's illegal. These men have to be stopped, and what you've done can help us stop them. But not if they find you first. They're searching for you now, and you know how desperate they are to find this ivory. You won't really be safe until the government steps in. I promise you, I can make enough noise so these men won't dare come after you."

Mulak smiled. "Yes, I think you can do that."

"Better believe it." The extraordinary warmth in the old Eskimo's eyes pleased her immeasurably. "Once the ivory is out of their hands for good, they won't have any reason to look for you. They won't risk that just for spite."

Mulak thought of Wolf Simpson's smile and wasn't so sure.

"Will you stay here, Mr. Mulak, where you'll be safe? I'll come back as soon as I can."

He was silent for a time, as if weighing her arguments. There was a gravity about him that suggested her words were worthy of his attention and must be considered. He was giving her respect. When he spoke, however, he said, "I will think about what you've said, and I'll meet you here in the bear's cave. But first I have to go to my village. I must know that nothing has been done that's harmful to my daughter and my son. I don't want to bring them harm through what I've done."

"You can't go there!" Kathy protested. "Someone is sure to tell the poachers."

"No one will tell them I'm there."

"But you said your son is with them. He—" She broke off, seeing the pain in his eyes.

"They force him to go with them," Mulak said stubbornly. "But he is my son. He helped me get away. Why would he betray me now?"

"If the weather clears, as you say it will, they'll be up in the air again, searching. They'll see you long before you can reach your village."

"This is my country," the Eskimo said. "My home. It has many paths. There is a fork in this river. If you traveled down the river, you have seen this fork."

"I remember it—there were some old fish racks there."

Mulak nodded. "My people go there often in the spring to catch fine salmon. The other river is smaller, the river that runs away from the mountains. It doesn't go all the way to my village, but it will take me to a place from where I can walk to my own house. I've done it many times. I will come there when it's dark. The gussaks will not see me."

Mulak's mind was made up, Kathy saw. Nothing she could say would dissuade him. "Can you be back here by tomorrow night?" she asked anxiously. "Will you meet me here then?"

"I will come to the cave."

"Then we have a deal, Mr. Mulak. And some nasty men are going to be in for a nasty surprise."

The weather cleared before noon, and Jeff Rorie began to make preparations for taking off. The engine started easily and was soon racing smoothly, before he shut it down to save gas. Take-off was going to be chancy—there was ice floating in the river—but Rorie thought there was enough open water to get air-borne, even with four men aboard the Cessna Skywagon.

He had spent the night in the aircraft with the heater on—more to keep his plane's engine warm and prevent its oil from freezing than for his own comfort, though the latter had been a bonus. Simpson and the young Eskimo had shared one of the tents in the empty camp, Mayberry taking the other, all of them enjoying considerably less comfort than Rorie.

The camp did not appear to have been abandoned—there was food in sealed, animal-proof lockers, along with clothing and the usual camp gear of stoves and utensils, blankets and sleeping bags. There had been speculation all evening about the whereabouts of the campers—two people, a man and a woman. Travis Mayberry had grown more thoughtful as the speculation took different turns. Who were the campers? What had they been doing here? It was late in the season for hunting or fishing, even later for bird watching or whitewater rafting, or any of the other wilderness adventures that lured vacationers from the Lower 48. Some of them had about as much common sense as a lemming, Rorie commented. He reminded Mayberry that he had a pair of would-be backpackers he was scheduled to pick up as soon as he deposited Mayberry and Simpson back at Nome. You could never tell what Outsiders might be into.

Now, eager to be under way, Rorie removed the wing covers he had put on the night before. In spite of the covers there was light frost on the wings. He used a rope he always carried with him to draw along each wing, sweeping it clean. He coiled the rope and stored it behind the seats. He was anxious to get into the air before the Arctic weather took another of its capricious turns.

"Hey! What have we got here?" Wolf Simpson called out.

Rorie followed his gaze. A figure in a red parka, layered pants and boots had appeared around a bend about a quarter-mile upriver, trudging slowly through the six-inch layer of powder snow that covered the tundra. To the surprise of the watching men at the camp, a large dog trotted along beside the figure.

"It's the woman!" Simpson exclaimed.

She had seen them, and waved. "Hello . . ." The call carried to them clearly in spite of the distance, sounding thin and brittle in the cold air.

The dog bounded ahead of her as the pair neared the camp. He was a husky, his curled tail waving as he approached. He looked friendly enough, but Wolf Simpson backed off, a furtive expression on his narrow face, as if he confronted a known enemy. The dog sensed the reaction. He was instantly wary, slowing to a stiff-legged pace, his ears pricked. A low rumble started in his throat.

"Survivor!" the woman called sharply. "It's all right!"

Reaching the camp just behind the dog, she took hold of his collar. "He wasn't expecting strangers to be here." She offered an apologetic smile as she glanced around the camp. "I hope you helped yourself to anything you needed. I was caught by the storm and couldn't get back to camp."

She was cool and relaxed, Jeff Rorie thought. A slender, attractive woman, thirtysomething. Her cheeks were pink from the cold, and there was frost on her eyelashes, suggesting that she had perspired as she labored through the snow. He wondered how far she had walked and why, beneath the surface composure, he sensed a thread of tension.

"I'm Travis Mayberry," Mayberry said genially, approaching the woman. "This is my associate, Mr. Simpson . . . and that's our pilot, Mr. Rorie. We had to sit down in the river last night when all that snow blew in. Couldn't see where we were going. I hope you don't mind, we took advantage of your tents, since no one was here." He didn't mention the cans of corned beef hash they had found in one of the lockers for breakfast.

"No, of course not." The woman's gaze drifted past Rorie, seeing more, he guessed, than she appeared to. "I'm Dr. Kathleen McNeely. I'm with a scientific expedition called ASSET. We're doing an environmental impact study here in Alaska . . . it's a long story."

Mayberry glanced at the two yellow tents. "You're alone?" He sounded incredulous. No woman would be out here in the wilderness alone.

She smiled at his tone. "At the moment. Unfortunately, my colleague, Dr. Cobb, was injured in a fall. He was flown out to a hospital yesterday. That's when I went for my walk, and was surprised by the storm." She hesitated. "Some other people from ASSET will be joining me today. They're coming down from our base camp, which is farther up the river.''

She's afraid of us, Rorie thought. *She knows something.* The perception confirmed his hunch that the woman had not been surprised to find four strangers at her camp. But how could she possibly have known? Rorie himself had not known where he was going to land yesterday in the storm, and since then the area had been blanketed by the storm. Maybe she simply had a keen woman's intuition, he thought . . . or she trusted her dog's reaction to Simpson.

"Do you mind my asking what you're doing here, Mr. Mayberry?'' The scientist sounded naturally curious.

"We're looking for a renegade Eskimo,'' Mayberry said. "A thief. The man stole some valuables from a village south of here, and the Native Council asked us to look for him. We believe he might have been heading up this way. You happen to see anyone . . . maybe in a boat on the river?''

She glanced curiously at Billy Mulak, as if seeing him for the first time. The young Eskimo seemed mesmerized by her. She shook her head. "No . . . we've been very isolated. Dr. Cobb and I . . . we hadn't seen another human face for weeks until yesterday when the plane arrived to fly him out.''

"He might be dangerous,'' Mayberry said. "He's an ivory poacher.''

"Ivory? You mean walrus ivory?''

"You know much about such things, Doctor?''

"I'm a marine biologist, Mr. Mayberry. I know more than you might think. And I can assure you, if I run into any ivory poachers, I'll notify the authorities immediately.''

"That might not be such a good idea,'' Wolf Simpson said.

She looked at him. Mayberry said, "What Mr. Simpson means is, this Eskimo is on the run, and you shouldn't give him any reason to be afraid of you.'' He smiled easily. "I bet you're hungry, bein' out all night.''

"I'm starved! I hope you had something—there's plenty of food in the lockers, especially now that Dr. Cobb is gone.''

"We helped ourselves to some hash for breakfast. Those others that are coming to join you, they'll bring their own supplies, I suppose.''

"I'm sure they will. And I can do better than canned hash, if you've time to stay for lunch."

"Well, I don't know . . . I think our pilot wants to get back in the air."

Jeff Rorie had come over to the big husky, who had relaxed somewhat as his mistress talked amiably with the strangers. The dog sniffed Rorie's boots and offered hand, and became friendly. In Rorie's experience huskies, however imposing they might be physically, and however unnerving their light-eyed gaze, were generally gregarious dogs, welcoming even to strangers. Rorie squatted beside the dog, which nosed and pushed against his hands, dancing around him. The scientist frowned as she watched.

When the woman mentioned bacon and powdered eggs and canned tomatoes, Mayberry changed his mind and decided they would stay for lunch. Rorie returned to the Cessna to put the wing covers back on, even though he hoped to be leaving within the hour. Although the snow flurries had let up, the temperature was well below freezing, with no sign of any warming this day. The night, Rorie guessed, would be even colder.

From the aircraft he watched the others at the camp: Billy Mulak staring covertly at the white woman as she moved about, setting up one of the Coleman stoves and putting the bacon on to sizzle while she went about the rest of her meal preparations with economy and efficiency; Simpson hanging back with an uneasy eye on the husky, who ignored him as long as he didn't move; and Mayberry, talking to Dr. McNeely as if they were old friends, asking her about her work along the river, how long she and this Dr. Cobb had been there, what they had seen and done. It was an ordinary, unremarkable scene, but something about it didn't ring true. *She knows something,* Rorie thought for the second time. It bothered him that Travis Mayberry might have had the same perception. Otherwise, why had he changed his mind and stayed for a meal he didn't need, when he had been so anxious to leave an hour ago?

Rorie joined the group for a plate of bacon, eggs and fried tomatoes, with some bread to mop up. He found himself wiping the plate clean, savoring every mouthful, and beginning to admire this cool, self-sufficient woman with something on her mind. He wished he could have a chance to talk to her in private before taking off. She might not understand the kind of men she was dealing with.

The opportunity came unexpectedly when they were preparing to leave the camp beside the river. Simpson and Billy Mulak were already aboard the Cessna, and Mayberry was standing by to cast off the last of the tiedown lines. Rorie walked back to the campsite and squatted beside the husky to say goodbye. The dog washed his face with his tongue, and the moisture almost immediately began to freeze on Rorie's cheeks. He grinned, patted the dog and murmured, "I wouldn't stay here long, ma'am. Not alone."

"I'm sure you mean well, Mr. Rorie. I'm surprised Survivor likes you so much."

"I don't know what you think of me . . ."

"I judge a man by the company he keeps," she answered coolly.

"Generally, that's a good idea, but—"

"Your friends are waiting for you. And watching."

Rorie gave the husky a final brisk rubbing on his head and neck, stood up and smiled. "You take care of yourself, ma'am," he said, loud enough for Mayberry to hear him.

Then he went back to the plane, Mayberry watching him with a scowl. The engine, still warm from its earlier startup, soon settled down to a steady roar. Mayberry climbed aboard, and Rorie taxied out into the river. The center was free of ice, a ribbon that appeared as straight and true as any runway. Rorie turned into the wind. He could see the woman watching them from the riverbank. As the plane picked up speed and the turmoil of noise grew around him, he felt grateful for about the thousandth time for the 185's manual flaps that always let him hop off the water faster. He coaxed the aircraft onto the steps of the floats until it was skimming on the water, a tail of spray boiling up behind. The propellor began to scream, and the wind whistles from the air leaks around the doors and windows and vents made it impossible to hear anything else. Then, suddenly, the river released its grip. They were in the air, lifting, flying free . . .

*   *   *

Kathy watched the floatplane lift cleanly from the water. Just as she had watched Jason Cobb's rescue plane the previous day until it dwindled out of sight, she stared after the poachers' aircraft. The feeling this time was starkly different. Not regret, and lingering concern, but sharp relief. She watched the aircraft's shrinking silhouette as if to make certain it was gone.

She turned back toward the camp. A stackful of pans and dishes to clean up, she thought ruefully. So much for wilderness hospitality.

Before leaving camp she had stored the short-wave radio in one of the lockers. She wasn't sure what that bush pilot had been trying to tell her—his words had sounded almost like a warning—but she intended to waste no time alerting the people at the ASSET base. Even if they brought all their clout to bear, it would take time for Federal agents to react. And—

Her thoughts froze. Her mind went blank.

She stared at the remains of the radio. There would be no immediate rescue, no Federal agents scrambling to respond.

The radio had been deliberately, systematically smashed.

SIXTEEN

IN NEW York City it was Indian summer. After a brief taste of fall, the city basked in warm sunshine, a last false promise before the hard, biting canyon winds arrived to lock the city into a gray autumnal chill. These were bright, sparkling days, unlike the heavy, humid heat of summer. The fall foliage in Central Park was a glorious blaze of reds and browns and yellows. Joggers were everywhere, competing with nature in their gaudy colors.

Harry Madrid stared unseeing from the window of his high-rise apartment. He was looking not at the beauty spread out below him in such lush splendor, but at the murky outlines of disaster. The little finger of his left hand ached, the way it sometimes did before rain—the finger that wasn't there. He absently touched the small rounded stub, knowing that the phantom pain was all in his head, feeling it all the same.

Two calls from Madam Lu Chang in a month. Her tone increasingly impatient and imperious. The mammoth tusks pictured in the magazine this past summer had acquired even greater importance in the interval, she had told Madrid. The delay itself had heightened the desire of collectors, as delay so often increased desire. No one else must have them. Madam Chang was relying on Harry Madrid's assurances that they would soon be in her possession.

Harry couldn't bring himself to tell her that the tusks were missing. Instead he offered details of the huge Japanese order for five tons of ivory. Sixty percent of the order had already been shipped, Harry told Madam Chang. The rest was being assembled from his most reliable sources, including those in Alaska. All of it was the best quality.

"That is excellent, Mr. Madrid," said Madam Chang, who knew all about the Japanese buyers and their negotiations with Harry, down to the smallest detail. "But I must also have those special tusks. You will inform me as soon as you are certain that they have been taken to a place of safety."

"Yes, yes, of course," Harry Madrid said. "My people in Alaska are working on it."

"Their value is almost incalculable. I would not wish my buyers to be disappointed." The Chinese matriarch paused a moment, then added, "There is another matter I would like to discuss with you, Mr. Madrid. It concerns my youngest son . . ."

The diminutive woman sat on the wide terrace of her white mansion on the Peak, overlooking Hong Kong and the world beyond. It was evening, and lights had begun to glow on the thousands of junks and other small boats packed into Victoria Harbor. She watched the landing lights of a jet airliner descending toward Kai Tak Airport, which pointed like an accusing finger into the gathering darkness of Kowloon Bay.

After breaking the telephone connection to America, Lu Chang sat in silence for several minutes, smoking a long, thin cigarette fitted into a slender ivory holder carved in the shape of a snake. She thought about the changes coming to the great city below in a few short years, ushering in the century of the Pacific Rim. Already many British colonials were leaving, fleeing to Britain or America or Canada, along with many wealthy Chinese who feared the imminent takeover of the city by the mainland Chinese government. Not the Chang family. Its connections reached deep into the heart of China. For Lu Chang, nothing would change in the long term. Greed and desire were not ideological factors. They remained constant.

There was, however, a short-term problem.

The warrant for Deng Chang's arrest.

Madam Chang had sent her youngest son into China, to the forests of Chingpu province, because a local, small-time poacher named Yen Sang Woo had succeeded in trapping a

Giant Panda alive. He had also killed a second panda in attempting to capture it.

The matter was of no small importance. There were now fewer than a thousand Giant Pandas still living in the forests of China, and the depredations of poachers were reducing their numbers every month. The live giant would bring more than one hundred thousand dollars on the black market in Tokyo or Thailand. Even the pelt of the dead panda would be priced at more than ten thousand dollars.

Deng Chang's mission was to supervise the smuggling of the live panda and the pelt out of China. Even a few years ago it would have been a simple matter of paying the poacher his minimal sum—a thousand dollars would be a fortune to him—and bribing local officials. But China was under increasing criticism and pressure from the international environmental community. The dramatic decline in the panda population had become a scandal. Increasingly stringent laws had been passed against killing or selling the rare creature that had become a symbol of China throughout much of the world. When fines did not prove to be a sufficient deterrent, more severe penalties had been decreed—including the death penalty.

The result had been the posting of rewards for information leading to the capture of poachers, and a new alacrity on the part of police in enforcing anti-poaching laws.

Deng Chang's smuggling operation was bungled. Local police were tipped off by an informant. Deng narrowly escaped a police trap, and had to be smuggled out of the province himself. There was now a warrant issued against him, and a reward posted for his capture.

It would be best, Madam Chang had decided, for her son to be far from the scene when Hong Kong officially became a part of China. In time the incident in Chingpu would be forgotten. The warrant could be made to disappear. In the interval, however . . .

She pressed a button fitted into the arm of her chaise. A white-suited servant appeared instantly. Madam Chang glanced pointedly at her empty champagne flute. Then she asked that her youngest son be summoned. She waited patiently, watching strings of lights appear above the decks of a large ocean liner anchored out in the bay, while she sipped the champagne that had hastily been poured into her glass.

Deng Chang appeared at her side. "Honorable Mother . . ."

"I have spoken to the American, Harry Madrid."

"Yes . . . ?"

"The splendid tusks you brought to my attention have become increasingly valuable. You did well."

Deng said nothing, waiting, his manner subdued in spite of his mother's praise. The humiliation of his venture into China was reason enough for silence.

"I believe there may be a problem with the tusks, however. Mr. Madrid sounds anxious. After assuring me that the old walrus in the photograph had been hunted down and killed, he is now being evasive. My impression is that he is not being entirely truthful with me."

"He wouldn't lie. He wouldn't dare risk your anger."

"Perhaps not," said Madam Chang, "but I think it is time, my son, for you to go to America."

Deng Chang merely nodded, as if the startling decision had been expected. He was maturing, his mother thought, watching him. Except for a barely noticeable flicker in his eyes, which no one else might have noticed, there was no visible sign of his reaction to say whether he was dismayed or elated.

"This is not banishment, my son, although it will be better for you and for the Chang family if your supposed transgression in China is allowed to die from lack of nourishment. I have another reason for sending you to New York. It may be that the time has come for us to consider a different arrangement with Mr. Madrid. You will be my eyes and ears. You will tell me what I need to know."

Deng Chang felt the weight of gloom lifting from his spirit. He was being given a chance to atone. His failure in China was not the end of everything!

Harry Madrid, when he spoke to Travis Mayberry on the phone, was in no mood to hear excuses. "I've been talking to my people in Hong Kong," he said. "They want to know whether there's a problem delivering the goods I promised. Do I have a problem, Mayberry?"

"I'd call it a temporary hitch," Mayberry said. "Not a problem."

"I see. Does that mean you've found the goods?"

"Well, not exactly . . . but we think we know who stole 'em."

"That's terrific." Madrid's sarcasm was unforgiving. "Am I supposed to be able to sell this knowledge? Is that your solution? Do you think it'll bring a good price in Hong Kong?"

Mayberry flushed. "It means we'll get the ivory. It's just taking a little longer than I thought."

"I don't like using that word over the phone. I've told you that before."

"Yeah, well . . . I guess you want that other order. The one that's been in storage."

"That would be nice."

"I was following up first on . . . on the pieces that were misplaced." Mayberry didn't believe it was really necessary to be so circumspect on the phone, but he had to go along with Harry Madrid's precautions. "I plan on taking care of the original order myself."

"When can I expect it?"

"It'll go out this week."

That was as explicit as Mayberry could be. He had various sources for shipping illegal goods out of Alaska. Some of it, boxed and labeled as office supplies, went through the U.S. Post Office with the help of a cooperative postmaster at Clark's Crossing, a small town on the Yukon. Even Federal agents could not tamper with the U.S. mail. The bulk of the shipment would go by air freight through Fairbanks, where another man on Mayberry's payroll worked as a freight handler. Mayberry was also able to ship some "machine parts" as cargo on a certain cruise ship that would be stopping at Nome in three days, on its last voyage south before winter froze the Bering Sea.

"I guess that'll have to do," Harry Madrid said. "But I need the rest of the material as soon as possible. Especially the oversize pieces."

"Yeah, I know." Muugli, Mayberry thought. "We're looking for them."

"Do better than that," Madrid said. "Find them. Or I'll find someone who can."

The threat evaporated from Harry's mind as soon as he broke the connection.

He was instantly thinking of the second reason for Lu Chang's latest phone call. Why was she sending Deng to America? Harry remembered the slick, arrogant young man in his American Dockers he had met in Taipei. Was Madam Chang telling the truth about having to send Deng from the country for a cooling off period because of a botched smuggling affair? The story seemed plausible, and Harry could check it out. Lu Chang had even sounded uncharacteristically conciliatory, as if she knew that she was asking a great deal in requesting that Harry take Deng under his wing.

But Harry's street smarts made him wary. He felt uneasy over the arrangement. He didn't want Deng Chang looking over his shoulder. Maybe Deng was the heir apparent in the Chang dynasty . . . but he wasn't going to take over Harry Madrid's life and times. Not now. Not after all these years.

The game wasn't being played out on the Taiwan Strait this time. It was in Harry's ballpark.

SEVENTEEN

THE MORNING after returning to that bleak outpost on the edge of the Bering Sea with Travis Mayberry and Wolf Simpson, Jeff Rorie left Nome. Mayberry wasn't too happy about it, but Rorie had told him of the commitment at the time he was hired. Rorie had booked a charter reservation back in March, and he couldn't get out of it. It would only be for a couple of days, Rorie said. In fact, he could be back the second night. He would fly to Anchorage the first day, and the next morning he would pick up these two tourists in their Abercrombie & Fitch wilderness outfits, and deposit them at a lodge on the Yukon a hundred miles north of Fairbanks, where they were to spend two weeks. He would still have plenty of time to return to Nome before dark. Barring changes in the weather, of course.

After Rorie left, Wolf Simpson went to Mayberry's office over the saloon. Mayberry had been dourly uncommunicative since talking to Harry Madrid shortly after returning to Nome. Simpson wondered if it had anything to do with Marie Lemieux's sudden departure. Mayberry's summer woman had left Nome while he was away, probably because she was afraid to do it while he was there. Simpson *thought* that Mayberry had grown tired of Marie, anyway, but that didn't mean he was happy to see her leave on her own before he kicked her out.

Mayberry glared at Simpson as if things were going very badly indeed, and he thought Simpson was to blame.

"What's goin' on?" Simpson asked. "What'd Madrid have to say this time?"

"The same. You know what he wants. He wants ivory."

"Yeah, well, we're trying to get more. Shit, we got our hands on the best haul in two years—"

168

"And we lost it," Mayberry interrupted curtly.

"We'll get it back."

There was a prickly silence. Simpson waited, then said, "That Marie, running out on you—"

"I don't talk about whores."

Another silence followed. Simpson waited as long as he could. "I tell you what's bothering me more than that ivory," he said, "is this hotshot pilot. I don't like him. There's something wrong about him."

"He's a damned good pilot. We learned that much. He saved our bacon. You can't fake being able to handle a small plane in the bush like that."

"Yeah, sure, but . . . I want to check him out, Trav."

"I need you to follow through with those Eskimos . . . find that old man, that's the first thing. I've got to do some of my own flying, damn it."

"You're going up to the cabin?"

"That's right."

The storage room in the back of the saloon, with its private stairway, held only a small quantity of Mayberry's supply of poached goods, mostly the pieces he would sell to tourists locally, either in the saloon or through a gift shop he owned on Front Street, or to private buyers whose discretion was known to Mayberry. Much of the ivory sold this way was first carved by a small group of native artisans who lived in Nome. Their most popular pieces were small images of sea otters and whales and polar bears. Their work did not generally compare to the exquisite craftsmanship of the carvers in Hong Kong, who carried on a centuries-old tradition, but the Eskimo carvers worked cheaply and they provided a legitimate facade for Mayberry's activities. For security, the bulk of the raw ivory, and the more valuable animal hides and other parts taken from protected species, were stored at an isolated mountain cabin in the appropriately named Raw Mountains north of the Yukon River and northeast of Clark's Crossing. The cabin stood at the edge of deep woods overlooking a small lake, the only place in that wilderness Mayberry would try to land since his accident. In the summer his Piper Cub was fitted with floats. When the lake froze, and there was snow cover, he switched to skis.

"Madrid has this big order from some Japanese buyers, and the Chinese are breathing down his neck to get it filled. He's emptied out his warehouse. He wants more ivory, as much as we can deliver, and he wants it yesterday. I'm going up to the hide-out. We've got two hundred tusks up there, maybe more. I'll have to ferry 'em out myself and get 'em shipped. It'll take me at least three trips. That'll have to hold Madrid until we find the other tusks."

Especially Muugli's tusks, he thought. Obviously, the prize tusks of the old walrus had become an issue with Madrid's Chinese connection. Mayberry was not sure exactly where Madrid stood with his Chinese partners, but he was beginning to realize that Harry sounded nervous and impatient whenever he talked about them. The way Mayberry felt when Madrid called *him*. He thought of a cartoon of a minnow about to be swallowed by a fish, a larger fish behind the second one preparing to gobble it up, and, waiting in line for the others to finish eating, a *really* big fish lurking in the depths . . .

"You're not going to wait until Rorie gets back?"

Mayberry stared at him long enough for Simpson to reconsider the stupidity of the question. Finally Mayberry said, "I like Rorie. I think you're wrong about him. But nobody knows about that cabin unless I want him to know, except for you and me and those two brain surgeons I have babysitting it. Nobody's going to know, including Rorie, even though it means I've got to fly up there alone and haul the stuff out myself."

Simpson had no comment. The two babysitters were Phil Torrance and Lester Paley, who had been under investigation by the Fish and Wildlife Service a year ago for poaching activities but had slipped through the legal net. Since Mayberry needed someone to guard the storage cabin, anyway—the major hazard was not theft but the possibility that some squatter would come along and adopt the cabin if no one occupied it—he had sent Torrance and Paley up there to keep them out of the way until the Feds forgot about them.

"Look, Trav, let me check Rorie out," Simpson argued. "So maybe I'm wrong, maybe I just don't like the son of a bitch. Anyway, I can't do anything here until he gets through ferrying these tourists and comes back here. I'll need him to fly me around. So let me tag along after him and see if he's what he says he is. He's gonna be gone two days, he says, okay, give me those two days. Then, if I don't find anything, I'm back here same time he is, and we go over to that Eskimo village and start banging heads."

Mayberry swiveled around in his green chair and stared out of the dirty windows toward the dirty gray sea. Looked like winter, he thought. Winter was rushing toward him. He wouldn't fly into those northern mountains when winter came, not even for Harry Madrid. He had to act now.

"Two days," he said without turning. "You get two days. It'll take me at least that long to move the stuff. As soon as Rorie gets back, you and him go back to the Eskimo village, find that kid, the old man's son, and use him. You know what he likes. Give him a taste, and let him look at a nice fat packet of the nose powder. Let all those natives know there's something extra for each of them if we find those tusks." Mayberry swiveled away from the window and its gloomy forecast. "And if you can find Muugli, there's a big fat bonus in it for you, Wolf. Rorie, too. You hear what I'm saying? Those big tusks, no matter what else happens, if we get those we're out of the woods."

Simpson caught a scheduled Alaska Airlines flight out of Nome for Anchorage, departing at eleven that morning. Jeff Rorie had taken off in his small plane shortly after eight. Simpson guessed, correctly, that the 727 airliner, flying above the weather in clear skies at six hundred miles an hour, would overtake Rorie in flight. Simpson would be in Anchorage waiting when Rorie's Cessna climbed over the last tier of mountains and dropped down toward Alaska's metropolis, home for fully half of the five hundred thousand residents of the state.

Anchorage International Airport saw more traffic daily than all but three or four major airports in the Lower 48, but Jeff Rorie's charter flight was booked by Far Eyes Charter Tours, a charter service located, Simpson had learned, at Anchorage's Lake Hood, home of the world's largest floatplane airport. A number of large and small charter services operated out of this facility, including Far Eyes Charter Tours. Simpson thought it was a dumb name—but at least Rorie hadn't made it up.

Simpson rented a Ford /Escort—Mayberry was tightfisted about paying for big cars on the tab. After booking a room at the Captain Cook Hotel downtown, probably the most expensive room he could find in Anchorage—let Mayberry squawk about the bill—Simpson drove out to Lake Hood. Traffic was light, but to Simpson it seemed like gridlock in Los Angeles. Like half the people in Alaska, the half who didn't live there, he envied and hated Anchorage, with its noisy, polluting traffic, its high-rise office buildings, its theaters, night clubs, chain stores and fast food outlets.

It was a bright, clear, autumn day in Anchorage, with the temperature just at freezing. The storm that had battered the northern coast, blocked by the towering Alaska Range, had not reached this far south. The snow-covered mountains ringing the city to the north, east and west stood in sharp relief against a brilliant blue sky, except for majestic Mt. McKinley, whose upper reaches were lost in clouds.

The floatplane airport was a jumble of small hangars, fuel storage tanks, Quonset huts and offices, including booking offices for a number of charter services—Bush Pilots Air Service, Alaska Air, Far Eyes Charter Tours, and others. Simpson walked by the Far Eyes office, glancing through a rain-streaked front window. A woman with a long jaw and formidable teeth sat at a battered old oak office desk pounding an equally ancient manual Remington typewriter, her mouth open in concentration. A man in a plaid wool shirt and baseball cap sat on a wooden chair nearby, smoking a cigarette and reading an outdated copy of Sports Illustrated, as if he were waiting in a barber shop.

Simpson found a pay phone at a nearby hangar and punched in the number for Far Eyes Charter Tours he had found in the yellow pages. A woman answered. She had what Simpson thought of as a whisky voice, the product of too many late nights and too many cigarettes. Simpson asked for Jeff Rorie.

"Mr. Rorie isn't here, but . . ." There was a momentary pause while, Simpson guessed, she consulted a schedule. "He filed a flight plan this morning at Nome that has him due in at any time. Can I help you?"

"I was thinkin' of booking a plane, and I was wondering if Rorie's available the next few days."

"Oh, is he a friend of yours?"

"Well, no, not exactly . . . a friend of mine flew with him and recommended him. He been with you long?"

"Almost a year. I'm sorry, he's booked for a charter flight tomorrow, and he's also been hired on an independent long-term contract we're not involved in. But we have several other fine pilots who are available. What kind of trip were you thinking about?"

Simpson was thinking he was glad he hadn't yielded to his first impulse and stopped in at the office in person, where this nosy woman could have pinned him down with questions. "It's not set in concrete yet," he said. "I just wanted to find out about Rorie. This would be a short run up near the Yukon and back."

"No problem. Why don't you give me your name and—"

"I'll give you another call when I have a firm time."

"You could book one of our pilots now and change the date if you have to."

"Yeah, well, I don't want to tie anybody up if it don't work out. I'll call back."

He hung up while the woman was still selling.

Simpson checked the area out, looking for a place where he could observe activity without being noticed. He found it at a used plane outlet located across a corner of the lake from the Far Eyes office and dock. Feigning interest, Simpson asked if he could poke around a bit on his own before talking details with the salesman. The salesman was used to independent Alaskan pilots who often had their own quirky reasons for liking one particular aircraft or another, and he was happy to let Simpson browse. Simpson climbed into the cabin of an Aeronca Champion with Edo floats. Sitting in the pilot's seat, he had a clear view of the small Far Eyes office across the lake.

He was sitting there when Rorie's Cessna 185 circled the lake and approached from the west. The lake was dark blue and calm, its surface lightly riffled. Rorie's plane seemed to skim along the smooth surface. He hit water, lifted briefly and settled down. The floats threw up long, twisting plumes of spray in a pretty landing.

Simpson watched Rorie go into the charter service's office. He climbed out of the Aeronca, told the salesman he would be back the next day for another look, and went to his rented Escort. He had to sit there for an hour before he saw Rorie emerge from the Far Eyes Tours office and climb into a red Ford pickup parked out behind the building. By then the low sun had set and it was cold sitting in the car.

It was early evening when Rorie drove away from the airport, but still light enough that Simpson had to be careful following the pickup out here in the boondocks. He lagged far behind to keep Rorie from spotting him. He expected the pilot to head north on Glenn Highway toward Fortune. The small town Rorie had given Mayberry as an address was about forty or fifty miles north of Anchorage up the Mat-Su Valley. Instead, to Simpson's surprise, the pickup headed toward Anchorage.

Still on the outskirts, Rorie turned into a small, U-shaped motel. While Simpson parked nearby in the Escort, the pilot booked a room, disappeared inside for ten minutes, reemerged and walked to a coffee shop a block away. Growing more disgruntled by the minute, Simpson could do nothing but sit in his rented car, turning the motor on periodically to run the heater. Through the coffee shop window he could see Rorie kidding around with a waitress who lingered at his booth, then dawdling after he ate, drinking coffee and reading a copy of the Anchorage *Times*. It was getting darker and colder in the Escort.

The rest of Simpson's vigil proved equally uneventful. From the coffee shop Rorie walked to a nearby bar, had a beer, and returned to his motel. Simpson walked by the room a half-hour later. He had a glimpse through the blinds of the television set flickering inside.

Simpson spent a restless night in his luxurious room at the Captain Cook Hotel, worrying about how Mayberry would scream over the hotel bill, and fretting over the possibility that Rorie might leave his motel room during the night. Up at dawn, Simpson took coffee and a couple of doughnuts in the car back to Rorie's motel, where he had to sit for over an hour before Rorie, appearing cheerful and refreshed, checked out. The pilot enjoyed a leisurely breakfast at the same nearby coffee shop, after which he drove back to Lake Hood and the Far Eyes booking office. Simpson, tired and chilled and disappointed, followed.

Rorie's charter passengers were already there and waiting. They were a couple of jovial, hearty types, loaded down with gear. Simpson could hear their laughter drifting across the lake in the early morning stillness while they helped Rorie load everything into the back of the Cessna. A half-hour after Rorie's arrival, he had the aircraft's engine running and his passengers aboard. Simpson listened to the now familiar scream of the propellor and the rasp of the engine as the aircraft picked up speed—it was much noisier inside the cabin—and followed its climb as it shook free of the lake and turned north along the Susitna River valley.

Simpson sat in the Escort, scowling, unsettled in his mind. He knew he should just drive back to the International Airport, drop off his rental and return to Nome. He had found nothing about Rorie that didn't ring true. But he couldn't make himself let go. He still wasn't satisfied.

Glenn Highway was a paved, divided highway. Simpson drove through the settled farming community on the route to Palmer at the head of the valley. He didn't encounter a single moose. At forty miles he turned onto a side road. It was also paved but only two lanes, and severely potholed even before the onset of winter. The road brought him to the small settlement of Fortune, Alaska. Population: 337.

Simpson had no trouble finding Rorie's cabin. He simply stopped at a gas station and asked. It was near the end of the town's one main street, with an airstrip behind it.

Simpson parked and walked. At the Sun Spot Cafe he had coffee and a chewy roast beef sandwich. The counterman knew Rorie, but not well. He'd lived there about a year or so, the counterman said. Nice fella, quiet, minded his own business. Simpson made other inquiries at a hardware store and a bar, where he had a beer and met the only taciturn bartender he had ever encountered. A couple of beefy men on bar stools stared at Simpson quietly. They made him uneasy.

Back at Rorie's cabin, Simpson made a show of knocking on

the door and shaking the clapper of a bell that hung beside it. He walked around behind the cabin and peered in through the back windows. There were dishes piled in a kitchen sink. Simpson couldn't tell if they had been washed. Behind the cabin were a number of small aircraft scattered along the fringes of the meadow strip, but no one in sight around them.

Simpson was wondering how troublesome the lock on the back door would be when he heard a sharp sound—the characteristic slide-and-clash of a shotgun's pump action chambering a round. It made the hairs stand up on the back of his neck.

Turning slowly, Simpson met the flat, unfriendly stare of a pair of bright blue eyes in a freckled face. They belonged to a tall, rawboned woman, middle-aged, with frizzy red hair, wearing jeans and a parka and one buckskin glove. The other glove had been removed so her finger could be inserted lightly into the trigger guard of a Remington shotgun that was pointed at Simpson's chest.

"Give me one good reason why I shouldn't fill those pants of yours with buckshot," the woman said in a calm voice that was more scary than a shout.

"Hey, what's wrong? What's this about?"

"You tell me. Start by telling what you're doin' skulking around my neighbor's cabin like you was fixin' to break in."

"You got it all wrong! Jeff Rorie's a friend of mine, I was hoping to find him—"

"If he was a friend of yours, you wouldn't have been askin' questions about him all over town. What are you, some kind of Federal agent? IRS?"

"Hell, no . . . hey, be careful how you wave that thing around." Simpson was edging backward, mentally cursing Alaska's small-town clannishness that bred suspicion of outsiders—especially outsiders asking questions. It made him recall the hatred of "revenooers" that had permeated the hill country where he grew up.

"I know how to use it. If it goes off it'll be because I want it to. Which is gonna be in about one minute if I can still see you within buckshot range."

Simpson bolted around the corner of the cabin and ran for the street. By the time he got there anger and humiliation were flooding through him. He forced himself to stop running. Slowed to a walk toward the Escort parked down the street. Willed himself not to look back, and couldn't keep the promise to himself.

The woman was standing at the front of Jeff Rorie's cabin, watching him, the shotgun cradled under one arm.

Simpson had intended to drive straight to the International Airport. Instead he diverted at the last minute toward Lake Hood. He found a bar amidst the clutter of buildings at the floatplane airport. It was called The Bush League. It smelled of stale beer and cigarettes. A half-dozen men sat on stools or in booths, smoking and drinking beer. A television set was suspended over one end of the bar, next to a mounted moose head. Simpson slipped onto a stool, ordered a Beck's, and glanced idly at the TV picture. It was an old black-and-white repeat of a Perry Mason drama. Raymond Burr was making Hamilton Burger look silly. The actress Burr was cross-examining must have been someone's relative, Simpson thought. She couldn't act.

He hadn't done much better in Fortune, Simpson reflected sourly. The memory of that woman making him run still rankled.

He wasn't sure exactly why he had stopped at The Bush League, except that, in spite of having discovered nothing new or solid to justify the feeling, in his gut he *knew* he was right about Rorie. He hated to go back and listen to Mayberry telling him I told you so.

He was nursing his third beer, thinking about leaving, when the man on the stool beside him said, "What're you flyin'?"

"Huh? Oh . . . I'm not a pilot. I was just here lookin' up a guy. Jeff Rorie. You know him?"

The man frowned in concentration. He was about fifty, Simpson judged, with a pepper-and-salt beard, a face burnished to the texture of leather by wind and sun, and light hazel eyes that had squinted so much for so long that the innumerable lines and creases around them were permanently etched into the leather. "I know most of the guys," he said. "Yeah, I remember Rorie. New guy. Worked for Far Eyes this summer."

"That's right," Simpson said. "And last year he was up at Prudhoe Bay with Les Hargrove, flying people around for ARCO."

The bearded pilot stared at him. "What's that? What'd you say about Les?"

"You know Hargrove?"

"Hell, yes, we've flown together a thousand times in the bush. I still don't figure him walkin' away from it, going back to sit under a palm tree and get red as a lobster."

"I guess he was tired of flying in the bush."

"You don't get tired of it, and you don't walk away. Not someone like Les."

Simpson studied the man curiously. He felt a nibble of excitement. Take it easy, he told himself. Don't rush it. "Buy you a beer?" he asked.

The old pilot's name was Kramer, and he didn't mind if he did have another. After some small talk Simpson said, "What was it you were gonna say about Hargrove?"

"Hell, it wasn't what I said, it was what *you* said. About Les flying with this guy Rorie up at Prudhoe Bay."

"Yeah, that's right, Rorie told me about it."

"Well, I don't know what he told you, but Les was one old-time sourdough who hated that damned pipeline. He wouldn't have been caught dead flyin' for ARCO or the Trans-Alaska, or for British Petroleum or anyone else had anythin' to do with it. You hear what I'm saying?"

Wolf Simpson heard. After a moment's careful thought he murmured, "So why did Hargrove take off for California?"

Kramer shrugged, wiped foam from around his bearded mouth. "Dunno," he said. "You're in this business, you do a little finaglin' here and there. Maybe Les did, maybe he didn't. But my guess is, somebody got to him. He didn't leave Alaska because he wanted to, not someone like Les. He left because he had no choice."

Simpson sat very still, a smile growing on his face. *Bingo!* he whispered to himself.

He had been right all along.

Les Hargrove had lied about his reason for leaving, and Jeff

Rorie had lied about working with Hargrove the previous summer.

Rorie was a plant.

And unless something was done about him, Simpson and Mayberry were in trouble.

EIGHTEEN

THE TWO tourists sat in the back during takeoff and stayed there while Rorie headed north along the course of the Susitna River. The noise inside the cabin during the climb precluded easy conversation. They flew over Alpine tundra in its autumn reds and golds, climbing over ranks of hills like steps leading upward to the mass of the Alaska Range. The two passengers watched, mesmerized as first-time lookers often were, by the unfolding spectacle. There were glimpses of dwindling forests, of waterfalls dropping hundreds of feet down the sides of the mountains into bottomless canyons, and, closer, of rivers of ice imprisoned between gray rock walls thousands of feet high. And as the Cessna leveled off at seven thousand feet, the horizon was dominated by Mt. McKinley, even though, as was often true, the cloud layer at about ten thousand feet covered more than half its bulk.

A half-hour out of Anchorage, Bob LoBianco, one of the two passengers, clambered forward into the seat beside the pilot. "How's it going, partner?" he asked.

"So far, so good," Rorie said.

He grinned, relaxing. It felt strange to let down his guard. It was six months since Rorie had made direct contact with any-one from the Fish and Wildlife Service. He was so deep into his cover it was unsettling to surface, however briefly.

Like Rorie, his two passengers were role-playing Fish and Wildlife Service agents. Everett Sanderson was tall, wide-hipped and heavy without being fat, like an NFL linebacker. His light brown hair was an inch-long brush cut. His habitual walk was an amble supported by size fourteen brogues, and he spoke at the same pace in a lazy South Carolina drawl. LoBianco was wiry,

180

compact, aggressive, a volatile Italian with the sound of Brooklyn in every word, and the habit of speaking out of one corner of his mouth like a movie tough guy. He had thick, wavy black hair, a beard so heavy it looked dark blue even when he had shaved, and black eyebrows that met to form a ridge above his dark brown eyes.

"Someone called the Far Eyes office yesterday, asking about you," LoBianco said.

"I know."

"What does it mean? Are you blown? You think they're onto you?"

Rorie hesitated. "I'm not sure. I doubt it. The guy who called, Wolf Simpson, is Mayberry's honcho. He's suspicious, but I don't think he knows anything. He's naturally suspicious of anyone he doesn't know."

"He should be." LoBianco hung on as the Cessna lifted on a thermal. He looked uneasy. "How do you know it was him?"

"They told me about the call, and I spotted him tailing me into town." Rorie grinned. "I took my time over supper in a coffee shop while he sat in his car. I'm sure he was there to see us off this morning."

Sanderson leaned closer from the back seat to make himself heard above the din. "If there's any chance you're burned, we pull you out right now. I know Simpson. He's got a record. He's a weasel with very sharp teeth. And Mayberry's nobody to fool around with."

Rorie knew the risks involved in working undercover for a prolonged period. There was always the chance of slipping up in some small way, of contradicting himself or otherwise tripping over his own story. For this reason, like most undercover agents, Rorie said as little about himself as possible. His current role, built up over the past year, was that of an easygoing, live-for-today bush pilot who, if he wasn't actually bent, had a careless attitude about activities that were either openly illegal or skirted around the edges of the law. He was certain that Mayberry had bought the story.

"I don't think I've made any mistakes. Simpson doesn't like me, and like I said, he's a skeptic by nature. I think Mayberry let him check me out to get it out of his system, that's all."

They were all silent for a time. The world below them now was white and bleak and cold, an unforgiving world of snow and rock, where nothing grew or survived for long. They were leaving sun and blue skies behind them, discovering gray cloud cover as far as the eye could reach across the breathtaking sweep of mountains and valleys.

"What about this search for the ivory? How do you figure in on that?" Sanderson was concerned about the narrow line between allowing a criminal to commit his crime and entrapment.

"I'm just the pilot," Rorie said. "I don't tell them where to go or what to do. It's not something I set up. I'm just going along."

"You're helping them, that's where it gets sticky."

"I think we're okay on entrapment," LoBianco growled. This was ground they had covered before.

"You have any problems with the situation, Jeff?" Sandy asked.

"No," he said. "No problems."

Rorie was not an undercover agent by choice. His superiors had simply discovered that he was good at it. Like a good actor, he was the kind of man who was able to submerge himself effortlessly into a variety of situations and roles. There was something believable about him. The people he became involved with tended to trust him—Simpson was the exception—even those whose business made them inherently cautious.

That believability, and his own tendency to find good in most people, had almost caused him to quit the Service. He had worked undercover first in Louisiana, and then in the Western states where the Service had become increasingly concerned about the killing of bald eagles and golden eagles, whose feathers, sacred to many Indian tribes, had become collectible items, used in Indian jewelry and in the roaches and bustles worn in Native American ceremonial dances. The magnificent birds of prey were also coveted by hunters running out of rare trophies to mount. For poachers, eagles had become a valuable target. The threat to these species had led to laws protecting them. Indians still legally used eagle feathers acquired through the death or accidental injury of birds that occurred naturally in the wild, but poachers didn't wait.

Working undercover, Rorie had entered the world of ceremonial Native American pow-wows and Western gatherings, some of the latter based on the nineteenth-century rendezvous, where trappers and mountain men got together to trade or sell their wares at a time when the bounty of the West seemed endless. Rorie had become a part of the scene, making friends with many of those who traveled the circuit of shows and gatherings where Indian jewelry, artifacts and collectibles were sold. He collected evidence on those who were selling items containing eagle feathers, or jewelry made with tortoiseshell or bear claws, both of which were now illegal. Most of these were ordinary working people who didn't think they were doing anything wrong. In the end, when Fish and Wildlife agents moved in for a crackdown on the most flagrant violators, Rorie saw himself through the eyes of those with whom he had shared drinks and family meals and birthday celebrations. He saw a liar and a traitor.

He had asked out—or at least reassignment. What he got instead was a stern lecture from Ron Haller, his superior, along with a short course in the ivory trade. "The poachers we're really after aren't selling trinkets at weekend shows," Haller told him. "They operate big-time. And whether it's elephants in Africa or walrus in the Bering Sea, snow leopards in Asia or alligators in the bayou, the animals are the real victims. The big-time poachers don't give a damn if they wipe out the species in our lifetime. They aren't people you should start feeling sorry for."

"I just don't think I'm cut out for this," Rorie had said.

"Wrong. You're good at it. In fact, right now you're the best we've got. Maybe the only one for this job I have for you in Alaska. We pulled off a sting in Nome a while back, and we caught some of the smaller fry. We can do better, but the same sting won't work twice. We need someone to get inside the trade. We need a new face. You're our number one pick. You can fly a plane through a knothole, which is one of the qualifications we need up there. You know how to fit in. Besides, you look kind of shady. Why do you think these guys all accept you?"

"Thanks a lot."

"Stop feeling guilty about doing your job, Jeff. Once you get up there and see what's going on in Alaska, you'll want to put these people away where they belong. This world is past the point where we can keep saying screw the environment, screw the Indians and the Eskimos, and screw the other animal species we share this planet with, as long as we get ours." Haller's voice took on the fervor of a true believer. "A walrus is kind of big and fat and ugly. It's not beautiful like an eagle in flight, or cute like a penguin. It's not even as majestic as an elephant or a whale. But if we keep letting them be slaughtered on a large scale, they won't be around in the next century. They'll be like the passenger pigeon and the buffalo."

"I know," Rorie said lamely.

"Keeping them as part of our world is a hell of a lot more important than someone being able to have a fancy ivory cigarette holder or amulet. If you don't believe that, then you're right, you *should* walk away. If you do believe it, like I know you do, you'll take your two weeks vacation, come back here and get ready to do your job."

A persuasive guy, Rorie thought. But what Rorie had seen in Travis Mayberry's back room, and in the Eskimo village, had been even more convincing.

"What's your line on Mayberry?" Sandy Sanderson said, interrupting Rorie's thoughts. "What kind of a guy is he?"

"You went fishing with him, or met him over drinks in a bar, you'd get along with him fine. Simpson's a slimeball, but Mayberry you could almost like."

"Don't start liking him too much," LoBianco growled. "He's dealing grass and other shit to the Eskimos for his ivory. That's the kind of good old boy who'd sell crack outside school playgrounds."

"There's something you should know, Jeff," Sanderson said. "We've turned up a haul of bear hides and raw ivory at a trading post in Fort Yukon. Not just a couple of tusks somebody had in a closet, but twenty-six pairs of high quality walrus tusks, and about a dozen polar bear skins. They just walked in out of the cold, like Sam McGee."

The owner of the trading post had purchased the bonanza from an apparent drifter, Sanderson explained, a man who was so anxious to sell he took a low-ball offer. Afterward the buyer started to worry. He realized that he was almost certainly dealing with illegal goods. After he became worried enough about keeping his license, he contacted a Fish and Wildlife Service agent in Fairbanks.

Rorie thought it over. What Sanderson described sounded like the product of large-scale poaching. Rorie didn't think that could be going on in Alaska without Travis Mayberry's knowledge or involvement. Then he remembered Mayberry's need to make special trips in his own plane, even after hiring a bush pilot for everyday junkets. "I think Mayberry must have a secret hideout," Rorie said. "A cache. What he keeps in that back room of his, behind the saloon, is for the everyday trade. There's only a small quantity of ivory, and a lot of that is tagged to pass off as legal. If he's the main source of Alaskan ivory for major dealers in the Lower 48 like Harry Madrid, or for the big Chinese cartels, then he has to have a lot more of it hidden somewhere."

"That ties in," Sandy said. "One of our agents showed the trader in Fort Yukon some mug shots. He nailed one right away. A small-time hustler named Lester Paley. You'll be pleased to know he was a minor league player on Mayberry's team. There was another guy with him when he sold the ivory. We don't have an ID, but Paley used to hang with another creep named Phil Torrance. They both did some poaching for Mayberry . . . and they both dropped out of sight after our sting operation last year."

"So what's going on?" Rorie wondered aloud.

"Mayberry's dumping some of his inventory," LoBianco suggested.

Rorie shook his head. "No, he needs everything he can put his hands on. I don't have all the details, but Mayberry's got a big order to fill and he's feeling pressure. He wouldn't be unloading tusks at a low price in Fort Yukon."

The three men were silent for a moment, piecing it together. The impatient LoBianco was the first to speak. "They're freelancing."

"It's possible." Rorie sounded dubious.

"Gotta be. If what you say is right about Mayberry having a

big shipment to get together, these punks have to be selling
without him knowing."

"So what do you think?" Sanderson said slowly. "Paley and
Torrance drop out of sight for a year. Mayberry has the two of
them up at his mountain cabin, out of harm's way."

"Where you can't find them, and they can look after his
ivory," Rorie said. "His main supply."

"Security," Sandy agreed.

LoBianco chortled. "Some security!"

"If we can pick them up before they leave Alaska," Sanderson speculated, boring straight ahead on his own track, "we
have a link to Mayberry that'll hold up in court. But finding
them won't be easy. If they've hijacked Mayberry's cache, you
know they're going to try to get lost in a hurry—not because of
us, but because of Mayberry."

"Yeah," LoBianco said with a wry smile. "We'd take 'em to
trial and they'd get six months probation if we're lucky. Mayberry finds 'em, they could disappear for good."

"This could play into our hands," Sandy drawled. "From
what you've heard, Jeff, Mayberry needs a lot of ivory to meet
what Harry Madrid and his clients want. He's had this big harvest stolen there on the coast. He'll go ape when he finds out
he's been ripped off a second time by his own people. That will
make this missing ivory you've been hunting even more important. He'll do whatever it takes to find it."

"The Eskimos will feel the heat," Rorie said. "Especially the
old man who got away from them."

"You really think the old Eskimo stole that haul?"

"I think it's a good bet. What I don't understand is why he
did it."

But he had an idea why, Rorie thought. He had been as impressed with John Mulak's quiet dignity as he had been dis-
gusted by the son's betrayal. Even there, the bitter truth was
that it was white men who had manipulated the young Eskimo,
just as they had used the other native hunters, buying them with
whisky, marijuana and cocaine. Against those enticements,
Rorie thought, Billy Mulak had never really had a prayer.

"Maybe the old guy wants to sell it himself," LoBianco suggested cynically.

"No." Rorie was emphatic. "He took it so Mayberry couldn't have it. Because that kind of killing violates everything the Eskimos believe about themselves and animals and nature."

The other two agents regarded him quizzically. After a silence LoBianco, peering nervously through the windshield, said, "How far is it to Fairbanks? I can't see anything down there now."

"We'll be over it in ten minutes. That is," Rorie added with a grin, "if we can find it."

"What's that supposed to mean?"

"We might run into ice fog. The guy who selected Fairbanks for an airport was probably the same Air Force colonel who picked all those sites for air bases located in foggy bottoms."

"Very funny."

"So where do we go from here?" Sanderson asked.

Rorie thought about it while he searched for the lights that would guide him into the Fairbanks airport. Even though it was now shortly past noon—there was no high noon so close to the Arctic, the sun riding close to the horizon—lights were mandatory. In the dense cloud cover beneath which Fairbanks was hiding, it might as well have been night.

"Mayberry was planning a trip to the hideout while I was away. If we get lucky, we might catch him with the goods."

"Plans have changed," Sanderson said. Rorie's glance showed surprise, and Sanderson leaned close to be sure he was heard clearly. "We've got a blanket over every possible way Mayberry can ship his stuff out of Alaska. We want to find the hideout, sure . . . but we'll let Mayberry take what's left. We'll track it wherever it goes. Our guess is a warehouse in New Jersey. If we can follow it there, then maybe we really get lucky. We want to shut Mayberry down up here . . . but we want Harry Madrid even more."

Rorie didn't like the idea of allowing Mayberry to get away with anything. "What if we find this other harvest . . . the big one?"

"Then you call for backup," Sanderson said, "and we take him down."

Rorie was still frowning. There was a rogue factor, an element he hadn't yet figured out. Briefly he told the other two agents about the scientist alone at her little camp on the river. He outlined his concerns. Why had Dr. McNeely been so cool to four strangers, barely concealing hostility? Why would she react that way to Mayberry and Simpson, whom she had never met? And to Rorie, rejecting his attempted overture? Because she was afraid of them? A woman alone in the wilderness would naturally be cautious, but Rorie sensed there was more to her hostility. She *knew* what they were (lumping Rorie himself with the other two). But how could she know?

"Civilians," LoBianco said disgustedly.

"She's as much right to be there in the wilderness as we do," Rorie pointed out. "Maybe more, considering what her group is trying to do."

"You think there's any way she could know something about the missing ivory?"

"That's what I've been wondering," Rorie said. "And there's only one way."

"What's that?"

"She's met John Mulak."

And if the possibility occurred to him, Rorie thought to himself, it would occur to a frantic, increasingly desperate Travis Mayberry.

"That's a reach," said Sanderson.

"I know . . . but it's one more reason I'd better get back to Nome tonight on schedule. Whatever you find in Fort Yukon or in the mountains, things are going to come to a head over that missing harvest on the coast."

"Play it close," Sanderson said. "This is no time to be a hero."

"No. But I'm not going to leave that old Eskimo twisting in the wind."

"Just make sure you're not the one left twisting."

Rorie returned his attention to the search for the Fairbanks airport. Unlike most smaller airports in Alaska, the facility at Fairbanks was used by large commercial jetliners. Going in blind in a small plane, even with tower clearance, wasn't an option of choice. Even scheduled airliners encountering the ice fog over Fairbanks, a potentially deadly combination of smog and fog and ice particles, routinely turned around and went back where they came from, or flew on to another destination.

Rorie raised the airport tower on his radio. "RO-1 calling tower. Do you see me yet?"

There was a moment's delay. Then, "We've got you on radar, RO-1." The bodiless voice floated eerily in the gray murk in which Rorie was now flying. He glanced out the side windows, worrying about ice collecting on his wings.

"How does it look?"

"Not good. You're cleared, and we can talk you down if you have problems. But if you've got an alternative, I'd take it."

"Thanks, I think I will."

In the Cessna the men were silent. Finally Sanderson said, "What does all that mean?"

"It means," Rorie said, "that I take you straight on through to Fort Yukon. I know a good place for lunch."

Mayberry had not yet returned to Nome—no way of knowing when he would be back. And Wolf Simpson knew that Mayberry wouldn't be happy on his return if he discovered that Simpson had sat around waiting for him instead of going after the missing ivory. The fact that Simpson had discovered something about Les Hargrove and Jeff Rorie wouldn't cut any ice with Mayberry. That problem could be taken care of after the ivory was found.

Simpson knew how Mayberry's mind worked. Take care of business first.

For now, Simpson needed Rorie and his plane. The pleasure of dealing with him could wait.

Planning ahead, Simpson knew how to work it. He would leave Nome with Rorie, fly to the Eskimo village to pick up Billy Mulak, and take care of business.

Afterward, the pilot wouldn't be coming back.

NINETEEN

THE NIGHT John Mulak returned to the village was the first time this season the temperature plunged well below zero. Driving winds created a chill factor of thirty below. Although there was no fresh snowfall, the winds scooped up the dry powder that covered the frozen tundra and hurled it into miniature storms of blowing, whirling, drifting snow. Blinded by the whiteout, Mulak sought shelter among craggy hills northeast of the village. There, huddled in a nest of rocks, he waited for the winds to die down. He knew it might be a long wait.

He had left his kayak grounded on a narrow gravel beach two hours earlier. Head down, he had plodded across the tundra on improvised snowshoes he had fashioned with willow struts. The snow was not deep enough to prevent walking without the snowshoes, but with them his progress was faster and less tiring. The wide shoes also lessened the risk of stumbling over unseen hummocks or sinking into invisible holes. He was less than four miles from the village when the winds forced him to seek cover.

Until now, hunched inside his fur parka and sealskin pants, with his L.L. Bean rubber boots pulled over sealskin mukluks, he had kept warm enough to survive. His head had been covered not only by his baseball cap with its ear flaps, but also by the fur-lined hood of his parka. Only part of his face had been exposed. Waiting, the nest of rocks providing only partial shelter from the cutting wind, his cheeks felt dangerously cold—his cheeks and his broken left hand. A white frosting of ice crusted on his eyebrows and clung to his lids. More ice froze in his nostrils, and he had to breathe through his mouth. His puffy lips were cracked from the cold.

He did not let himself think about the warmth of his house

with its oil-fired furnace, now so close that, through gaps in the whirling ground snow, he imagined that he could see a halo of light over the village. He couldn't be sure. He knew that such visions could be false in whiteout conditions, like a mirage in the desert.

He found it very hard to imagine living in a desert. Hard to believe that people would choose to remain in a place where there was only sun and heat and sand, a place without water or life. He did not see the familiar tundra as bleak or empty. In spring, summer and fall it sprang into bursts of color. Even now there were bright red cranberries frozen on their bushes. Earlier in the day he had feasted on frozen berries. And in all seasons of the year, the tundra was alive with creatures. Even winter had its white Arctic hares and foxes, its snowy owls and white-feathered ptarmigans, and, out on the margins of the ice, magnificent polar bears and the seals they hunted.

He thought of the woman in the cave. A white woman, watcher of birds and sea animals. It was good to know there were such people among the gussaks. His daughter Ruth had often spoken of meeting white men and women of this kind when she went away to school, but Mulak was glad to have met such a woman himself.

However, Mulak wasn't as confident as the woman was in the justice she wanted to bring down upon the walrus hunters. White men's justice was not predictable. It seemed to Mulak that this justice was very harsh at times, while at others it allowed men like Simpson to do whatever they wished. He had reached the conclusion long ago that white men should make laws only for white men, and Eskimos should make laws for Eskimos. How could he, Mulak, make laws for people whose way of life was a mystery to him? And how could the gussaks tell Eskimos how to live when they did not understand the Eskimo way of life?

As a practical matter, though, Mulak knew that white men would continue to decide things for Eskimos. And even if the woman in the cave spoke truly and not only from the heart, and the white hunters were to be punished for taking so much ivory in violation of their own laws, what of the Eskimos who had participated in the slaughter? Were they also to be punished?

Would Mulak bring harm to his own people if he returned to the cave where the woman was to wait for him?

Mulak's troubled thoughts trickled off, unresolved. Some time later he woke suddenly, stiff with cold. Alarm drove him to his feet. He had dozed. The knowledge carried its own chill. He must not sleep again. He flexed his arms and legs, took off one mitten briefly to touch his face. His cheeks were numb, without sensation.

Stepping away from his warren of rocks, he felt again the full force of the wind. It was not as strong as before, he told himself. He could even see ten or twelve paces in front of him, sometimes more.

No matter. He could rest no longer. He had to stay on his feet. He had to keep moving. If he slept again, there would be no awakening.

When she saw him in the doorway, Ruth burst into tears. Quickly she pulled him inside and closed the door, shutting out the cold. He moved stiff-legged with his arms away from his body, like a robot in a science-fiction movie she had seen on television. One look at his blue cheeks told her that he had frostbite. She put a pan of water on the stove to heat. She ran to the thermostat and turned it higher. On a night like this the searching wind found cracks in the prefabricated government-built house, and the furnace struggled.

When the water was almost hot enough to scald, she dipped a small dishtowel into the water and wrung it out. Then she began to bathe her father's face. Mulak flinched but did not pull away. He was still bundled inside his fur parka and double-layered pants, and he was still shivering.

The ice that had clogged his nostrils and rimmed his eyes melted quickly in the warmth of the house. Water ran down his face and under the collar of his shirt.

All this time he had not spoken.

Ruth retreated to the kitchen, where she began to heat some leftover stew. By the time it was ready Mulak had stopped shivering. He took off his parka and sat at the table at the dining end of the living room. His hands trembled, and his fingers seemed thick and clumsy. He ate slowly, chewing each mouthful of stew methodically. Like most older Eskimos, he had lost some teeth and others were bad. Mulak jokingly blamed it on the white men's sweets, which had never been part of the Eskimo diet. She cringed when she saw how badly his swollen lips were cracked and bleeding. The bleeding had started after he was inside for a few minutes.

Ruth watched him in silence, her heart aching, until he had finished eating. Only then did she trust herself to speak. "The gussaks have left the village."

"They will be back."

"Yes . . . I know."

His left hand was swollen, and she noticed that he winced whenever he tried to use it. It wasn't frostbitten. It had been injured. Ruth found gauze and a roll of bandage tape in the ten-dollar first-aid kit she kept in the bathroom. She bound the hand with great care. Her father accepted the attention—and the pain—in stoic silence. When she had finished he simply nodded. She had the impression that, behind the swollen mouth, a smile was concealed.

Tears returned as she studied him. Where had he been? What had he been doing? How far had he come on this cold night?

"You can't stay here," she said. "They'll look for you here when they come back."

"Where's Billy?"

"He . . . he's with some of his friends. He doesn't sleep here, in his family's house. I think he's ashamed."

"He shouldn't be ashamed. He helped me to get away. He broke the lock on the door of the storage house."

Ruth looked at him, puzzled and uncertain, remembering the anger of the white men when they came to the house to get her brother. "Are you sure it was Billy?"

"Who else would have tried to free me?"

"I don't know, but . . ." Her next words came reluctantly. "Billy went with the gussaks to find you. He was helping them."

John Mulak considered this, and nodded with understanding. "He could do nothing else. They would have punished him if he hadn't pretended to help them."

"How do you know he was only pretending?"

The cracked, puffy ghost of a smile reappeared. "They didn't find me."

Mulak did not tell his daughter where he had been, or about the white woman he had met, or anything about the ivory he had stolen. It was better for her not to know.

In the comfortable warmth of the house his fatigue began to crush him. He would rest for a while. The white men would not return tonight. Later he would talk to his son—

The old man and Ruth heard the footsteps outside at the same time. Running steps, thudding on the porch. They both looked toward the front door, Ruth's expression suddenly anxious. The door burst inward. It was never locked. No doors in the village were locked against friends or strangers alike. Billy Mulak appeared in the doorway, dusted with snow. The bitter cold blew into the room with him.

"Pop! Someone said they saw you—I couldn't believe it!"

Billy glanced back over his shoulder. Closed the door quickly, as if afraid that someone might have followed him. Turned to stare again at his father in disbelief, as if he regarded a ghostly apparition.

"Are you crazy, old man? Why did you steal the ivory? The white men know you took it. They're angry. If they find you . . ." He faltered, his eyes turning away from his father's. "I don't know what they'll do."

"How can they know it was me?"

"There's no one else." Agitated, Billy began to pace the room, leaving wet footprints on the tile floor and the braided rug in the living area. Ruth said nothing. "Why did you run away? You can't keep hiding from them."

"If you didn't want me to run away, why did you break the lock on the cabin?"

Billy's face registered incredulity. "Why would I do that? I didn't break the lock, I thought you did it yourself."

He dismissed the puzzle. His arms flailed the air in frustration as he paced. His movements were jerky, and his eyes darted about. Mulak realized that this agitated energy was nothing new in Billy's conduct. It fell into the recent pattern of sudden angers and periods of exaggerated euphoria. The boy's appearance had even changed without Mulak remarking upon it. Billy had always been thin, but now he was skinny to the point of appearing gaunt, hollow-eyed and drawn. These were signs that Mulak had seen but refused to recognize because he didn't want to. Even now he resisted admitting the truth to himself.

"You've got to tell them where the ivory is, Pop, don't you see that? Or tell *me* where it is so I can take them to it. They'll leave you alone once they have the ivory."

John Mulak felt many things in that moment. Confusion, disappointment, sadness. Dismay as Billy's words sank in. Billy hadn't helped him escape. Then who? An old friend in the village brave enough to defy the white men? Mulak had no answer.

Billy had joined the gussaks to search for him. That was why the airplane had flown over the river not far from the cave—why it had come so close to discovering him. Billy knew that he fished in that river, that he went there often. That, if he were trying to hide from the white men, he would choose a place that he knew well.

Billy had told the gussaks where they might find him.

The sadness overwhelmed everything else. He felt very tired, and old.

Billy didn't know about the cave. Mulak hadn't been there in many years, but it was only by chance that he had never mentioned the bear's cave to his son, or taken him there even when Billy was a boy, for the cave was the kind of secret place that would have been fun for a boy to explore. Mulak remembered once being on the river with Billy, maybe six or seven years ago, and thinking about the cave. But it was early spring, and Mulak had wondered if the bear that wintered in the cave would still be there. He had decided this secret could wait for another time. He had not mentioned the cave.

Ruth saw the understanding in Mulak's eyes, and the grief it awakened. Her anger erupted at Billy. "What did they promise you to betray your father? Tell us that!"

She knew the answer. She wanted to force Billy to admit it before his father. But Billy avoided the hot accusation in her eyes. His expression became sullen. "You know nothing about such things."

"I know about loving my father," Ruth retorted scornfully. "I

know enough to see how much it hurts him when he sees that
his son would sell him for the white men's drugs! No Eskimo
would even sell his *dog* for so little!''

"That's enough!" John Mulak had heard enough.

"You're as bad as he is!" Billy shouted at his sister. "Don't
you know what he's done?"

The youth stormed about the living room, shoving a table out
of his way. An arm swung savagely, knocking a lamp off the
table beside the worn sofa. It landed on its side, unbroken, the
shade askew so that the light shone upward.

Billy stopped, breathing hard, and glared wildly at Mulak.
"What am I supposed to feel when my father is a thief! That
ivory was *ours!* It wasn't yours to take. It belongs to all of us, not
just the white men! You stole it from *us!*"

"No," Mulak said heavily. "Such killing is not the way of the
people. You've become more white than brown. You no longer
think like an Eskimo."

"If you mean I think there's more to life than fish and seal
blubber and berries, you're right!" Billy's defiant words turned
bitter. "The white men have everything. We have nothing! We
would still be living in mud huts if it weren't for the gussaks.
We'd be living with seal oil lamps and no heat, and half our
babies dying."

"We have ourselves. We have a good life. The white men I've
met are not happier than Eskimos. You won't be happy trying
to be one of them . . . trying to be something you're not."

Listening, Ruth felt heat in her cheeks. In an anguished way
she understood Billy's torment. He was like so many of the people of her village, especially the younger ones, especially the
men. The world outside had imposed on their lives inexorably
until they didn't know where they belonged. They were pushed
this way and that. They had come to depend on snow machines,
Evinrude motors for their boats, generators to provide electricity, refrigerators, television sets, white men's packaged foods.
Their children played electronic games. And to pay for the oil
and the food and the machines they could no longer rely on
the furs they could trap or the fish they could catch, or even the
ivory they obtained in a walrus hunt. More and more the men
had to leave the village for the cities where they could earn

dollars, or if they were lucky, to find work on the pipeline. They came back to the village restless, dissatisfied, confused, their dollars soon squandered . . . or they remained in the cities, derelicts where they had no place.

Ruth thought of her own longings to experience more of the world beyond her small village, a world of unimaginable beauties and wonders and surprises. Billy would not find those in the white men's drugs, but even though his dreams were different, he longed for an escape she had also imagined for herself.

But she would not betray her father for her dream. Or betray her people.

"I know the truth," Billy said to Mulak. "This isn't about me at all, it's about you. You wanted Muugli's tusks for yourself."

"Billy!"

Wearily John Mulak waved away Ruth's protest. "Go," he said to his son. "Go to your white men. Tell them they'll never find the ivory."

"They'll find it. They'll find *you,* crazy old man!"

"No," Mulak answered. "Not even with my son helping them. And tell them their bullets will never kill Muugli. Tell them he's not dead. He is part of our lives, he belongs to the people."

The old man turned away. He did not look up when Billy stormed out of the house. Ruth, watching him closely, saw his body flinch when the door slammed.

There was a long, painful silence. Her father's slumped figure seemed smaller, frailer in that moment, and Ruth had a frightening vision of the house without him, without Billy, a house emptier and colder than any mud hut. She shivered, hugging her chest with her arms.

"You must get some rest, Papa," she said softly. "I'll have some food ready for you to take with you. But you must be gone in the morning. You must be gone before the gussaks come back." Ruth paused at a sudden inspiration. "You can take the sno-go. There's enough snow on the ground." The snow machine was one of the marvels of the white man's world that had been enthusiastically adopted by the Eskimos, who had virtually abandoned traveling by dog sled in the winter. A hundred-mile journey across the frozen tundra, once a daunting expedition of several days, could now be completed easily in less than one day in good conditions. "You could get far away."

John Mulak's puffy smile was heavy with irony. "No," he said. "Billy is right about me. I will go my own way. The Eskimo way."

TWENTY

THAT SAME night in the river bottom, where the two small yellow tents stood out sharply against an endless sea of white, was the coldest Kathy McNeely had experienced north of the Arctic Circle. The Coleman stove struggled. Winds tore at her tent, and the flapping and keening kept her awake. The cold seeped into her sleeping bag and she could not get warm.

The darkness and cold and, especially, the fierce winds transported her in her thoughts to Antarctica—and Brian Hurley.

Seasons in Antarctica were the opposite of those in the Arctic. Where winter was setting in for her, Hurley was now experiencing spring on The Ice. He had planned to make his dogsled run at the Hartsook Glacier in Antarctica's spring and early summer, October to December, with the goal of reaching the South Pole before Christmas.

He would be there now, she thought. Too busy to send a radio message halfway around the world. She'd had no word from him during the past two months, not even while she had had a working radio. For Hurley and his dogs all the frantic preparations, all the intense conditioning and trial runs were over now. They would be quickly forgotten as the real test began.

When Hurley reached the bottom of the earth, others would be there to cheer him. Television cameras would record the event. After their quarrel, did he still believe that she prayed for him? That she would rejoice for him at the end?

Lying alone in her tent, she felt impossibly remote from Hurley, divorced from everything he faced, and the feeling unnerved her. Even success—the success she ardently wished for him—would take him further away.

She listened to the wind scouring the snow-covered tundra, prowling outside her tent like a malicious force. Every sound was magnified. She remembered being alone in her family's big old house as a child during a storm, hearing all the familiar creaks and groans of an old house with unfamiliar anxiety. On a bright sunny day, when she knew her parents were nearby, it was the most inviting, sheltering home. But in darkness, with chaos outside, hearing no reassuring voices, she would conjure up in her imagination all kinds of menacing shapes in the unseen shadows of the hallway, the back stairway, the attic. The ordinary became strange and threatening. Like that child she could barely remember, she found herself lying rigid in her tent, listening tensely. Something rustled just outside. But Survivor slept there, having dug out his own shelter in the snow. He would sense another animal's presence.

Stupid to start feeling vulnerable because she was alone. No comforting male presence in the next tent, or in her bed.

No Jason Cobb to challenge her.

No Brian Hurley lying beside her.

The night was not that much different from many others she had experienced here in Alaska. A little windier, she admitted, the euphemism provoking a small smile in the darkness as the tent shook, ballooned outward and threatened to fly away. But no more dangerous.

Except for one thing. One factor that changed everything, and it was not a product of the wilderness.

Her smashed radio.

Kathy read an unmistakable message in the deliberate destruction of the radio. It told her Travis Mayberry and his men would be back. She was uncertain why Mayberry had felt the need to isolate and silence her, unless he had guessed that she might somehow have linked up with John Mulak. Or maybe the poacher was simply a careful man, leaving nothing to chance. Either way, he would be back, and she didn't want to be here when he came.

She thought of the old Eskimo. In less than twenty-four hours Mulak would be returning to the cave where the ivory was hidden. Relying on her promise to meet him there. And on her confident assurance that she would notify Federal agents of the stolen ivory and Mulak's dangerous situation—a promise she could no longer keep.

She would wait at camp until noon, she thought, on the chance the ASSET plane would arrive. No later. If it didn't come, she would go to join Mulak, and . . .

She didn't really have a Plan Two.

In the morning it was still fiercely cold, her thermometer registering twelve degrees below zero, but the winds had died. In their place was a dense, penetrating fog that obliterated the mountains to the north, and funneled the immensity all around her into a tiny stage less than a hundred feet square, with her at the center.

She waited through the morning, increasingly ill-at-ease. No cavalry arrived. If the fog persisted, no plane would come. She spent three hours in the comparative warmth of her tent, updating her notes on the habitats she had observed along this coastal river plain. She thought of John Mulak's people hunting, fishing and trapping along this river for generations past, and tried to assess the impact a pipeline and supporting service road would have on the river and the natives who had used it for thousands of years unchanged. Would the salmon still come to spawn in polluted waters? How soon before they would begin to disappear, as they had almost completely from the rivers of the Sacramento Delta in California?

At noon she heated a can of chicken chili and finished it off with the last of a package of Carr's English water crackers. She tried once again to think of a Plan Two.

By this time her ASSET colleagues would be concerned over their inability to establish radio contact. They hadn't been comfortable with leaving her alone, anyway, after Jason Cobb was flown out. Initial worry would be turning into alarm. She knew that the supply plane would be dispatched promptly to her campsite with a rescue team as soon as it returned to the base camp. Even if the plane were grounded somewhere by bad weather, or delayed by other demands on its services, the ASSET group had other resources, principally a large, sturdy Kodiak that had proved itself in Alaska's rivers. The downriver trip was one Kathy and Jason Cobb had taken slowly, in stages. By air it was a short two-hour flight. By boat, however, with floating ice now escalating the normal hazards of a stream mined with hidden snags, shallow riffles, sandbars and whitewater rapids, it would be a hazardous journey of several days.

She couldn't count on an early rescue. She would have to work something out with John Mulak. The old Eskimo knew the land, the rivers, all the hazards of the wilderness. He also had his kayak, roomy enough for two people. But the thought of asking Mulak to take them up the ice-laden river was daunting. It would also make the two of them visible from the air if the poachers returned. Their pilot, Rorie, seemed more than competent for such a search.

Kathy frowned as she thought of Rorie. Something about him was missing. The sleaze factor. It was all over the man called Simpson, and visible in glimpses beneath Mayberry's bonhomie. So what was the pilot, then? Simply a mercenary? A man who sold his services wherever there was a demand, no questions asked? It seemed to fit.

Something tugged at her memory. She couldn't quite pin it down. What had the pilot said just before he left? *"I wouldn't stay here long, ma'am. Not alone."* In retrospect the words sounded even more clearly like a warning.

After lunch she cleaned up, storing the empty chili can with other refuse in a plastic bag in one of the animal-proof lockers. She packed everything away that she couldn't easily carry. She would have to come back for most of her equipment and supplies, along with the accumulated refuse she would not leave behind in the wilderness. She filled her backpack with lightweight foods—dried fruits and nuts, freeze-dried eggs, M&Ms, oatmeal, cocoa—no canned goods because of their extra weight. She added such necessities as a flashlight, change of socks, her folded tent and sleeping bag. It made a bulky but manageable pack. Carried over her quilted parka and layered clothing, it made her feel top-heavy and extremely clumsy.

She stared for a long moment at the Coleman stove before accepting the reality that she couldn't take it with her.

Banishing the longing, she called Survivor. The husky, who

had been watching her preparations, pranced around her eagerly. He was a traveler. Ready to go.

She started east, following the general course of the river while picking her way across the tundra. In a way she was grateful for the fog. Visibility at ground level had improved a little since morning, but it was still no more than fifty or sixty steps. The mist was thick enough to make her invisible from the air, from anything but a low-flying plane passing directly overhead.

The snow lay in uneven drifts across the land. Here and there the surface had been swept clean by the winds. Elsewhere the snow piled several feet deep around brush and tussocks and mounds. The ground was frozen—the underlying permafrost regenerating itself—eliminating the soft, boggy patches that had made hiking so difficult in past weeks. But the damp fog was condensing and freezing on the snow, creating a crust of thin ice she broke through with every step. After a while she began thinking nostalgically of the good old mushy bog.

Survivor, as usual, trotted on ahead, unhindered by snow or uneven terrain, eagerly looking about. Head up, sniffing the icy air. What did he smell or sense that she didn't? Or was he simply excited to be on the move again?

No trace of a limp anymore. He had probably been fit enough last spring to rejoin Hurley's dog team for the great adventure. Instead Hurley had made him a gift. A link.

Good thinking, Hurley.

Good luck . . .

She brought herself back to her own predicament. Isolated, her radio destroyed, most of her food and supplies left behind. Was it a mistake to abandon her camp? If the poachers couldn't find her there, neither could a rescue party.

She shook off the question. She had to return to the cave.

Ten yards ahead of her, Survivor suddenly stopped, at full alert. The hackles rose on his shoulders. He stared off to the left. Following the direction of his stance, which was like a hunting dog's point, she felt her heart thump.

On a rise to her left, some forty yards away, almost at the edge of the clear envelope within the surrounding curtain of fog, closer than Kathy had seen her before, was the gray-white female wolf. She stood immobile while her pack of adolescent pups milled about her. Kathy could see her coloring distinctly, more white than gray, with the darker coloring across her neck and shoulders, and a wide chest patch like a shield. Her pups were all darker, gray shading out of black. They would become whiter as they matured. One of them, obviously the largest male, was already almost as big as his mother, and the white was beginning to show clearly throughout his coat.

Kathy's heart beat faster. Even that gangling youngster was taller than Survivor. She could hear the pups whining and yipping with excitement, but their mother continued to stand motionless and quiet, looking down the slope toward the intruders.

"Easy, Survivor," Kathy murmured, using her voice like a leash to restrain the husky. "They know us by now. Let's just keep walking."

She reached the dog's side and seized his leather collar. She could feel the tension in his neck, the faint quivering in his powerful body. She walked straight ahead—not the normal way of progressing across the tundra, which required constant diversions this way and that to find the easiest path. But she had lucked upon an animal trail, beaten smooth over countless years, that made walking easier. She and Cobb had come across many such trails while traveling toward the coast. She hoped this one didn't end the way most such trails did, as suddenly and inexplicably as it appeared.

Her mittens were stiff with cold, offering minimal sensation, but she became aware of something. A wedge of paper dislodged by her grip and working loose from under Survivor's collar. She plucked it out and stuffed it into her pocket. No littering in the wilderness. Her attention was focused on the wolf pack.

They were following. They trailed a little behind, keeping to the higher ground. Sometimes, as Kathy and Survivor proceeded on, she would glance back and find the wolves had disappeared from view, but as soon as she began to relax they were back.

She wondered what she would do if they came down toward the river, creeping closer.

Odd, that piece of paper. How had it got caught under Survivor's collar? She realized suddenly why it hadn't worked loose earlier. It had been *stuck* there. A piece of gum now adhered to the tip of her mitten.

She wanted to stop and dig out the wedge of folded paper, but the urge wasn't strong enough to override her nervousness over the following wolf pack. She thought of all the articles and studies she had read that tried to settle the argument about whether wolves were dangerous to humans, whether they would attack without provocation or only when threatened. The flood of words, so reasonable on paper, evaporated before the specter of real wolves in a real wilderness. Wolves not running or hiding from a human threat, but following.

Stalking?

Kathy shivered, as if the clammy fog had stolen under her parka and her Irish cableknit sweater and the soft wool shirt and two layers of underwear. Her skin prickled with gooseflesh.

The strange procession continued through the afternoon. The cave where Mulak had hidden the ivory was not far from her camp in miles—no more than three or four miles on the river, she guessed, though nearly twice that overland, with the constant detouring the tundra demanded. The journey took most of the afternoon. Near the end she was laboring, her pack grown into a monstrous burden. She felt her legs quivering with strain, but she resisted the urge to stop and rest.

When she finally paused, dismay threatened to overwhelm her. She was convinced that she had come far enough—perhaps even overshot her goal. She had thought she would be able to recognize distinctive landmarks—a broad thicket of cranberry bushes spread over the bottom of the slope near a bend in the river, the profile of the ridge to the west of the cave, the shallow strip of beach where Mulak had drawn up his kayak. But even though the morning fog had lifted through the afternoon, the snowfall had changed everything. It blurred outlines, altered contours where drifts had piled up, turned the entire landscape into a homogenous sea of white. Even the unchanging mass of the Brooks Range to the north and northeast appeared different, its snowy peaks hidden in the lingering mist.

Kathy stared back along the path she had followed beside the river. She-wolf was not in sight. Nothing else in the landscape jumped out at her. Could she risk climbing to higher ground? She might be able to recognize some feature she had missed while she walked.

Head down toward the last, she admitted ruefully to herself. Plodding wearily, her concentration flagging, she could easily have missed spotting the cave. If she had, then she was ahead of Mulak. She was convinced that she hadn't overlooked his tracks in the snow. And she didn't see how he could have beached his boat and climbed to the cave without leaving a clear trail.

A shock ran through her.

She pictured Mulak's footsteps in the snow. Like the clear trail she had left behind her. She might as well have been sending up signal flares for the poachers to follow!

She wondered how she could have overlooked something so obvious. Her only consolation was that it was already late in the day, with no sign of Mayberry or his plane. By morning, especially if the night winds moved the snow cover around, or even if it warmed and there was melting and packing of the snow, her tracks would no longer be as obvious.

She wondered if Mulak, a skilled hunter, would have thought of leaving tracks. Of course! *She* was the amateur. But that meant she might very well have overrun the site of the cave, presuming the Eskimo had managed to hide his kayak and somehow make his way to the cave without leaving a clearly defined trail behind.

As Kathy stood there, chagrined over her clumsiness, her eye was drawn toward a brow of rock a quarter-mile north of the river, at the crest of a rise made so smooth by its covering of snow that it was almost indiscernible in that white landscape. She hadn't recognized it in passing. Now she did. The overhang was a few steps from the entrance to the invisible cave.

Although the cave seemed so near, distances in the Alaskan wilderness were notoriously deceptive, and this time was no exception. Backtracking along the river bottom to the point where Kathy could climb to the cave took her nearly half an hour. By then she was too near exhaustion to worry about the trail she left behind her in the snowpack.

She dragged herself through the mouth of the cave. The clammy darkness assaulted her senses. She was too tired even to look around for the she-wolf and her brood. Survivor was reluctant to enter the cave, preferring to linger outside, but she lured him in with dry biscuits and chocolate. She wasn't sure that chocolate was good for dogs, but the husky had developed a craving for it almost as great as her own.

There was no sign of John Mulak.

The stack of ivory gleamed as before at the back of the cave.

Kathy ate a cold meal of dried fruits and peanut butter sandwich crackers. Would the old Eskimo come tonight? Had he run into trouble with the poachers at the village? Did he believe what she had told him, believe enough to trust her? She recognized the futility of the questions. She didn't relish the prospect of another night alone in the cave. And what would she do now if Mulak didn't return at all?

As twilight brought a deeper gloom to the interior of the cave, she suddenly remembered the wedge of paper that had worked loose from under Survivor's collar. She fumbled in her pocket. What had she done with it? She—

Her fingers closed on the piece of paper. She unfolded it and, to her astonishment, saw a hasty scrawl written in pencil on a page torn from a small spiral note pad. She dug out her flashlight and flicked it on. Felt renewed astonishment as she reread the words slowly: *Don't stay in this camp, not safe. Contact Fish & Wildlife if you know anything about poachers, esp. missing ivory. J.R.*

Rorie! It was but a short leap to the conclusion that the pilot of Mayberry's plane was himself a Fish and Wildlife Service agent, working undercover. Trying, at considerable risk, to warn her.

He hadn't known about the smashed radio, she thought. Mayberry or Simpson must have done that while Rorie was busy with his plane. So Rorie didn't know that she was incapable of contacting anyone—that she was, in fact, more isolated than ever.

While she stared at the note, reading it for a third time as if she might find some new meaning or reason for hope, a long, spine-tingling howl rose into the stillness outside the cave. The cry, deceptively mournful to human ears, rose and fell, and became a chorus, so close by that it filled the night with its outpouring of sound. Survivor was on his feet, an answering moan in his throat.

Kathy and the husky had indeed been followed to the cave. Not by poachers, but by the she-wolf and her pack.

TWENTY-ONE

JOHN MULAK listened patiently to the growl of sno-gos. Only two of them now. It was getting dark, and there would be snow tonight. Mulak read the signs in the thick pile-up of black clouds over the Chukchi Sea. The only question was how long the storm would last, and how much snow would fall.

He wanted to be gone before the snow came. It would hide his trail.

Mulak had been awakened that morning by the snarling chorus of snow machines, which, as usual, set the village dogs barking and howling, as if they knew these growling machines had replaced them in the affections of most villagers. Ruth had suggested that Mulak take one of the sno-gos on leaving the village, but he had not been tempted. In fact, he did not like the noisy machines, although they were sometimes useful. He remembered the days of traveling by dog sled as good times.

The old Eskimo rose quietly. The house was still. Billy had not returned during the night, and Ruth, exhausted, still slept. Peering outside, he saw thick fog—a welcome sight this morning. It had crept inland while he slept.

He did not awaken his daughter. Instead he made a bundle of the food she had fixed for him to take, shrugged into his heavy parka and boots, and prepared to set off. In place of the makeshift pair of snowshoes he had worn out by the time he returned to the village, he slipped on his best snowshoes, handcrafted of a willow frame and tough sinew.

A mile from the village he knew that he was being followed.

Mulak continued inland for another half-mile, where he diverted toward a cluster of cranberry bushes near the river. For the next half-hour he picked berries, not looking up, making

209

no attempt to determine whether he was being watched. When he had enough berries to justify his morning walk, he returned once more to the village.

From a corner of the storage shed behind his house, which vantage offered a clear view of the eastern end of the village, he saw two men trudge into view, following the bend of the river, their labored breathing making small puffs of mist in the cold morning air. They were coming from the same direction Mulak had taken. They had not, he knew, been picking berries.

His son no longer cared to pick berries, but he would follow his father, as a hunter stalked his prey.

"We're grounded," Jeff Rorie had told Simpson curtly that morning, frowning at the same coastal fog that John Mulak welcomed.

"What's the problem? You're supposed to be the hotshot pilot."

"Good enough to know better. Getting us smashed into a mountain isn't going to get your ivory back." Rorie refrained from offering up the tired Alaskan joke about there being old bush pilots and reckless bush pilots, but no old, reckless bush pilots.

The fog, frustrating his plans to get to the Eskimo village as soon as possible, seemed to threaten Wolf Simpson's new spirit of agreeability, but after a moment of glowering the poacher nodded and stalked upstairs to the office in Travis Mayberry's Front Street saloon. Rorie ordered a breakfast of bacon, eggs and country fried potatoes, figuring that Mayberry's cook couldn't do too much damage there. The scrambled eggs were hard, the potatoes from a frozen package, the bacon burnt. The toast, however, was surprisingly good, made from fresh baked bread . . . which told Rorie only that the cook must have got the bread from somewhere down the street.

Munching toast and drinking thick, black coffee, Rorie looked across Front Street and a narrow strip of gravel beach directly at the Bering Sea. Only the skirts of waves pounding the beach were visible, the rest hidden behind the solid gray wall of mist. He was puzzled by the joviality Simpson had displayed toward him since his return to Nome. Because Simpson had put his suspicions to rest? Because he was ready to accept Rorie at face value? Rorie wasn't sure, and the uncertainty made him uneasy.

After breakfast Rorie went to look after his Cessna. The evening before, he had talked himself into using a corner of a hangar for the aircraft. The hangar was unheated but it was sheltered from any snow or rain that might come, and from the fog's heavy dampness. Standing by the doorway of the hangar, feeling the chill work its way through his layered clothing, Rorie could see Mayberry's private hangar. He talked casually with a mechanic who sometimes worked on Mayberry's Piper Super Cub, learning that Mayberry had taken off twenty-four hours earlier for the interior, after having the aircraft fitted with skis.

"Must be planning to go where there's plenty of snow," Rorie said idly.

"Well now, it might be harder to find any place where there *isn't* snow, from now until spring," the mechanic said. "You oughta think about skis yourself, 'stead of usin' those itty-bitty two-way floats."

"They sit down all right on snow. And I'd hate to have to land in the water on skis." After a moment's silence Rorie said, "Mayberry give you any idea when he'd be back?"

The mechanic peered at him. "When he's ready to, I reckon."

"I reckon so," Rorie said easily, turning away. Mayberry's town, he thought.

He looked back toward the buildings along Front Street, picking out the back wall of Mayberry's saloon that concealed his local supply of poached goods. Rorie wasn't comfortable with Wolf Simpson's new attitude, or with not knowing where Travis Mayberry was.

The future of his mission was about as impenetrable as this morning's fog, he thought. He was on his own, left to wonder about the outcome of Travis Mayberry's solo expedition to his mountain hideout. Rorie had stayed in Fort Yukon with his fellow Fish and Wildlife Service agents only long enough to learn that one of Mayberry's babysitters, Phil Torrance, had been picked up in Anchorage and was singing loud and clear. Since then, nothing. Rorie knew only that he was to stay on top of the search for the missing ivory harvest somewhere along the Chukchi coast. When and if the ivory was found, Rorie was to "act on your own initiative." Whatever that meant.

Don't let it get away, was what it meant. And try to stay healthy until some troops can reach you.

Three thousand miles away, autumn had come to New York that morning with a vengeance. Harry Madrid's finger was hurting. Cold winds blew leaves and paper and trash along Park Avenue as Harry alighted from his Mercedes limousine near the entrance to his showroom. He was carrying a Danish in a brown paper bag from a deli where he had stopped en route. People hurried past him with their eyes averted, shoulders hunched inside their coats. Harry's overcoat, an elegant black cashmere with a matching sable collar, effectively shut out the biting winds. If it hadn't been for the finger, he wouldn't have noticed the cold. His black leather gloves didn't keep the phantom finger from hurting.

He ducked into the entry to his shop. There would be little action today. This wasn't one of those brisk, invigorating fall mornings that invited you to get out; it was a chilly, forbidding day, a good time to stay inside by a fire. Harry was actually surprised to see his manager, Paul Kaminski, talking to someone in the gallery, standing before a display of antique Dresden china. Harry had hired Kaminski away from the Metropolitan, where he had been working as a flunkie cataloging items in dim back rooms. Kaminski was a treasure, Harry said, borrowing a word upscale New Yorkers usually applied to their maids or secretaries. He gave the place some class, and his genuine expertise with fine art objects and collectibles freed Harry for his real work.

The client with Kaminski was slender, well-dressed, black-haired. The glossy black hair was pulled back into a ponytail, Harry noted with disapproval. His back was to Harry, who peeled off his gloves as he walked toward his private offices at the rear of the building. Just before the customer was cut off from view by an intruding display wall, he turned around.

Harry dropped a glove. Reaching for it, he felt as if his stomach were on the cold tile floor with the glove. He covered the trembling of his hands by removing his other glove. The smile on his face as he straightened felt carved in ice. "Mr. Chang! What a pleasant surprise! I wasn't expecting you until the end of the week."

The young Chinese, heir apparent to what Harry thought of as the Chang dynasty, wore a western-cut suit in a dark gray pinstripe, a white silk shirt and floral silk tie. He carried a camel's hair coat draped indolently over one arm. He looked like some Ivy League playboy, Harry thought, come to the Big Apple for a week of slumming.

"It has been a long time, Mr. Madrid. You are looking well." Deng Chang made the compliment sound like an insult—or perhaps it was Harry's visceral resentment that lent hidden nuance to the polite words.

"Yeah, well . . . we didn't exactly meet in the best circumstances."

Chang raised an eyebrow. "I trust that what occurred in the past will not be a hindrance to our working together, Mr. Madrid."

Working together! There it was, right out in the open— Chang had come to stay. Harry hadn't been fooled by Madam Chang's story about having to send her son out of China for a cooling-off period because of an incident involving the police on the mainland. But even if the story were true, there were many places where Deng could have been sent, most of them a great deal closer to the family's seat of power and influence than New York. Why send him into Harry Madrid's territory? Harry didn't think he was there merely to learn the ropes of the operation on this side of the Pacific.

"Hell, no, Chang," Harry said, still smiling. "Hey, we've been doing all right by each other, haven't we? I told Madam Chang I could deliver, and I have. We've both done okay."

"As you say," the Chinese agreed. He glanced around. "Your gallery is most impressive."

"Wait'll you see our real operation. I'll show you around this afternoon. But yeah, this business is making a buck, too. Listen, you see anything you like, let me know. I hope Paul has been able to answer any of your questions."

"He has been most helpful and illuminating."

"That's why he's here," Harry chuckled. "I hired him for his illumination."

Harry took Deng Chang to the Four Seasons for lunch to impress him. The maitre d', who knew Harry, found them a good table in the Grill even though it was packed. Harry pointed out a few of the celebrities in the room. Chang seemed particularly interested in the model Niki Taylor. When Harry said he would see if he could arrange an introduction, Deng's dark eyes for the first time held a hint of respect.

Over English sole with lemon dill, Harry asked casually about the "little problem" in Chingpu that Madam Chang had mentioned. When Harry saw Deng's lips tighten, he was glad he had asked.

"In China I am a wanted man," Deng said, as if this were amusing. "If this were your Wild West, there would be posters with my picture on them."

"Offering a reward?"

"Of course." Deng smiled. "I can assure you, no one will be eager to collect it."

"I can imagine. Madam Chang wouldn't approve."

"My mother does not tolerate betrayal. The man who informed on me has already been found. He has been made a lesson for others to see."

Harry shivered. He didn't really want to know the nature of the informant's punishment. He remembered something Madam Chang had said about a Chinese method of killing by inches.

He cleared his throat. "Wasn't it a bit risky, sending you into the jungle personally?"

"There was risk, of course." Deng was offhand about the danger. "But the prize was worth it."

"How much is one of those big pandas worth alive, anyway . . . like the one you lost?"

Deng's mouth flattened again, and there was a flare of anger in his eyes. Harry decided he had better not push it too far. "In U.S. dollars, more than a hundred thousand," Deng said. "I believe the five-foot tusks of the old walrus, which you have promised to my mother, will bring several times as much. They are even more rare. That is," he added softly, "if they are not lost."

Harry felt an autumnal chill.

When they drove over to New Jersey that afternoon in Harry's limousine, two men accompanied Deng Chang. They were burly men, short but powerfully built, and they sat stiffly on the backward-facing middle seats of the limo, their expressionless faces making Harry Madrid uneasy. They were not as obviously thugs as the men Harry had encountered on the junk in Quanzhou harbor, but there was no doubt about what they were. Deng would meet Harry alone on Park Avenue or dine with him alone at the Four Seasons, but the young Chinese wasn't going to visit Harry's wharfside warehouse without his bodyguards.

Chang didn't trust him. Which was okay, Harry decided. The feeling was mutual.

They spent the whole afternoon at the warehouse. Deng wanted to see everything. He wanted to know how many alligators were killed in a month or a year in Louisiana swamps, who the poachers were, what was the price of a good hide. He was fascinated by Harry's stories of the bayou-raised Cajuns who supplied most of the trade. He shook his head in world-weary resignation over U.S. environmental laws designed to protect everything from bald eagles to species of ducks to small stream wrigglers. He asked seemingly innocent questions about Harry's sources in Africa and South America, as well as markets in Europe. Harry Madrid smiled, answered politely, and seethed.

Harry knew that Deng was trying hard not to act impressed, but he had to be. Hell, Harry's warehouse covered an entire city block, three stories high, every foot of it crammed with animal skins and heads and teeth and bladders and furs.

The Chang family didn't want to admit how well they had done with Harry as their principal American manager and source.

And Deng Chang hadn't been sent to America to cool his heels until after the approaching Chinese take-over of Hong Kong.

The young Chinese dropped his indolent air when they talked about walrus ivory from Alaska. Harry showed Deng the shipping records for the recent large sale to the Japanese buyers, but Deng brushed these aside. "It was I who showed my mother the photograph of the old walrus with the magnificent tusks," he said proudly. "We're delighted that your source in Alaska was able to find this walrus."

"Yeah," Harry said, resenting Deng even more.

"Do you know when these tusks will be arriving from Alaska?"

"I'm waiting to hear from my man. Should be any day now."

"Any day?" Deng prodded. "You are not in close touch with him?"

"Alaska's a big place. Getting around up there isn't like running around Hong Kong in a ricksha."

Deng smiled. "We do not run around in rickshas anymore. My mother prefers the Lexus sedan."

"We also have to slip our goods past the Federal agents who are trying to shut off the ivory trade in Alaska. You should know what that's like, after what happened to you in China. It's not going to do us any good if the government ends up with those tusks."

"That would be most unfortunate," Deng murmured.

It was at that moment that Harry knew he was going to have to go to the mat with the Chang family. It had been a long time coming, and Harry discovered that he wasn't as scared as he thought he would be. Meeting Deng Chang again, not in Quanzhou but in New York and Newark, measuring him face to face, had brought the fear down to human scale. Harry found himself looking at a thin, cocky young man with soft hands and a punk's grin who wouldn't have lasted a week in the old neighborhood. Harry would have dusted him off himself.

Instead of shaking in his boots, Harry was looking forward to going eyeball to eyeball with Madam Lu Chang's heir apparent.

Harry had a score to settle.

Niki Taylor was tied up that evening, Harry told Deng Chang regretfully. But one of the other models who worked for the same agency was free as a bird and delighted to start out an evening at Club 21 with a visiting prince of the powerful Chang family of Hong Kong. Harry's limo was at Deng's disposal.

When Chang returned to his hotel, eager to prepare for his date, Harry tried to raise Travis Mayberry on his private line in the saloon in Nome. Mayberry wasn't there. Harry left a coded message on the answering machine. The buyer from Hong Kong was becoming impatient. When could Harry say the goods would be delivered? A prompt reply setting a firm date was of paramount concern.

Mayberry would read the message between the lines: What the hell is going on? Where are Muugli's tusks?

Wolf Simpson played the message back when he saw the red light blinking on Mayberry's answering machine. He knew what Mayberry would say. Forget about fog. Get off your rear end and get down to that Eskimo village and find that ivory!

Simpson went downstairs to the saloon. It was afternoon in Nome, and he found Jeff Rorie enjoying a beer. Rorie didn't look enthusiastic about having company, but the new, friendlier Wolf Simpson insisted that Rorie let him buy another round. The fog had thinned out and Simpson said they were leaving for the Eskimo village at dawn, weather be damned. Mayberry wouldn't stand for any more dragging their feet.

Rorie didn't comment. He wondered when Mayberry would contact Simpson, surprised that it hadn't happened already.

Over Moosehead beers Simpson was happy to share his plans. Starting early the next morning, he'd have the natives scour the coastline looking for Muugli, he said, while he and Rorie hunted down the fugitive old Eskimo. They'd take the native's kid along. There was a lot of ice around now, Simpson pointed out, that hadn't been there even a few days ago. John Mulak had to have his boat, he wasn't going to get far on foot, and the ice spreading through the wetlands near the coast would limit his options. "It's like when you're hunting a wolf," Simpson said eagerly. "Once you find out where his territory is, you can zero in on him. Then you work him into the open where he doesn't have any place to hide. Then you can chase him down, tire him out, close in on him. He'll snarl and show you his teeth, and if you get close enough you'll see the hate in those bright eyes. But he won't be able to do a damned thing. He can't get at you, and he can't get away. . . ."

Jeff Rorie thought he liked it better when Simpson didn't trust or confide in him.

He declined another beer and stepped outside, glad to be alone. On Front Street he felt the full force of the wind driving inland from the sea. Great black clouds filled the sky. They appeared ominous, but the weather forecast was for brief snow flurries passing through overnight, and clear, cold weather behind them. Good weather for flying, he thought . . . and for hunting.

Mulak had spent the rest of the day in the village, staying indoors much of the time, going out to talk to old friends in the afternoon, welcoming a cousin and his family for dinner, offering no visible sign of his concern, which was chiefly directed toward the white woman who was a watcher of birds and sea animals. She would be at the cave to meet him tonight, and he would not be there.

He waited for darkness. Billy would not expect him to travel over the snowbound tundra at night, especially during a storm. And even if Billy anticipated such a move, Mulak was too old a hand at the hunt to be easily tracked in darkness.

An hour after the last snow machine coughed and sputtered into silence, Mulak slipped from his house by the back door. The black clouds were now directly overhead, and the night was very dark. The wind had quickened, and Mulak could smell the snow that was coming. He thought of it as an old friend. It would hide him in its shroud, and it would fill his footsteps.

Ruth, her protests unavailing, watched anxiously until she could no longer see her father's dark shadow in the lee of the shed. It was as if he had melted into the night.

TWENTY-TWO

THE FOG that lay over the north Alaskan coastline that day had not penetrated to the interior, and even though the sky was overcast Travis Mayberry had been able to take off immediately after breakfast. Visibility was twenty miles or more, and when he reached the vicinity of his mountain cabin the first inkling he had that something was wrong was the absence of smoke.

In the clear Arctic air, even on a cloudy day, the stain of wood smoke spreading against the sky was visible for many miles. Mayberry searched the horizon, his expression part squint, part scowl. He was edgy, some of that tension left over from yesterday's flight from Nome to Clark's Crossing. This morning's run had tightened the strings.

He glimpsed the lake in the distance, picture perfect, white-rimmed with ice and snow like a salted Margarita glass. A ribbon of deep blue ran along the center where the lake had not yet frozen. Mayberry hated his involuntary shiver of relief, recognizing it as a sign of weakness. Since his accident, the exhilaration of flying was gone. No matter that he had flipped out during a landing. The fear stayed with him every moment he was in the air, the knowledge that he was always an instant away from losing control of his fate.

Why was there no smoke? Dammit, Torrance and Paley wouldn't be doing without a fire in freezing weather. What was wrong?

Mayberry had been more annoyed than alarmed when his attempt to raise the cabin by radio before he left Nome had failed. There were any number of reasons why the two men he had left at the hideout might be outside, hunting or fishing or cutting wood. Besides, where could they go?

He could just make out the cabin at the northern rim of the lake. Built of logs, it was camouflaged by the stand of spruce behind it. But even in summer there was almost always a plume of smoke curling above the cabin.

Never had the area appeared so empty, bleak and deserted. Snow covered the lower hills as well as higher peaks, and, below the tree line, mantled the evergreens in white. The shore ice extended outward into the lake, leaving only that blue highway along the centerline. In all that open expanse, nothing moved.

The hideout's isolation was one reason Mayberry had chosen it as a storage site, but there should have been some sign of life. Smoke. Figures appearing on the far shore at the sound of his aircraft approaching. No one in the wilderness ignored the buzz of a small plane passing close by.

He came in low over the lake, the silhouette of his plane with its slender skis a dark shadow skimming over the snow. Before leaving Nome he had called the weather station at Fort Yukon, confirming that the smaller mountain lakes above two thousand feet were already frozen or in the process of freezing solid, and there was a foot of snow across most of the interior, even more in the mountains. He had had his Super Cub fitted with its winter skis before taking off.

He flew over the cabin. Glanced across a wing as he banked, saw tracks in the snow. Human tracks.

Torrance and Paley should have been outside by now. Mayberry's nervousness fueled his speculations. The two men had been attacked by wolves or, more likely, a bear. They were too sick to get up from their cots. They had run out of food and were too weak to respond.

The notion that they might have deserted flicked through his mind. But they knew better than to cross him.

After another pass over the cabin Mayberry decided he saw no sign of immediate danger. And he had to land. He hadn't come all this way, sweating out every mile in the air, to leave without the ivory he had come for.

This was the moment he had come to dread most of all. He felt only light winds buffeting the plane as he lowered the flaps. He had done this a thousand times, on wheels and floats and skis. It was a piece of cake. The yielding resiliency of the

snowpack made setting down on skis easier than touching down
with floats on water or a wheeled landing on macadam—or one
of the bumpy grass meadows that often served as landing strips
in Alaska. He approached tentatively, sweating in spite of the
cold drafts whistling through the cabin. Fought the desperate
urge to haul back on the stick. His hands shook and perspira-
tion dripped into his eyes.

The skis touched. The aircraft floated a little, but somehow
Mayberry willed his hand to remain steady. The skis found snow
again, skipped once, and then he was down. Feathery arcs of
powder snow flew up in his wake. The plane slid effortlessly
across the expanse of white, as sleek as a skate on ice.

Mayberry taxied slowly back along the beach toward the
cabin.

No one came out to greet him.

When he opened the cabin door and stepped out onto the
snow, Mayberry had a Heckler & Koch M91 military assault rifle
in his hands, ready to fire.

Thirty minutes later Mayberry's rage had simmered down
enough for him to assess his situation with some degree of ratio-
nality. Trashing the interior of the cabin had vented his anger,
but it didn't solve anything.

Torrance and Paley had left behind a half bottle of Canadian
whisky. He poured a tumbler half full of whisky and forced himself to examine his situation methodically, a step at a time.

His two babysitters had bailed out on him—men he'd stuck
his neck out for, helping them to evade the government agents
seeking to question them last year. Maybe they had gotten tired
of hiding out. Maybe, staring at all that ivory week after week,
they had become greedy. Maybe they were hungry for city
lights, bars smelling of stale beer, the crash of voices. Maybe
they wanted a woman. Maybe he had left them alone too long.

The reason didn't matter now. It wouldn't buy them clem-
ency when he caught up with them, and it wouldn't alter Mayberry's predicament. The fact was they were gone. And nearly
half of his store of walrus tusks with them.

As soon as he discovered that the cabin was empty—with indications that it had been abandoned for some days, ashes cold in the fireplace and dust and ice beginning to accumulate inside —Mayberry had counted the remaining tusks in the storage room beneath the cabin. There were ninety-three tusks—forty-three pairs and seven assorted individual tusks, the latter taken from walruses with one damaged or broken tusk. Mayberry estimated that he had had nearly twice as many stored at the cabin, which meant that his loyal employees had stolen nearly half the ivory along with some bear skins and other items. He would have to make a complete inventory to discover everything that was missing.

How had they managed it? They had no transportation. They had to walk out of the mountains, probably dragging a sled loaded down with ivory. Mayberry hoped they'd been caught in the last storm, that they had bogged down in the snow and frozen to death. But that wouldn't bring back his ivory.

He would find them eventually. On his mother's grave, he'd find them.

Meanwhile, he would need every remaining tusk to placate Harry Madrid—and that wouldn't be enough. He would have to locate the harvest from the recent hunt. He would have to find where Muugli's body had washed ashore. If he didn't . . . Madrid would likely come visiting.

It took him the best part of an hour to load most of the ivory— forty-three pairs of tusks and three of the best individual tusks— and all of the polar bear skins. He estimated the weight of the load at between seven and eight hundred pounds. The Super Cub sagged where it waited in the snow, sitting on its slender skis.

The small aircraft had a factory-estimated useful load of 750 pounds, including the pilot, any passengers and a full tank of gasoline. There was over half a tank of gas, say about 150 pounds; and Mayberry himself, dressed for the cold, hit a solid two hundred on the scales.

The aircraft was going to be overloaded by at least three hundred pounds. Maybe four hundred. The workhorse Piper Super Cub was famed in the bush for its ability to haul far more than the factory estimate, but a four-hundred-pound overload? On a short field with thirty-foot trees climbing the side of a hill at the end of it, and snow-covered ridges above the treeline?

He would never make it.

Mayberry ground his teeth. Some day, sooner or later, he would be alone with Phil Torrance and Lester Paley . . .

Mayberry retraced his steps to the cabin, replaced the floorboards to conceal the storage area beneath and sat at a wooden table with another tumbler of Canadian whisky, studying the quiver in his hand to see how much liquor he spilled. He thought about getting drunk enough to believe he could make it.

Everyone ripping him off. Torrance. Paley. The Eskimo. That smartass scientist McNeely. Even Harry Madrid, who sold the ivory Mayberry supplied to him for many times over the price he paid. Even the damn Feds, their own pockets well lined, who couldn't stand seeing a man make a buck.

No longer did Mayberry doubt that Eskimos had been involved in the theft of his ivory. John Mulak was surely involved, acting on his own or in league with others unknown. Mayberry might not be able to run Torrance and Paley down quickly, but he could damned well find the natives who had stolen from him.

He thought of the woman camped by the river. He wondered what it was about the scientist that nagged at him. John Mulak's son Billy had led them to that river, a favorite of his father's. It was not far from the site of the walrus hunt, which made it a logical route for the ivory thief or thieves to have taken with his stolen goods. The woman claimed not to have seen anyone. Why would she lie?

A do-gooder, Wolf Simpson had suggested. Mayberry could not see her as someone eager to make a few quick bucks on the side, smuggling some ivory tusks out of Alaska along with her scientific gear. But he could imagine her siding with an old Eskimo who told a plausible story about evil white poachers.

Something about Dr. McNeely hadn't rung true. She had been evasive, trying to hide a hostile reaction that was visible in her cool gaze. Mayberry had sensed it, strongly enough to take the impulsive precaution of disabling her short-wave radio. She had lied about an ASSET rescue team being due that day. A boat wouldn't reach her on the river for days. And without a radio she wouldn't be calling for immediate help.

Simpson and Rorie should be at the Eskimo village by now. Tomorrow they could head for the river and the scientist's camp. Mayberry could also approach that campsite from the interior. Between them they could scout the whole length of the river. If Mayberry's gut instinct was correct, and the woman knew anything about Mulak and the ivory, the tusks had to be hidden close by her camp . . . and the tundra offered few safe hiding places.

Walking distance, he thought. Where she had been before she came strolling back to the camp where they waited? She had been gone overnight. And she hadn't seemed surprised to discover three strange men standing beside her tents.

He should have acted on his instinct then and there. But messing with scientific or environmental groups was a touchy business. Anything happened to a woman like that, alone in the wild, there would be a major flap. But he had been too cautious, he decided. The next time they met he was going to enjoy asking that lady some tough questions. . . .

After a while the smoldering anger drove him to his feet.

The engine was still warm enough to start instantly. Mayberry revved until it ran smoothly, or as smoothly as it ever did. He taxied slowly to the beginning of the natural runway of snow and ice. From this vantage point it appeared long enough, the length of a football field, but Mayberry knew how quickly that distance could be eaten up. He had the heater going, fighting the drafts inside the cabin, but he was sweating again. If he had to leave the relative warmth of the cockpit in a hurry, he knew his sweat would freeze in his beard.

He was forced to abort the first attempt at taking off when he ran out of room. Throttling back, he swung out over the frozen lake and taxied back to the starting point, cursing his enemies in a string that ran from Torrance and Paley to the Fish and Wildlife Service to Marie Lemieux and Alaska itself.

The second time he revved the engine until it was screaming before he released the Cleveland brakes and the small plane lurched across the snow. The white field danced before his vi-

sion. The distant line of trees rushed toward him. He could feel
the overburdened Super Cub straining to gain enough speed
and lift. Another thirty yards flew by under the skis . . . forty
. . . a low snowbank loomed dead ahead. The cacophony of
engine roar and wind and the pounding vibration from the
undercarriage filled his brain, overwhelming thought, drown-
ing his fear. Suddenly, without his conscious effort, the skis
broke free of the snow. He was in the air.

He peered through the windshield, and his heart seized. The
little plane seemed to crawl upward, like a climber clawing at a
wall with his fingernails. Mayberry dug the controls into his
belly. The treeline rushed toward him. The angle of ascent
steepened, but suddenly the trees were there in front of his
eyes, a wall of green.

He felt the shock that jolted through the plane as one of the
skis hit the tip of a spruce. The aircraft wobbled, threatening to
careen out of control, then straightened, took aim at an approaching ridge and began to climb. A tiny bug droning in that
vast wilderness, it cleared the ridge and flew on.

TWENTY-THREE

MOMENTS AFTER the Piper Super Cub cleared the trees at the far end of the lake and swung west, heading for the pass through the mountains, two men stepped out of the woods behind Travis Mayberry's cabin. They walked down to the edge of the frozen lake.

"I didn't think he was going to make it," Bob LoBianco said, sounding disappointed.

"I believe he spit out some pine needles," Everett Sanderson drawled. "He's more overloaded than Santa Claus."

"I'm surprised he risked his neck for a load of ivory. Is it worth dying for?"

"He must be under some heavy-duty pressure to deliver."

"Yeah." LoBianco fidgeted, stamping his feet, more from cold than nervousness. "You see that automatic rifle he was carrying? You think we made a mistake lettin' him go?"

"We can always pick him up," replied Sanderson. "Mayberry's not leaving Alaska."

"But the ivory might."

"It'll be tracked, whether he ships it out of Clark's Crossing or Fairbanks, or takes it back to Nome. And we can identify it now."

Sanderson spoke with satisfaction. He *wanted* the ivory to be shipped out of Alaska. He wanted it to go all the way to Harry Madrid's warehouse in New Jersey. Catching the poachers in Alaska wasn't enough. The Fish and Wildlife Service was now hoping to hook even bigger fish.

The agents had had their first real break on arrival at Fort Yukon in Jeff Rorie's plane with the news that Phil Torrance had been picked up in Anchorage trying to unload a dozen

227

pairs of raw ivory tusks to a dealer in native artifacts. The dealer had been pressured recently by Fish and Wildlife agents to report any unusual trading in walrus ivory.

Torrance had tried to stonewall it. He denied selling ivory at the trading post in Fort Yukon and claimed to have no knowledge of Lester Paley selling ivory there. But agents had quickly discovered an air-freight shipment outbound on Alaska Airlines to an address in Seattle belonging to Torrance's brother. Confronted with the information, the air-freight clerk's identification of his photograph, and eyewitness testimony that he had indeed been with Paley in Fort Yukon, the poacher had decided to make the best deal he could for himself. That meant informing on Travis Mayberry's entire operation. Once he got started, he talked freely, even eagerly. He identified several of Mayberry's clandestine shipping arrangements out of Clark's Crossing, Fairbanks and Nome. And Torrance's specific directions had led Sanderson and LoBianco to the cabin on the lake in rugged mountains north of the Yukon.

The two federal agents had reached the lake three hours ahead of Mayberry in a Fish and Wildlife Service floatplane that had taken off immediately after they stepped onto the ice.

They found Mayberry's hideout unlocked. Torrance and Paley had left in a hurry. According to Torrance, their primary motivation had not been to steal from their employer. The problem was that Paley was going crazy from the isolation of the cabin. With the approach of another winter, he had become increasingly agitated. Finally he told Torrance that he couldn't hack it. He was bailing out. Nothing would dissuade him, and Torrance knew he couldn't face staying in the hideout alone. When they left they had taken the ivory only to provide them with a needed stake. "Once we walked out on Trav," the poacher said, "we had to leave the state. There wasn't no other choice."

According to Phil Torrance's confession he and Paley had hauled out thirty-eight pairs of walrus tusks, all they could manage in two trips overland to the Yukon, where they had hired a boat. The rest of Mayberry's stock they had left behind.

Following the poacher's directions, Sanderson and LoBianco took up the floorboards in the cabin and found a large storage room—effectively, given the underlying permafrost, a cold storage room. The two F&WS agents counted ninety-three tusks remaining. They also found dead eagles, a stuffed polar bear and ten polar bear skins, and a barrel filled with bear claws and assorted teeth. Working quickly, they marked the tusks and the skins with an invisible marker that would show up under infrared light. Then they left everything in the cabin as they had found it and retreated into the woods. They had less than an hour to wait before Mayberry's Piper Cub climbed into view over the hills at the southern end of the lake . . .

Sanderson surveyed the lake, frozen along its edges with a dark blue ribbon at its center where their floatplane had landed earlier that morning. He could see the path Travis Mayberry's skis had left in the snow, starting along the flat beach near the cabin and disappearing down the long length of the lake. The small plane had been overloaded, all right, and for a moment there Sanderson had stopped breathing, fearing that Mayberry wasn't going to make it and the whole operation was going to crash with him.

A deep, cold lake, Sanderson thought. The kind that could hide a lot of secrets.

"Better alert the boys at Clark's Crossing that our man is on the way."

"Yeah, sure." LoBianco didn't argue. When Sandy said let's do something, he usually meant for LoBianco to do it. Sanderson was the weighty member of the team in more ways than one, the thinker and planner. LoBianco, who couldn't sit still for five minutes to watch the SuperBowl game, didn't really mind doing most of the donkey work, even though he groused about it. "I'll get on the horn."

Agents were on standby in Clark's Crossing, Fort Yukon and Fairbanks to monitor any shipments Mayberry made. Everything would be allowed to go through, but it would be tracked every step of the way. Meanwhile, other agents would be dispatched to impound the hideout, remove the illegal goods from the secret storage room and seal the building. Sanderson and LoBianco would be flown toward the coast to provide Jeff Rorie with any needed backup.

Sanderson continued to study the lake. It gave seclusion a

different meaning. The stillness defined it, he thought. Absolute stillness. As if the world had stopped turning and everything was waiting.

Sit outside your cabin here and, nine months out of the year, you'd become a frozen statue.

Running to the store for a six-pack would mean an hour's flight, minimum, in your trusty floatplane. Weather permitting, of course.

You could go crazy, waiting for a twig to snap or a loon to cry.

"I wonder," he murmured.

"What?" LoBianco was back from the cabin, where he had radioed the time and track of Mayberry's Super Cub to agents on alert at Clark's Crossing.

"Those two goons who were staying here," Sanderson said. "You buying Torrance's story about Paley getting cabin fever?"

"Why not?" Lo Bianco paced back and forth, wearing a path in the snow. "Myself, I wouldn't last two weeks here. I don't see how they made it through a whole winter. Must've been goin' nuts. I'm surprised one of them didn't hack the other up with an axe and eat him."

Sanderson listened to the stillness. Felt it all around him. "You're probably right. We're not talking about a couple of Thoreaus here."

"Yeah, right, whatever." LoBianco peered anxiously toward the western horizon. Possibility of a storm moving in overnight, the agent at Clark's Crossing had said. It might affect Mayberry's actions. It might also delay the agency plane getting back up to the lake, a prospect LoBianco did not look upon with any enthusiasm. "You think we'll catch up with Paley?"

"Not anytime soon. My guess is he's already on his way to the Lower Forty-eight, hoping to God he never meets Travis Mayberry again even in his dreams."

"Yeah." LoBianco grinned at the thought.

They were silent for a moment. Sanderson drank in the feel of the wilderness, wondering if he could handle that kind of isolation any better than Mayberry's babysitters. But LoBianco could not remain silent for long. "We're gonna be here the night, I better get a fire going."

"Good idea, Bobby."

"Where do you think Mayberry's going from here? He can't be a happy camper."

"My guess is he'll head straight for the coast, soon as he drops off his cargo. He needs more ivory. It's going to be on Rorie's shift now. I just wish we didn't have to play that scenario out."

"Why not? It's one more nail in Mayberry's coffin. This time he's gonna do some serious time."

"As long as it's not Rorie's coffin," Sanderson said.

A half-hour after leaving the cabin behind, Travis Mayberry cleared the last tier of mountains and came into view of the long Yukon River valley. Clearing the mountains greatly improved the probability of clear radio transmission to the coast, but that wasn't the reason Mayberry had waited. His paranoia about government eavesdropping extended from his office telephones to the radio in his aircraft. Tuning in on airborne transmissions—like listening to cellular phone conversations back in the States—wasn't even illegal.

He raised Jeff Rorie's plane on the third try. By then he was approaching Clark's Crossing. "Where the hell you guys been?" Mayberry demanded.

"We've been grounded." Mayberry recognized Jeff Rorie's voice. "I just happened to come down to check out my plane."

"Damn it, why aren't you at the Eskimo village?"

"It's been foggy, like I said. But it's supposed to clear out tonight and we're taking off at first light. How about you? Where you been? Are you coming back to Nome?"

"Never mind where I've been. I'm coming over your way in the morning. I'll want to keep in touch, so stay tuned."

"What's going down?"

"We're gonna find some ivory." Mayberry's voice was flat, cold. "Get Simpson. I want to talk to him."

While he waited Mayberry came in sight of the tiny cluster of huts and cabins that made up the settlement of Clark's Crossing, a smudge on the white surface of the snowbound plain. The river appeared black against the snow, edged with a silvery crust of ice.

Simpson's voice over the headset caused Mayberry to jerk in his seat. His nerves were frayed, and he faced another tricky landing, this time with the Super Cub handling like an overladen semi. "Trav?"

"You alone?" Mayberry snapped.

"Better believe it." Static crackled over the headset, and Simpson's voice faded a little before coming back. "—like I told you. Our pilot's a plant."

"Don't say too much on this open line. You sure?"

"I'm sure."

Mayberry was silent. He could see tiny figures on the ground now, his arrival a moment of excitement for the isolated river settlement. "We still need him . . . for now. I'll be with you tomorrow, we can handle it then. We need to coordinate."

"Sure, Trav. You want to meet us at—"

"No names, okay? No places, no specifics. You learn anything new from those natives, you let me know. Otherwise, we go back to where we stopped on the river overnight. We'll go from there. You understand?"

"You thinkin' about that woman?"

"This isn't a talk show." Mayberry cut him off. "I said no details. Just be there."

The landing strip at the edge of Clark's Crossing was a field of snow. Mayberry came in wobbly, scared, to a perfect landing, light as a snowflake.

TWENTY-FOUR

THE NEXT morning was another world, clear, bright and cold. Kathy McNeely woke to sunlight pouring in through the entrance to the cave.

Silence clotted her ears. Something unnatural about it struck her. Not even the sound of breathing, or claws clicking on the floor of the cave as her husky dreamed. Kathy's pulse quickened. The clinging webs of sleep obscured the immediate cause of her anxiety.

She rose, shivering, and called out. "Survivor?"

It had snowed during the night, and in the glare of a low-riding sun, white against a brilliant blue sky, the sweep of snow assaulted her eyes. It was as if the entire earth were dressed in a silver-sequined gown. She squinted at the cave mouth, shielding her eyes, trying to remember if she had had sense enough to include her dark glasses in her pack when she abandoned her camp.

She called the husky again. "Survivor?"

It wasn't unusual for the dog to be awake ahead of her, prowling around outside. But this morning was different from others. As soon as she understood why, she turned back into the cave, fighting off a quiver of alarm. She searched the interior quickly. The husky was not there.

And there were no tracks in the fresh fall of snow outside the cave.

Survivor hadn't simply awakened ahead of her and gone outside to lift his leg. Sometime during the night, before it stopped snowing, he had left the vicinity of the cave. He was gone.

* * *

Survivor paused at the edge of a bluff, his flanks heaving. Below him, broken scree formed a ragged slope leading down toward the tundra plain. His mouth was open as he panted, and his tongue flicked ice crystals from his muzzle. His legs quivered from the long run.

A few yards away the female wolf had flopped onto her belly in the snow. She, too, was exhausted, but she watched him with the glitter of excitement still bright in her eyes.

Their romp had begun before dawn.

Survivor had heard the wolf pack prowling close outside the cave during the latter part of the night. Once, a shadow fell directly across the mouth of the cave, and he was instantly on his feet, snarling a warning. The answer, moments later, was a long, soaring howl.

The typical human response to the howl of a wolf in the night is the prickle of gooseflesh and the uneasy shiver. The husky's reaction was to prowl back and forth across the floor of the cave. The howling awakened a song in his blood, ancient and long dormant. He glanced at the woman, who slept undisturbed. The call came again. The ferment it had awakened intensified. It compelled him toward the exit.

He stepped out cautiously onto a narrow shelf, wary and alert. The darkness was not total, and he saw the she-wolf instantly, not twenty feet away. Behind her other shadows writhed, low figures slinking back and forth. Survivor took a few steps toward her, stiff-legged, ears and tail up, hackles rising. The smaller figures—her pups—retreated hastily, scattering across the snow, but the female stood her ground.

Then, as Survivor drew close, she began to squirm, lowering herself closer to the snow, as if to make herself smaller. She began to whine. When the husky stopped a few feet away, she pulled herself closer, front paws scraping the snow. Finally she dropped onto the snow and rolled over, her exposed belly totally vulnerable.

The age-old message meant the same to dog or wolf, and Survivor's spring-loaded muscular tension eased. His muzzle approached the wolf's, tentatively sniffing.

Out of the shadows in a rush, the largest of the pups charged the husky, lips drawn back in an erupting snarl.

Survivor's early upbringing had been that of a contentious trail dog. Fights for position and role were common, and in his early age he had been put in his place many times by older, larger huskies. But he was now full grown, mature and confident. The weeks on the tundra had hardened his muscles, and he was broader-chested, better fed and heavier than the rangy young wolf. With a lightning quick jump he eluded the pup's rush. Spinning instantly as the wolf hurtled past him, its jaws clicking on air, Survivor attacked. The pup was turning, floundering a little in the snow, and the husky was on him before he could brace himself. The weight of his charge bowled the young wolf over. In a flash Survivor was on top of him, pinning the lighter animal to the ground with his weight, his jaws raging at the young wolf's throat.

It had happened too quickly for the other pups to join the fight. And suddenly it was over, the ferocious snarling stilled, the figures of husky and wolf frozen in place.

The husky stepped back, and the young wolf who had tried to claim his place as the alpha male beside his mother slunk away. Survivor watched him closely, but there would be no repeated challenge. And the adult female, the leader of the pack, came squirming toward him again, a whine in her throat.

Their romp began shortly thereafter as the white dawn seeped across the tundra and the neighboring foothills. It was not the female's time for breeding—that would come in early spring—but she was alone except for her pups. Wolves are sociable creatures, and she had somehow fixed upon the husky as a suitable alpha male to run beside her, to hunt and race and rest, and howl against the night. His quick, ferocious quelling of the young male's challenge had settled matters.

She led the way through thinning snow flurries across the plain to the north. Where the river bent away to the southeast, she veered toward the mountains, following an old, invisible trail. Once she spotted a snow rabbit, and Survivor joined the wild pack's pursuit across the snow. It ended when the rabbit dove into a hole and disappeared. For a few minutes the hunters milled around the hole, pawing at the opening in frustra-

tion, but the alpha female quickly tired of the fruitless quest
and set off once more.

Sometimes the pack ran snarling and yipping across fields of
snow in sheer exuberance. Sometimes they stopped to howl in a
chorus that was not mournful but joyous. And at other times
the female led them in a steady, purposeful trot across low
plains and over rounded foothills, gradually climbing toward
higher ground, still treeless but more broken, with steeper
bluffs and gullies and sharp-edged scree. The miles vanished
underfoot, and as the day came bright and clear, and the ice-
mountains reared ahead of them, they had traveled more than
twenty miles north and east of the bear's cave where Kathy
McNeely slept. They came to a rocky outcropping, a cave-like
shelter that the female had chosen as a winter den. She stopped
there, as if this morning's run had had this destination all
along, as if she had brought the husky here for a purpose. This
is where we began, she seemed to say, looking around at her
pack of leg-weary pups lying in heaps in the snow. Here you can
stay with us, and lead us.

After resting awhile, Survivor rose and trotted off. The wolves
did not follow him. A half-hour later he reappeared, carrying
not one but two dead rabbits by the ears. He presented them to
the female wolf. She deferred to him, waiting for him to eat, but
he turned away indifferently. The female ate a little, quickly and
voraciously, before sharing most of the small feast with the hungry pups. Pack wolves generally hunted game larger than themselves, but winter was coming and prey in the vicinity was scarce.

Survivor rested happily, surrounded by the wolf pack in the
bright, cold morning. It was an hour before a vague restlessness
began to disturb him. He gazed back along the flanks of hills
and the irregular carpet of the plain, seeing from this elevated
bluff the twists of the river winding its way westward toward the
sea, and a familiar longing grew within him. The strange, exciting song that had lured him this morning was quiet now. He
was remembering other mornings, other attachments forged
over long months of close companionship.

A distinct sound brought him to his feet, alert. He lifted his
nose to the wind, as if it might confirm what his sharp ears
recorded. Sounds carried great distances in the windy silence of

the wilderness, and this clear crackle of sound had traveled easily across more than the twenty miles Survivor and the wolf pack had run that morning.

When the sound came again, reverberating across the tundra, the husky began to growl. The female wolf heard him, and watched, as if she sensed the conflict within him. Survivor glanced at her, but there was no question in his eyes. After a moment's hesitation he turned away.

He trotted off once more. This time the female was on her feet, watching him go.

TWENTY-FIVE

Jeff Rorie was becoming very tired of his undercover role. Watching Wolf Simpson hustle and bully the Eskimos at the village, and being unable to do anything about it, was bad enough. Seeing young Billy Mulak tiptoeing around, high on cocaine on the morning he was to lead a search for his father, was more than Rorie could watch. He walked out of the village recreation center, where Simpson was pumping Billy and several other natives about John Mulak's whereabouts.

Rorie thought about the information obtained so far. John Mulak had reappeared in the village the night before last and had stayed for over twenty-four hours. Billy and another Eskimo hunter named Kirfak, one of those involved in the ill-fated walrus hunt, had followed the old man from his house the previous morning, thinking that he was leaving the village and might lead them to the ivory cache. "But all he did was pick some berries," Kirfak told Simpson. "Then he come back. I never seen him after that."

Several others had seen Mulak at different times during the day. One of his cousins and his family had visited the old man. One man swore that Mulak had still been present in the village this morning when the poachers' plane flew over the village preparatory to landing. "I saw him look out his front door. I don't know where he could be now. He was here."

It seemed unlikely, but Simpson had gone to Mulak's house. His daughter had been openly defiant. Her father wasn't there, she said. She had no idea where he was, and if she did, she wouldn't tell the gussaks who bought Eskimos' lives with drugs and whiskey.

Simpson had bristled with anger, but Rorie, Billy Mulak and

238

several other natives were listening to the exchange. Rorie
didn't have to speculate overlong about Simpson's reaction under other circumstances. As it was, the poacher eyed Ruth Mulak with an insolent, head-to-foot appraisal that brought a dark
flush to her cheeks. "We'll talk again, you an' me. Count on it,"
he told her.

Rorie hadn't left the recreation center long before Simpson
followed him. He found the pilot in the Cessna's cabin, the
heater turned on. "You got a problem, Rorie?"

"No problem. I'm just the chauffeur, remember? This stuff
you're into, it's not my business."

"You work for Mayberry, you better make it your business."
Simpson's glower shaded into a sneer. "What's the matter, Les
Hargrove didn't tell you what you might be gettin' into?"

"Les didn't say anything about drugs. Or pushing the natives
around."

"What drugs? That stuff is legal tender in these parts. And
there's only one Eskimo we figure to give us a hard time. That
old man ripped off his own people. Who do you think shot all
those walruses to get the ivory we been talkin' about? They
didn't fall over scared. Eskimos shot 'em. And that old man
stole the tusks from his own friends and relatives. That don't
make him no hero to me."

Rorie said nothing for a moment. It wasn't a debate he could
safely get into without revealing too much about himself.
"That's a big country out there, looking for one Eskimo," he
said finally. "What makes you think we have any better chance
of spotting him this time than we did before?"

Simpson's smirk turned sly. "Because I learned something in
there, Rorie, after you went soft on me and walked out. I
learned old John Mulak didn't have his kayak when he came
back to the village this time, he was on foot. So we're not gonna
be searchin' along the whole damned coastline this time. We
know which way he went. We got a trail to follow."

Rorie managed to conceal the thread of tension that ran
through him like a hot wire. "Billy knows where he went?"

"That's right. You can start warmin' up this beat-up old flyer.
And lemme at that radio. I gotta raise Mayberry. He should be
on his way to meet us."

*　　*　　*

From the small shelf before the entrance to the cave, Kathy McNeely surveyed a scene of breathtaking beauty. The dazzle of new-fallen snow was everywhere—drifting on islands of river ice, filling the channels of the wetlands to the southwest, lying in seamless blankets of white over empty miles of the tundra plain, and rising along sweeping slopes toward the hills and mountains—a universal whiteness, pure and unmarked. She remembered something Jean-Jacques Cousteau had written about first stepping onto the untouched ice of Antarctica, the explorer's feeling of guilt and regret that the dirt on the soles of his shoes would despoil the purity of a landscape of snow and ice where no one had stepped before him. This Alaskan morning inspired the same reverential awe.

The air was cold and sparkling, so clear and clean that the view, with no trees or other familiar objects between land and sky to give it scale, seemed to stretch to infinity. The overwhelming sense of limitless space all around her was magnified by Kathy's feeling of being completely alone, without even the company of her husky, Survivor.

And there was no sign whatever of John Mulak.

She searched the surrounding emptiness for some evidence of the dog. She walked along the spine of the ridge above the cave, calling out. "Survivor! Survivor!" The name echoed over the tundra and through the hollows and hills to the north. Silence answered her.

She would have to leave the area of the cave to search. There had to be tracks somewhere, the snow couldn't have covered everything. Retreating into the cave, she stuffed chocolate and biscuits into her pockets, and dug her sunglasses out of her pack. Outside once more, she had momentary misgivings. The sun made the day appear deceptively mild. In fact there was a hard crackle of cold in the air.

She plodded through knee-deep snow along the ridge to reach an accessible trail that offered easier progress down the sloping terrain toward the river. Every few minutes she paused to survey the wilderness. The emptiness was so complete, the stillness so absolute, that her attention strayed. She almost missed the rustle of color and movement in the brush down near the river.

Shielding her eyes with one hand, she searched for a repetition of that fragmentary glimpse out of the corner of her eye. She suspected an illusion born of anxiety, a kind of mirage. Then she saw it again.

A short distance to her right—no more than fifty paces—a long, dense thicket of cranberry bushes sprawled along the river bottom, their branches decorated with sleeves of snow. Suddenly small clouds of snow erupted from the brush, flying in every direction with furious energy. Something silvery gray moved in the tangle of bushes. Survivor? A wolf? She had the sense of a creature larger than either the husky or a wolf. What—?

The bulky shape reared up, taller than a man. "My God!" she whispered aloud.

A huge male grizzly swung his massive head around slowly, as if sensing another presence.

Airborne, Billy Mulak sat in the back seat behind Rorie, looking as if he was already coming down from his temporary high. Rorie didn't have to guess what Simpson had given Billy to start off his day. A small sample of coke would explain the young Eskimo's jittery high and his quick comedown with its inevitable slide into depression.

Simpson was in the front passenger seat, and Rorie felt that he couldn't look at the poacher without his contempt showing. He was also less than happy about the Remington 30.06 rifle Simpson had propped beside him. Rorie's rifle was in a rack in the rear of the cabin, out of reach. His government-issue Smith & Wesson .38 automatic was taped to the underside of his seat, but he hoped he wouldn't have to dig it out in a hurry.

"Where to?" he asked once they were in the air.

"You tell him, Billy boy."

Speaking in a jerky monotone, Billy directed the plane inland over some low hills. A shallow pass led between the hills out onto the tundra plain, here threaded with a network of waterways hidden under the snow—most of them frozen solid. Less than ten minutes from the village Billy pointed at a larger stream, through which a gray ribbon of water was visible, and a fingernail-shaped gravel beach.

Billy pointed at the beach. "That's where he leaves his boat when he comes this way."

"Why'd he come this way this time?" Simpson demanded.

"So no one at the village would see him come and go," Rorie interrupted, thinking it was a stupid question. "Like going out the back door when the husband's comin' in the front."

The stream was perhaps twenty yards across, smaller than the river to the north Rorie had followed the other day to the scientist's camp. Shore ice shrank the passage to only a few yards of open water. Dangerous for a kayak, though wide enough for a skilled boatsman like Mulak to squeeze through if the ice didn't suddenly close the door.

"Where does this river go?" Simpson pressed the young Eskimo.

"There's a fork not far from here where the big river meets this one. Our people go there to fish for salmon in the spring. My father knows it very well."

"There's a camp?" Simpson leaned close in his eagerness. Rorie wondered if he ever brushed his teeth. "Could he be hiding there?"

Billy shook his head. "There might be a few fish racks, and a dump, and some wood the people use to make temporary shelters. But no place for him to stay . . . or to hide the ivory."

"How far is this fork from that camp where we stopped overnight?"

"I'm not sure. It's different in a plane. It is many miles in a boat, but . . . not so many flying like this."

Simpson studied the empty white plain that passed slowly beneath them, like a panoramic shot in a film. If they spotted the old man now, he was thinking, there'd be no place for him to hide. The thought shot a jolt of adrenalin into his bloodstream. "We get to that fork, we'll swing back toward the coast."

"Maybe he went further inland," Rorie suggested.

"He's goin' for the ivory. And he wouldn't have ferried that much ivory so far up the river. He didn't have time. Besides,

Mayberry's flyin' in that way. No matter which way the old man went, we'll have him in a bind."

Rorie reluctantly accepted Simpson's logic. Ahead of them, as clearly defined as a wishbone, the fork appeared, framed by gravel bars. Rorie saw what appeared to be a crude fisherman's lean-to collapsed in upon itself, and several typical Eskimo fish-drying racks erected on a wide bar in the point of the V where the two streams came together. He circled over the area briefly before turning the Cessna's nose toward the distant coastline. The horizon was now defined by a low bank of clouds. Fog, he thought. Over the inland tundra plain the day remained sunny and bright, the sky almost cloudless.

He could feel Wolf Simpson's excitement, and it brought a rising tension into the small cabin. "We're getting close, Rorie. You know what I told you about a wolf on the run? I can feel him down there. And this time he's mine!"

TWENTY-SIX

STANDING ERECT and looking around, the grizzly seemed almost human. Kathy estimated him to be at least eight feet tall, and the sight of him took her breath away. "The grizzlies of the Brooks Range aren't as large as some members of the species." Words from one of the wildlife specialists who had briefed the ASSET scientists before they went out into the wilderness. "Those in the forests and mountains inland will run five or six hundred pounds. In the coastal area where food is plentiful, they weigh more like a thousand pounds . . . and some North American grizzles weigh up to a ton."

Kathy's heart raced. The grizzly's gaze passed over her. She couldn't move. Random details from the cautionary briefing tumbled through her mind. This was grizzly country, and you didn't fool with them. You tried not to encounter one directly or at close quarters. If you did, there was one cardinal rule: don't run. Running simply brought you to the bear's attention and stamped you as prey. Grizzlies had poor vision, she remembered. Could he see her at all at the distance of a quarter mile? Or was she only an inconsequential blur as long as she didn't move?

Grizzlies made up for poor eyesight with sharp hearing and a keen sense of smell. But she was downwind of him, and he had not caught her scent.

Survivor! Where had he gone? The huge bear with his six-inch claws would make short work of any dog. But the scene Kathy overlooked was serene, unmarked by any sign of violence.

What had brought the bear to this section of the river bottom? Grizzlies covered a wide-ranging territory, she recalled, up to a hundred miles. More to the point was the presence of the cave. *It is a bear's cave,* John Mulak had said. With the premature arrival of winter weather, had the grizzly returned early to the vicinity of his cave? If he saw her near it, there would be no question of whether or not he would attack. Her presence would be an immediate challenge.

She had to get away from the cave. The bear was drifting up the slope, once more busily attacking the cranberry bushes, sometimes pulling up whole bushes in his search for the coveted frozen berries. He might browse there among the berries for the whole day, Kathy realized, clearing out the entire thicket, which measured about fifty yards long and at least twenty yards wide. At this time of year he would already have begun storing up reserves of food for his approaching hibernation.

She began a cautious retreat. Distancing herself from the cave without attracting the bear's attention meant traveling east, away from the coast. Instinct told her also to withdraw upslope. The ridge that formed a brow over the cave's entrance would soon shield her from the grizzly's view.

The bear reared up again on his hind legs, and Kathy stopped to stare down the white slope at him. She was filled with admiration. He was a king. This was his territory, and she was the intruder. Struck by his size and power, she felt puny and defenseless, unable to shake the fearful wonder the grizzly demanded even at this distance.

Suddenly she realized that, pausing on the line of the ridge, she was silhouetted against the skyline. The bear had seen her!

He didn't hesitate. He broke out of the patch of scraggly brush and lumbered up the slope toward her, gathering speed. A grizzly could outrun a horse, reaching speeds up to forty miles an hour. Surely not that fast in the snow, she tried to reassure herself, stumbling back from the ridgeline. But the snow, which seriously hampered her every step, seemed no impediment to the bear at all. He ploughed up the slope like a runaway bulldozer.

The explosion of a shout startled her. It also stopped the grizzly in his tracks.

"Halloo! Mr. Bear!"

The direction as well as distance of sounds were deceptive

across the tundra, and it was a moment before she located the source of the cry. A stocky figure, face concealed by the hood of a fur-lined parka, stood near the riverbank in plain view. Recognition cut through Kathy's fear. The small figure began to flap his arms and shout. "Here, Mr. Bear! I am here! Mulak the bear hunter!"

Kathy McNeely was astonished as much by the quirky humor in John Mulak's cries as by his unexpected attempt to divert the bear's attention from her. The huge grizzly stood irresolute for a moment, his head swinging back and forth. But Kathy remained downwind. Her human scent was carried away from him, and he could see her only vaguely. The Eskimo, on the other hand, was a noisy, challenging presence. He was also upwind, and the grizzly could not only smell him but could also see his dancing figure with its flapping arms and hear the taunting shouts.

The bear's regal arrogance was decisive. He started down the slope, slowly at first, then quickly gathering speed. He charged straight toward the man on the riverbank, not swerving for brush or snowbank or mound.

Kathy couldn't tear her gaze away. My God, why was Mulak standing his ground? Why did he continue to shout and wave? Why didn't he run?

The gap between the charging bear and the Eskimo shrank swiftly while Kathy watched. Then something in Mulak's shouts caught her attention. They were not random cries or noises—he was yelling at *her!* "Bird watcher! Go now—hurry!"

The words shattered her trance. She floundered up the slope from the ridge, putting more distance between herself and the grizzly. Mulak seemed to know what he was doing, there was obvious purpose in his madness. He meant to save her, but what of himself?

Climbing out of a hollow into full view of the river below, she glanced down, anxiety a tightening band of pressure around her chest. The grizzly was almost on top of Mulak—he had waited too long! But the Eskimo scrambled behind some brush at the edge of the riverbank, and for the first time she saw the dark spearhead of his kayak slide into view. Mulak was in the boat, his arms paddling furiously. Floating ice crashed against one side of the kayak, turning it sideways to the shoreline just as the grizzly reached the riverbank.

A roar of frustration thundered up the slope and reverberated over the tundra. The grizzly waded into shallow water, breaking through the shore ice in pursuit of the kayak. But Mulak was into the main stream of the current now, and as the bear's paw slapped water at its stern the narrow boat shot clear and sped away.

Kathy began to breathe again.

And in that moment she heard another sound that made her throat catch: the drone of a small aircraft swiftly drawing near. A rescue flight? Her leap of hope was instantly sobered by a darker possibility, far more likely than an ASSET rescue.

Had the poachers returned to hunt for her and Mulak?

The answer came almost immediately. She recognized, darting low above the river, the familiar silhouette of the poachers' plane.

As the minutes had ticked by, flying above the river, Jeff Rorie had grown more hopeful. The farther they went without spotting the old Eskimo in his kayak, he felt, the less chance there was. Wolf Simpson's hunter's instinct was scary, but it could just as easily be wishful thinking.

"Not so fast, Rorie," Simpson said. "Slow it down. We could miss something. And take us lower so I can see what's down there. Like to a hundred feet."

"That's too low," Rorie objected. "I'm not playing games with this beat-up old flyer, as you call it. It's my living."

"Don't give me that bull," Wolf Simpson said. "You can hedgehop this crate close enough to shed leaves. I've seen dozens of pilots in the bush like you. Take it down."

It was an order. Rorie dropped to an altitude of a hundred feet, throttling back to a speed of seventy mph. The little plane seemed to crawl over the limitless white landscape. At the poacher's direction, Rorie followed the twisting course of the river. Forward visibility at ground level was not one of the

Cessna's virtues, and Rorie banked frequently to give Simpson a better view out the side windows.

They had been flying seaward for about twenty minutes when Simpson suddenly exclaimed, "Will you look at that bastard!"

Tilting on a wing, Rorie saw a patch of silvery brown in the river near the bank. A thousand-pound grizzly, alarmed by the noisy aircraft passing so low above him, floundered out of the water and ran with surprising speed away from the river. As if in reflex, Wolf Simpson's rifle appeared in his hands. "Take us back!" he ordered as he peered down. "Take us back!"

"That's not what we're here for."

"I don't give a damn. I want a shot at that big son of a bitch."

"Then you can do it in your own damned plane," Rorie said, "not in mine."

All the hostility that had lately been missing blazed in Simpson's eyes. His hand went to his side and reappeared with a gun. There was no room within the narrow confines of the cabin for his rifle, but the short-barreled Walther PPK .380 automatic he thrust toward Rorie's belly was, at this point-blank range, just as lethal. Brandishing a gun in a noisy, bumpy, small aircraft was stupid, Rorie thought angrily. Pointing it at the pilot was insane. Simpson's readiness to do it, and the vindictiveness in his expression, confirmed Rorie's suspicion that Simpson's attitude toward him hadn't really changed, that he had simply been hiding his hostility. The poacher knew something about him, or thought he did. What had he learned in Anchorage, or in Fortune if he was persistent enough to go that far?

Rorie concentrated on flying. He could feel Simpson's hard stare as the poacher debated with himself how far to push the confrontation. While he hesitated, the distance between the Cessna and the bear swiftly lengthened. Feeling the ache of taut neck muscles, Rorie let himself relax a little.

Then Billy Mulak broke the tenuous truce. "There he is! That's Pop! There—on the river!"

In an instant the grizzly was forgotten. Wolf Simpson pressed his face close to the side window, a vicious grin distorting his mouth. "Where? I don't—yeah, I see him! For God's sake, Rorie, stay with him! Don't lose him now!"

*   *   *

Mayberry had left Clark's Crossing at dawn. His hastily made arrangements for shipping the ivory recovered from the hideout were in place. Two boxes would go out parcel post on the next mail pickup. A larger consignment would be sent upriver by boat to Fort Yukon, and from there on a short flight to Fairbanks, where it would be loaded as air freight bound for the Lower 48.

He had stopped at Bettles to refuel when he received Simpson's message that he had discovered John Mulak's route on leaving the Eskimo village. Simpson sounded eager, excited.

The pieces were falling in place. Mayberry had the feeling that this day would bring him a break. God knew, he was due for one. Finding Muugli's tusks would do it, he thought, feeling the frustration. But even without them, the rest of the missing harvest from that single aborted hunt would bail him out as far as Harry Madrid was concerned.

And he was closing in. He could sense it. Simpson was hot on Mulak's trail . . .

An hour later Mayberry was feeling less confident. He had crossed a half-dozen similar ranges of hills and mountains, all of them dwarfed by the bulk of the Brooks Range to the north, and he had traced the passage of a score of rivers threading across the tundra toward the distant coast. He had expected no trouble finding the river where he was to meet Rorie and Simpson, but he had approached the river earlier from its mouth where it flowed into the Chukchi Sea. Now he was coming from the interior, and all of the rivers and mountains looked the same.

He abandoned one stream after following it for nearly half an hour and could feel a nibble of panic. It was easy to become lost in this wilderness north of the Arctic Circle. He wouldn't be the first pilot who disappeared. . . .

"We got him, Trav! We got him!"

Simpson's raucous shot made Mayberry's heart race as he thumbed the speaker switch on the stick. "Mulak? You're sure?"

"It's him, all right. We overshot him, lost him again, but we know he's down there now, and he can't hide for long. Where the hell are you, Trav?"

"I don't . . . wait a minute! I think I see something ahead. It's a big fork in the river. I think there's some fish racks and some old shacks down there—"

"That's it!" Simpson yelled. "You're just east of us. Haul your ashes and you can still get in on the fun!"

"I'll be there!"

The confidence was back. By God, this *was* going to be his day!

TWENTY-SEVEN

Retreating up the snow-covered slope away from the river, the grizzly and the shocking arrival of the poachers' plane, Kathy McNeely quickly lost sight of both the bear and John Mulak's kayak. Soon even the river was cut off from her view, and the rasp of the aircraft engine faded away. Through heavy snow that dragged at her knees and thighs, she fled eastward, away from the cave and its treasure of ivory into the emptiness of the Alpine tundra.

The land itself began to control her steps. A broad, flat slope ended abruptly at the rim of a ravine. She had to climb above it to another higher ridge. Cut off from the familiar river valley, she realized that she could easily become lost. Orienting herself by the white sun, she plodded on until she came upon another animal trail that dipped away from the ridge and created a twisting path that angled south. The snow here was not as deep. A few minutes later, her frosted breath wheezing from her chest and her legs quivering from the strain, she emerged between two mounds and saw the river directly below.

She stopped, shaking with exhaustion. How far had she come from the cave? Half a mile? A mile? Given the twists and turns of her panicky flight, she had no way of judging.

No sign of Mulak and his boat on the river. She could hear the buzz of the aircraft in the distance, no louder than a fly in a quiet room.

No sign of the grizzly.

Then, thin and sharp like a dry branch snapping, an alien sound racketed across the white wilderness: the unmistakable crack of a rifle shot.

* * *

The Cessna quickly overshot the slower moving kayak, and Rorie swung into a steep turn. As he leveled out he throttled back close to a stall. He glimpsed the long, narrow skin boat shooting a strip of white water. A face turned upward, hidden in the folds of a fur-lined hood. Torn between his sympathies and the constraints of his secret role, Rorie brought the Cessna around behind the kayak. He flew back and forth, a maneuver designed both to harry the man in the boat and to stay behind him.

But a low bluff worked against the strategy. It forced a sharp bend in the river and caused Rorie to climb quickly to three-hundred-feet. He swung left to intersect the river again, and Simpson began to swear. "Where'd the son of a bitch go? God-damn it, Rorie, I told you not to lose him again."

Rorie turned back, flying just south of the river and peering down. He glanced back at Billy Mulak—silent since spotting his father on the river—trembling in the seat behind him, his eyes wide with fear. Or was it only the drugs? Rorie wondered bitterly.

Rorie was the first to spot the kayak again, no longer in the river but paddling along a narrow creek that dipped southward, where the tundra was laced with innumerable creeks and smaller streams. Rorie said nothing. Maybe Simpson wouldn't see it. The Eskimo in the boat was in trouble, slowed by his struggle to break through surface ice.

Then Simpson spotted Mulak. "There he is!"

Simpson kicked the right side-door open. Icy air howled through the cabin. The wing struts prevented the door from opening a full ninety degrees, offering Simpson only a limited sightline toward the side and rear. He shoved the automatic pistol under his waistband and grabbed the Remington rifle. He propped the door open and braced himself at the opening, half sitting and half kneeling, the rifle in his hands.

"Are you crazy?" Rorie shouted over the screaming of the wind. "You'll get us all killed!"

"You just fly the damned plane! Gimme a line-of-fire—get out in front of him. He's not going far with all this ice."

"You can't shoot him—you'll never find the ivory!"

"I can wing him! He's not getting away this time."

Billy was shaking, his brown face sickly pale. He stared help-lessly at Wolf Simpson as the poacher took aim at the old man in the kayak.

"Even if you only wing him, he could die out here," Rorie shouted. "You can't risk it!"

He reached for the panel-mounted microphone, flipped the speaker switch. Before he could speak, Simpson swung the butt of his rifle, two-handed, smashing it into the black box. Plastic splintered and sparks sizzled.

Rorie stared at the radio, momentarily stunned. "Mayberry will skin you alive."

"To hell with Mayberry!"

There was a glitter in Simpson's eyes that didn't answer to reason, and Rorie realized that the poacher was so caught up in the excitement of the moment that he was beyond caring about the consequences of his actions.

Rorie's grip tightened on the stick in front of him. His hand moved an instant before Simpson's fired. The slam of the rifle bucked through the small cabin and sluiced away on the wind.

A burst of static on his headset was so loud that Mayberry jerked the set free. Suddenly it went silent.

He thumbed the speaker button. "Simpson? Rorie? What's going on?"

Silence. In the normal tumult of noise inside the Piper Cub's cockpit, the abrupt radio silence seemed ominous. He peered ahead through the windshield. The Cessna had to be nearby.

A thermal lifted the small plane, and Mayberry rode it up-ward over a ridge overlooking the river valley. The area was beginning to look familiar. That scientist's camp was—

A moving speck caught his eye. He dipped lower as he shot over the area. The speck took human shape. Laboring through deep snow. A face turned upward. A hand waving at him as he flew overhead.

He'd guessed right all along! It was the woman from the camp . . . and to Mayberry that meant only one thing. Let

Simpson take care of the old Eskimo . . . *she* would lead him
to the ivory!

The shock of the distant gunshot pulsed through Kathy Mc-
Neely's mind. She wouldn't believe that John Mulak had fired
on the grizzly, not after she had seen the old Eskimo make his
escape on the river. It seemed incredible that the poachers
would shoot Mulak, their only link to the missing ivory. Could
there be sportsmen hunters in the area? For one moment the
possibility buoyed her spirits. She was alone on foot in the wilderness with little food and minimal survival skills. Hunters
might have a working radio. They would also provide a buffer
between her and John Mulak and the poachers.

The sound of a second shot extinguished the flicker of hope.
If the Eskimo was under fire, she had to do something . . .
surely a witness would make the poachers hesitate. She had to
find a way to get back to Mulak without crossing paths with the
grizzly. The Eskimo had been carried downriver while her flight
took her in the opposite direction. She faced the daunting prospect of another long hike across the snow-covered tundra on
feet that already felt like lumps of ice.

The growl of a small plane came again, closer. Puzzled, Kathy
squinted skyward. Her eyes raw from snow glare, she had trouble seeing. Then the aircraft slipped out of the sun's white or-
bit. Relief left her slightly giddy, her weary legs quivering. This
was not the poachers' plane! Its landing gear were skis, not the
small floats on the poachers' Cessna. And this plane, although
not new, was smaller, less grungy, the red of its fuselage freshly
painted, everything about it bright and polished. It reminded
her of one of those vintage old cars that collectors kept undercover, chromed and lovingly maintained.

As the plane passed overhead, Kathy waved frantically, but
the aircraft continued on its way. She began to run, shouting.
The small craft passed over the long meadow she had crossed.
Just when she became convinced the pilot had failed to see her,
the plane began a wide circle, turning back.

Elated, certain that the plane had come from the ASSET
group's base camp to search for her, Kathy plodded up an in-

cline. She reached the lower side of the snow-covered meadow as the plane began its descent at the far end of the level shelf. Her fatigue now forgotten, she hurried across the snow, still concerned not only for John Mulak but also for the missing Survivor. But an ASSET rescue plane changed everything. Its presence meant the poachers would have to pull back from any open attack against the Eskimo. And the plane made an air search for the husky possible. She wouldn't let herself believe the worst until she was forced to.

The aircraft's landing was anything but smooth. It touched down, lifted into the air and settled down again. Crow-hopping a third time, it wavered erratically before the skis finally gripped the snow and the aircraft steadied.

It taxied toward her across the open expanse of snow. As she ran forward she could see a goggled face behind the windshield, one face only, which surprised her a little. But the aircraft's cabin was small, and her ASSET colleagues would have expected Survivor to be with her.

The little plane taxied within twenty feet of her before it stopped, the propellor wash creating a small blizzard of snow behind it. After a moment the cabin door opened. Kathy started forward, grinning through cracked lips, thinking what a wreck she must appear. Then something about the man stepping from the aircraft stopped her.

She stared at the pilot as he clambered down. Not a stranger. She recognized a familiar bulk in the heavyset body, an aggressive forward thrust of his head on his thick neck, as if he were trying to get a better look at her. She knew who it was even before he pushed up the big sun goggles and the brown eyes stared at her, cold above a disarming grin.

Even before she saw the weapon in his hands.

She began to run back the way she had come. The snow dragged at her legs, and before she had covered twenty yards she heard the airplane taxiing after her, growling closer and closer. It cut in front her, blocking the way, and swung around. She ran back, the aircraft dogging her tracks. She couldn't reach uneven terrain where it would be unable to follow, but she refused to give up.

The aircraft drew alongside her and pulled slightly ahead.

Once more it stopped. The door popped open. Kathy veered away, stumbling in the knee-deep snow. The hard slam of a single gunshot was so shocking that it dropped her to her knees.

Travis Mayberry climbed down from the Piper Super Cub and started toward her. Kathy stared at the ugly assault rifle in the poacher's hands. "That's what they call a shot across the bow, Dr. McNeely," he said, his tone almost genial. "Give it up, doctor . . . you've got no place to run. I've been lookin' forward to meeting you again. I think you have somethin' that belongs to me."

TWENTY-EIGHT

"SLOW *down,*" Wolf Simpson yelled at Jeff Rorie. "He's gettin' away again!"

"It's not a damned helicopter!" the pilot yelled back.

Rorie already had the Cessna under partial power and full flaps, holding the aircraft above a stall at about 45 knots. A hundred feet below, the kayak veered suddenly, and the Cessna roared on by. The maneuver had become part of a pattern. Constantly breaking through the thin surface ice, John Mulak had sent his narrow boat skimming along branch channels that twisted this way and that, his abrupt changes of direction too quick for the Cessna to follow without overshooting him. The Eskimo was like a rabbit eluding a pursuing dog. The dog was faster on the straightaway, but it couldn't make a ninety-degree turn like the rabbit.

And Jeff Rorie, walking a tightrope to avoid giving his own game away, was doing his best, with small nudges and twitches of stick and flaps, to prevent Simpson from getting a direct shot at his prey.

For Wolf Simpson this kind of pursuit—like the wolf hunts that had given him his nickname—was the ultimate high. Such hunts were usually carried out in a helicopter, but the added difficulty of pursuit in a conventional small aircraft added zest to the game. Some others might see nothing either sportsman-like or humane about shooting an animal, using a high-powered rifle, from the safety and comfort of a hovering helicopter. Simpson loved the prey's ultimate helplessness. He had been delighted with the latest subterfuge adopted by the state to get around the usual indignant protests and their corollary threat to Alaska's tourism. It required that the wolves could not be shot within one hundred yards of the hunter's aircraft after

257

landing. Of course, there was no way to prove when a wolf was actually shot, or whether the hunter had killed from the air or after landing. The carcass didn't talk.

Simpson kept up a fevered commentary. "There he goes . . . after him, Rorie . . . left, left! . . . son of a bitch, he broke loose again! . . . dammit, Rorie, what's wrong with you? Where's he goin' now . . . he's looping back . . . slow down, slow *down* . . . come in on his left . . . good, good, get on top of him, he's not gonna get out of that creek easy . . . come on, baby, give me one clean shot, that's all I ask, just one clean shot . . ."

Even before accepting his undercover assignment Rorie had thought about the kind of dilemma he faced now. His pontificating superior Ron Haller had once compared the undercover agent's moral predicament to Winston Churchill's agonizing wartime decision to remain silent about an impending air raid on the English town of Coventry to avoid betraying the fact that the Allies had broken the top-secret German radio code. What Rorie confronted was not such a monumental choice. It didn't embrace the fate of nations or of hundreds of innocent people. But it did involve one Eskimo's life. Rorie wasn't sure John Mulak had taken Mayberry's ivory, or if he had, what his motive was. But he knew he couldn't let Simpson shoot him in cold blood. He kept hoping that the poacher would cool off enough to make him see a little reason. They needed to question Mulak, he kept insisting, not fish his body out of a frozen creek. Simpson ignored him—and Rorie knew he was running out of time and options. He had overshot the kayak—or allowed the Cessna to bounce and rock in imaginary turbulence—too many times.

"Now!" Simpson gloated. "You thievin' old man—gotcha!"

Rorie had nudged the Cessna to the right, spoiling Simpson's angle of fire once more, but unexpectedly the kayak had changed course at the same instant and in the same direction Rorie took. Suddenly Mulak was in Simpson's sights.

Rorie flattened the manual flaps. The aircraft's nose lifted a moment before Simpson fired.

The poacher spun around. "You bastard! You think I'm not on to you? You did that on purpose."

"I don't know what you're talking about. This isn't a Coney Island shooting gallery."

"What is it, Rorie? Save-the-Eskimos-Week?"

"You think you can do better, you take the stick."

"Maybe I will. Take us down."

"Don't be stupid. There's no safe place to land down there. Look for yourself."

"You can find a place. You're good, Rorie. Ain't that why they picked you?"

"Who? What are you talking about?"

"The Feds, who else? The same ones who put the arm on Les Hargrove to get him to disappear."

"You're hallucinating, Simpson." Rorie wondered how much the poacher really knew and how much was a bluff. He could feel himself beginning to sweat in the cold cabin.

"Take us down."

"No," Rorie said, his voice tight. "You want to kill all of us, go ahead. Pull that trigger."

"He . . . he's stuck!" Billy Mulak's anguished cry broke through the deadlock between Rorie and Simpson. Both men followed Billy's bug-eyed gaze toward the ground. The kayak was hung up, wedged in the grip of thick ice. The old Eskimo in the boat battered at the ice with a paddle. He peered upward. Rorie thought of one of Simpson's exhausted, helpless wolves at the end of his desperate run.

"Take us down!" Simpson raged. "Close to him! You hear me, Rorie?"

"I heard you, and you can go to hell."

Simpson swung the muzzle of the rifle in a vicious arc—not toward Rorie but at the young Eskimo in the back seat. In the tight limits of the cabin the muzzle stopped inches from Billy Mulak's chest. "He goes first. We're not on the way down in three seconds, you're gonna have a messy cabin to clean up. Do it, Rorie—now!"

Kathy McNeely stared at the weapon in Travis Mayberry's hands. Her ears were still clogged from the harsh slam of the shot—across her bow, as Mayberry had sardonically put it. "Are you out of your mind?'' She looked at him in disbelief. "You can't go around shooting at people—''

"You gave me no choice, doctor. You have some ivory that belongs to me, or at least you know something about it. You know where it is—''

"I don't know what you're talking about.''

"I think you do. If I had any doubt, you took care of that when you tried to run away. What reason did I give you to run? It won't wash, doc. You know about the ivory. You know about me.''

She met his gaze. "I know *nothing* about your ivory.''

"I don't believe you, doctor.'' Travis Mayberry seemed faintly amused by her defiance. "Isn't there anything in your code of ethics about lying?''

"There's a great deal about viciously exploiting animals. You're a poacher. You might as well know I won't do anything to help you . . . and I don't believe you're prepared to shoot me and face the consequences.''

"I wouldn't be so sure about consequences,'' Mayberry said mildly. "We're a long way from civilization. Someone would have to find you first.''

She stared at him in silence, sobered by the cold indifference in his quiet words—and by the realization that he was right—there was hardly any risk for him at all. He could do anything he wanted . . .

"You must think me some kind of monster, Dr. McNeely. Who put such ideas into your head? That old Eskimo? A thief hardly makes a good witness.''

She refused to rise to the bait. No way that he could know about her and John Mulak. She wasn't going to give away information that easily. "That gun you're carrying gives me a clue,'' she said. "It's what they call an assault rifle, isn't it? An AK-47? Hardly the kind of weapon a legitimate sportsman carries in the wilderness. What do you propose to do with it, Mr. Mayberry—slaughter more walruses?''

He smiled. "I can see I'd better not get into a debate with you, doctor. But this weapon has an unfair reputation, thanks to the anti-gun hysteria back in your Lower 48. On semiautomatic, the way I have it set right now, it fires only one bullet for each squeeze of the trigger, no different from a dozen semiautomatic hunting rifles no one tries to outlaw. It's not an AK-47, by the way, it's a Heckler and Koch M91, a much superior gun.''

"It must make you proud."

"Let's say appreciative of a fine piece of equipment."

"For slaughtering helpless animals?"

Mayberry's good humor vanished. He was tired of the argument. "I'm a businessman, doctor. I buy and sell ivory, among other things. Don't try to make it into something else." Adjusting his sun goggles, he turned to peer off across the tundra. "I think we'll walk. I doubt we'll need the plane right away. I don't want to land on this snow any more often than I have to."

"I won't tell you—"

"You don't have to tell me anything. We'll just follow your tracks . . . it can't be too far." Kathy wasn't quick enough to conceal her dismay at that, and Mayberry smiled. "Once I have the ivory, you'll be free to leave, Dr. McNeely. I really mean you no harm, you know."

"Leaving me free to tell the authorities what I know?"

"It won't matter. The authorities, Fish and Wildlife or whoever, already know I deal in native artifacts, including ivory carvings."

"Dealing in *artifacts?* Is that what you call killing an entire walrus herd? Using your damned automatic rifles?" She was stopped by Mayberry's satisfied grin.

"So, doctor, you *do* know all about the ivory." The poacher clicked his tongue against his teeth, mocking her. "Who can a fellow trust anymore?" He gestured with the M91. "Shall we stop playing games and get started? You never know how long a nice sunny day in Alaska is going to stay nice and sunny."

Dismayed by her compromising outburst, Kathy hesitated. She had little doubt that Mayberry would use force if he found it necessary—or he could decide to abandon her on the tundra and simply follow her trail through the snow to the cave. She saw there was little to be gained by refusal to go with him. If she went along there at least might be—

"There's something you should know," she said suddenly.

Mayberry waited, eyes hidden behind his goggles.

"The ivory is hidden in a cave. A grizzly's cave," she added pointedly. "The bear wasn't there when the ivory was taken to the cave, but he's there now. I saw him this morning." She nodded toward her path in the snow. "That's why I'm out here in the middle of nowhere. I was running from him."

Mayberry seemed to weigh her words, then smiled and shook his head. "That's very good, doctor, off the top of your head. But you can hardly expect me to believe you."

"I'm *not* lying, not this time. Listen to me. Going back there now is dangerous. You didn't see him. He . . . he's huge. And he was angry."

"Well then," Mayberry said, impatience resurfacing, "I'll be glad to have this handy-dandy version of a machine gun, won't I?" He pointed the barrel of the M91 along the tracks leading across the meadow to the west. "After you, doctor. You know the way."

TWENTY-NINE

Rorie's mind raced to keep up with his pounding heart. He tried to guess how crazed Simpson was and whether he would carry out his threat against Billy Mulak. In the fleeting seconds he had, there wasn't enough time to calculate the odds. He simply couldn't take the chance.

He shoved the stick forward, and the Cessna started into a downward glide.

"We go through the ice into the water, in this cold air, we're all going to freeze," he told Simpson.

"Then you better make sure we don't take a dunk."

Rorie couldn't see enough open water to gamble on. He would have to come down on the snowpack. The book distance for landing a Cessna was over five-hundred-feet, but in the real world of the bush this figure was meaningless. Landing on snow with the amphibious floats, with the extra drag from the penetrating wheels, he estimated that he could cut that distance in half. "No guarantees," he muttered.

"What's that?" Simpson barked above the whistling and howling of the wind.

"You better hang on!" Rorie raised his voice so Billy Mulak could also hear him.

He was already flying too low to allow room for much maneuvering. He saw what appeared to be an open stretch of snow-covered tundra—no way of telling what treacherous holes or bogs or creeks might be hidden under the deceptively smooth white surface. The level strip was parallel with the creek where John Mulak was trapped, struggling to reverse course.

No trial run. Rorie felt he couldn't risk Simpson losing it. He would have to take his chances on the ground. Lining up his landing area, he came in nose-high at full flaps and close to a stall at under fifty knots. At the last moment Wolf Simpson put his Remington rifle aside and grabbed his seat with both hands.

Kissing the snow, Rorie dumped his flaps and killed power. He came in for what would have been—on a normal, solid runway—a perfect three-point, full-stall touchdown. Then the edge of the floats dug into the snow a little and he was fighting for control, feeling the pounding from the landing gear slam up into the fuselage as he tapped the brakes, the whole plane shaking and bucking as it skidded over the snow. The level strip before him was no longer two hundred feet or even a hundred, it was shrinking fast, a hump in the tundra dead ahead, streak of water to his left . . . now, now's your only chance, *do* it.

As he braked hard he felt the tail lift and the Cessna teetered on the edge of a ground loop. The air went out of Rorie's lungs as the aircraft skittered once, tilted up, settled back, then came to rest in a pounding silence.

Rorie had hoped for an opening at the moment of shutdown when he could release the controls and lunge for Simpson's rifle, but the poacher was ready for him. He hadn't been bluffing. He *did* know who and what Rorie was. His Walther PPK was back in his hand, pointing at Rorie's chest.

In her flight from the grizzly it had seemed to Kathy as if she were crawling across the tundra. Wading through the fresh snow blanket was like walking in water up to her knees. She had no idea how far she had come before she began to feel safe. Returning now, prodded by Mayberry a few steps behind her, the distance seemed to fly by. Ten minutes after they set out she was recognizing landmarks. She scanned the snowy slope angling down toward the river, searching for the grizzly, the berry patch, John Mulak in his kayak. . . .

The bear's presence would change everything. Once Mayberry actually *saw* him, for all his confidence in his assault rifle he would, she hoped, think twice about approaching the cave. When you met a grizzly up close in the wild, his elemental force could change your perspective in a hurry. Even Mayberry's.

"How much farther?" Mayberry grunted.

His breath made sharp puffs of vapor in the cold air. She wasn't the only one struggling, Kathy thought with satisfaction. She squinted against the snow glare, uncertain. The profile of the ridge slightly below them, perhaps two hundred yards ahead, seemed familiar. She wasn't anxious to reach it. Could she somehow stall? Mayberry would be suspicious of any diversion from her tracks that led straight toward the ridge.

"How far?" he repeated impatiently.

"I'm not sure. I was running scared . . . I don't know."

"Yeah, sure, you were scared."

"I was, Mr. Mayberry."

"Let's not start that again."

"Just pray you don't find out the hard way."

As they drew closer to the ridge, she felt her chest constricting. She had trouble breathing. It was more than simple fatigue or the ice clogging her nostrils, or her reluctance to give Mayberry free access to the treasure in the cave. She was thinking of the grizzly at close quarters, defending his territory.

Thirty paces now. If she was right, the cave was just over that brow of rock. She glanced back over her shoulder, trying to refresh her memory of the terrain. She gasped aloud.

Mayberry jerked around, instinctively raising his rifle. "What—? What the hell—?"

She saw him nervously lift the gun to his shoulder and called out "Don't shoot!"

"What the hell . . . what is it? A wolf?"

"No! It's Survivor—my dog!"

The husky had burst over a rise in the distance. Spotting them immediately, he bounded down a hillside, creating small craters in the snow until he came upon their tracks, which made running easier. He raced toward them.

"He'd better stop or—"

The roar behind them chilled Kathy to the marrow. She knew what it was even before she spun around. She and Mayberry had been distracted by Survivor's sudden appearance out of nowhere. They hadn't seen the grizzly climb onto the ridge above the cave. Not sixty feet away, he rose to his full height, a thousand pounds of massed bone and muscle. Mayberry's jaw literally dropped as the silver-tipped bear roared once more, and charged.

"Nice work, Rorie," Wolf Simpson said. "You're good . . . good enough to keep me alive and get you killed."

"What are you going to do, Simpson—walk out of here? You need me to stay alive."

"Mayberry will find me. And you're a dead man."

Simpson hadn't been paying attention to Billy Mulak. He had written the young Eskimo off as a non-person, someone easily manipulated and controlled . . . Without warning Billy threw himself across the back of the front passenger seat to get at Simpson. The Eskimo was young, wiry and strong. The impact slammed Simpson backward against the frame of the open door. Momentum carried the two men through the opening, Billy awkwardly on top, Simpson sprawled halfway out the door. The gun in the poacher's hand went off outside the cabin, tearing a neat hole in the fabric of the high wing. Billy was screaming incoherently. "—gussak! Pop isn't . . . you never said nothin' about killing him! You can't . . . I won't let you kill him!"

By this time Rorie had dug his Smith and Wesson revolver from its hideout under his seat. He lunged across the cabin, but he moved too fast, and when Simpson kicked out in his struggle to free himself from Billy, his boot accidentally caught Rorie flush in the head. Rorie's nose smeared over his face and blood gushed. He sagged near the small doorway, ears ringing, a red haze filming his eyes.

Simpson and Billy Mulak thrashed around at his feet. Pushed out through the doorway, Billy grabbed a wing strut with one hand. Simpson clubbed at him with the automatic. His finger was still on the trigger, and the Walther fired on impact. The explosion must have deafened Billy and momentarily stunned him. His grip on the strut slackened. Simpson's hard shove sent him tumbling, and Simpson fired again as Billy was falling.

Raging, Rorie dove into Simpson from behind, driving his shoulder into the small of the poacher's back. The tackle carried both men through the doorway and into the air. They landed in the snow, Simpson on top, his weight exploding the breath from Rorie's chest. Rorie fought for air, the cold searing his lungs. He was momentarily helpless, unable to fight back, but Simpson didn't realize it. He had lost the Walther in the fall from the cabin. He looked around, scrabbling at the snow, digging for the gun, and the delay gave Rorie the moment he needed. His right arm was pinned under his body. He still gripped the revolver. He dragged it clear just as Simpson whooped in triumph.

"Now, you fink, report this!"

But his hands, exposed to the cold for only a few seconds, were already clumsy. It was a moment before Simpson's suddenly thick fingers could find the grip and trigger of his automatic. Rorie had time enough to wonder if the snow clogging the muzzle of the Smith and Wesson would cause it to misfire.

He felt the gun kick in his hand, saw the sudden surprise in Simpson's eyes turn to bewilderment and then, like a curtain rising over an unpainted wall, to a gray emptiness.

"You're John Mulak," Rorie said to the gray-haired Eskimo.

"Yes . . . I remember you. You are a very good pilot."

"Not as good as you are with a boat."

"You were at the village. You broke the lock on the storage shed and let me get away."

"Yes, I hope I did the right thing."

"I was glad to get out." Mulak paused. "I thought it was my son who did it."

"Your son saved my life," Rorie said. "But I believe he was trying to save yours."

Billy rested with his back against one of the aircraft's pontoons. Simpson's last bullet had gouged a furrow in Billy's right shoulder, missing bone as it passed on through. Shock had covered the pain, Rorie thought, but Billy would be feeling it soon enough.

"He is my son," the old Eskimo said. "He lost his way, but he is still my son."

Both men stiffened at the crack of another rifle shot rolling across the tundra. They exchanged glances. Mulak said, "There is another hunter. . . ."

Rorie was already moving toward his plane. "You stay with Billy. I'll be back. I think I know who the hunter is . . . I have to find out what—or who—he's hunting."

The speed of a charging grizzly, given his great size and weight, defied credulity. It completely unnerved Travis Mayberry. He had the Heckler and Koch automatic rifle in his hands, chambered for .762/NATO bullets with great stopping power even for game as large as the grizzly. In his panic, though, he forgot to click the weapon over to full automatic. A full burst might have stunned the bear, but Mayberry fired only a single shot. It struck the grizzly high on his massive chest but didn't even slow him down. It merely increased his rage.

Mayberry gaped at the angry force bearing down on him. He glanced at the assault rifle in disbelief, stumbled backward a step before the grizzly got to him. In one sweeping blow the bear's six-inch claws tore through Mayberry's layers of clothing and ripped flesh away to the bone along his right side from his shoulder to his waist. His scream was lost in the bear's thunderous growl.

As she tried to run, Kathy floundered in the snow and stumbled to her knees. Scrambling to her feet, she slipped and fell on her back. She looked up as the grizzly's attention turned from the rag doll he had made of Travis Mayberry toward the other intruder. At that moment Survivor reached the front of the ridge, and the bear saw him.

His weak vision attracted more by a moving object than a stationary one, the grizzly's attention focused immediately upon the dog. Survivor circled the bear, barking furiously. He kept darting forward, dancing back each time the grizzly swung toward him. Survivor's aggressive actions drew the bear away from Kathy, who got up, legs unsteady. She remembered reading about someone who had survived a grizzly's attack in the wilderness by lying absolutely still and playing dead. Probably good advice, she thought, but hard to take.

She backed away. *Wrong!* The bear saw the movement. His

massive head swung from the dog toward her. He hesitated, deciding between them. Then suddenly his head lifted. At the same moment Kathy heard the rapidly approaching snarl of a small aircraft in a dive.

Jeff Rorie's Cessna pulled out of a steep plunge directly over the ridge, the engine's scream bottoming out like a small explosion. The size and speed and thunder of this unknown thing hurtling toward him out of the sky was finally too much for the grizzly. He turned and ran down the long slope toward the river, ploughing a small highway in the snow. He never looked back.

THIRTY

"THIS IS becoming like an emergency hospital flight," Jeff Rorie said. "I don't think there's room for everyone."

Travis Mayberry was alive but he had lost a great deal of blood and his long wound was sickening to look at. If he lived, Rorie speculated, he would probably lose his right arm, or the use of it. Though in much better shape, Billy Mulak also needed emergency care. Even after Rorie had taken out the Cessna's rear bench seat, the two wounded men lying on the floor in back took up most of the space in the small narrow cabin. Only one person could ride in the front seat next to the pilot. That left an odd person out, and the big husky.

"I will wait with the dog," John Mulak said. "He will be good company, I think."

"I'll stay too," Kathy said. "If the ASSET people are coming down the river looking for me, I want to be here when they arrive."

Rorie frowned. He had contacted the ASSET base camp over the radio in Mayberry's Super Cub. A rescue team had left the base thirty-six hours earlier, he was told, coming downriver in a Zodiac. They should reach the area of Kathy's abandoned camp by the following day. Even so, Rorie didn't like leaving her behind.

"Don't worry," Kathy said with a grin. "You've done your job, Mr. Rorie. Now I can get back to doing mine. And in the meantime, Mr. Mulak will be good company, I think."

"I'll get back as soon as I can. I don't think staying near the cave is such a hot idea with a wounded bear around. Your old camp makes better sense. Your people will be looking for you there. You have a heater there, too."

"I doubt our grizzly will be coming back soon," Kathy said, less sure than she sounded. "I know he was hit once when Mayberry shot at him. How badly do you think he's hurt?"

"They're hard to kill," Rorie said. "My agency may want to send someone up here to look for him."

"If he comes back before you do . . . well, I don't know how the government feels, Mr. Rorie, but as far as I'm concerned, he can have the ivory!"

"He will take good care of it," Mulak said quietly. "I think when the snow melts in the spring and he decides to leave, he will not care so much if we come back for the ivory." He studied the Fish and Wildlife Service agent, perhaps not sure of his reaction. "It belongs to my people, I think. I took it from the white hunters but they won't get it now. I never wanted to take it from my friends."

Rorie looked at him for a long moment. If agents recovered the ivory, it would be physical evidence against the poachers. But they already had the ivory Mayberry had shipped as evidence. Simpson was dead, and it would be a very long time before Mayberry recovered enough to stand trial. Besides, Rorie had never actually seen the white harvest.

Aloud he said, echoing Mulak, "Neither do I."

Muugli raised his head when he heard the drone of Rorie's aircraft flying south. It was a faraway sound, but it reminded him of the buzz of an outboard motor in the water, a grimly familiar threat. The fog bank that lay over the coastal shelf all that day muffled the buzz, but the huge old walrus continued to listen for a long time after the threat faded away. Then there was only the battering of the waves against the ice floe on which he rested, and the grinding and tearing and crashing of the ice smashing through a disintegrating barrier.

Beneath the smothering fog over the straits and the coastal shelf, the temperature had risen slightly. With the easing of hard freeze, some of the ice that had begun to pile up near the entrance to the straits broke loose noisily and drifted on the current. Muugli had been imprisoned at the ice barricade for nearly two days. Now his island moved, slowly but steadily southward toward the Bering Sea.

Although he had not regained all his strength, his ugly wounds had largely healed. What he suffered now was a malaise that time and nature alone could not heal. Walruses were sociable creatures. The herd instinct was strong, and Muugli's herd had been destroyed.

The droning sound continued to worry him, for it was associated with the recent memory of pain and turmoil all around him, of his own kind screaming on the ice or sinking into the darkness of the sea. It was the sound of creatures in boats, and of death.

It was a long time before he put his head down.

The old walrus drifted through the afternoon and into the lengthening night. His wounds might have healed but he was no longer doing well. The urge to move, even to feed his prodigious hunger, was dying.

Sometime in the darkest part of the night he was awakened by another sound. Something stirred in him. He listened to the continuous crunch and rumble of ice, the roll and crash of the sea. Then his head tilted, as if to hear better.

A tolling, as if bells boomed in the darkness of the sea. Muugli's response was instinctive: he bellowed at the night, again and again. For a few moments there was silence. Then other voices answered him, first one or two, then more, in a strange bodiless thunder that filled the darkness.

When the first pale light of dawn filtered through the mist, Muugli saw that another large cake of ice, perhaps forty yards across, had bumped into his own floating island during the night, and they had drifted together. Dozens of reddish-brown bodies lay on the adjoining island. Other individuals swam or surfaced in the water nearby, and other groups were scattered about on smaller ice floes. There were females as well as males, the former surrounded by the smaller shapes of their calves. The barking and bellowing began again.

Muugli's voice, the oldest and deepest of them all, became the centerpiece of a raucous celebration of reunion.

Soon some of the walruses swimming in the sea hooked their tusks over the edge of Muugli's island of ice and heaved their heavy bodies onto the table. Others flopped over from the neighboring floe. Using their powerful flippers, one by one they walked across the ice toward the huge old walrus. Their bodies gradually surrounded him. Grunting and snorting, they lay close together, some back-to-back, or lying across other bodies, or piled two-deep.

Muugli rested in the center of the herd, at peace. The weight that had lain across his spirit dispersed, as light as the fog, which lifted slowly to unveil the white splendor of the Arctic sun.

EPILOGUE

ONE COLD morning in the first week of November, Harry Madrid hurried out of the lobby of his apartment. His limousine was waiting. Harry was startled when he saw that Sal, his chauffeur, wasn't behind the wheel. But the man who jumped out to open the door for him could have been Sal's muscle-bound cousin. "Sal's sick," he mumbled. "Got the flu."

The flu, Harry thought irritably. Probably had it all week, filling the limo with his germs. "Stop by the Waldorf," he ordered as he climbed in. "We're picking up the Chinese."

"You got it, boss."

Deng Chang was in a typically cheerful mood after a night on the town with another of Harry's models. He had also been delighted to hear from Harry that a substantial shipment of ivory had arrived from Alaska. Chang chattered happily all the way to Newark, even though traffic crawled through the Lincoln Tunnel. Two bodyguards sat on the seats facing Harry and Chang, their faces expressing nothing.

They reached the warehouse shortly before ten-thirty. The electronic remote in the limousine opened the heavy iron gates, nine feet tall with a roll of concertina wire on top, and the Mercedes slid through quietly into a walled yard formed by wings of the three-story brick warehouse. The gates were automatically swinging shut when Harry stepped out of the car and glanced around the yard. Nothing out of line, a few cars parked near the heavy entry door to the row of offices, a truck backed up to a loading dock at the far end of the frontage road. Good, just as he had laid it out for Tony Manero, his foreman at the warehouse and his primary heavy-duty muscle. Nothing to make Chang or his goons suspicious.

274

Harry walked briskly toward the entrance. "I'll make sure those boxes have been brought down for you to look over," he called over his shoulder. He wanted to be inside quickly, out of the way while Chang and his men were still in the open. Fish in a barrel, Harry thought.

He had the morning's second small jolt when the door opened and he saw another strange face, a chunky block with old acne scars and cold eyes. The man had knee-breaker written all over him. One of Tony's recruits, Harry decided with relief, hired for the occasioh.

Seeking reassurance, he glanced down the hallway, looking for more of his own men. No one was in sight. Through a half-windowed wall to the right of the corridor he could look directly into the main offices. His own office was in the far corner, also partitioned off with half-glass walls. His secretary's desk was out front. Surprisingly, she wasn't at her desk. In fact, no one was there—not the secretary, not the receptionist, not the accountant. The offices were empty.

Harry quickly turned. Three wrong notes in one morning were too many. There should have been some action behind him by now. Chang and his goons had to be taken quickly, by surprise.

Chang stood smiling in the doorway. "You were expecting someone else, Mr. Madrid?"

"Huh? Yes . . . no! What are you talking about?"

"My mother has spoken to your principals. They are in agreement."

"What's that supposed to mean? I don't have any principals."

Chang smiled. "I doubt very much you intended that as a joke, Harry, but it's a good one. What I mean, of course, is that you could not operate on the docks without the cooperation of . . . certain people of influence. But you should have understood that Madam Chang has long had an arrangement with them. And you were trying to act on your own initiative, without seeking their approval for what you planned to do to me."

"You been sniffing too much opium, Chang—"

"No." The Chinese spoke sharply for the first time. "You planned to kill me. Your men, those who were uncooperative, have been removed. Most of them went willingly. Your foreman, however . . .''

"Tony? What's happened to Tony?"

"He . . . resisted. Most unfortunate."

Harry saw his future opening up before him like a deep black pit. No way to escape it, but at least on the way into the pit he would take Deng Chang with him.

Harry's shoulders sagged. Bending as if in surrender, he turned away. And as he turned he reached for the small hide-out gun in its neat shoulder holster under the London-tailored suit that had been so artfully fitted to hide the minimal bulk of the concealed weapon. He actually got his hand on the pearl handle of the Beretta .25 automatic before a soft-nosed bullet from a much more powerful gun struck him in the back and broke his spine. The bullet expanded as it tore through flesh and bone, making a much larger exit wound in Harry's chest than the nickel-sized entry hole in his back. Blood and bone and tissue spewed in a large circle across the glass partition.

Deng Chang spent the rest of the morning going over the inventory records in Harry Madrid's office. He was familiar with most of the information but was pleased to verify the extent and variety of Harry's operation. He was also anxious to inspect the newly arrived shipment of walrus tusks from Alaska, which had provided Harry with his excuse to lure Chang into a trap. Chang had the boxes brought to the offices and opened up. The contents, handsome walrus ivory tusks packed along with several polar bear hides in mint condition, were impressive in themselves but disappointing in light of Deng Chang's expectations. The spectacular tusks of the huge old walrus he had spotted in the wildlife photograph were not included in the shipment.

Harry Madrid had lied.

Deng placed a transPacific call to Hong Kong and was informed that Madam Chang was not immediately available but would return his call shortly. While he waited, Deng heard a commotion outside the offices near the front entry and saw several men push through the main doorway. Inexplicably, one of Deng's bodyguards was backing away from the intruders, offering no resistance.

Chang was on his feet when two men reached his office. Both wore what he thought ill-fitting, obviously inexpensive suits. One was large, heavyset and slow-moving, the other small and energetic. "What is the meaning of this? Who are you?"

"We might ask you the same question," the big man said in a lazy drawl. "We're looking for Harry Madrid."

"You will not find him here."

Now he realized that the two men had the unmistakable arrogance of policemen everywhere. He thought of Harry Madrid's body, safely packed in a box and stacked on the dock, ready to be shipped that night along with other goods bound for the Orient. Harry was to be buried at sea. The blood in the hallway and on the walls had been cleaned up. Of course, modern forensic methods would detect the presence of blood and possibly even human tissue, but there was no reason for such an inspection to be made. Chang relaxed.

"Mr. Madrid has retired. He is no longer involved in the business. My name is Deng Chang. I represent the Chang Asian Import-Export Company. Our main offices are in Hong Kong."

The two men looked at each other. Behind Chang the telephone rang. He ignored it. He was perspiring slightly.

"You've taken over?"

"That is correct. Now if you'll tell me your business with Mr. Madrid, perhaps I can help."

Another exchange of glances. The big man nodded and the smaller one produced some papers from his suit pocket. "Then these are for you," he said. "We're with the United States Fish and Wildlife Service, Mr. Chang. That's Mr. Sanderson there, and I'm LoBianco. We have a warrant to search these premises and to impound any illegal goods found in them." He paused, studying Chang's reaction. "I think you'd better call a lawyer, Mr. Chang. From where I'm standing you're gonna need one."

The telephone kept ringing. Deng Chang, the reality of his situation becoming clearer by the second, made no move to answer it.

Sandy Sanderson smiled. "Do you want me to answer it for you, Mr. Chang?"

Anchorage lay under twelve inches of new snow that first week of November. Outside the windows of the television studios, in a high-rise building in the heart of the city, the peaks of the Alaska Range were crowned in white.

Alaska's governor, Tom Brady, turned away from the view and took his place on the set facing a local news anchor. He smiled automatically at the young woman sharing the hot seat with him on "Alaska Speaks." A scientist, Brady had been told, part of the ASSET group that had spent the summer conducting environmental impact studies near the Arctic Circle. The governor hated these TV interview programs, but with a Congressional subcommittee convening hearings the next morning in Anchorage on the proposed new Northern Slope oil development, he couldn't risk turning down the invitation.

The newsman caught his attention. A red light was blinking over one of the cameras. "How would you sum up your view of the proposed new oil pipeline, Governor Brady?" the anchor asked.

The governor turned toward the woman beside him. A slender woman in her early thirties, Dr. Kathleen McNeely seemed ill at ease facing the cameras under the hot studio lights. To the television-wise politician, she looked like an easy target.

"Let's face it," the governor intoned in his rich baritone, "most of Alaska is uninhabitable and always will be. It's a fantastic place and I love it, but eighty percent of our land is too remote, too harsh and too cold for human beings to survive on it. But it's incredibly rich in natural resources. Not to develop those resources for the good of the entire country would be both shortsighted and incredibly wasteful."

"Aren't you being the shortsighted one, Governor?" Kathy McNeely cut in quickly. "You're talking about oil and mineral resources. How long are they going to last before being exhausted? Twenty years? Fifty years? What is Alaska going to be left with at the end of the next century, if these limited resources last that long?"

The governor smiled indulgently, an expression that played well on the television screen, which did not capture the steely glint in his eyes. "We're talking about carefully controlled development that will benefit us and those of you in the Lower 48 who still want to drive around in your automobiles and live in your air-conditioned houses." He leaned forward, his professional smile suggesting tolerance for an opponent who didn't know any better. "You live in Santa Barbara, I believe, isn't that right, doctor? Most of the people in the United States would enjoy living there, savoring the sea and the sunshine. You won't find them colonizing the Brooks Range. But what we here in Alaska can extract from those mountains, and from the Northern Slope, will help make it possible for millions of people to continue to enjoy their way of life in the places where people want to live and will continue to live in ever growing numbers."

"It will also destroy the habitat of millions of birds and animals that have been thriving there for centuries," Kathy shot back. "Not to mention the native Alaskans who were here long before we came. ASSET's full report will be released tomorrow morning, Governor Brady, prior to the opening of the Congressional hearings. It documents the serious impact of the development not only on birds but on scores of land and sea animals, the fish in Alaska's river systems along the route, and on the land itself. I think you'll find our report a revelation, Governor. I'm sure the subcommittee will."

The governor flushed. He had the feeling he had been sandbagged. "What we don't need in Alaska," he snapped, "is another spotted owl controversy stopping development and driving business away. I don't plan to stand by and see that happen in Alaska!"

Kathy McNeely's Irish temper was two generations removed from the real thing, her paternal grandmother had told her, but it was strong enough to make Tom Brady blink. "That's the heart of the matter, isn't it, governor? The development you're so anxious to see will also make some individuals a great deal of money. Isn't that what it's all about?"

"You're damned right it is! It will bring *jobs* here for Alaskans —and *jobs* for those natives you're so concerned about, just like the first pipeline. It will benefit this state and the United States.''

''The way the Trans-Alaska Pipeline benefited Prince William Sound?''

The governor's red-faced reply was lost in the general uproar as the studio audience reacted and the news anchor tried to intervene while Kathy and Brady talked over each other. Watching from the control room, the producer of ''Alaska Speaks'' grinned with delight. Tonight's show was going to be a ratings bonanza.

Jason Cobb limped up to Kathy McNeely. She turned away from a couple of spectators who were ready to continue both sides of the televised debate. Her eyes sparked with pleasure. ''Jason! They told me you'd gone back to the States.''

''The Lower 48, you mean. I did . . . but I wouldn't have missed your show today for the world.''

She made a small grimace of discomfort. ''That's the problem . . . instead of addressing the issues together we were giving performances, competing for points as if this were a Nintendo game.''

''You're not going to change politics overnight. Or TV.'' Cobb grinned. ''Not even you, Kathy.''

She looked at him with obvious affection, but, he regretted to note, with nothing more . . .

''You're looking great, Jason. I expected to see you in a wheelchair or at least limping around with a cane.''

Cobb shrugged, wryly noting to himself that it was not one of his better roles. ''It turned out I fractured my pelvis. The doctors had me walking the corridors in one of those hospital gowns in two days. It wasn't a disk or anything like that, thank God.''

''I'm glad. I was afraid I'd crippled you for life, hauling you all that way over the tundra.''

An amiable silence fell between them. The noisy confusion in the emptying television studio swirled around them. Cobb saw Alaska's governor, still obviously angry, stalking toward an exit with a phalanx of aides surrounding him.

"I heard what happened with those ivory poachers," Cobb said. "Someday I'd like to hear the whole story. What about the poacher who was attacked by the grizzly? The last I heard he was still alive."

"His name is Mayberry—they say he'll recover. His trial has been postponed indefinitely but I understand Fish and Wildlife has impounded all the skins and ivory he had. I'll probably never be called to testify."

Cobb studied her admiringly. "You do seem to be a lightning rod, McNeely . . . as his honor the governor discovered. The people who wanted you for ASSET's expedition weren't wrong about you."

"He's one of those nature-be-damned developers, but I wish the discussion hadn't fallen apart like it did."

Cobb shrugged. "From ASSET's point of view, having Brady lose his temper was the best thing that could have happened. It will open up the whole subject to strong debate throughout Alaska, right on the eve of the Congressmen's arrival in Anchorage. Now at least our viewpoint will be heard. There's just no way, after tonight, that it can be swept under the rug."

Some well-wishers interrupted them, one congratulating Kathy on her television confrontation, another wanting to talk about her encounter with the ivory poachers. Finally, when they were left alone again, Cobb cleared his throat self-consciously. "Have you heard . . . that is, from Brian Hurley?"

Kathy brightened. "Someone handed me a note just before the telecast saying there was a radio message for me. I sort of expected it before now . . ."

They both saw Carl Jeffers moving through the crowd toward them, a broad grin on his round face. He pushed up to them, nodded at Cobb and thrust a yellow teletype into Kathy's hand. "What you've been waiting for, my dear."

Kathy's hand trembled a little as she took the message. It read:

I HAVE THE D.O.P. ON THE WAY HOME. I LOVE YOU. BRIAN.

"The D.O.P.?" Cobb murmured. "What . . . ?"

Jeffers laughed. "Damned Old Pole. It's what Admiral Peary

put in the first telegram he sent after he returned from the North Pole in 1909.''

"In those days our newspapers were more prim,'' Kathy said with a smile. "When they quoted Peary they never did use the D-word.''

Watching Kathy closely, Cobb could not miss the glow in her eyes. It answered the question he had been unable to bring himself to ask. Nothing left to say but . . . "Congratulations . . . to both of you.''

Kathy looked up at him quickly. "You are . . .'' She seemed to grope for the right word, then impulsively stepped close and hugged him, and as he felt the warmth and strength in that slender body, his regret deepened.

"A prince of a fellow,'' he said, and turned away.